SUNRISE
AT DUSK

 FriesenPress

Suite 300 - 990 Fort St
Victoria, BC, V8V 3K2
Canada

www.friesenpress.com

ISBN
978-1-5255-2901-6 (Hardcover)
978-1-5255-2902-3 (Paperback)
978-1-5255-2903-0 (eBook)

1. FICTION, URBAN LIFE

Distributed to the trade by The Ingram Book Company

SUNRISE AT DUSK

ALAIN FOURNIER

PROLOGUE

Jesse grabbed him from behind, locking him in a stranglehold, one elbow wedged under his father's jaw, his other hand holding the arm in place. "Not this time, old man!" he yelled. But, though his strength was formidable, he was no match for the bigger man. Jesse's last recollection was flying through the air. Then there was a crash and a scream and... Lights out.

CHAPTER 1

Jesse Decruz opened his eyes slowly for the first time in three weeks. His life had changed profoundly, but he knew neither how nor why, nor when he came to be in this place. The haze began to lift from his eyes ever so slowly as the world came back into focus.

Where the hell am I?

Lying on his back, Jesse moved his eyes slowly around the room, attempting to make sense of his new reality and the circumstances that brought him here. He attempted to speak but felt obstructions in his throat; it was raw and dry as he swallowed, waiting to feel some relief from saliva that wasn't there. As frustration promoted to panic, his instincts told him to rise from where he lay and extricate himself from this place. His head struggled to lift away from the pillow, the motion sending a sharp, piercing pain through his head, as if a spear had penetrated his brain. His left arm ached and the pain resonated through his torso. Panicked at the thought of paralysis, he tried wiggling his toes and fingers. Everything appeared normal, but something just wasn't right, something was off on his left side.

What the hell happened to me? Come on, Jess. Get your shit together. You can figure this out.

His head dropped back onto the pillow. Once again, he scanned the room, moving only his eyes this time to avoid the pain that would surely accompany any further attempt to rise. His focus now turned to sounds, voices, and commotion coming from outside the room. At that moment, a buzzer went off, repeating intermittently. The noise penetrated the room, piercing his ears every two seconds in succession.

The fries are ready, must be at Mickey D's… Shit! No, you're not in a goddam fast food restaurant!

The fog from his brain started to dissipate as he moved onto smells. Definitely a clinical odour in the room. Best guess was disinfectant or rubbing alcohol.

He closed his eyes again as the buzzer went silent, opening them again at the sound of a female voice above him. "Hello, Jesse, welcome back. We've been waiting for you." A woman dressed like a nurse stood within his line of sight.

"You're in the hospital. You've had an accident and we've been taking care of you for the past three weeks." He read her name tag. Carol Phillips. "Jesse," she said, "I need you to remain very still and calm. Dr. Ambrosia will be here shortly to talk to you. He'll explain everything. It's very important you don't attempt to rise from this bed. You have tubes in your throat. You're not able to speak right now, but that's only temporary. Can you blink twice if you understood everything I just said?" Jesse blinked twice. He was more than happy to communicate with another human being and assure her there was someone inside, someone who understood what she was saying.

Three weeks? What the hell have I been doing here for the last three weeks?

Jesse listened intently as Nurse Phillips spoke into the phone. "He's awake doctor. He just woke up."

Jesse could faintly hear the doctor's voice on the other end.
"Good news. Is he coherent? Were you able to reach him?"
"Yes, sir. He gave me a non-verbal indication, but his eyes are
still glazed and obviously disoriented for the moment."
"Excellent. I'll be there in ten minutes. Keep a close eye on
him till I get there."

Jesse fought hard to focus his mind, trying desperately to tap
into his most recent memories. Flashes of his father and mother
entered his mind's eye. There'd been an altercation of some type.
But that was it. There was no context or semblance of events.
His frustration mounted. Where was his mother and why wasn't
she here with him? What happened to her? Jesse had always felt
a deep love and affection for his mother. Not knowing where she
was caused him great anxiety.

Several minutes passed before Dr. Ambrosia entered the
room and stood over Jesse along with Nurse Phillips. "Hello,
Jesse. I'm Dr. Ambrosia. You've been under my care since you
arrived. You're a lucky young man. I'm just going to do a few
checks on you now and then I'll explain your current condition
and status."

Jesse remained calm as the doctor probed his head, arms, and
torso. The doctor shone a bright light into both of his eyes and
snapped off the light.

"Jesse, you came to us nearly three weeks ago. You were the
victim of a violent altercation. You sustained significant injuries
throughout your body, particularly to your head. Your left radius
was broken, which we reset and placed in a cast. The radius is
one of the two bones below your elbow on the lateral side of
your forearm. The x-rays show a clean break so we fully expect
this will heal 100 percent. Your torso experienced a good deal
of trauma, mostly bruising in the ribs but you did show some
minor rib fractures on the lower right side. Your kidney was also
bruised but we expect a full recovery there as well."

Jesse listened intently but this was not what he wanted to know. He was more interested in the circumstances leading to his current condition, not a dry clinical summation of his injuries.

Dr. Ambrosia continued. "My primary concern is the injuries you sustained to your head. You were brought here unconscious with obvious signs of trauma to the head. After several hours during which you were unconscious, we quickly diagnosed a severe brain injury and elected to operate immediately to relieve some of the swelling you were experiencing. I was the surgeon who operated on you. Following your surgery, we made the decision to keep you in a medically induced coma. We do this to give our patients the best chance at recovery. Remaining still while you heal is paramount for these types of injuries, providing you the best chance at a full recovery. This morning we brought you out of your coma."

Jesse attempted to process the information. He tried to ask a question but to no avail. His mind was now focused on thoughts of his mother. Where was she and what happened to her, and why wasn't she here with him? Tears began to well up in his eyes.

Nurse Phillips dabbed his eyes with a tissue and attempted to comfort him. "It's okay, Jesse. You're going to be okay. Dr. Ambrosia is one of the best doctors in the country and he'll get you well again. Don't despair."

"That's right, Jesse," Dr. Ambrosia said. "Gaining consciousness today was the first big step in your recovery. We have excellent people, including Ms. Phillips here, who will care for you. I can see you are young and strong. These are two very important factors that will work in your favour. You need to rest. I'll be back to see you later and we'll talk more then."

Jesse took some solace in the doctor's words. He knew his past conditioning and fitness had made him strong. He thought back to the countless hours he spent, from the age of twelve, working out in the small spare room of his apartment on Sackville Street.

His father had fashioned a makeshift workout room in the apartment with equipment from his earlier boxing years. The room was filled with a jumbled collection of free weights, gym equipment, and punching bags. Now, at the age of seventeen, Jesse stood at 6'2" and weighed 185 pounds with barely an ounce of fat on his chiselled body. He had consumed a great deal of his spare time getting his body into top physical condition, an activity he enjoyed and could afford given the impoverished life he lived with his family in the government projects of Regent Park.

The makeshift gym was also the place he first learned to fight. It represented the only useful skill his father had ever passed on to him. It brought back painful memories, however. He recalled coming home one day from school during the seventh grade, having suffered yet another beating at the hands of his tormentor, Jason Sanderson. His nose bloodied and his eye swelled, he dreaded having to explain to his drunken father how he'd allowed someone to abuse him again.

Roger Decruz had a dominant presence and a body to match. He stood at 6'4" and weighed 230 pounds, with long hair pulled into a tight ponytail and narrow piercing eyes, hazel in colour. At forty-two years of age, the alcohol quickly pushed him past his prime. Yet he was still solid and ruggedly handsome with a menacing look that would strike fear into any man, much less a twelve-year-old child.

"What the hell's wrong with ya, kid? What kind of pussy lets someone beat on him like that?" Roger Decruz yelled as he knelt forward, getting into his son's face. "Who did this to you?" he screamed.

Jesse, repelled by the smell of cigarettes and 'Jack' on his father's breath, replied sheepishly, "Jason Sanderson. He's in Grade 8. He's way bigger than me." This reply was met with a strong slap to the side of his head.

"Quit makin' excuses, ya dumb little shit! Ya don't let someone mess ya up like that no matter how big he is, ya understand?" In spite of the abuse delivered at the hands of his father, the elder Decruz proceeded to coach his son in the art of hand-to-hand combat. Not out of some sense of loyalty or protection, Jesse concluded, but to save himself the embarrassment of raising a wimpy kid. In time, Jesse's size and fighting skills progressed to a point where the Jason Sandersons of Regent Park no longer presented a threat to the younger Decruz.

Jesse's hatred for his father started very early in his life as he was forced to endure the mental abuse and venom that frequently spouted from his father's mouth. He was a mean drunk and Jesse witnessed far too many beatings unleashed on his mother. The experiences played over and over in his head, poisoning his mind. He came to fear, a condition he would slowly overcome as his age, size, and strength grew. But his hatred never wavered. He resolved at an early age that one day he would stand up to his father and stop the hell he inflicted on their lives.

Jesse's head began to throb once again as painful thoughts and memories consumed his mind. Mentally exhausted and physically spent, Jesse closed his eyes and receded back into sleep.

CHAPTER 2

Jeanie Decruz sat patiently in the waiting area in front of the nurse's station on the fourth floor of Toronto's SickKids Hospital. This had become her second home over the past several weeks where she held vigil. Jeanie had worn a groove in the stretch of floor separating Jesse's room and the mini cafeteria located at the end of the hall, where she complemented her daily diet with a steady supply of cigarettes and free coffee.

Born in 1948 as Rejeanne Perreault, she was the product of a devout Catholic family from Laval, Québec—fourth oldest child in a litter of nine. Her childhood regimen was simple. She attended school and returned home to complete a litany of chores and homework bridging her time till bedtime. In spite of numerous siblings in the home, she felt isolated and largely invisible within the family unit. Attention and love from her parents was mostly non-existent.

Her life was an open book with the exception of a painful secret she kept buried in the darkest regions of her mind. It haunted her every single day of her life. Jeanie had neither the maturity nor support system to confront her demons. She had long ago left her home in Québec but the nightmares followed her. Jeanie was once a strong, practicing Catholic. That too she abandoned. Most children feared the dark and the bogeyman at night time, a harmless phobia shared by most kids growing up. Jeanie's bogeyman was real and it lived in the place she once called home.

How could a loving God allow such things to happen to a defenceless little child?

She suffered her pain in silence, without medication, without guidance, and survived nonetheless, just barely. The birth of her first and only child was her salvation, her saving grace, and her entire purpose in life.

When Jeanie first met Roger Decruz in 1965 at the age of seventeen, she was drawn by his good looks and bad boy qualities. Roger rode a bike and frequented the café where Jeanie worked as a part-time waitress. He had eyes for her and never missed the opportunity to strike up a conversation. He was a charmer and provided the attention she so desperately craved that was absent in her personal life. But Roger had a dark side, something he concealed very well. She knew little about the real man beneath the handsome façade, long hair, and buffed body, and the path their relationship would take.

Jeanie sat nervously in her chair, sipping coffee, awaiting news from Jesse's doctor. Dr. Ambrosia had informed her earlier in the week that today was 'wake up day' for Jesse, the day they would bring him out of his medically induced coma. Jeanie was told this would be a pivotal day where her son's results could range from very good to very bad, including possible brain damage they couldn't assess until he was fully awake.

I'll never forgive myself if he wakes up a vegetable. It's all my fault. I'll never forgive myself.

Jeanie tried hard to remain positive but guilt consumed her mind. Her malnourished and sleep-deprived body allowed only negative thoughts to creep into her conscience. She fought hard to remain positive but time and guilt kept her conflicted. Her 5'2" frame had depleted to just under 100 pounds since the incident as she replayed the events of October 4th in her mind over and over again.

Why couldn't I have left it alone? Why did I provoke that drunken asshole?

Jeanie attempted to push the painful memories of that evening from her mind, but failed. Just as she was starting down another dark path, Nurse Phillips distracted her. "Hello, Jeanie. Dr. Ambrosia is ready to speak with you. Can you come with me, please?"

Jeanie's heart fell. This was it, the day she had long awaited but dreaded. Now that it was finally here, she began to unravel. She filed in behind the nurse as they walked down the hall. She could no longer resist the urge and blurted out, "Is he awake? Is he okay? Tell me now, please!"

"Dr. Ambrosia will explain everything to you," Nurse Phillips responded calmly. "We're almost there."

Jeanie felt sick. The news must certainly be bad. Her mind now moved down the dark path and she struggled to find her breath.

Oh, my God. My son has died. He must have died!

Jeanie began to sob as they turned the corner and moved into the small office off the hallway where the doctor was waiting.

"Mrs. Decruz, why the tears? Is this how you're planning to accept good news?" Dr. Ambrosia asked, an impish smile on his face.

"What? What do you mean?" Jeanie shot back, dropping into a chair.

"Jesse awoke this morning and the results are as good as we could have hoped for at this point. He can't communicate with us yet, with all the tubes still present, but he appears to be aware and responsive to our instructions, which is an excellent sign."

Jeanie sat back, collecting herself, and drew in a long breath of relief. Then she leapt to her feet and ran to hug the doctor. "Thank you! Thank you both!" She turned to Nurse Phillips, sharing her moment of gratitude.

"We're just doing a few more minor checks on Jesse. Give us another thirty minutes and you can come by to see him," the doctor instructed.

Jeanie went back to the waiting area. She felt a sudden emptiness in her stomach as her appetite came back for the first time in weeks. She went over to the nurse's station and opened a box filled with muffins, a snack she'd been offered earlier but had refused. She picked at a chocolate chip muffin and delivered small pieces into her mouth. It tasted good, she thought, as the strain of the past weeks fell away from her face. She felt a tremendous sense of calm come over her and had to resist the temptation to fall asleep right there and then.

Thirty minutes seemed like two hours but finally the nurse summoned her. "Okay, Jeanie, you are free to see him now. Go on in. He's on some strong pain medication right now so keep that in mind. He'll seem a bit groggy but he's awake."

Jeanie moved to the entrance of Jesse's room, staring down at her broken son. Her lungs felt void of air. A flood of emotion washed over her. The love she felt for her son and the responsibility she accepted for his current predicament caused her to feel lightheaded and unsteady. As Jesse became aware of her presence, he shifted his gaze to her. Jeanie's eyes welled up with tears as she moved swiftly to him sobbing uncontrollably.

"I'm sorry, Jesse. I'm so sorry. This was all my fault," she whispered softly as she embraced him, burying her head into his shoulder. She cupped his head delicately. "I love you. I love you so much. Thank you for coming back to me."

Jesse looked at his mother in obvious distress. He lifted his right hand to her eyes and wiped her tears with the tips of his fingers, attempting to console her. He had not seen his mother cry like this in a very long time. In spite of being a battered wife, Jeanie rarely cried in his presence. It was her stubborn French Canadian background that allowed her to never give her abusive husband the satisfaction of seeing her cry. She had a strong will. But her failure to protect her son filled her with guilt, a guilt she had not yet reconciled.

Jeanie laid her head next to her son's and they remained there in silence for a good long while. "I don't know how much you remember about what happened," she said, "but now is not the time. I want you to get well first. We'll have lots of time to talk once you are able. Just get some rest now and I'll be right here when you wake up." She kissed his forehead.

Jeanie turned and pulled the cushioned armchair in the corner of the room closer to the bed. She sat down, removed her shoes, and fell quickly asleep. Jesse followed suit. They would indeed have much to discuss but, right now, fatigue had taken its toll on them both.

CHAPTER 3

Room 244 at Lakewood Public High School in Regent Park was settling in for the morning session following the weekend. The final stragglers for Mrs. Berger's Grade 12 homeroom slowly filed into their seats. Taking in a deep breath and preparing herself for another week, Marianne Berger wondered what adventure the new week would bring. As she scanned the room, taking mental note of vacant seats, she could only imagine what they'd experienced over the weekend. She had only a small window into their world to help her understand the challenges many faced on a daily basis. She wondered how many of them were sad, angry, scared, or perhaps even hungry right now. Empathy was all she could provide. Anything more would come at a personal cost to her own well-being.

Drugs, alcohol, violence, and single-parent homes were commonplace throughout the Regent Park and Cabbagetown areas of Toronto. Most of the children were born and raised in the RGI (rent-geared-to-income) units strewn throughout the area. These kids were tough and resilient, but their wounds were not always visible. Their minds carried the memories, the pain, and often the abuse they endured at the hands of those entrusted with their care. In spite of everything, each class had those rays of sunshine, those diamonds in the rough, and this kept Mrs. Berger hopeful and motivated to make a difference in their lives. Quite often, she represented the only smiling face and inspiration in their young lives and that was good enough for her.

Only six of thirty kids absent today. Not bad for a Monday morning.

"Alright, settle down everyone. I hope you all used these past few days to rest in preparation for another week here at school." Mrs. Berger's comments generated some smiles and mild laughter. The students had become accustomed to their teacher's subtle sense of humour. They had accepted Mrs. Berger early on in the year as her style of teaching resonated with them. A good mix of authority and humility was the hook that had served her well here and in the past.

"Now, as you know, your classmate Jesse Decruz has been hospitalized for the past several weeks downtown at SickKids Hospital. He was placed in a coma while his head injuries healed. I'm pleased to report today that he's now awake and appears to be on a good path to recovery. His mother has asked me if I could gather some school reading and work to help him catch up with his studies." This information garnered several smiles and nods around the classroom. Jesse was a very quiet student but had grown quite popular among his peers.

"In addition, I'm also looking for a volunteer to come with me to the hospital this Wednesday to act as a support person, a liaison or tutor, someone who can help me bring materials back and forth to the hospital and Jesse's home. This would only be for a short time, just while he gets back on his feet. We expect Jesse will be back to school within a few short weeks."

One student raised a hand to volunteer. Amanda Perone. Her history with Jesse was well documented; in fact, it had become legendary among the school population. The irony was not lost on Mrs. Berger. As Amanda sat there, her hand raised high above her head, the room filled with whispers. Mrs. Berger instructed the class to quiet down.

◻

It was the second week of the new school year after football practice. Amanda was waiting at the back of the school near the players' locker room exit for her boyfriend, Owen Reed, the Lakewood Bulldog's starting quarterback. Handsome, popular, and charming were among his best qualities; possessiveness and controlling behaviour rounded out his worst. Jesse Decruz was also nearby waiting for his best friend Robby (Goz) Gosling and the Jackson brothers, Trey and Jamal (JJ). They were all close childhood friends of his from the neighbourhood.

Reed finally emerged from the school door exit and immediately got into a heated argument with Amanda behind the large waste container parked at the back of the school. Their voices rose in volume.

Jesse stood nearby watching the pair intently. The verbal altercation quickly turned physical as Reed grabbed the back of Amanda's neck and pressed her face to the container. Jesse's face flushed red. It was a move he'd seen his father make dozens of times with his mother. "Back off of her right now, Tarzan," he ordered loudly.

Standing at 6'1" with a solid build, Reed was no slouch. He slowly turned his head towards Jesse. "Take a hike, bitch, or you're next." He continued holding Amanda's head against the metal.

Jesse went to stand directly behind Reed. In a flash of movement, he grabbed Reed's left wrist and yanked the arm up behind his back. With his other hand, Jesse grabbed Reed's neck and shoved him up against the container. Clearly in pain, Reed struggled, letting go of Amanda. "Get the fuck off of me!" he screamed. "Let go, you asshole!"

Keeping a strong hold of Reed, Jesse calmly instructed him, "Tell your girlfriend you're sorry."

"You're fucking dead! I'll kill you, man!" Reed shot back.

Jesse yanked the arm back even further and calmly repeated, "I said, tell your girlfriend you're sorry." Reed was now in extreme pain. As the pain grew unbearable, Reed could no longer hold his bravado. "Okay, okay. I'm sorry. I'm sorry."

"That wasn't so hard now, was it?" Jesse asked. He released Reed, pushing him forward with force. The 6'1" athlete hit the metal structure with a thud.

Amanda stood between them in tears. She pleaded with Jesse to stop hurting Reed any further. Jesse complied, turning away and heading back towards the school. He had learned early on, however, that you never turn your back on an enemy, so he waited for it.

Patience, patience… wait for it…

And there it was. Jesse's keenly tuned ear could hear the shuffling and heavy breathing coming his way from behind. It was the sound of blind rage and retribution charging in his direction. Jesse waited patiently then quickly swung around and jerked his head back before Reed's ample right fist could land. Reed's momentum drove him past Jesse. From behind, Jesse locked both of his arms under Reed's armpits and forced his weight forward while cupping both of his feet to the front of Reeds legs. Both behemoths fell forward. With Jesse's arms locked in position, Reed no longer had the benefit of his arms to break their fall. Jesse allowed gravity to take his entire weight and squared his right shoulder to the back of Reed's head as they came crashing to the earth. A sickening crunch followed as Reed face-planted into the concrete. Blood flowed freely from his nose and mouth as he moaned in agony.

Jesse positioned his mouth by Reed's right ear. "Who's the bitch now?"

In addition to a broken nose and a few missing teeth, the fall tore ligaments in Reed's right shoulder, his prized throwing arm. Season's over! For his troubles, Jesse was awarded a one-week suspension. He didn't care. He'd always disliked Reed and took pleasure in tuning him up. No man should ever strike a woman, he thought. In his mind, he held the high moral ground.

□

Amanda addressed Mrs. Berger. "Jesse's place is not that far from mine. I would like to help out if that's okay, Mrs. Berger."

"Well, thank you, Amanda, that's very nice of you. Can you come see me after school? We'll plan a Wednesday visit and see how you can help."

By this time, Amanda was well aware of the numerous stares she was receiving from her classmates. She was pleased with her decision. She had never properly thanked Jesse for rescuing her that day. In fact, she'd gone out of her way to avoid him in the weeks that followed, although she never quite understood why. She wanted to make things right with Jesse and looked forward to the opportunity.

CHAPTER 4

Dominic Nardelli stared pensively out the window of his spacious office at the back of Lakewood Public High. Hardly avant garde, it was functional, providing a panoramic view of the baseball and football fields; more importantly, it had excellent line of sight to the general student population. At the age of thirty-five, Nardelli was the youngest principal to serve in the largest school board in Canada. Brains and ambition moved you up the hill; knowing the right people got you up the mountain.

What the hell did I do to deserve this place?

Nardelli was a rising star at the Toronto District School Board. He was in his second year as a principal, first year at Lakewood, and on the fast track to a school board executive posting, and he had a solid pedigree to boot. His ambitions aimed high. Always impeccably dressed and groomed to a fault, Dominic Nardelli was a contradiction, an oxymoron of sorts, working at arguably the most challenged secondary school in the nation. Nardelli stood at 5'10", with short hair and a short-cropped goatee over sharp facial features. He was professionally manicured, and walked with authority; his edgy attitude and intelligence were supplemented with a quick wit and charm.

Nardelli was far too busy for a wife but he certainly had the time to move through numerous girlfriends—like candy through a pez dispenser.

It was no coincidence he had achieved this station in life so early. Nardelli had established himself as a change agent, Mr. Clean-up, the master of conversion if you will. He knew how to clean a mess and had successfully transformed the last three high schools he'd served, 'cesspools of decaying youth' as he commonly referred to them. He introduced innovative and radical new programs aimed at elevating the sparks within the school and eliminating the fizzle. He had genuine intent and a desire to help those students who wanted to succeed and meet their potential. He was quickly accepted and respected among his peers and subordinates as being tough but fair. His hair-trigger temper was his kryptonite, a personality trait carried down from his father.

Dominic Sr. was the past Director of Education for the school board; he cast a long shadow over his son, a legacy the young Nardelli was determined to not only match but surpass, in spite of the cold-hearted indifference he'd endured at the hands of his father throughout his early life. Dominic Sr. was a disciplinarian with an odd way of showing his love, likely the product of a similar upbringing back in his native Italy. Nardelli no longer had that dark cloud hanging over him. Dominic Sr. had long since retired and moved his wife and himself back to Italy. Dominic Jr. pledged he would never become like the man he called his father.

There was a knock at the door and his executive secretary, Maria Garcia, entered the office. "He's arrived, Mr. Nardelli. Shall I show him in?"

Nardelli had been dreading this meeting all week. Anderson Malvoy was the current Director of Education for the school board, a former protégé of his father. To say that Malvoy was ambitious would be a tremendous understatement. Malvoy was the embodiment of ambition on steroids. His sights were set on provincial politics. He had set a personal goal to become the premier of the Ontario Liberal Party within the next term, now four years away. His current posting and successes would be the stepping stone and launch point to get him there.

Nardelli had quickly become Malvoy's golden goose. Malvoy recognized talent and forged an alliance with Nardelli early on, placing him in some of the most challenged schools in Toronto. His plan was to showcase dramatic turnarounds and successes at the worst schools within the Toronto district. In exchange, Malvoy pledged to be the wind beneath Nardelli's wings, elevating him to achieve his ambition, Director of Education, by the age of forty. A lofty goal for mere mortals, but Nardelli was never short on confidence.

A deal with the devil, that's what this is, plain and simple.

"Thanks, Maria. Yes, please show him in."

Maria retrieved Malvoy from the outer office. He entered the room with purpose, wearing no sense of humour. He stood close and glared at Nardelli but said nothing, a power play Nardelli had seen many times before.

"Good morning, Anderson. Can we get you a coffee or a juice?" Nardelli asked, finally breaking the silence.

"Nothing for me, thanks," Malvoy said, quickly dismissing the offer.

"Okay, thanks, Maria." Nardelli motioned to his secretary. "That will be all. I don't want to be disturbed unless it's an absolute emergency." Maria retreated to the outer office.

Malvoy sat and removed several files from his briefcase. Riffling through several pages, he finally pulled out the documents he wanted, likely the purpose of his visit. Nardelli sat waiting as Malvoy silently reviewed each document in a slow and deliberate fashion. Growing impatient, Nardelli turned to his computer and occupied himself with matters of the day. After what appeared to be an eternity, Malvoy addressed him. "Dominic, look at me. Do I look like someone who accepts lip service, mediocrity, failure?"

"I'm sorry, Andy," Nardelli responded. "I don't follow."

"Do I need to speak slower for you, Dominic?" Malvoy asked condescendingly.

Nardelli turned to look at Malvoy. He was accustomed to this type of handling and had trained himself not to react negatively or defensively despite his temperament. "No, that's about the right speed, thanks," he replied.

"Okay, let me get to the reason for my visit."

Malvoy stood up and extracted from his briefcase a large piece of graph paper, which he proceeded to unfold. He walked towards a large white metal board hanging behind Nardelli's desk and carefully tacked the corners of the document using four small circular magnets. Nardelli was very familiar with this line chart. It represented a key performance metric Malvoy would be using to measure the effectiveness of Nardelli's goals and initiatives for the school year or, in his mind, lack of performance. "Now, do you see the bottom two lines on this chart, Dominic?"

The question was rhetorical and intended to diminish him; however, Nardelli did not react as he waited for the explanation.

"These two lines represent the average overall suspension and expulsion rates across the Toronto District School Board for the last ten years. Let's just focus on suspensions for the moment, shall we? The average suspension rate for the entire board is currently sitting around 2.75 percent of the student population per individual school. Now, do you see this line up here?"

Malvoy's forefinger moved to the solid red line running significantly higher than the average blue line he'd just presented below.

"This line here represents Lakewood Public High School's suspension rate, which is now trending at a whopping 5.89 percent, more than double the board average and projecting to trend nearly 15percent higher than last year's figures for this school. We're only two months into the new school year, Dominic," Malvoy said, stating the obvious for dramatic effect.

Nardelli remained silent. He had been tracking the same numbers himself and was quite familiar with the metric.

"Let's carry on, shall we?" Malvoy continued. He reached into another folder and pulled out more documents. "Let's break this all down. I'm going to ignore the demographic breakdown for now and get into the causal effects or infraction types, which are far more interesting."

Familiar with this next topic of discussion as well, Nardelli anticipated the discussion would move to the Achilles' heel of Lakewood High and the focus of his many sleepless nights since the start of the school year.

"I'm just going to hit the highlights here, Dominic. Otherwise, we're going to be here all day. I'm going to list the top infraction types leading to suspensions at this school. Physical assault and fighting. Lakewood is number one across the board. Possession of alcohol and drugs. Lakewood is number one across the board. Swearing at teachers or persons in authority. Again, Lakewood is number one. Breach of board or school code of conduct. You guessed it. Lakewood is number one."

"Okay, okay, I get it," Nardelli said, attempting to stem the tide of criticism.

"Fine. Have I missed anything? Have I misrepresented any facts so far?" Malvoy retorted.

A prominent vein began forming across Nardelli's forehead, stretching to the back of his right ear. He paused a moment to gather himself and find his words. "I'm intimately familiar with everything you've presented here, Anderson. You seem to forget, I'm the guy you sent to this hellhole. I live this every day so there's nothing you can show me from your bulging briefcase that I don't already know. You also seem to forget I've been down this road before. I know what I'm doing and I don't need to be reminded of where Lakewood's status stands from Mount Olympus. To answer your question, yes, you have missed something. You may have all the statistics but you certainly don't have the context."

"What do you mean?" Malvoy shot back.

"Do I need to speak slower, Anderson?" Nardelli asked, testing him.

"Don't fuck with me, Dominic, not today! If you have a point, get to it!" Malvoy snapped.

"Extortion," Nardelli said simply.

"Extortion?" Malvoy's eyebrows lifted. He began leafing through his spreadsheets and stats, quickly retrieving the number. "Student extortion makes up less than one percent of your suspension numbers. What are you trying to tell me?"

"You see, Andy, that's the problem when you stare at a page full of numbers without understanding the environment that's generating those numbers. In fact, all the numbers are right there staring you in the face but you couldn't possibly put it together without the proper context. You don't have the luxury of knowing what I know."

"If you're planning on educating me here, Dom, I wish the hell you would get to it and quit jerking me off!" Malvoy snapped. He hated losing the moral high ground.

Nardelli gestured to the infraction stat sheet in front of him. "Look at these lines. Uttering threats to inflict bodily harm. Bullying. Theft. Aid to incite harmful behaviour. Now, add all those numbers onto the extortion number. What do you get?"

Malvoy studied his spreadsheet intently. As he attempted to quickly add up the percentages in his head, he was cut short by Nardelli. "Should come out to just over 15 percent."

Malvoy looked at Nardelli, impressed with his familiarity with the statistics without the benefit of a single stitch of paper in front of him. "Comes out to exactly 15.3 percent."

"Yep, it's a huge problem in this school. Most of those infraction types are related to one form of extortion or another. It mostly points to the older students preying on the niner's for lunch money and other possessions. And that's only the ones we know about, the ones that get reported. I suspect the real number is much higher. "

Malvoy's expression turned solemn. "Are you sure? This is very disturbing, Dominic."

"It's a symptom of a bigger problem in this school, Anderson. All these infractions lead to drugs and alcohol; that's the source. Extortion is a means of financing the substance abuse of those students in this school. You add up all the infractions tied specifically to drugs and alcohol, you get nearly 35 percent. Then you add up all the other infractions supporting this activity, you're over 50 percent. Drugs and alcohol, Anderson, that's the source of all evil at this school."

Malvoy's mood turned sour as he attempted to process everything Nardelli had shared. "You seem to know everything that's going wrong at this damn school, Dom. What the hell are you doing about it? Why are your numbers still rising when apparently you have a clear understanding of the problem?"

"I explained this to you weeks ago. Things will get worse before they get better. Why do you think my numbers have gone up? I'm attacking this problem head on, and because I am, the numbers will rise as I flush out the bad guys. I know you don't want to hear this, but the problem is likely much worse than your stats indicate. All you need to know is that I'm not sitting on my hands here. I'm taking care of it and our numbers are going to tank in the short term." Nardelli's voice moved to an aggressive tone. "You need to be patient."

"You can't even fathom the scope of my responsibilities!" Malvoy shot back.

Nardelli recognized the preamble. Malvoy was about to launch into full-rant mode.

Oh shit, here we go!

"As Director of Education at the Toronto District School Board, I'm responsible for a total of 510 schools in this region including nearly 196,000 students. This board is divided up into twenty-two wards, which means I have to sit in a boardroom every week for eight hours listening to twenty-two super-intendents and school trustees gripe about how impossible it is to create effective change at their schools without additional funding.

"After I finish listening, I proceed to tell them to quit pissing and moaning about everything and do the job we pay them to do. Then I get my chance to bend each of them over and deliver a spanking because they're not meeting expectations. That's all I'm asking you to do, Dominic. You need to do your job. Did you know God created the universe in just one week? And he even took a day off."

"If I was God, I'd deliver myself from this hell. I have no problem doing my job. In fact, miracles I can perform. The impossible just takes a little longer. You need to trust me, Anderson. I know what I'm doing."

"I've got a meeting next month with the minister of education, including some of his disciples, the deputy mayor and an assortment of law enforcement brass. I can't go in there with just my dick in my hand, Dom. They'll eat me up. I've been down this path with them before and it's not pleasant. It's like experiencing a colonoscopy during a double root canal."

Nardelli had always enjoyed Malvoy's metaphoric expressions. He bowed his head slightly and started to snicker. Malvoy, caught off guard, looked sternly at Nardelli. A smirk spread across Nardelli's face as he fought the urge to laugh, but to no avail. Malvoy reluctantly began laughing along with Nardelli. In the end, they surrendered to the moment, hysterically busting a gut.

It was the sound of laughter that caught Maria's attention. She was making photocopies just outside the office and turned her ear to the door to listen. The exchange confused her given the angry shouting she'd heard earlier. Unable to make sense of it all, she simply shook her head in confusion and headed back to her desk as Malvoy wrapped up the meeting and saw his way out.

Nardelli sat quietly at his desk. He was happy the meeting was over but remained troubled by his situation. He had done an excellent job convincing Malvoy he had the situation under control, but Nardelli knew better. The reality was, he had never felt so defeated or lost before. This school was like no other he had ever experienced and his old bag of tricks weren't having the desired effect. He needed to figure it out soon or watch his ambitions fade away.

What the hell did I get myself into?

CHAPTER 5

Jesse sat up in his hospital bed, leafing through a *Sports Illustrated* as he inhaled his second tub of green Jell-O. He had progressed to solid foods including pasta, soups, and of course his favourite, Jell-O. His mother entered the room with coffee in hand. She was spending more time with Jesse now since he was free and clear of his breathing apparatus. Jesse's recovery was exceeding expectations and Dr. Ambrosia was pleased with his progress to date. His memory was improving but the details of that fateful night of October 4th remained a mystery. He had probed the subject with his mother several times but she was reticent, refusing to share or recount the events of that evening. She said she didn't want to stall his recovery or harm his mental well-being. She did reveal his father was being held in prison but that was the extent of it. The situation continued to frustrate Jesse.

"I would kill for a cup of coffee right now," Jesse said as he stared at the warm brew cradled in his mother's hands.

"Not till the doctor clears you first, kiddo. Clear liquids only. I can get you another Jell-O if you want, or some juice," his mother offered. "How are you feeling today?"

"If I eat one more Jell-O, I'm going to turn into the hulk," Jesse chuckled. "Listen, mom." His tone turned serious. "I'm really getting tired of not knowing what happened. You can't keep me in the dark forever."

"Sorry, Jess. It's been difficult for me, too. I feel responsible for you being in here. Because of your father's actions, he's sitting in jail for now. The doctor says it's best to let your memory do the work rather than dumping all the gory details on you at once. Yesterday was your father's arraignment date. He pleaded no contest to all the charges in exchange for a deal. It's not official yet but his sentencing hearing is next week.

"The lawyer says he's expected to get a five-year sentence with possible early parole in three for good behaviour. He's had a few priors for drunk-and-disorderly and minor assault charges that'll be factored in. An occupational hazard, I suppose. His early parole is conditional on his entering some new intense rehab program for substance abuse. He's agreed to go. Can you imagine that? A sober Roger. I wonder what that even looks like," Jeanie chuckled. "He's been drunk from the day I met him. My bet is he doesn't last a day in there. The good news is, we don't need to testify or go to court and relive this whole nightmare."

"Well, that's awful nice of him, isn't it? Five years, huh? Good thing I didn't die. I guess I did him a favour," Jesse said. "Just doesn't seem like much for all the crap he's put us through, mom. What are we going to do for money? Isn't that what caused this whole thing to blow up?"

"Don't worry about that. I still have some money and I've picked up a few more evening shifts at the diner. We'll manage. I also have your father's car right now so my transportation situation has improved. Right now, I'm trying to figure out your father's bank account and finances. There never seems to be much money in there but he always carried a wad of cash in his pocket to pay the bills. I never questioned him about that. They always paid him cash at Club eX, all under the table."

Roger Decruz was a long-time employee at Club eX, a local strip club filled with unscrupulous characters. He'd worked primarily as a bouncer for the past nineteen years. His job paid the bills but he spent a lot of time there; many nights he wouldn't make it home. Needless to say, his vocation was risky and filled with danger. Roger was certainly capable of handling himself but he also suffered a number of injuries over the years of breaking up brawls and manhandling drunks. Nothing serious, but it took its toll. At times, his overzealousness landed him on the wrong side of the law. As an alcoholic, it was the worst possible environment to be working in and likely a contributor to his spiralling condition in the weeks leading up to October 4th.

"I'm going to leave now and get ready for my night shift. You get some rest, honey, and I'll be back tomorrow. Don't forget, your teacher, Mrs. Berger, and her helper, Amanda, will be by later this afternoon to see you. They're bringing some gifts for you from school," Jeanie said tongue-in-cheek. She'd already arranged with the school to bring over reading materials for Jesse.

"Nice try, mom. Would those gifts have anything to do with math, English, and history? Goz already gave me the heads up."

"Isn't that the same Amanda you got in trouble with back in September?" Jeanie asked. "You lost a week of school over her, didn't you?"

"I already explained that whole story to you, mom. She was in trouble and I helped her. That's it. I got booted out a week for my troubles. I'm still very pissed about that."

"Anyways, nice of her to help you out. She seems like a nice girl. Don't forget to thank them both," Jeanie instructed.

"Okay, mom. I'll see you later."

Jesse laid his head down on the pillow for a short rest. He had read every magazine available in his room, including the newspapers he'd requested from the day nurse. He was now walking the halls unescorted as a form of daily exercise with strict instructions to return to his room if he felt dizzy or his headaches returned. His physical state was still fragile and he'd been placed under close watch by the nursing staff.

Dr. Ambrosia entered the room and sat down next to Jesse.

"Hello Jesse, how goes the battle? Have you walked much today?"

"Yep, I wandered the halls all morning," Jesse said, pulling himself off the pillow. "I think the nurses are planning to put me on a leash soon."

"This is good. Your physical health is tied to exercise and nutrition. You are progressing well on both fronts. Your head dressings are in good shape. The swelling on your kidney is down. However, your rib cage will be sore for a while yet so let us know if you require some help in the pain department. If all goes well, the cast on your left arm will come off in a few weeks. Unless you're experiencing headaches or discomfort, we will look to release you within the next few weeks. I'm very pleased with your overall progress."

"Listen, Doc. I never properly thanked you for everything, but thanks for saving my life. I really mean it." Jesse shook the doctor's hand.

The doctor smiled, nodded his head, and left to return to his rounds.

Jesse pondered his return to school. His good friends Goz, Minoo, Trey and JJ had all been by to visit him shortly after he awoke from his coma. He wasn't able yet to speak at that point and the conversations were mostly one-sided. He had much to say to them but couldn't. They managed to keep him smiling, a regular travelling comedy show when they were all together. He was thankful to have such a loyal circle of friends. Growing up in Regent Park, they always had his back and he had theirs.

Nurse Phillips poked her head into the room. Jesse was resting on his side but still awake. "I have a few visitors for you here, Jesse. Are you up to it?"

Jesse turned to face the nurse and sat up immediately. His teacher and Amanda Perone were waiting at the door. "Oh, hi, Mrs. Berger, Amanda. Just pull up a seat over here. Sorry for the mess. I'm going to have to let the housekeeper go. It's just not working out," he quipped.

"Everyone back at Lakewood homeroom 244 says get well," said Mrs. Berger. "We're so happy to have you back, Jesse. You've certainly been through a lot. Amanda here will be helping me get you caught up with your studies but I understand you may be back sooner rather than later?"

"Yes, looks good for either next week or the week after."

"We brought you a few books and assignments that should help you get back into the swing... math, English, and history. Your favourites," she kidded. "There's no need to overexert yourself. Just do what you can and we'll get you the help you need. Amanda has been nice enough to jump in and tutor you through some of the lessons since you're both in the same classes."

"I'll stay back with Jesse for awhile, Mrs. Berger. If you need to leave, I can make my own way back home so no need to worry about me," Amanda assured her.

Jesse watched Amanda intently, his heart starting to race slightly. He had always thought she was hot but knew she was a real magnet for the popular guys. Guys like Owen Reed. It always baffled him how girls like her could fall for such monumental jerks. He'd always felt Amanda was a bit naïve, with low self-esteem motivating her poor choice in guys. She was well-proportioned from head to toe, with long black hair combed over to the side that reached the middle of her back. Amanda could fill out a pair of jeans like no other girl at Lakewood. Her long slender legs started at her shoulders, but that was surely Jesse's imagination hard at work. She had a pair of firm and prominent breasts that complemented her slender build, and accentuated her assets with a tight-fitting top like the ones she frequently wore to school. Amanda's beauty was natural and she wore little makeup; her perfume was intoxicating.

The scent brought Jesse back to that day he rearranged her boyfriend's face. She had been very standoffish since that day and, with the exception of a passing nod or acknowledgement in the classrooms and hallways, they barely spoke to each other. Her presence at the hospital was perplexing but he didn't mind one bit.

"Okay, Jesse. I'm going to leave you now. If you have any questions, either Amanda can assist you or she can pass them along to me. Glad to see you're getting better," Mrs. Berger said, moving towards the door. "Good bye."

Jesse raised a hand in gratitude. "Thanks, Mrs. Berger, for everything."

Amanda gathered the books together and placed them on the vacant chair. She turned to Jesse and started to speak but stopped herself. Then she moved her chair closer to the bed, sat down, and looked at him.

"You're probably wondering what I'm doing here, right? I volunteered to help you out until you get back but the real reason is…" she hesitated, trying to find her words, "the real reason is, I wanted to clear the air with you and apologize."

Jesse looked at her, puzzled. "What do you mean, Mandy? Apologize for what?"

"I was real crappy to you after what happened in the schoolyard. I'll be honest. I was real pissed with you at first for hurting Owen. Can you imagine that?" She let out a nervous laugh. "I even got back with Owen for a short while after that because that's what girls like me do. We go back to guys that treat us like shit. It's a pattern with me. I always manage to pick the wrong guys, you know, good looking guys on the outside but certifiable assholes on the inside." Amanda began to tear up a bit and wiped the moisture from her eyes.

"What were you guys arguing about that day?" Jesse asked, attempting to cut the tension. "Couldn't have been good since he got all physical on you like that."

"That's exactly what I'm talking about. He turned out to be this jealous maniac I couldn't even relate to any more. Every time I even talked to a guy, it made him crazy, asking why and what we're talking about, like, what the hell's that about? I'm just having a conversation with somebody and he assumes I'm sleeping with the guy. It's nuts. Anyway, we lasted for about another week and it started all over again. Same thing. Who am I talking to and why am I talking to him? Shit, like, what the hell's wrong with this guy? So then I decide I need to just cut him loose, walk away. He went crazy. Good thing I did it in a crowded hallway at school or I'd probably be in here with you. I'm telling you, Jesse, he's a scary guy!"

They both chuckled briefly and the tension started to clear from the room. Amanda seemed more relaxed, as if she'd lifted a tremendous weight from her shoulders. "I really wanted to clear this up between us. You deserved better from me. Instead of thanking you, I shut you out and that just sucks, Jesse. I'm so sorry."

"Apology accepted." Jesse then leaned over and wrapped his only functioning arm around her. Her head fell into his chest as he pressed his face against the back of her head.

Oh ya, intoxicating.

CHAPTER 6

Roger Decruz stumbled through the door for the first time in two days. It was 2 a.m. and Jeanie was fast asleep on the couch as the television played to the four walls. He opened the fridge door allowing the front side to slam up against the sink, startling Jeanie out of her slumber. "Where the hell's my beer? Who drank my goddam beer?" he said, slurring his words.

"You drank it all, and where the hell you been for the last two days, Roger? I've been trying to reach you," she shot back.

"I been workin'. I'm always workin', goddamit." He continued to rummage around looking for a bottle to calm him. "Ah, there ya are. There's my best friend, Jack. Come to poppa." He reached to the top shelf of the kitchen cabinet, retrieving his trusty go-to bottle of Jack Daniels.

He sat at the kitchen table and drew a big swig from the bottle, then looked down at the table. "What the hell's all this crap? Ya really need to clean up around here, woman. Everything goes to shit when I'm gone." His eyes were extremely red and swollen.

"Those are all the bills you been ignoring for the past two months, Roger. We're in trouble here. Look at these." Jeanie attempted to get him focused on the bills spread across the table. "Electrical, gas,

rent, water, everything's behind. I'll take care of getting these paid like usual but you really need to give me some money right now," she pleaded.

Jeanie had always taken on the role of looking after the monthly bills and was meticulous, ensuring everything was paid on time. She always needed to coax him for cash but never anything like this. Eventually, Roger would always pull a wad of bills from his pocket and leave it on her dresser. The past few months had been difficult. She'd seen a change in Roger, worse than usual. He was largely absent and appeared to be shutting down on her. "That's all ya ever want from me now, money, money, money!" he said, his voice raising.

Jesse, who'd been fast asleep in the adjoining room, began to stir as the commotion grew outside his bedroom.

"Here's what I think of these fuckin' bills." Roger rose, grabbed one end of the kitchen table and flung it across the room. Papers flew everywhere and lay scattered on the floor. "Ya want money? Here's your fuckin' money!" He reached into his pocket and withdrew a thick pack of bills, pulled back his arm and threw the money violently at his wife. Dollar bills, five, tens, and twenties, now covered the kitchen everywhere.

Jesse stood watching from the doorway of his room, rubbing his eyes, trying to make sense of what was happening. Jeanie turned and noticed him there. "Go back to bed, honey. Everything is fine. We'll be fine," his mother assured him as she always did.

"Ya, go back to bed, ya little puke, before I really lose my temper." Roger glared at his son and grew more agitated by the second.

Jeanie placed herself between them and shouted at her husband, "Why do you have to talk like that to him? Why do you have to be such an asshole?"

Roger was now reaching his tipping point and moved towards his wife. In one motion, he backhanded her, knocking her across the room. Jeanie landed hard on the floor, struggling to regain her feet as Roger lunged towards her. Jesse grabbed him from behind, locking him into a stranglehold, his elbow wedged under his father's jaw, his other hand holding the arm in place. "Not this time, old man!" he yelled.

Jesse's strength was formidable and he held onto his father long enough for his mother to scramble to safety. But in spite of his intervention, Jesse was no match for the Sr. Decruz. Roger had not worked at Club eX for the past nineteen years without acquiring a special set of skills. Even in his current condition, escaping a death hold posed no challenge from a patron, much less a seventeen-year-old kid.

Roger reached back and grabbed his son's crotch, squeezing with force until he felt the arms release from his neck. He turned and grabbed his son by the throat and pressed him to the wall. "What the fuck ya going to do now, kid?" he asked, goading his son.

Before Roger could say another word, he felt hands grabbing his scalp from behind. Jeanie was pulling his hair violently and yelling, "Leave him alone! Let go of him, you asshole. He's just a kid!"

Roger turned his attention to Jeanie again. He swung around grabbing her arm and bending it back until she released her clutch on his hair. "You bitch! That's going to cost ya." He advanced on her again.

Jesse recovered quickly, grabbing a kitchen chair and swinging it as hard as he could against the back of his father's knees, causing him to yelp in pain as his body buckled backwards onto the floor.

Roger was now in full bouncer mode and his fighting instincts fully engaged. He moved towards Jesse with purpose. Jesse backed into the living room trying to distract his father away from his mother. Roger moved forward as Jesse cocked his fist, taking aim at his father's head. As he swung out, Roger blocked and countered with a single blow to the Jesse's forehead. He grabbed Jesse as he stumbled and swung his son hard into the wall. Then he picked him up and threw him onto the coffee table. As Jesse landed awkwardly on his left arm, his head smashed into the side of the solid oak table supporting the TV. There was a sickening crunch and his son rolled to the floor. Lights out.

□

"Jesse, Jesse, Jesse, are you okay? Wake up, Jesse." Nurse Phillips' voice came to the forefront. She was clutching him, shaking his shoulder.

Jesse opened his eyes. He was sweating profusely, his breathing unsteady; he was very disoriented. The events of October 4th were no longer a mystery. He had just relived it.

"You've just had a bad dream, Jesse. You'll be okay now. Let me get you a drink." She quickly returned with a glass of water and a cold, moist cloth that she placed carefully across his forehead.

Jesse was exhausted. His head was throbbing. He lay back against the pillow, waiting for the pressure in his temples to recede.

"Here, take a drink and lay back. Dr. Ambrosia did mention you would likely experience some dreams as your mind gets stronger over these next few weeks. I assume this one was closer to a nightmare?"

Jesse simply nodded. This was not a subject he wanted to discuss with her or anyone else right now. "Thanks, I'm fine now. Just a slight headache but it's starting to fade."

He rested the remainder of the morning, the scenario continuing to replay in his mind; he refused to close his eyes. Lunchtime arrived and the nurse entered his room. "Your lunch is ready, Jesse. Here's your tray. You'll feel better after having something to eat."

Jesse devoured his entire lunch, which included red Jell-O today. He preferred green. Still reeling from the nightmare, he turned his attention to his studies. Jesse had not yet started his math or history lessons and thought it would be a good distraction. He had missed over a month of school and was now procrastinating; he needed to get caught up.

Jesse had never been one to hit the books hard but he managed to keep himself in the high C's and lower B's for grades. He demonstrated a higher potential but school was a burden and his tumultuous home life kept him distracted. His mother always pushed school on him. "You don't want to end up like your father and me, Jess. You need to do well in school. That's your ticket out of Regent Park," she would say.

Jesse propped himself up in bed and started to read through his math book. The next time he looked up, it was nearly 5 p.m. and the nurses were coming around with dinner. He'd been reading for nearly four hours straight. He'd completed most of the required reading in one sitting. Impressive, he thought. But it felt odd.

It occurred to him that he'd spent the entire afternoon with his nose in a math book, a task he'd never accomplished before at home. In addition, the fatigue and frustration that normally followed his math studies were absent. His mind felt clear and centred as he recalled the subject matter. He quickly flipped to the sample questions Amanda had provided him and turned to the algebra section. He randomly chose a sample question and began reading it through.

Question #15. A car travels from A to B at an average speed of 50 km/hour. At what average speed would it have to travel from B to A to average 60 km/hour for the whole trip?

Jesse picked up a pencil and started to work through the answer.

A. Let d be the distance between A and B
B. $T1 = d/50$: travel time from A to B
C. Let S be the speed from B to A
D. $T2 = d/S$: travel time from B to A
E. $60 = 2d/(T1 + T2)$: average speed for the whole trip
F. $60 = 2d/(d/50 + d/S)$: substitute T1 and T2
G. $S = 75$ km/hour: solve the above equation for S

Jesse was impressed with his ability to quickly organize his thoughts and formulate a response. He reviewed his solution a few times before checking the answer sheet. "Yep, that looks about right," he said out loud, impressed with himself. The answer sheet validated his assumption—he was 100 percent correct.

Jesse felt a clear presence of mind, clairvoyance, a keen sense of focus he had never experienced before. His heart started to race slightly as his anxiety level rose. He felt a sense of exhilaration; it scared him, but in a good way.

The nurse entered the room with his dinner. Jesse was pleased to move his attention away from his studies for the moment. He was hungry. Although time appeared to stand still, his appetite did not. He directed his attention to the food on the tray.

Excellent, green Jell-O!

CHAPTER 7

"Let's start off with some good news, shall we, Jesse?" Dr. Ambrosia asked as he examined Jesse's chart hanging on the backside of the bed.

Jesse was up early in the morning, unable to sleep further. Boredom was creeping into his daily routine. He had already completed all his homework and circulated the halls of SickKids before breakfast. The nurses knew Jesse very well by now and understood his personal situation. They were attentive to his needs and aware of the history and trauma he'd endured at the hands of his father. They worked hard to keep him positive and get him well; it was a reputation the staff enjoyed at this facility. SickKids Hospital had become renowned in Canada for its unique ability to provide not only physical support but also specialized care around the emotional needs of its young patients, who were often victims of violence.

"I can always use some good news, Doc. Lay it on me," Jesse said in anticipation.

"Your recovery has been excellent. We're planning to release you next Tuesday. In addition, we also plan to remove your arm cast the same day so it's a double win for you."

"That's awesome, Doc. Thank you." Jesse was hardly able to contain his excitement. He had missed the routine of daily life at school and the camaraderie of his friends; they gave him purpose in his otherwise empty life. He was also anxious to spend more time with Amanda. She had been visiting nearly every day with new assignments, which he would complete with ease. He did his best to hold her attention at the hospital under the guise of homework support. He often asked questions about problems he'd already found solutions for earlier. He felt a spark with her and was fairly confident the feeling was mutual. Little did she know he required little help with his schoolwork; it had become effortless for Jesse. His reading and comprehension had improved tremendously. Jesse attributed his transformation to the rest and quiet the hospital provided him. Whatever the reason, he felt prepared to re-enter his life at school with a heightened sense of confidence.

As Dr. Ambrosia left, Goz and Minoo entered the room. Goz and Minoo were Jesse's very best friends growing up in Regent Park, residents of the government housing projects there, a short distance from Jesse's Sackville Street apartment. Both had challenging lives at home, a common thread for kids growing up in this area of Toronto.

Goz was large for his age, standing at 6'3" and nearly 210 pounds. He was the star defensive tackle for the Bulldogs senior football team, an all-star three years straight. Growing up had been difficult for Goz as tragedy struck early in his life. Following a fatal car accident that took his parents when he was seven years old, his aunt and uncle became mom and dad, which introduced a whole new set of challenges. Although he was seemingly normal and engaging on the outside, a groundswell of anger, grief, and disappointment was brewing just below the surface. During those early years growing up in Regent Park, Goz and Jesse first met serendipitously under strained circumstances. Afterwards, the bond became strong and their friendship inseparable.

Minoo was the product of a hard-working family back in Croatia. He immigrated to Canada as a refugee with his uncle when he was eight years old following the sudden disappearance of his parents. The Croatian Spring and ensuing political unrest brought instability and danger to life back home.

Minoo thrived in his new home country of Canada. He grew very popular at school, particularly with the ladies. He was silver-tongued, never at a loss for words or a quick joke. A natural salesman, Minoo could sell a refrigerator to an Eskimo. Most notably, he once negotiated a complete unconditional release from police custody one evening after illegally entering a Brewers Retail store where he proceeded to access the inventory and drink himself to oblivion.

Minoo had a dark side, however. He remained very guarded where his home life was concerned. Both Jesse and Goz became aware of Minoo's involvement with black market distribution in the area but he didn't attempt to recruit or talk about it with his friends. Minoo was always dressed to kill and never short of cash in spite of his paltry existence in his uncle's RGI unit on Pashler Avenue. He was always generous to his closest friends where money was concerned and willing to help out financially without question. Over time, the three developed a strong attachment to each other.

"Hey, Goz! Minoo! Where the hell you guys been? I'm dying here, man!" Jesse lit up at the sight of his two best friends.

"Last time we saw you, you didn't say a fuckin' word. Ignored us the whole time we were here. Just lying there saying nothing," Goz shot back with a grin.

"I was on life support, you dick. Had tubes coming out of me everywhere like a Chia Pet. Were you expecting me to get up and do the macarena with you or something?"

"By the way, you look like shit, JD. Thought you could handle yourself," Minoo said, joining in.

"Oh, I can handle myself alright. You should see my old man. I kicked the shit out of his fist with my face!" Jesse quipped.

The room filled with laughter. They were freewheeling now. Nothing was off the table and no subject taboo. Jesse continued laughing. He doubled over and started to favour his lower right abdomen as the laughter irritated his bruised and fractured ribs.

"By the way," Minoo continued, "did you get a load of that Nurse Valdez out there? Please tell me you get a daily sponge bath from her."

"No, she doesn't work this side of the hall, but I head out every morning for a walk to look for her. She gives me purpose in life, no word of a lie." Jesse patted his right hand to his heart.

"So what's going on with your old man? They strap him up to the chair yet? Shoot a couple hundred thousand volts through him? Fry him good?" Goz asked, fuelling the discussion.

"Ya, all you'd have left is a boiling puddle of whiskey," Minoo added. They cracked up again.

Jesse explained, "As a matter of fact, they're giving him five years, out in three for good behaviour. He's at Millhaven Penitentiary and apparently in rehab right now drying out in some new radical rehab program he agreed to take."

"Rehab? Rehab? Your old man?" Minoo asked. "I'll bet a thousand bucks he's doing shooters right now with his counsellor!"

"No kidding, tokin' weed with the guards and snortin' coke with the warden more like it," Goz added.

Taking cheap shots at those they detested most in life was a form of therapy for the trio—the more distasteful, the better the therapy.

"Before I forget, Jess. You need to know something before you come back to school," Goz said. "Reed's got a real hard-on for you and I think he's up to something. But don't worry. I'm keeping my ears to the wall. I got your back. To be honest with you, most of the guys on the team loved the way you tuned him up even though you fucked up any chance we had this year of winning the title. Most of them realize he's a dickhead so you've become real popular in the change room. He does have a few loyal losers in his camp, so just keep your head up," Goz warned.

Jesse listened to his friend but offered no reaction. He merely shrugged at the notion of some revenge plot Reed may be hashing.

"So, when are you busting out of here, JD?" Minoo asked.

"Glad you asked," Jesse said. "Matter of fact, the Doc just told me today they're releasing me next Tuesday. Happens to be the same day they're cutting this fuckin' anchor off my arm. Life will be beautiful again."

"I'm sure it will be. Now you can go back to using both hands," Minoo shot back as he flashed a stroking motion over his crotch. They all laughed hysterically.

"What's the deal with Mandy doing the daily Jesse run over here?" Goz asked. "Maybe she's been giving you the sponge bath," he teased.

"Careful now, you're talking about my future wife. Keep it clean. Nah, she's just helping me out with homework and assignments. I don't think there's anything there." Jesse remained coy, not willing to show his hand just yet where Amanda was concerned.

"Before I forget, Trey and JJ say hi. They're helping out Mr. Alverez tonight with the junior football team. They also pass on their thanks to you for the wonderful job you did on our star quarterback. They plan on raising a monument in your name when you get back," Goz explained.

The three continued back and forth for another hour. They truly enjoyed each other's company. Mostly, they kept each other grounded and provided genuine life support for each other growing up in the 'hood.

CHAPTER 8

Ring... ring... ring...

Jeanie ran to the phone in the kitchen to retrieve the call. She was preparing Jesse's room in anticipation for his return that day.

"Hello," she answered, slightly out of breath.

"Hello, am I speaking with Mrs. Decruz? Rejeanne Decruz?" a man's voice asked, sounding very proper and official.

"Yes, this is her. Who am I speaking with?"

"Good morning, Mrs. Decruz. My name is Zach Simon. I'm the lawyer representing your husband, Roger. Do you have a moment to speak with me?"

"I want nothing to do with him and I don't appreciate you calling me at home like this," Jeanie shot back.

"Please, Mrs. Decruz. Roger has been in rehabilitation for the past month and he was just released yesterday. I can tell you first-hand that he is very much a different man from the individual who went in. He is now clean for the first time in decades and his first request to me was to arrange a meeting with you and Jesse here at the Millhaven Penitentiary."

"Then you've fallen for the best con man in history, Mr. Simon. Roger Decruz is still the same man that beat his son to within a thread of his life and the only reason he's not doing life in prison is my son's will to live!"

"If you could just give him a chance to explain. All he wants is to sit down with you and Jesse and explain. He wants to come clean about everything, there so much you don't know about him, and—"

"Please don't call me again, Mr. Simon," she said, cutting him off and hanging up. *Click.* Jeanie sat back in the kitchen chair. Her hands were now trembling and her face ashen. What could he possibly want or say that would be of interest to her?

There's so much you don't know about him…

Jeanie wanted to push the call from her mind but she continued to replay it, trying to understand Roger's true motivation for this meeting. She grew very conflicted. Memories of a warm and nurturing Roger contrasted with the drunk and abusive man he had become. She concluded the negatives outweighed the positives and her choice to dismiss the lawyer was ultimately the right decision.

After a long while sitting at the table, Jeanie finally collected herself and got ready to head out to SickKids Hospital. She was excited at the prospect of having her son back home, sleeping in his own bed, and getting his life back to normal. Jeanie understood the challenges ahead. Besides the physical and mental healing ahead for them both, she understood they were now financially vulnerable. But she convinced herself they would manage; as long as they had each other, they would manage.

□

Jesse stared anxiously at the nurses working to remove the cast from Jesse's left arm. He was excited to finally be free of his 'anchor,' as he called it. The plaster mold was the last physical reminder of his terrible ordeal, with the exception of an incision at the base of his skull and the hair they'd shaved away to save his life a month earlier. His recovery was impressive, as the doctor and nurses kept reminding him. He would miss their company but he was overjoyed with the thought of finally going home to his mother, eating her food, and sleeping in his own bed.

Dr. Ambrosia entered the room and smiled at Jesse.

"Well, Jesse, this is it. Your last day with us, failing any unforeseen surprises. I'm here to do a few last checks on you, kick the tires, as they say. Remember to take it slow. Ease back into your life. In fact, I suggest you remain at home the rest of the week and start up at school next Monday."

"Sure, Doc. I'll take it easy. No heavy lifting for sure," Jesse reassured the doctor, knowing full well he had every intention of attending school the next morning. *No more sitting around for this guy.*

Nurse Phillips entered the room and looked down at Jesse's bare left arm. "You may need to do a few pushups and get some sun on that, Jesse," she teased.

They shared a laugh, both staring at his left arm. Now extremely pale and somewhat emaciated, it was quite a normal look for a limb following weeks inside a plaster cast.

"Your mom is on her way. She called earlier and said she'd be here shortly. You should gather your things. I know she's excited to have you back."

Within half an hour, Jeanie Decruz entered the room and greeted her son with a full body hug. "Okay, let's see it," she demanded.

"It's not so bad," Jesse chuckled as he held out his arm for full viewing. "I just need to pump some iron and maybe hit a tanning salon on the way home."

Jeanie laughed. "Small potatoes, kiddo. Things could have been much worse. I'll take bruises and a pale-looking arm any day. Let's go!"

Both Jeanie and Jesse sat quietly in the car as they drove back to their Sackville Street apartment. Jeanie felt compelled to share the phone call she'd received earlier in the day but was unsure how to broach the subject with her son. Once again she was conflicted and her instincts told her to shelter her son until he was completely healed. Instead, she chose full transparency. She owed him that.

"Listen, Jess. I need to tell you something. Your father's lawyer contacted me this morning by phone." She paused, waiting for some reaction from her son, but nothing came.

She broke the silence again. "Guy's name is Zach Simon. He says your dad just finished up rehab. Apparently he's a whole different man now," she said with a twist of sarcasm in her voice.

"What's he want from you, mom?"

"Us. What he wants from us is a face-to-face visit at Millhaven Penitentiary. He wants to clear the air, wants to sit down and explain things, things we don't know about him apparently. He wants to come clean about everything." Jeanie tried to frame the discussion for Jesse's sake.

"So, what'd you tell him?"

"Basically told him to pound sand. Told him not to call me again, wasn't interested." Jeanie looked at her son for some reaction. "Do you think I did the right thing?"

"Of course, mom. He's a maniac. Can't change a man like that in one month. What the hell can he possibly need to tell us? 'I'm sorry I beat the shit out of you for the last twenty years, Jeanie. I'm sorry I beat you to an inch of your life, Jesse.' I'm not interested in going there so he can clear his conscience. Let him rot in jail for the next three years and think about what he did. Far as I'm concerned, he's dead to me. I did him a big favour already just surviving." Jesse turned sour at the idea.

"Thanks, Jesse," Jeanie acknowledged. "I'm glad we're on the same page with this. I don't want to keep any secrets between us. Open book from now on, you and me."

Jeanie drew a deep breath as they pulled away from SickKids. She understood the challenges ahead and was ready to face them head on. Having her son back gave her strength and resolve. They both sat quietly the rest of the trip home; however, the wheels in their heads were certainly turning.

CHAPTER 9

"Are you sure I can't drive you to school, Jess?" Jeanie asked as she sat and shared breakfast with her son. "I don't mind. The doctor said you should take it easy the rest of this week."

"I'm fine, mom. Besides, Mandy's coming over. We're walking over together this morning." Jesse was pleased at the prospect of spending time with Amanda outside of the hospital.

"What's going on with you two? You've been spending a lot of time together these past few weeks. Have you taken this past the tutor–student level yet?"

Jesse left the comment alone and gathered his books as he packed up for school.

Knock... knock... knock.

"Hey, Mandy. I'm ready," Jesse said, greeting her at the door.

Amanda stepped inside. "Oh, hi, Mrs. Decruz. Big day today. I'll make sure Jesse gets to school on time."

"Hey, thanks so much, Amanda, for everything you've done. We owe you big. You've been a life saver."

"I really didn't work that hard. Jesse made up all the ground he missed. Like he never left."

Jesse and Amanda headed out, chatting as they walked to school. Amanda wasn't herself this morning. She was more quiet than usual; something was definitely on her mind.

"What's up, Mandy? You're a million miles away this morning. You're killing my buzz. Out with it," Jesse coaxed.

"It's Owen. He's not harassing me or anything, but... but... it's like he's always around, watching me. He's like my shadow. You know what I mean?"

"Guys like him have trouble letting go. Typical alpha male. They're not used to getting dumped. He's 90 percent ego and 10 percent hair. It may take a while before he moves on. Don't worry. Once he picks his next victim, he'll forget all about you," Jesse reassured her.

"You're probably right. He just gives me the creeps these days. You should really be careful too, Jess. He's got a long memory and he's said a few things my friends have repeated. You probably got a target on your back. You can't trust this guy."

"I'm a big boy. I can take care of myself," he said dismissing it. "I need to peel away. My locker's over this way. See you later in homeroom."

Jesse moved down the corridor towards his locker, chatting with friends along the way. They were happy to see him again. He received a rock-star welcome on the way to his locker. As he approached, he noticed a large red heart-shaped poster taped to his locker with everyone's signature on it and WELCOME BACK JESSE written across the top. It brought a smile to his face.

He began to work his combination and then felt an uneasy presence behind him. As he continued, the presence grew stronger. He quickly turned and caught Wesley Dragos staring at him. Jesse knew Wesley very well. He was commonly referred to as Wesley the Weasel. Wesley's locker was near Jesse's this year. He was an odd kid with a dark sense of humour and a slanted smile.

Wesley had no filter between his brain and his mouth, a characteristic that often got him in trouble. He always had a scam going, was always looking for a shortcut, always ready to make a quick buck somewhere. Jesse often thought he would do well in life if he could ever channel his enterprising nature towards something meaningful. But at this moment, he was just Wesley the Weasel and he gave Jesse, and many others, the creeps.

"How's it going, Jesse? Heard your dad kicked the shit out of you. I'd be real pissed if I were you," Wesley blurted out in his typical brash manner.

"I'm fine now. Gotta go," Jesse replied making quick work of the conversation and vanishing down the hallway.

Jesse settled into his seat in homeroom. He glanced briefly over at Amanda and shot her a quick smile as she gestured back.

"Good morning, everyone," Mrs. Berger started. "We have a special guest among us this morning." She motioned to Jesse. "Please give Jesse a proper room 244 welcome back."

Jesse blushed as the class erupted into applause. He had always been well liked among this group of peers and had received numerous well wishes from his classmates while he was laid up at the hospital.

"Jesse, can you stay behind for a moment after we finish this morning, please? I have some instructions I need to give you."

After Mrs. Berger dismissed her homeroom, she waited for the class to clear before approaching Jesse. "We've set up a meeting this morning with you and our student counsellor, Mrs. Yang. She will talk with you briefly on some personal matters and then discuss a recovery plan with respect to your studies. Please go see her in her office at 10 a.m. this morning. We've already briefed Mr. Nardelli about our plans and he's approved them. Our primary concern is to get you back on track as quickly as possible. Good luck today."

"Thanks, Mrs. Berger," Jesse said as he left the room. He turned the corner to go to his locker when he noticed Owen Reed, the Weasel, and a few of Owen's football goons gathered at the head of the hall. Owen stood at the centre of the group looking directly at Jesse. Then he extended his right arm, pointed his index finger at Jesse, the thumb straight up, and pulled the mock trigger. A large smirk spread across his face.

Not much doubt what that means, Jesse thought. He stared Owen down, blew him a kiss, and proceeded down the hallway. *Goz wasn't kidding. This guy's got more than just a hard-on for me. More like infatuation.*

Jesse reached Mrs. Yang's office, situated near Principal Nardelli's office. A small auxiliary room often used for interviews and small meetings separated the two offices.

Lian Yang was an excellent student councillor. She was easy to talk to and approachable with a warm disposition. This was a strong quality to possess, a definite asset in this school. Many of the kids at Lakewood High had trust issues with adults and getting them to talk openly was the largest obstacle she faced.

"Hello, Jesse. It's great to see you back. How are you feeling?"

"I'm fine now. They removed my cast. Just a bit of bruising left."

"SickKids Hospital is an excellent facility. I'm very familiar with their programs there. They treat both the mind and body. I was glad when they decided to take you there," Mrs. Yang offered. "We want to get you back into the flow as quickly as possible, but don't worry, we'll take it as slow as you want. We'd like to set up some makeup tests for your English, history, math, and science classes to recover the marks for assignments and tests you missed. We were thinking one subject per week would be reasonable. Is that a schedule you think you can handle or should we spread it out further?"

"If you don't mind, Mrs. Yang, I'd like to take those tests four days in a row next week if that's possible. I'm ready to go."

She looked at him strangely. She was familiar with Jesse's academics records. He was a solid C+, possibly a B- student at best. What he was proposing did not sound like a formula for success in her mind.

"Are you sure, Jesse? That's awfully ambitious. We can easily spread this out till Christmas break if you want."

"Seriously, Mrs. Yang, I'm ready. I can handle it. I've been studying hard and Amanda's been a great tutor. I'd like to get through this sooner rather than later if that's okay with you."

She looked at him apprehensively but didn't want to crush his spirit. She decided to give in to his wishes but was prepared to change course if the results came back negative.

"Okay, Jesse, we'll do it your way. But if you change your mind, please come see me. We'll conduct the testing right here next door in our meeting space. I'll have your math teacher prepare something for you for Monday morning."

◻

Jesse remained after school to watch football practice. He enjoyed the sun on his face and finally finding a quiet moment to think. He'd been bombarded with well-wishers all day long and felt exhausted. As he watched Goz and JJ ripping through the offensive line during scrimmage, he was pleased he had turned down the opportunity a few years back to play football for his high school. Goz had attempted to recruit him numerous times to no avail. It was not Jesse's thing. He didn't relish the thought of knocking heads with gorillas like Goz. His head injury eliminated the possibility of that in any case.

Jesse reflected back to his first encounter with Goz. They were both nine years old at the time and Goz had recently moved to the area with his adopted family. Jesse had just become the target of some neighbourhood bullies and hadn't yet found the strength and confidence to defend himself. As he walked home from school one day, he took a short cut through a local playground when he was suddenly confronted by a few larger ten year olds. He cowered as they stripped him of his backpack and rummaged through his belongings. They continued to taunt Jesse verbally then began getting physical, eventually knocking him to the ground. Before Jesse could find his feet, he turned just in time to see Goz tackle the larger of the two onto the ground. Goz quickly straddled the bully and delivered two quick right-handers to his face. Blood began flowing from the bully's nose. His partner had already fled by the time Goz rose from the ground, leaving his victim bloodied and beaten. Jesse thanked him and the rest was history. The two were as close as brothers ever since.

Practice was done and Goz sprinted over to speak with Jesse before hitting the showers. "Welcome back to paradise, homey. Ready for a vacation yet?" Goz jested.

"Not yet, but soon. I was just thinking of something as I watched you practice. Your mom must spend half her paycheque just trying to feed a gorilla like you. Wouldn't it be cheaper if she just traded you in for two smaller apes?"

"Look who's talking. I'm only an inch taller than you," Goz shot back.

"I was thinking more horizontally than vertically," Jesse joked. "By the way, I think you could be right about Reed. I don't think he's over me yet. It would appear I'm in his crosshairs."

"Oh ya? So what happened?" Goz asked.

"He keeps popping up every once in a while. Likes to stand there and watch me close like some fucking lion stocking its prey. He probably thinks he's intimidating me or something."

"So what'd you do?" Goz asked.

"Well, I didn't want to be impolite. I did what I normally do when someone shows me personal attention like that. I blew him a kiss and stroked my ass for him. He really needs to stop flirting with me."

The pair broke into laughter.

CHAPTER 10

Ring... ring... ring...

"Hello," Jeanie said, answering the phone.

"Hello, Mrs. Decruz. It's Zach Simon. We spoke the other day. Please don't hang up," he implored.

"I thought I was very clear, Mr. Simon. We have nothing further to discuss."

"I know, I know, but your husband is a very persistent man and I want you to understand. I'm completely sincere when I say that I have never witnessed a transformation in a man as I have with Roger. You simply will not recognize him. He truly is remorseful but, more importantly, he insists he owes you and your son a full disclosure of his past, things he's never shared before. He believes it will help you heal as well as him."

"I'm not here to offer forgiveness, Mr. Simon. I've spent the last twenty years as his punching bag and it's not in me to forgive all that. I've already discussed this with Jesse and we are agreed. This is not a good idea and we just want to be left alone to live our lives. Do not call me again," Jeanie finished and hung up. *Click.*

"Who was that?" Jesse asked knowing full well as he'd been eavesdropping from his room.

"It's that damn lawyer again. He's a sucker for punishment. He won't take no for an answer but I made it pretty clear where we stand."

"If you change your mind and want to go, mom, I'll go with you, you know, like, to get some closure. You know, be done with him once and for all," Jesse offered.

His comments caught Jeanie off guard. She was resigned to the meeting never happening, yet her son had just opened the door to that possibility. She pondered for a while and concluded he was testing her resolve and had no desire himself to meet his father.

"No, we've already discussed this, Jesse. Let's stick to our guns. I don't want to open up any old wounds. We've been through enough. End of story."

Knock... knock... knock.

"That's Amanda. I'm off to school, mom. Thanks for the lunch. I might head over to Yonge Street after school with Amanda but I'll be home for supper."

Jesse and Amanda headed out down Sackville Street towards Lakewood High. They were a regular pair now and enjoyed each other's company.

"You want to hit Yonge Street after school? I want to check out the new Van Halen CD at Sam the Record Man. Big sale going on right now."

Amanda was pleased at the proposition as they had spent little time together outside of school and quickly jumped at the offer. "Ya, I'm in. There are some CDs I wanted to check out too. I'll meet you at your locker after."

"Perfect, see you then," Jesse said, heading to his locker.

□

Jesse was anticipating the first of his four days of makeup testing. He was not required in homeroom and had been instructed to see Mrs. Yang over the next four mornings until the testing was completed. Surprisingly, he was not nervous in the slightest. The uneasy feeling he normally experienced before testing was absent. He felt prepared, confident, unencumbered by doubt. He was perplexed by this newfound confidence but accepted it as a good problem to have.

Jesse finished up at his locker and turned to leave. Wesley the Weasel was standing there, staring at him again. He had an uneasy feeling about Wesley. His mere presence made his skin crawl. He felt Wesley may have a man crush on him but just simply nodded and attempted to walk past quickly without engaging.

"I was just looking at the back of your head. Don't worry, man. Your hair should grow back soon. It'll only look shitty for a little while till it grows back," Wesley said, attempting to engage in the way only he could.

"Good to know," Jesse shot back, making quick work of him again before fleeing down the hallway.

Fuckin' psychopath.

Jesse made his way to Counsellor Yang's office. She was busy talking to Principal Nardelli but he elected to rap on the door and enter the room anyway.

"Good morning, Jesse. Just take a seat in the office next door while I finish up with Mr. Nardelli, thank you," she instructed.

Jesse walked through the door to the adjoining room and took a seat. The room was small and sparsely furnished with only a desk, a few chairs, and a phone. On the opposite side of the room was another door leading into Nardelli's office.

Jesse reached into his bag, removed his notes and began reviewing some of the algebra questions he anticipated to be on this morning's test. Mrs. Yang finished up with Mr. Nardelli and vanished down the hallway. Nardelli made his way into the room to greet Jesse. "Welcome back, Jesse. I understand you and I will be neighbours over the next several days. I'll try to keep the volume down but that's a real challenge in my job," Nardelli quipped.

Jesse looked up at the man who'd suspended him just a few short months back. His altercation with Owen Reed was surely fresh in Nardelli's mind; Nardelli was new to the school and had already established a hard-nose approach to troublemakers. He had suspended and expelled a trove of problem students at a pace never seen before at Lakewood High. Jesse, however, respected Nardelli and felt he had been handled fairly given the circumstances. Reed was a high-profile student and Jesse had taken out Lakewood's star quarterback for the season. The infraction cast a spotlight on him and didn't go unnoticed by the entire student population. Nardelli had taken a measured approach. He'd considered the mitigating circumstances and elected suspension over expulsion, issuing a one-week penalty. No one challenged his decision.

Jesse smiled, looking up at Nardelli in his three-piece suit and flawless features. He concluded his principal likely did very well with the ladies. He envied Nardelli's looks, confidence, and general swagger. "Don't worry about me, Mr. Nardelli. You won't even know I'm here."

"Well, it's good to have you back in the swing of things. Good luck on the tests," he offered and headed back to his office.

Mrs. Yang returned with the math test in hand. There were five pages in total, mostly problem format—solving the problem and showing your work. Jesse took the test from her. He felt anxious for the first time, wondering whether his new-and-improved focus and memory was just a fluke, wondering if he was about to bomb badly. This was his first bout of self-doubt since leaving the hospital.

"Take your time, Jesse. We've scheduled two-and-a-half hours for this test, which should be enough time for you. Don't forget to show all your work. Even if you can't arrive at an answer, show your work. That will earn you partial marks. I'll be right here most of the morning in the next office. If you need me for anything, don't be afraid to ask. You can start the test anytime now. Good luck."

Jesse turned the test paper over and started to read the questions. He began working through the document, one question after another. It came to him fast and effortlessly. Jesse worked through the entire exam and finished it in just over an hour. He looked for additional questions he might have missed, but there were none. He felt good. He felt confident as he reviewed his answers.

Jesse chuckled to himself. Nardelli wasn't kidding, his booming voice carried right through the walls. The door did little to muffle the numerous conversations and phone calls Nardelli conducted that morning.

Jesse poked his head out of the office. "Mrs. Yang, can I be excused? I need to go to the washroom."

"Certainly, Jesse," she replied. Jesse headed out the door towards the men's washroom located around the corner. He noticed Anderson Malvoy on his way in to see Nardelli. Malvoy had been a regular visitor to the school this year and made his presence well known with the faculty. Malvoy stuck out like a sore thumb. He was tall with jet-grey hair slicked straight back, dark black pinstripe suit, red tie with designer Italian shoes and black-rimmed glasses. He could easily pass as the prime minister. It was not a secret that Malvoy had a special interest in Lakewood High given the number of visits made here already by the Director of Education. Given the scowl on his face, it was clear Malvoy was not in good humour and Nardelli was about to have his hands full.

Jesse quickly finished up in the washroom and headed back to the test room. He had finished reviewing his test now and had another hour to kill. He could hear rumblings from Nardelli's office and shuffled his chair a bit closer to the shared door. Sitting about a foot away from the door, he turned his ear to listen, ready to be entertained.

Jesse could hear Nardelli's secretary, Mrs. Garcia, enter the room and address the principal. "Mr. Malvoy has arrived. Are you ready to see him now?" she asked.

"Yes, send him in please, Maria."

Malvoy entered the room, acknowledging Nardelli. "Dominic," he said simply and a chair creaked as he took a seat.

Nardelli spoke up. "You sounded urgent when you called me last night. What's going on?"

There was the sound of a briefcase opening and a shuffle of papers that were slammed down on the desk.

"You know what this is, Dom?" Malvoy asked.

"Your recent attempt to destroy our trees and forests?" Nardelli shot back.

Jesse was now engaged in full eavesdropping mode. He held his mouth tightly with both hands, desperately attempting to muffle the laughter trying to escape.

"In addition to all the other issues we're dealing with at this school, imagine my surprise when this lands on my desk. These, Dominic, are the math and English literacy test results from your Grade 9 and 10 students conducted earlier this year. Are you familiar with these results?"

"Why don't you enlighten me, Anderson, since you spent half the evening at the photocopier."

"I'll save you all the hard reading and detail to peruse at your leisure. Let's just have a look at these pretty bar charts here and get to it, shall we? Grade 9 math literacy, less than 30 percent of your students achieved an acceptable level against the standard.

Your Grade 10s, not much better, less than 40 percent of them are hitting the mark. Grade 9 English literacy, only 50 percent are meeting standard. Grade 10 marks are slightly higher at 55 percent. This is abysmal, Dominic. These figures will get published, and once they're out there, we got a full-on shitstorm coming our way."

"I'm way ahead of you, Andy," Nardelli deflected. "I'm in the process of assembling an after school program to improve the literacy in this school. I've been here for exactly two months. Did you actually believe I was going to resolve all the sins of the past by this point? I told you before, miracles I can perform. The impossible takes a little bit longer."

Nardelli was an accomplished escape artist. Mr. Teflon as they referred to him at his previous administrations. He understood the best defence was a good offense; never let your enemy see you flinch or sweat. He knew, however, trying to establish such a program in a challenging school like Lakewood would be uphill against the wind. The faculty was already overburdened, and trying to recruit teachers to spend another few hours a day in this environment, especially to teach math and English to a bunch of challenged students who didn't want to be there in the first place, would be mission impossible.

Malvoy quickly dismissed Nardelli's comments and moved onto the next subject. "What are you doing about the extortion problem you have at this school?"

Jesse, still listening intently, tried to process the question. *Extortion? Did he just say extortion?*

"I've got to be honest with you, Dominic. When you revealed this problem to me last time I was here, the whole subject disturbed me greatly. The idea that our kids are extorting cash and possessions from the younger students bothers me greatly, and it should you as well. Please tell me you have a plan to deal with this."

"We're still gathering intel on that. The problem is the kids are terrified to talk. They go home and their parents are the ones who come to us, not the kids. The kids start making excuses to stay home and then the parent's start putting it together. They see the missing money, lost watches, wallets. They bring the problem here to me and my vice-principals. Best we can tell at this point, the majority of the kids extorting money are not even from this school. Our kids are getting intercepted before they get here in the morning or get back home at night."

Jesse continued to listen. What he was hearing shocked him. He had no idea, like most students at Lakewood, about the dark underbelly of their school. That this was happening in plain sight right out there on the streets angered him. He imagined he and Amanda likely walked right past such kids in the morning on their way to school and were totally oblivious to what was really happening.

"Absolutely incredible. We are harvesting the future criminals of Toronto within these four walls," Malvoy said, framing it.

"You're not listening, Anderson," Nardelli shot back. "Most of this is being perpetrated by kids outside this school. But to your point, you're responsible for all the schools around here and I'm sure Lakewood's hands are not clean either. There's likely a criminal presence here in our own school. You just need to know I'm all over it."

"I want to believe you, Dom, but it would be easier if the statistics supported your results. It's in your best interest to turn the tide and quickly. The school year will disappear just like that," Malvoy said with a snap of his fingers.

"Don't forget our deal, Andy," Nardelli reminded. "I clean up this mess and you put me on the fast track to your job. I expect you to live up to that agreement."

Agreement? Jesse thought. *What the hell are they talking about?*

Mrs. Yang entered the room and Jesse quickly straightened, shuffling the papers in front of him.

"Is everything all right, Jesse?" she asked. "You've been very quiet in here. I thought you had left already."

"No, no, I've finished writing my test but I'd like to use the remainder of the time to review everything if that's okay."

"Of course, use the entire time allotted. That's very smart and prudent of you, Jesse. I'll give you some privacy." She exited but left the door slightly ajar. Jesse moved back to the opposite door to pick up the conversation again.

"You seem to forget. In order for you rise to this position, I need to vacate. In order for me to vacate, I need to showcase successes to my superiors and my future constituents if you understand what I mean. That means you need to take some bleach to this place, Dominic. Do what you need to do. Time's running out, Dominic. Tick, tock, tick, tock."

"You have a short memory, Andy. I need to remind you the source of all major problems at this school is the drugs and alcohol. Aside from the extortion problem we have, theft is a significant problem here as well. We need to go after the root cause. These kids are stealing money to fuel their substance abuse issues. Theft and extortion are just symptoms. It's like shooting water at the top of the flame. You need to hit the base of the flames to put out the fire. We need to go after the source of the drugs and alcohol. I've suspended dozens of kids already for possession but it keeps flowing in here like water. I need to find out how this stuff is getting in and who's feeding the kids this poison." Jesse heard a fist pounding the desk and then a chair being pushed back.

"Okay, Dom. Good talk. I'll be by next week. Let me know what you need, but I want to see some concrete action plans. I like what you're saying but I need some action." There was a shuffling of paper, the snap of a briefcase closing, and footsteps as Malvoy vacated the office.

Jesse rose from his desk and quickly surrendered his test back to Mrs. Yang.

"Good job, Jesse. We'll see you again tomorrow. Same time, same place."

□

Jesse waited outside for Amanda after school. He was deep in thought, still trying to process everything he'd heard that morning. He had a totally different perspective of Lakewood High now. The school had just lost a bit of its lustre in his mind when he considered the gravity of the issues it was experiencing. He'd had no idea. He also started to understand that Malvoy and Nardelli were not just figureheads. They were real people with their own ambitions and goals. It was interesting to hear them converse and strategize. He was particularly impressed with Nardelli's confidence and ability to handle himself and wondered if he could ever rise to such a level some day.

"Penny for your thoughts?" a soft voice asked behind him.

"Hi, Mandy. You ready to go?"

As they made their way off the school property, Jesse glanced around and saw Reed standing near the student parking lot. He watched him closely and, although he continued forward, got an uneasy feeling. He decided to ignore Reed this time.

Jesse shared some of his experience from the morning session with Amanda as they walked downtown. He felt close to her and trusted her completely; conversations grew more intimate the more time they spent together. He was desperate to move their friendship ahead and it was painfully obvious to them both they had not yet shared their first kiss. He longed for her lips, her body. He was anxious to move their relationship to the next level and hopeful the feeling was very mutual.

CHAPTER 11

Sixteen... seventeen... eighteen... nineteen...

Jesse counted off the arm curls as he continued to pump iron and work up a good sweat in the mini gym in the back room of his apartment. He enjoyed the struggle, the muscle burn, and the fresh flow of blood coursing through his body that only a good workout could provide. He was pleased to be back in his after-school routine at home and slowly felt the strength coming back to his body. He was nowhere near his pre-October 4th form. His focus right now was to work his upper body, particularly his left arm, and bring some symmetry back to his upper limbs. There was a decent assortment of weights and equipment in the small room but Jesse preferred a repetitive cycle of push-ups, sit-ups, chin-ups, and any type of resistance exercise that worked his cardio and muscle definition.

Jesse was having a very productive week. He had completed all of his makeup tests over four days. He felt very much in control of his academics for the first time in his life. The same pattern had repeated following his Monday math exam. He made quick work of his next three exams and enjoyed the entertainment that Principal Nardelli's office provided.

A continuous stream of faculty, parents, and students paraded through Nardelli's door all day long. Each meeting was more interesting than the one before. It opened Jesse's eyes to the true goings-on at his school, the real dynamics and challenges faced by teachers, students, and parents. Nardelli was like a maestro. He was able to orchestrate and manage a seemingly impossible schedule. He dealt with people's frustrations, fears, and tears. He could be an aggressive asshole one minute, then turn on a dime and show the type of empathy only a seasoned psychiatrist could pull off. He was impressive, Jesse thought. In addition to the relentless demands within the school, Nardelli continued to handle Malvoy and keep him at arm's length. His phone calls from the director offered the greatest source of entertainment.

What stood out most in Jesse's mind was the plethora of new programs Nardelli was attempting to implement at the school. These programs were innovative and outside the box. There was the Anti-Bullying Program that involved peer-to-peer and senior student involvement, an effective strategy, he thought, given the size of the school and student body. There was the Parent–Faculty Focus Council he was contemplating, which departed from the typical parent–teacher meetings most every school conducted. These sessions would focus on the real-life issues affecting students in this environment, including drugs, alcohol, theft, violence, home life, abuse, and so on. Bake sales and cookie drives were not likely to make it onto the agenda for these meetings, Jesse mused. He followed a short discussion Nardelli had with Mrs. Yang that he called the Last Chance Program. Although he couldn't completely follow the discussion, Jesse concluded the strategy included a mentorship involving both the principal and counsellors. The basic premise targeted the inclusion of suspended or behaviour-challenged students. The program was designed to provide them positive role modelling and offer the support their personal home lives surely lacked. This program resonated with Jesse. He understood the challenges of single parents and the absent parent syndrome so typical in the Regent Park community. It was an epidemic and likely the major contributor for many students turning to substance abuse as an escape from their seemingly hopeless lives. In the end, these programs were great on paper but the reality was that the school system could only reach so far. The gist of most discussions he heard ultimately came down to the same things: resources, staff, and funding, or lack thereof. The sad reality was apparent to Jesse, and likely Nardelli. Making effective change within the school required more than just will or desire. It would require money that the board didn't likely have or weren't prepared to invest.

"Supper's ready, Jess! Wash up! It'll be on the table in five minutes!" Jeanie yelled from the kitchen.

Jesse cleaned up quickly. The delicious smell of lasagna filled the air of their small apartment as he worked out. He always contended his mom made the best lasagna around, the type that would put a seasoned Italian momma to shame. He was so happy to be out of the hospital and back in his home where his mother's cooking had become a regular staple in his life again.

"Tough week so far, huh, Jess? How did today's testing go?" she asked as they both sat down for dinner at the kitchen table.

"Same as the others. Everything went well this week. Hard to explain. I just seem to remember what I read. It just comes to me."

"I'm so happy, Jess. After they told me you would pull through, my biggest concern was that you would fall behind at school. I really want you to do well in Grade 13 next year. You'll need better marks to get into a college or university, you know," she pressed.

"How about I get through Grade 12 first. Then we can worry about next year," Jesse reassured her.

"I need to tell you something, Jess. That guy who called earlier this week, you know, that lawyer guy handling your father? He reached out again."

"He called again? What the hell's wrong with this guy? You want me to scare him a bit, mom? I won't touch him, just a scare." Jesse was clearly irritated by the constant harassment and angst this was causing his mother.

"No, Jesse. Don't do anything. I'm handling it and I don't want you involved. I just think it's important I share this stuff with you. We're a team now, you and me. In fact, I wouldn't be surprised if he tries to approach you next on this. He might try to hook me in through you, you know what I mean? I don't want you acting out on this guy. Don't forget he's a lawyer," Jeanie reminded him. "This time he just left a letter in the door. There was a short note with his business card attached. The note basically says the same things he mentioned before, but this time it said if we agree to go see your father, they will make it well worth our while, whatever that means."

"Sounds like he's offering something now. Maybe money?" Jesse verbalized what his mother was likely thinking.

"That's what I made of it as well. I'm sure he thinks the ball's in my court now but I've decided to just ignore it," Jeanie said with resignation.

"We could definitely use the money, mom," Jesse added. "I'm just saying. If he calls again, you might want to ask him about that."

"I'm just leaving it at that. I have no intention of calling him, Jesse."

"On the subject of money, I picked up another couple 4 to 10 p.m. shifts for tomorrow and Saturday at the diner. I won't be around for supper so just help yourself to leftovers or whatever's in the fridge, okay?" Jeanie said, changing the subject.

"I'll be fine, mom. I'm trying to pick up a part-time job right now at the gas station so I can help out around here with expenses. Goz was telling me about an opening at the Esso station on Parliament Street. I might head out over there tomorrow after school."

"No, Jesse!" she implored. "Please don't. Not right now. We've got enough to survive on for now. I just want you to concentrate on school and getting better. You've only been back for less than two weeks. That's too soon. I'll let you know when things get bad. I won't lie to you. I promise." Jeanie felt a deep sense of responsibility for him, now more than ever. Her priority was her son and to make their new lives work. Although she had fallen out of love long ago and cared even less what happened to Roger, she knew he was resourceful and would continue to follow their lives no matter what. She would not give him the pleasure of failing to provide for her son and their home. She would make things work even if it killed her. She had left her home in Laval long ago and survived the hell it imposed on her life. Surely she could survive this and make it on her own with Jesse here in Regent Park. The thought scared her and doubt crept into her mind daily; however, she would not allow that to dissuade her so long as she had air in her lungs and the will in her mind.

CHAPTER 12

Amanda rose from her bed and made her way slowly to the washroom to get ready for the school day. She could hear her momma getting breakfast ready for her and Gina, her older sister. Poppa had already left for work by now as he did every day at this time.

Gina stormed in. "You going to hog the mirror all morning?" she barked.

"Almost done. Just combing my hair and it's all yours," Amanda replied. She usually rose early, knowing her sister's temperament and routine of monopolizing the washroom each morning. Amanda was kicking herself for getting a late start this morning and having to deal with her sister's wrath. Gina was not very pleasant at the best of times. Amanda avoided such encounters with her at all costs, certainly until Gina's face was on, her hair was up, and her stomach was filled.

Gina was commonly described as 'a three dressed up as an eight' by most guys. Heavy on the makeup and hairspray, Gina stuffed her portly body into uncomfortably undersized clothing each morning as she prepared for school. Amanda concluded Gina suffered from an overly high impression of herself. She envied her sister's self-confidence but deplored her self-righteousness.

"I don't even know why you bother. You hardly use any makeup and you do nothing with your hair," Gina said disparagingly.

Amanda had learned over time to drown out her sister's critical assaults but they took their toll on her nevertheless. It made her question herself and her self-worth. She concluded her sister was just plain nasty. What's worse, Gina was her momma's favourite.

Amanda walked into the kitchen and kissed her momma good morning on both cheeks. Her parents were traditional Italians who had immigrated to Canada shortly after Amanda was born. Breakfast more closely resembled a smorgasbord but Amanda preferred a simple helping of toast and coffee each morning. Her slender build provided a stark contrast to her sister, Gina.

"Why you not eat more, Amanda? You so skinny. No one gonna marry a skinny woman, momma mia!" her mother preached.

Amanda had learned to ignore such comments and just smiled at her mother out of respect. Gina finally emerged from the washroom and came to the table, filling her plate to capacity.

"See, look atta Gina. She eat well and look atta her hair anda her face. So beautiful. Thissa how you getta good man," her mother continued in her broken English. "How issa Rino doing, Gina? He's sucha good lookin' boy."

"He's great, momma. Look at what he bought me." Gina reached into her blouse and pulled out a necklace to show her mother. She shot a glance at Amanda to gauge her reaction to the gift.

"Thatsa beautiful! He's such a good boy, Rino. You gotta gooda one there, Gina."

Amanda ignored the exchange. Her mother's glowing references to Gina's boyfriend, Rino, amused her. She knew Rino and how he operated. She also knew at least three other girls who 'knew him well'… very well. She quickly finished the rest of her breakfast and headed out to the door.

Jesse was outside waiting for her and they set off for school. It was Friday morning, the last day of the school week, jammed full of tests and assignments. Jesse felt good about himself. He was finally back on track. He enjoyed this part of his day, particularly spending time with Amanda who was now occupying his thoughts around the clock. It occurred to Jesse that his life had changed; it had changed for the better both at school and at home. He felt strange, undeserving in a way, now that he was no longer burdened with the anticipation of conflict in his home. No more screaming, no more physical or mental abuse, all things he'd come to expect in his life living with his parents on Sackville Street.

"Hey, Jess, can I ask you something? And I need you to be completely honest with me," Amanda started.

"I don't like the sound of this but sure, Mandy. What's wrong? What's on your mind?"

"Do you think I'm too skinny?" she asked, stepping away from him.

"Is this a test or something, Mandy? You're joking right?"

"No, I'm serious. You think I should wear more makeup or do something different with my hair?"

"I'm not sure where this is coming from, Mandy." Jesse stopped walking and turned her body square to his. His eyes met hers. "Look at me, Mandy. You're absolutely perfect just the way you are and don't ever let anyone convince you otherwise." He wrapped his large arms around her and they shared a moment.

"Speaking of perfect, my mom's working tomorrow night. Won't be home till some time past 10 p.m. They're playing the original Rocky movie on TV. Why don't you come over and we'll hang out at my place. I'll cook you dinner and we'll watch some

Rocky Balboa. *Whadda ya say, Adrienne?*" Jesse asked projecting his best Sylvester Stallone voice.

Amanda chuckled. "You're going to cook me dinner? Do I get fries with my Big Mac?" she asked jokingly.

"Nah, no McDonald's for you. I'm going all out because you're very special to me. Tomorrow we'll be dining on a large bucket of Kentucky Fried Chicken. And since I really like you, I'm going to splurge on a large container of coleslaw. How's that sound?" Jesse asked with a confident smirk on his face.

"Well, how can I turn down an invitation like that? A girl would have to be crazy to turn down some KFC followed by a fine Rocky movie. Sounds perfect. What time shall I come by?" Amanda asked.

"Dinner will be served at 6 p.m.," Jesse responded, using his preppy voice.

"I'll bring dessert. Poppa just got a new load of Jos Louis and May Wests," Amanda added.

A huge smile spread across Jesse's face. Amanda's father worked for Vachon as a delivery driver, transporting their dessert cakes to various grocery outlets in the Toronto area. One of the perks of his job was first dibs on the slightly imperfect cake boxes occasionally damaged in transport. He would bring home boxes of desserts for his family from time to time. She would need to hide some away from Gina, who had a similar weakness for the dessert cakes. Amanda had started bringing the Jos Louis cakes for Jesse at lunchtime, which he loved and devoured. She knew this would please him greatly.

"That's awesome. By the way, did you—"

"Yes, yes, I brought some for lunch today," Amanda said, reading his mind.

"I think I love you!" Jesse exclaimed unable to contain himself. They both laughed.

Once they arrived at school, they went their separate ways. Jesse approached the hallway leading to his locker. As he was ready to make the turn, he decided to slow down and peer around the corner first.

Fuck, there he is again!

Jesse had grown accustomed to bumping into the Weasel every morning at his locker and, sure enough, there he was again. He was like a housefly on dogshit, Jesse thought. Unwilling to endure another awkward conversation with Wesley, Jesse elected to circumvent the hallway and take an alternate route. He was willing to wait it out until the Weasel left.

□

Mrs. Berger was organizing and packing her things away. It was the end of a long day and a long week. She was looking forward to the weekend and some much deserved R&R.

Mrs. Yang entered the room holding a blue file. She approached Mrs. Berger. "Hi, Marianne. Have you got a sec? I need to show you something and it can't wait till next week."

"Sure, Lian. What's up? Is there something wrong?" Mrs. Berger detected a note of reticence in her voice.

"Maybe. I'm not sure. You need to see this," Mrs. Yang said as she opened the blue file. "We've just compiled the results of Jesse's makeup exams. Here's the results summary sheet." She handed the document to Mrs. Berger.

"Oh my God. Are you certain this is correct?" she asked in amazement.

"Yes, we've double checked everything. It's all accurate," Mrs. Yang assured her.

"We need to bring this to Dominic right away," Mrs. Berger insisted.

"Agreed," she replied.

They bolted from the room and headed towards the principal's office.

CHAPTER 13

"Good morning, come on in boys. Haven't seen you two in a long time," Jeanie said, inviting Trey and his brother, JJ, into the apartment. They lugged their football gear inside. The brothers came to scoop up Jesse on their way to Saturday morning football practice.

"Jesse! Jesse!" Jeanie yelled from the doorway. "Trey and JJ are here for you!"

"Okay, coming," Jesse responded from the washroom where he was putting the final touches on his hair.

"How you boys been?" Jeanie asked. "How's Winnie been? Haven't seen her in a long time," Jeanie said, referring to the Jackson matriarch, Winifred Jackson.

"S'all good, Mrs. D," Trey replied.

"Must be real quiet 'round here without Rog, huh, Mrs. D?" JJ asked, attempting to make conversation. His comment was met with a head slap from his older brother.

"What's wrong witchu, man? You don't be asking that, fool!" Trey reprimanded his younger brother.

Of all Jesse's friends, the Jackson boys were Jeanie's favourite. She loved them to death from the time they were little boys growing up in the neighbourhood, always mischievous and getting into trouble, innocent-type trouble. Real boys, she thought.

The brothers were born into a single-parent family ruled by Winnie, the matriarch. The Jackson boys lived in the RGI units on the south side of Shuter Street, growing up in the '70s and '80s in a tough neighbourhood in Regent Park. The boys' father physically abused them until Winnie decided to boot him to the curb when Trey reached the age of ten.

In spite of all their challenges, Winnie was a strong woman, even though she stood barely 5'4" tall and about as wide. She ruled with an iron fist and did a formidable job of keeping her kids out of trouble. She had pushed them hard into sports, reasoning that it would do them well growing up and help maintain a distance from the criminal element that lurked everywhere in the Regent Park community. Winnie had decided to start both boys in school at the same time despite Trey's advanced age; Winnie recognized the challenge of keeping JJ under control at an early age. He was a hyperactive child and always getting into trouble. JJ was a stark contrast to Trey, who matured very quickly and adopted a protective role where JJ was concerned. Winnie believed the best chance for JJ was to keep his older brother close by to watch over him until he matured, a process that was clearly still in progress. She worked closely with the school system to ensure her sons were teamed together in the school classroom each year, an arrangement they always accommodated.

"That's okay, Trey. JJ's absolutely right. It's been real quiet around here these days," Jeanie replied in amusement. She had grown accustomed to JJ's candour. You never had to wonder what was on JJ's mind. He was never too shy to share.

The dynamics within the Jackson family unit had amused Jeanie from an early age. The Jacksons were an animated group and had perfected the fine art of the head slap, a behaviour the boys picked up growing up under the heavy hand of their mother. It was normally applied to the boys when they acted out, and that was quite often. The head slap, when perfectly executed, created a sound much like in the '70s comedy series, The Three Stooges.

Jeanie recalled an incident a few years back during a Lakewood League football game. The high school football games were always well attended with a mixture of students, friends, and parents lining the field; it would normally draw 200 to 300 spectators. Winnie Jackson was in her element at these games. She had a clear presence and a voice to match. She could be seen screaming at her kids throughout the game. This particular game was tied late into the fourth quarter with Lakewood's rival innercity team, Cabbagetown High.

It was third down and short yardage. Cabbagetown was in possession of the ball. They elected to run a play instead of punting. JJ jumped the line from his right defensive tackle position and was called offside. The penalty gave Cabbagetown a first down and they went on to score a winning field goal in the dying seconds of the game. It was a real heartbreaker. Following the game, Winnie was so enraged she charged down to the field where the players had gathered after the game. After she arrived in the scrum, an infuriated Winnie could be seen yelling at the top of her lungs at her son JJ.

"What's wrong witchu? Whatchu be doin' jumpin' offside? You done cost your team the game, fool!"

She continued to berate him in front of his peers, much to their amusement. This was nothing new to the Lakewood players; they were all quite familiar with Winnie and conditioned to these types of outbursts. Winnie's grandstanding was always a huge source of amusement to players, coaches, and spectators alike.

"Take off your helmet!" she screamed.

"No, mama, not now," JJ replied, anticipating what was next.

"I said, take off your helmet!" she yelled again.

JJ relented and sheepishly removed his helmet. *Here it comes.* Winnie drew her right arm down and, in one quick and efficient motion, swung her hand upwards landing a perfect head slap on JJ's head. The team erupted in laughter as Winnie stormed off the field leaving JJ holding the side of his head and his pride. JJ had come to expect this from his mother. He understood her emotional outbursts and always took it in stride. Trey, on the other hand, was embarrassed and tended to distance himself from the drama when he anticipated a situation was about to come unhinged. In the end, they both loved their mother and knew this was just her way. The bond and love within the family was strong and Winnie Jackson could take full credit. They were living a reasonably normal life thus far, in spite of where they were being raised.

Jesse finally emerged from the washroom. "Hey guys, ready to go?"

"Maybe the boys would like to take a few chocolate chip cookies with them, Jess." Jeanie presented a tin of cookies to the boys.

"No thanks, Mrs. D," Trey replied. "I'm good."

"Oh ya, thanks, Mrs. D. You don't mind I score a few?" JJ jumped in quickly to seize the opportunity.

Trey took a quick swipe at JJ's head but missed. JJ had done well to anticipate it.

"It's okay, Trey. JJ can help himself to as many as he wants. Here you go, honey." Jeanie held the container for JJ who proceeded to pull four cookies from the tin.

Jesse looked on in amusement. There was never a dull moment with these two. They had an endearing quality and were completely oblivious to the comic relief they provided to those around them.

The three boys headed out to Lakewood's football field, situated at the back of the property. Jesse took his seat in the stands as he waited for the team to dress and hit the practice field. He had brought along the latest issue of *Sports Illustrated* to read while he waited. As he flipped through the pages, he felt footsteps coming his way from behind. As he put the magazine aside, he turned around and stiffened when he saw who was standing over him.

"How's it going, Decruz?" Owen Reed greeted him.

"You seriously talking to me right now, Reed?" Jesse sat up, keeping his gaze on his adversary.

"Come on, Decruz. Don't be like that. Just came to say hello," Reed offered.

"Okay, hello, have a good day." Jesse attempted to wrap things up quickly.

"I heard what happened to you. Real tragic," Reed continued. "Didn't know your old man was such an asshole. You seem to be okay now."

"Did you have anything specific on your mind, Reed? You come over here to ask me out on a date?" Jesse asked sarcastically.

"Look, I'll admit, the idea of taking some revenge on you crossed my mind." Reed started to bring some context to his visit. "After all, you did set me back a year on my football career, not to mention I'm still having trouble breathing and my smile's not so nice anymore. Oh ya, almost forgot, you were also good enough to start things up with my girlfriend as a final act of gratitude," he added. "But I figure, life has a funny way of making things right, making things even, you know. I figure what happened to you is some kinda karma thing, figure you paid your dues now."

"We're not about to hug this out here, are we?" Jesse asked flippantly. "I'm not sure I can handle that." Jesse focused on

Reed, trying to figure out his end game; the interaction was very odd and confusing.

"No, no kissing, I promise," Reed played along. "Just a handshake to put this whole mess behind us." Reed stretched out his right hand and offered it to Jesse.

Jesse looked at Reed strangely, taking his hand apprehensively and shaking it. "Fine, no hard feelings." Then, Reed departed just as quickly as he came.

Jesse tried to read his *Sports Illustrated* but remained stuck on the same page for ten minutes; he was still distracted from the conversation he'd just finished with Reed.

What the hell's this guy's game?

The Bulldogs took to the practice field. The team looked solid. They looked quick and in excellent shape this year in spite of Reed's absence. Their backup quarterback, Reggie Jones, was a senior, a very steady and competent athlete. They would no doubt be contenders again this year. Jesse took a strong interest in this year's team. He understood any shortcomings on offense from the quarterback position would likely reflect badly on him. As a result, he became a huge Reggie Jones fan. With Goz and JJ as defensive tackles, and Trey at halfback, Jesse concluded the Bulldogs did indeed have a contending team for their '85 season.

Following practice, Trey and JJ stayed back to help Mr. Alverez with the junior football team practice that followed right after the seniors'. Manny Alverez was the physical education leader at Lakewood High and took on the assistant coach's role for the senior team in addition to his head coaching role for the juniors. He was a dedicated teacher who seemingly spent all his time at school supporting the football program including numerous other sporting events the school organized. Nardelli had taken a shine to Alverez early on and appreciated his dedication to the job and school. He often took the opportunity to wander down to the gymnasium after school let out to chew the fat and share a cup of coffee with him. Jesse noticed Trey's leadership qualities developed significantly under Mr. Alverez's guidance. He was more like the father figure Trey never had.

Goz emerged from the school after showering and made his way over to the bleachers where Jesse sat. "Hi, sweetie, thanks for waiting for me. Come here and give me a kiss." Goz leaned into him mocking a fake kiss to the cheek.

"Get off of me, you fuckin'"mo," Jesse said, pushing him away; he'd endured this type of greeting from Goz in the past.

"Speaking of kisses, did I see you and Reed deep throating each other over here earlier? You guys looked pretty chummy from where I was."

"Ya, I'm pretty sure he's trying to fuck with my head. Strangest conversation I ever had. Still trying to figure out his move," Jesse replied.

"Well, I wouldn't let my guard down with him. He's slippery and you can't trust the bastard. I haven't heard anything yet, but nothing would surprise me where he's concerned."

"So after he reminds me all the bad shit I did to him, including stealing his girl, he wants to make nice and shakes my hand. It sounds fucked up, don't you think?" Jesse asked, looking to Goz for validation.

"Ya, just stay away from him, JD. You don't need the drama and you definitely don't want to mix it up with him. Don't forget, you can't afford any more hits to the noggin till you heal up," Goz warned.

"I'm not planning to duel with this guy, if that's what you mean. I'm staying on my best behaviour till I get back to 100 percent," Jesse assured him.

"You got plans tonight? Want to hang out?"

"Can't. Date night with Mandy tonight."

"You trying to tell me she's got a nicer ass than I do?" Goz asked shaking his backside.

"Don't give me a hard time. I'm actually a bit nervous about this. It's really our first time alone together where we're not at the hospital or school," Jesse said apprehensively.

"Do you need me to explain the bases to you again? First base is kissing, second base is—"

"Fuck you, Goz. I'm serious. I really like this girl. Don't want to mess things up," Jesse said. "Can you pick me up a bottle of white wine from the LCBO? I got some cash here for you."

Jesse and others often used Goz to acquire liquor. Given Robby Gosling's size, maturity, and facial hair, he disguised his true age quite well, easily passing for a nineteen year old.

"There we go. There's a plan that never fails. Always willing to assist the desperate and underaged," Goz added chuckling. Goz was always willing to help his friends acquire alcohol. The task would normally yield enough cash to procure his own booze, a small price he thought for his valuable services.

"I'll come by your place around 4 p.m. to pick it up. Thanks, buddy," Jesse replied as they headed back home.

□

"You sure you don't want me to whip something up for you guys tonight, Jess? I don't mind," Jeanie offered.

"No, mom. I'm just going to pick up some KFC and we're going to watch a movie. We don't need a fancy meal, but thanks for offering."

Jesse waited till his mom went off to work before he headed out to pick up the chicken on Dundas Street. He swung by Goz's apartment on the way back to pick up the wine. He heard shouting from inside the apartment as he approached.

Fuck! His mom must be off her meds again.

Jesse had witnessed the pattern many times with Goz's mother. She tended to blast off a few days a month, although her bipolar condition had become more controlled over the years. Usually lasting only three days on average, the severity of the event was sometimes extreme; it took its toll on Goz and his younger siblings. This usually only occurred if she missed or neglected her medication. In spite of his dismal home life, Goz appeared fairly normal outwardly, but his temper had worsened. He generally kept his temper under control but you didn't want to be anywhere near him when it went off. Football was a perfect outlet for Goz; it gave him purpose and a distraction from his daily responsibilities at home.

Jesse knocked on the door.

"Hey, Jess. Figured it was you. Got your homework right here." Goz shot him a wink and handed a bag to him while his mother looked on.

"Hey, Mrs. G. How you doing?" Jesse asked, acknowledging her.

"I'm well, Jesse. Great to see you back. How you feeling, honey?" she asked.

"On the mend. Much better now, thanks."

Mrs. Gosling left the room as she said goodbye.

"Thanks, man. I owe you," Jesse said as he checked the bag's contents for wine.

"Good luck tonight. Did you want me to review third and fourth base with you first before you go?" Goz offered.

They both chuckled as Jesse turned and departed.

It was shortly after 6 p.m. when Jesse heard the knocking at the door. He was pleased he'd tidied up the apartment. It was normally well kept, but Jesse wanted to impress Amanda.

"Hey, Mandy," Jesse greeted, leaning in for a hug. "Is that what I think it is?" he asked, looking down at the bags Amanda was holding.

"Yep, but it's not for now. Keep it till after we eat," Amanda instructed as she spilled the contents onto the table.

As promised, she had brought over a trove of Jos Louis and May West dessert cakes that her father had foraged from Vachon the night before.

"Okay, okay, after dinner," Jesse submitted. "First things first." Jesse shuffled over to the far end of the kitchen cabinet and pulled two wine glasses off the top shelf. He then fashioned a pirouette as he swooped over to the fridge, pulling out a bottle of white wine.

Amanda watched Jesse intently. She flashed a smile, impressed to see he had actually put some thought into their evening. Jesse uncorked the bottle and filled each glass halfway. Handing a glass of the Chardonnay to Amanda, he took his glass in hand and slowly raised it towards hers.

"Here's to our very first real date. And to Kentucky Fried Chicken and Vachon cakes for making this evening memorable," Jesse toasted, taking a sip. "And finally, here's hoping my mother doesn't return before 10 p.m. tonight."

Amanda laughed, amused by Jesse's toast. They clinked their glasses and drank. Then Amanda boldly moved towards Jesse and kissed him. It was their first kiss. Startled it was happening so soon, Jesse grabbed their glasses, set them on the table and pulled Amanda into a full embrace. He could feel her tremble in his arms, or perhaps it was him; he didn't care. They were both feeling the rush of endorphins flooding through their bodies with the excitement and intimacy of the moment. They separated, smiling, then put their attention to the food, pulling out the chicken and coleslaw.

They continued to drink from the bottle of wine, enjoying each other in conversation and feeling very comfortable together. After they cleaned up, Amanda pulled out the Vachon cakes as Jesse turned on the TV and flipped to the channel where Rocky was scheduled to begin. It was one of Jesse's favourite movies. He knew most of the dialogue by heart as he'd watched it numerous times. He started referring to Amanda as Adrienne, getting back into his Sylvester Stallone persona. Amanda was amused and enjoyed his playful side.

They sat side by side and watched the movie, sipping the last of the wine. They both started to feel the effects of the alcohol and began making out again. Amanda placed her glass down on the side table and rotated her body towards Jesse. Then she climbed onto him, straddling his lap, facing towards him. Jesse felt the excitement starting to grow within him. He wondered which base Goz would classify this current configuration. Amanda was now kissing him hard and slowly grinding her pelvis down on his lap. Jesse could now feel the pressure from inside his jeans growing as he slowly moved his hands under her blouse from the back. He made a clumsy attempt to unclip her bra and was surprised when Amanda reached back to assist him. It became clear to Jesse now he would not likely be viewing the final fight sequence tonight with Apollo Creed versus Rocky Balboa.

CHAPTER 14

"Breakfast, Jess!" Jeanie yelled out towards her son's bedroom. Jesse was already up; he'd been lying awake in his bed for the past hour, thoughts of the previous night replaying in his mind.

"Be right there!" he shouted back, somewhat annoyed the moment had passed.

"You were awfully quiet last night when I got home. How was your evening with Amanda? Based on the empty containers in the trash, looks like KFC and Vachon were a real hit," Jeanie observed.

"Ya, might have over done it. My stomach's a bit off this morning," he shared with his mother, attempting to disguise a mild hangover. "Saved you a few pieces of chicken in the fridge for later if you're interested. I'm going to pass on the leftovers. How was work? Any generous tips worth talking about?"

"No big tips but I did get a couple of romantic propositions," Jeanie quipped.

"In other words, typical night," Jesse added.

The two sat quietly eating breakfast. Sunday morning was always a down day they both enjoyed. It gave them time with each other to reconnect and decompress from the week.

Knock... knock... knock.

"Who could that possibly be at this time of the morning? You expecting anyone, Jess?" Jeanie looked to her son.

"Not me."

Jeanie peered out the front door before she opened it. "Jesus Christ, I can't believe it," she said out loud. "This goddam lawyer's got a death wish!"

Jesse rose from his seat with a scowl on his face. "Let me take care of this, mom. Please."

"No, Jess. Sit back down. I'll deal with him. I don't want you involved, okay?"

Jesse complied and sat back down reluctantly.

"Hello Mrs. Decruz, sorry to—"

"What part of 'don't call me again!' did you not understand, Mr. Simon?" she demanded, glaring at him. "You should know that request also includes 'don't knock on my front door'!"

"I'm not here to sell you any further regarding your husband, Mrs. Decruz. I'm simply here as a messenger today and was asked to deliver this letter." He held out an envelope to her.

"What is this?" she asked Mr. Simon, refusing to accept the letter from him. Jesse watched the exchange closely from the kitchen table.

"This letter was handwritten by your husband, Mrs. Decruz. He gave me specific instructions to hand deliver to you. Although I don't have any first-hand knowledge of its contents, he asked me to provide you my card and instruct you to contact me regarding any further contact with him."

Jeanie finally reached out her hand to receive the envelope. "Okay then, I guess your job is done here, Mr. Simon," she said, dismissing him.

"Thank you, Mrs. Decruz. Have a good day." Simon departed in haste.

"What did he give you, mom?" Jesse asked with a heightened sense of interest.

Jeanie dropped the envelope on the kitchen table in Jesse's direction. "Love letter from your father, I suppose."

Jesse took the letter, holding it up to the kitchen light, trying to decipher any markings on the contents inside but to no avail. He looked at his mother. "Okay, you didn't take this letter from numbnuts if you weren't planning to open it," he said, coaxing his mother to reveal the contents inside. "More than just a letter in here. Too bulky for just a letter. There's something else, but I can't tell what it is." Jesse held the envelope up to the kitchen light again.

"You really want me to open this now, Jesse?" She sensed her son's uneasiness to get on with the inevitable.

"It's not what I want, mom. It's what you want," he replied, turning the tables on her. Curiosity was killing him, however.

"Okay, let's get this over with then," she said with resignation in her voice.

Jeanie carefully tore through the flap of the envelope with a kitchen knife. She slowly peered into the envelope before placing a hand inside. The outer document was a letter of some type. She removed it from the envelope and unfolded the document to discover a significant packet of bills inside.

"Is that money?" Jesse blurted as his mother started to feather away the stack of twenty-dollar bills from the package. Jeanie made a quick count of the cash in her hands.

"What the hell?" she said with a hint of trepidation. "There's at least fifteen hundred dollars here, Jess." She looked at her son in bewilderment. Jeanie then took the handwritten letter and spread it out on the table. She positioned the letter between herself and Jesse so they could both read together:

Dear Jeanie and Jess,

By now ya know I done my time in rehab. First time in decades I bin clean and sober, best I ever felt, no word of a lie. Docs in here are amazin. They didn't just flush the crap out of my veins, they also fixed my head, I aint been right up there for a long time you know, no need tellin you guys that. Only an asshole hurts the people he loves, that's what I done and that's what I been, a real asshole, 100 percent. Doc says the key to gettin better, key to healin, is tellin the truth, all of it, no matter how bad, just tell the truth he says. He keep sayin *the truth will set you free* and I believe him. I talk to him bout all the bad stuff I did, like a big weight off my shoulders, felt much better after. Best part, he can't be tellin no one what I tellin him. Called it doctor patient confidentiality. That's why I told Zach to set up a meetin here, got so much I need to say to both ya. I hurt both ya real bad, specially Jess, so don't spec you to forgive me. Jus want to tell ya both sorry and tell the whole truth bout me, then we can all move on, its like closure, the Doc says. Figure I owe ya that much. I spec you guys need some cash by now. I put some money in the envelope for ya, hope that fix some of the bills for now. If ya come see me at Millhaven, I got lot more where that come from. Not goin to ask ya for nothin, just want you to listen to what I gotta say, and then you can go. Just contact Zach, he'll set it up. I know I never say this but Doc says it helps me heal, but I do luv you guys even though I don't know how to show it. See ya soon I hope.

Roger Decruz

Jeanie finished reading and looked at her son, unsure what to say or how to react. She looked at him for some reaction. She had never witnessed her husband be quite this contrite, much less apologetic. She was conflicted, still trying to process the letter. "What do you think, Jess. What do you make of this?" she finally asked.

"I don't know, mom. He's either the best con man ever or… it could be the real deal. Maybe he found God. I'm not sure."

She thought about it for a moment. "It sounds sincere. He's not asking for forgiveness. Just wants to meet us. Outside of that, he's not asking us for anything."

"Hell, mom. What've we got to lose. Besides, he's *got a lot more where that came from*, the letter says. Worse case, we get more money out of this. We can sure use more money, mom." Jesse looked to her for affirmation.

Jeanie stared at her son who was seemingly less resigned at the thought of a future meeting with his abusive and now imprisoned father. Sensing her son's resolve, she relented. "Okay, I'll call Zach this afternoon. Besides, if we don't do this, he's just going to keep coming back over and over." She smiled at Jesse as he nodded in agreement.

CHAPTER 15

Jesse arrived at school Monday morning with Amanda. He retrieved a few books from his locker and headed to homeroom. He'd thoroughly enjoyed the events of the past weekend and was feeling particularly good on this morning. Even the letter from his father had now moved from disturbing to intriguing. He and his mother were tentatively scheduled to meet Roger the following weekend at the Millhaven Penitentiary pending arrangements through Zach. Jeanie had contacted the lawyer the previous day and informed him they would be willing to meet with her husband on the following Saturday.

Jesse entered room 244 and saw his teacher, Mrs. Berger, in discussion with a substitute teacher who was seated at her desk reviewing the day's agenda. Mrs. Berger addressed the class, indicating she was required at another meeting this morning and a supply teacher would be filling in her place. She approached Jesse. "Jesse, can you come with me, please? We have a meeting scheduled this morning with Mrs. Yang and Mr. Nardelli in his office."

Jesse assumed the meeting would be to discuss his progress and next steps as he recovered his schedule at school. Mrs. Berger was not herself this morning, he noticed. There were the normal pleasantries exchanged but, as they approached Nardelli's office, Jesse began to feel uneasy.

Mrs. Garcia waved them both through as they arrived in the office. Nardelli was seated at his desk while Mrs. Yang sat at a side desk. There were a number of documents in front of him. He glanced up and acknowledged their presence.

"Have a seat here, Jesse." Nardelli pointed to a vacant chair as he rose from his desk. He pulled a single document from the blue folder at the front of his desk. He quickly perused it then sat on the side of his desk closest to Jesse.

"What I'm looking at here, Jesse, are the results from your examinations conducted last week." Nardelli looked down at the document in his hand examining it again. "I'm curious, how do you think you performed on these tests?"

"I don't know. Pretty good I guess," Jesse replied, now feeling uncomfortable with the dynamic of the meeting.

"Pretty good? I should say so. Why don't you have a look for yourself. Here's the summary sheet of your results." Nardelli handed him the paper.

Subject	Score
English	89
Science	93
Math	92
History	90

Jesse examined the document and reviewed his marks. A smile spread across his face. He was clearly impressed with himself. This meeting was obviously to congratulate him, to recognize him for the excellent results. He looked up at the threesome but their faces were serious and disconcerting.

Nardelli studied him hard. He was highly attentive to facial expressions. He was looking for some crack in Jesse's armour but saw none. "Now Jesse," Nardelli started again, "can you please explain to us how a student who has just suffered through a life-threatening injury, a student who has missed over a month of school, and someone who typically scores C's and sometimes B's on his tests is able to produce these types of results?"

Jesse no longer felt uncomfortable; he felt toxic. Nardelli had clearly asked a leading question. Jesse thought carefully how to best respond.

"I studied hard for these exams. I worked with Amanda and we spent a lot of time reviewing the lessons I missed. I don't understand. Why are you asking me this? Do you think I cheated?" Jesse asked, finally addressing the elephant in the room.

"No one is accusing you of anything, Jesse. But given the circumstances I just outlined, these results are nothing short of remarkable. We'll be sitting down with Amanda Perone later to talk with her as well."

Mrs. Yang spoke up. "If there's something you haven't told us, Jesse, this would be the best time to explain how you were able to achieve these results."

Jesse looked at them and attempted to explain. "After my accident, Amanda brought reading material to the hospital for me. I just bore down and started reading, and it all kind of made sense to me. I was able to read a lot quicker and was able to remember almost everything I read. Probably because it was real quiet at the hospital, no one there to disturb me. I was able to focus. I mean, that's about all I can say."

Nardelli began to probe. "How did you think you performed on your math test after you completed it?"

"Actually," Jesse began, "I thought I answered all the questions right on that test."

Mrs. Yang thought it was a bold statement but wondered where Nardelli was going with it.

"You did answer every question correctly, or at least, all your answers were correct," Nardelli responded. "You lost some marks for not showing all your work, but all your answers were correct. We contacted your mother this morning to let her know what was going on. She's on her way in now. Just a heads up, she's not very happy with us at this moment. She believes we are accusing you of cheating but I want to be very clear, that is not what we are doing here. I'm going to ask you one last time, is there anything more you need to tell us about this before we bring an end to the meeting?"

"No, sir. And if you still have any doubts, I'll gladly take another test, anytime, anywhere," Jesse challenged. It distressed him to know this would cause his mother a great deal of anxiety, something she didn't need right now in her life.

"Okay, Jesse. Can you just wait outside please until your mother gets here? Thank you." Nardelli dismissed him.

Jesse left the room and closed the door.

"Well, what do you think?" Nardelli looked across at both Mrs. Yang and Mrs. Berger. "How about you, Marianne? Why don't you start first."

Mrs. Berger looked pensive. "I'm not sure. I've had only a limited exposure to Jesse this year but I've always believed he was more capable than what he showed. He's a bright kid from a broken home. I don't know. Maybe he wakes up in the hospital and realizes his alcoholic father is no longer around to hurt him. Free of his tormentor, maybe he taps into a part of his brain that was once paralyzed with anxiety and fear. Now he utilizes his mind productively to its full potential unencumbered by any fear or threat. I don't know. I'm not a psychiatrist. Just thinking out loud here."

Nardelli considered her comments closely then turned to Mrs. Yang. "Lian, what do think?"

Mrs. Yang was less forthcoming. She had been feverishly taking notes throughout the meeting and was on a different tangent. She finished her notes and collected her thoughts before looking up and addressing Nardelli.

"I have a different theory on this. I'm less inclined to believe there was anything underhanded going on here. Jesse was sitting in a room directly next to mine the whole time we tested him with the door open. It would've been difficult to cheat on one test, but all four? I don't buy it. Marianne hit on something when she was speaking. The only difference between the Jesse today and the Jesse a month ago is he woke up in the hospital following a trauma and a long coma. Otherwise, he's the same kid."

"What are you thinking?" Nardelli asked, his interest perked.

"Well, it's extremely rare but it is possible that Jesse's brain may have been altered slightly following the trauma. It's been known to happen. Most brain injuries lead to cell damage. Perhaps in Jesse's case, it's the opposite effect. The only way to be sure is to have him tested. I will need permission from Jesse's mother to speak with his doctor."

At that moment, Jeanie flew into the outer office with barely a notice to Maria Garcia seated at her desk or her son nearby.

"Mrs. Decruz… Mrs. Decruz…" Maria attempted to stall her progress with no success. Jeanie Decruz was on a mission and Nardelli was clearly in her crosshairs as she busted through the door and headed towards him.

"How dare you! How dare you accuse my son of cheating! Who the hell you think you are!" she screamed at Nardelli as she approached him.

Nardelli was accustomed to these types of parental outbursts, having dealt with several of them every day since the beginning of the year.

"Please, Mrs. Decruz, please have a seat. No one has accused your son of anything. We'll explain everything," Nardelli said in a calm and empathetic voice. Jeanie glared at him, realizing she needed to calm herself, and sat down.

"Why is my son getting the third degree for doing well on his exams? Why?" she pressed.

"Jesse has not been accused of anything," Nardelli repeated. "However, he has scored several grade points above his normal average. Under the circumstances, it certainly raises questions."

"He studied hard for those exams. His head was in those books every day while he was at the hospital and when he got home. He's just been studying real hard is all," Jeanie attempted to explain.

"So far Jesse's admitted to doing nothing wrong and we have no reason to believe otherwise. You need to understand, Mrs. Decruz, these results are highly unusual and it's my job to apply due diligence when it's warranted. We do have another theory and it may explain some unanswered questions. We need your cooperation to test our theory."

"Theory? What kind of cooperation? I don't understand." Jeanie looked at him, confused.

"Mrs. Yang here indicates this may be quite rare but it is possible that Jesse's recent trauma may have contributed to his sudden improved capacity for comprehension and retention," Nardelli explained.

"You mean it's changed his brain?" Jeanie asked.

"It's not quite that dramatic, but it may have cleared a pathway to areas of his brain that were not there before. Possibly, we don't know. The only way to be sure is to perform some noninvasive tests on him. Don't worry. These are performed in a classroom. No slicing or dicing of any kind," he assured her.

Mrs. Yang spoke up. "I just need permission to speak with his doctor at SickKids, Mrs. Decruz. Once I have that, I can discuss testing with his doctor. This would clear up a lot of questions. In addition, we can get some clarity on his condition," she said, pitching the idea.

"Fine. If this will clear everything up, let's do it. We've got nothing to hide." Jeanie sounded resigned.

"I just need you to sign a permission form and I can take it from there," Mrs. Yang assured her.

□

Amanda entered the outer office and saw Jesse seated in front of Mrs. Garcia's desk. "What the hell's going on, Jesse?" she asked with concern.

"Apparently you can't ace an exam around here without causing a Spanish Inquisition. I did so well on my tests they think I cheated. Maybe I should have dumbed myself down or something," Jesse replied with a half-smile on his face.

"What do they want with me then?" she asked.

"Probably think we're in on some scheme together, like we're a team or something. Just tell them the truth, Mandy. I'll be fine," he assured her.

Amanda sat next to Jesse without speaking. She pondered their conversation. It was certainly on her mind, wondering how he could have scored so high after such an extended absence. Very strange, indeed.

CHAPTER 16

Jesse lingered outside after school, waiting impatiently for Amanda to emerge. He imagined she was getting grilled about his exam performance. He continued to pace outside the front doors of Lakewood High until she finally exited the school and caught Jesse in her sights.

"Relax," Amanda offered immediately as she approached him. "They didn't ask me anything different than what I told Mrs. Berger this morning. Complete waste of time."

"Did they accuse you of feeding me answers?" Jesse's tone turned aggressive.

"Nothing like that. They were more interested in how much you hit the books while you were in the hospital and at home. I told them the truth. You plowed through the readings and seemed to understand everything, like you never missed a class," she explained. "In fact, I thought that would surprise them but it almost seemed like they understood. It was like that's what they expected, I would say. The whole interview was real strange to be honest."

"Okay, thanks for having my back and sorry you had to get involved. Now I've got to go home and talk my mom off the ledge. She's so pissed right now and I'm not sure at who," Jesse reflected.

"I don't think you need to worry about your mom. People are implying her son cheated. That's where her anger's coming from. She's just defending her son. Period."

"Ya, you're probably right," Jesse said, unconvinced, as they both headed for home.

□

"Thank you for returning my call, Dr. Ambrosia," Mrs. Yang said as she attended to her phone call. "I faxed a permission form from Mrs. Decruz to your office earlier today."

"Yes, I have it here so we are clear to discuss Jesse's condition and treatment. Is there something specific you needed to know regarding his status?" Dr. Ambrosia probed.

"Nothing serious," Mrs. Yang began. "We are attempting to explain some very unusual results following the makeup exams Jesse completed here recently. Specifically, his scores are well beyond expectations. In fact, his results finished in the 90th percentile where he would normally perform much lower. Under the circumstances, we are having difficulty making sense of it all."

"That is strange given his scoring history. How can I assist you?" Dr. Ambrosia asked in a pensive tone.

"We are fairly certain there was no foul play on Jesse's part so we are running down a theory that might provide a plausible explanation for his improved level of performance. We know that Jesse sustained a brain injury last month. Under normal circumstances, we assume that would slow a person down, particularly during the recovery cycle."

"That's correct," Dr. Ambrosia offered. "These types of injuries are very unpredictable, but normally we ask our patients to take it very slow at first and re-enter their lives at a practical pace and not overexert themselves. Although I must say, in Jesse's case, his recovery has advanced remarkably well given the trauma he endured. My last examination showed he was quite alert and progressing well ahead of schedule. He exhibited very few side effects to his head injury, aside from some minor intermittent headaches."

"We are seeing the same thing here. He appears to be back at full capacity and then some," Mrs. Yang said.

"How do you mean 'and then some'?" the doctor asked.

"Based on our interviews internally with Jesse's teachers, a close friend, and Jesse himself, his study habits appear to have improved significantly. His reading speed, comprehension, and retention have vastly improved. That is really what I would like to explore with you, doctor. Are there examinations that can be conducted that would confirm this theory?"

"I must admit, Mrs. Yang, what you are telling me is intriguing. I would like to schedule a battery of tests for Jesse. We will conduct them here at SickKids since we have all the equipment and facilities on site. I will contact Mrs. Decruz directly and have her bring him in once I set it up. Thank you for coming forward with this, Mrs. Yang," Dr. Ambrosia said and hung up.

□

"Okay, it's all set up for this weekend," Zach Simon advised as he sat across the table from Roger Decruz. "I'm going to have to charge you danger pay for this kind of work going forward, Rog. She was about to rip my head off the last time we met. She's quite the firecracker, your wife," Zach said with amusement.

"Ya live long enough with an asshole like me, you're gonna develop an attitude, no avoidin' it. Good work, Zach. We jus needed to get her and the boy here. Got lots I need ta talk with them about. Seems the more I tell, the better I feel. Gotta tell her the truth about me. The whole thing."

"I hope you can trust them, Roger. You don't want this to blow up in your face. They won't be listening to your private conversations here, but you're taking the risk they may repeat something you say that could be incriminating down the road. It's risky and you just need to be aware."

"Lived my whole life on the edge, Zach," Roger assured him. "Not worried my kin's goin' to the authorities or gonna stab me in the back. I'll jus take the chance. All I know, every time I unload some of my past, I feel better. I'm a selfish son-of-a-bitch. This is all about me gettin' better. First time in my life I can actually feel somethin', you know. I jus don't wanna be in here next three years feelin' like shit the whole time, ya understand?"

"Got it, Rog. Good luck Saturday. Oh, and one more thing, Rog. Don't expect them to show up here with big smiles and open arms. I can assure you, based on my last phone conversation with your wife, you're going to have your hands full. In fact, you may want to pat her down for weapons when she comes through." Zach threw him a sarcastic smile.

□

"You got what I told you to get?" Reed asked.

"Yep, right here in my pocket. We got a deal, man," Wesley Dragos reminded Reed.

"Listen, you fuckin' weasel. Don't mess with me. If you got what I want, you'll get what I promised you. Now pass it over!" he demanded.

"Wesley dug into his pocket and produced a slip of paper. Reed grabbed it, unfolded the crumpled piece of paper, and examined the three numbers written on it. A smile came across his face as he deposited the slip into his pocket.

"Well done, Weasel Man. This better be right, for your sake," Reed said as he placed a hand on Wesley's shoulder and squeezed hard, causing Wesley to wince in pain. Reed pulled out a wad of cash from his pocket and peeled away the agreed-upon booty. "I'm sure I don't need to remind you this conversation never happened, right?" He grabbed Wesley by the hair forcing a nodding motion.

Wesley scooped the cash from Reed's hand, disposed of it into his pocket, and made a hasty retreat.

CHAPTER 17

Jeanie and Jesse headed down Highway 401 East towards Bath, Ontario, home of the infamous Millhaven Penitentiary. The institution boasted it was the home of the country's worst criminals. Both Jeanie and Jesse were dreading this day but happy to finally spend some time together and catch up a bit along the three-and-a-half hour car ride. There was a nip in the air but the sun was peaking around the clouds and the roads were sparse at this time of the morning. It had been a long, trying week for them. Jesse's integrity was still in question at school and Jeanie had worked long hours at the diner three days in a row, rarely getting home before 10 p.m. each night.

"You were in bed early last night, Jess. Not like you at all. I wanted to talk to you about your visit at SickKids yesterday. Are you feeling okay?" Jeanie asked.

"I'm fine, mom. It was just a long week and then I spent the whole afternoon at the hospital going through one test after another. I felt like a guinea pig. I'm not even sure what they're looking for. They asked me all kinds of questions. They made me read stuff then repeat things back to them over and over. And then, just when I thought they were springing me, they kept me back another half hour asking a whole bunch of questions about a story I read when I first got there. Memory-type stuff. At the end, they shoved me into this human oven kind of shaped like a tube. I felt like a slab of pizza. They called it an MRI machine. It's supposed to give them a nice picture of my brain. Hope I still got one up there," Jesse joked, showing some levity.

"Well, I'm glad you went. And I'm also glad it's over. I think they're trying to prove your mind might be better now than before the accident. It's all very confusing if you ask me," Jeanie said, trying to rationalize it.

"Best part was, they gave me a meal ticket for the cafeteria downstairs afterwards. I loaded up big time. I made it worth my while. They definitely lost money on me yesterday. I didn't have to dirty any dishes last night when I got home." Jesse chuckled in amusement.

"Yep, that sure sounds like you," Jeanie shot back.

After several hours on the highway, Jeanie finally pulled into the small town of Bath. The maximum-security facility had a housing capacity of over 400 inmates and had transferred in the country's finest convicts from the illustrious Kingston Penitentiary following a major riot there in 1971. The Millhaven property was diamond-shaped from an aerial view and surrounded at the perimeter by double thirty-foot razor-edged fencing with four lookout towers positioned at each point on the diamond. Just inside the perimeter fence was a four-foot warning fence the inmates were forbidden to cross without deadly force being used. All entry points were equipped with state-of-the-art scanning equipment to prevent any weapons from breaching the perimeter.

Jeanie parked the car in the visitors' area and walked to the entry point with Jesse where they were questioned and their belongings were scanned.

"We're here to visit Roger Decruz. We have a 1 p.m. appointment," Jeanie announced through the plexiglass-covered kiosk. The guard slowly perused the daily log schedule on the desk in front of him.

"Alright. Pass through the gate and wait in the outer room until someone comes to get you," the guard instructed as he hit the buzzer to free the gate.

Jesse and his mom moved quickly through the gate, surveying the outer room and the endless number of keypads and lights installed at each doorway. The facility seemed extremely clean and sterile for a prison. Other civilians were sparsely spread throughout the room—other visitors, they assumed.

"Wonder what the food is like here," Jesse whispered to his mom.

"Hope you never have to find out," Jeanie quickly replied. "This place gives me the creeps."

Jesse nodded in agreement as they both sat silent for a while. Their anxiety levels were elevated. The anticipation of meeting Roger was starting to weigh on them both as they waited patiently for someone to retrieve them.

After what appeared to be an eternity, a floor guard finally entered the outer room and announced, "Rejeanne and Jesse Decruz."

Jeanie motioned him with her hand.

"Okay, follow me please," he instructed them.

They penetrated the outer core of the housing block. Buzzers engaged at each entry point as they weaved through numerous hallways, finally arriving at a small, private visitors' room. The room had basic furnishings, including a single table with numerous chairs and communication equipment situated at the entry point. There were large metallic eyebolts protruding from the floor on one side of the table.

"I'll be back in a few minutes. Please remain seated. When I bring the inmate to the room, there will be no physical contact of any kind as he will be secured on this side of the table. Understood?" the guard asked, waiting for confirmation. Both Jeanie and Jesse nodded in agreement.

Five minutes passed and they could see through the glass encasement Roger Decruz being brought forward to the room by two guards. He was secured with chain bracelets on both his hands and feet. They looked at him as he approached. His physical presence was nearly unrecognizable. Roger was now clean-shaven and no longer sporting a ponytail, a signature of his since his teenage years. His hair was now shoulder length and neatly combed straight back. His jumpsuit was clean and presentable.

Roger's eyes first met Jeanie's; his features softened and he entered the room. He sent a smile to Jesse and looked back to Jeanie. The guards sat him in the chair and then secured his chains to the metal eyebolt located on the floor. Roger paid no attention to the guards going about their business. He fixed his eyes on Jeanie who was now trembling in her seat as she held Jesse's hand for support.

"You have thirty minutes, Roger," the guard reminded him.

"Thanks, guys." He gestured to his escorts and waited for them to leave the room. They both sat outside the room and engaged in conversation, presumably till the meeting ended and they would return Roger to his cell.

Roger sat calmly across the table from his family. He had a look of relief on his face. His eyes scanned his wife and son for a long moment. Jeanie sat quietly looking at Roger and trying to absorb this new persona. His eyes were clear, aware, and present like never before. Jesse examined his father as well, wondering where the anger he felt before the meeting had gone. This was nothing like the person who had assaulted him a few months earlier. The moment was surreal to him but he remained steady and kept his emotions in check.

Roger finally broke the silence.

"I can't tell ya how happy I am right now to see ya both." Tears began to well up in his eyes as he tried to speak again. "I-I-I..." he finally surrendered to his tears and dropped his head into his hands, unable to fix his gaze on them further.

Jeanie began sobbing quietly and continued to squeeze her son's hand. Jesse remained sturdy, unwilling to show any emotion. He comforted his mother while Roger regained his composure.

"What kinda animal hurts his own family? What kinda animal nearly kills his own son?" Roger blurted out. "That's what I been askin' myself the whole time I been here, Jeanie. I'm so sorry. I'm so sorry..." Roger once again buried his head in shame, letting the tears flow freely this time. "I been drunk for the last thirty years. Then I came here, now I'm not drunk no more. I can finally see clear for the first time in my life. Ya know, sometimes the sun only rises after it gets dark. Ya know what I mean? It's like that moment at dusk, when the sun hits the horizon? Only time ya really notice the sun is when it starts to get dark and it disappears off in the horizon, ya understand? I'm jus tryin' to say I'm sorry best way I can, is all."

"Too late for that. We're not here for your apologies, Rog." Jesse stood up from his chair in disgust. Refusing to acknowledge the emotion flowing from his father. "You don't get a second chance after what you did, Rog," he said, continuing to hammer at his father.

"I don't blame ya, son. I don't blame ya at all. I didn't ask ya to come here lookin' for forgiveness but I still wanna say sorry. It's important I say sorry."

"You didn't ask us here just to say sorry. So why are we really here?" Jeanie asked, attempting to break the tension. She grabbed Jesse's hand and motioned him to sit down. They had never seen Roger as contrite as he was now.

"You're right. Got lotsa explainin' to do," Roger started. "By the way, my boy Zach, he scared to hell of ya, Jeanie. Thought you were gonna mess him up last time he was out at the house," Roger said, attempting to lighten the mood. "What I gotta tell ya is the truth 'bout myself. My doc keeps sayin' the truth will set me free and I believe it 100 percent. I sure do!"

Roger turned his gaze to Jeanie. "When I first met ya, Jeanie, I fell in love straight away, no word of a lie. If ya believe nothin' else I tell ya today, I want ya to believe that. Back then, I was runnin' with the Hells Angels bikers out of Laval. They were some badass SOBs back then, into girls, guns, and drugs. I told ya back then I was bouncin' at the Excalibur Club. That there was true. But, I was also doin' bad shit with them boys. Got involved movin' drugs from point A to B. At first, that's all it was. I was jus transportation, that's it. Well, later on, they took a shine to me cuz I was a tough guy, you know? I could really handle myself. Good with my hands, ya know what I mean? At that point, I was just a drunk. Never used the drugs, jus transportin' them, is all.

"Well, the landscape started changin' in Laval back then. New rivals come to town lookin' to shave our business. Things started gettin' dangerous and demand for muscle like mine went up. I started makin' more money, gettin' drugs to where they got to be. They paid me well. This is how ya get sucked in, by the money. First, I'm just a bouncer at some titty club. Before ya know it, I'm movin' drugs around Quebec. Once you're in the life, no gettin' out. Jus the way it works. Well, one night, the boys and me were movin' a huge haul downtown Montreal. Long story short, we get into it with some rival gang. Knives and guns start comin' out. One of them goes down. Before we know it, heats comin' down on the whole club and cops got their boots on our throat. Jus a matter a time before they find out who the shooters are. Leader decides it's best I hit the road before they connect the dots. He sends me out to Toronto. That's why I asked ya to come out with me to Regent Park, Jeanie. Told ya I had a new job at Club eX. I was so happy you agreed. Ya jus picked up your stuff and came out with me. That's real luv. You and me started a new life out here. Got married and had Jesse. Only two things in my life I ever did right."

"You were running from the law? You're a wanted man for that crime?" Jeanie gasped.

"Na, had nuttin' to do with it. Eventually one of the brothers fell on his sword and took the heat off us all. We're all clear now on that count," Roger assured her. "Anyways, started to work Club eX as a bouncer there, which ya already know. That's all I did for years, 'cept, same pattern starts up in Toronto. Club eX pretty much biker controlled back then, mostly movin' girls and firearms, but the drug scene started ta change during the '70s. Hard to tell who the bad guys were cuz everyone gettin' bought off, law enforcement, politicians, lawyers, judges, you name it, real cesspool of corruption. We no different. Bikers start branchin' out, bringin' in drugs and distributin' out to the local areas. Course, now they need muscle again movin' drugs around so that's where I get sucked into the vortex. Jus like déjà vu as they say in Quebec.

"So now I'm involved movin' drugs around again. Dangerous shit cuz the players keep changin', 'specially in Toronto. The boys at the eX hooked up with Colombians for a new source of drugs. Bad motherfuckers, them Colombians. They cut you up jus lookin' at them wrong, no word of a lie. So now my time's split between bouncin' at the eX and transportin' drugs. Ya remember, Jeanie, when I started workin' long hours at the eX? You got all over my ass 'bout not spendin' time at home with you and Jess. Fact was, I had no choice. I was in the life and I did what I was told, plain and simple, or I don't breathe no more, you know what I'm sayin'?"

"Why didn't you tell me back then? I would have understood. You could have told me then," Jeanie cut in.

"Less you knew, Jeanie, the better. I didn't want you guys anywhere near them animals. We had some guys there brought in their wives into the life with 'em. Bad decision. The women became expendable. Throw ya under the bus to save their own hide. Seen it many times. Back then, I was under lots of pressure. Start doin' pot to settle myself. Jack Daniels jus wasn't doin' it for me anymore. That's around same time I started slappin' you 'round, Jeanie. I'm so sorry for that." Roger's voice started to crack with emotion. He collected himself again. "Kept tellin' myself this was jus temporary, jus do another job and things get better. Problem was, drug business was shootin' through the roof, couldn't keep supply on the shelf.

"So they brought in more partners. Eventually club management responsibilities changed. Bikers took the girls and Colombians moved the guns and drugs. Course, I spent more time dealin' with the Colombians now. Needless to say, business was boomin' and, course, I was being more compensated for my services. All under the table. That's why I never missed payin' for anythin', always paid cash. After a while, was nothin' I didn't know 'bout Toronto's drug market. Where it comes in. Where it goes out. Like that."

Jeanie and Jesse were trying to absorb this revelation as quickly as it was coming out of Roger. It all started to make sense and explained a great deal in the context of their lives.

"Big problem with bein' around drugs all the time, handlin' it all the time, ya start lettin' it control your life. Workin' long hours around bad dudes with guns and drugs, ya get stressed, tired. Ya start dippin' into the inventory, ya know what I mean? At first, I jus turned to the weed to mellow me out, settle me down, get me through the night. Then the lack a sleep get to ya. Can't stay up no longer so ya take somethin' harder. Started doin' the coke. Bad shit that is, real bad. Once ya got that monkey on your back, bitch don't wanna come off. That's what went down that night at home, Jeanie. I been workin' two days straight, no sleep, wired like I never been before, jus kept takin' the coke to stay awake. Demands of the job, ya know. Came home jus to get away from it for a bit. Bad decision, started lashin' out at you Jeanie... then I see Jess comin' outta his room, jus tryin' to protect ya like I taught him... then I-I'm sorry, Jess, I'm sorry..." Roger was unable to finish his thought as he broke down, crying harder now than before. Unable to control himself, his body was now trembling with grief. Unable to hold his eyes on his son, he slowly lowered his forehead to the table.

Jeanie attempted to console him. "He's okay now, Roger. He made it through."

She stared at Jesse, who was now starting to soften for the first time. His eyes started to moisten slightly as he stared down at his abuser, his tormentor. His father was clearly in the deepest depths of despair at what he had done.

Roger slowly lifted his head off the table, leaving behind a pool of tears. "Moments like that happen in a second, without thinkin'. All I could think was how to take it all back the second it happen, ya know. Then ya realize, ya can't un-ring a bell. It was done. Nothin' I could do to fix it. Too late." Roger bowed his head again, fighting the urge to fall.

They all remained silent for a moment while the emotions passed. The guards outside were now staring in as they fixed their gaze on Roger who was visibly distressed. Roger wiped away his tears and collected himself as he had more he wanted to say.

"Damn, haven't cried like that since I was a baby. Maybe that's why babies are so happy after a good cry. Kinda how I feel right now. Feel like the weight of the world off my back. Needed to tell you all this. Best therapy ever," Roger said in a moment of levity.

"Got one last thing I need to tell ya both before ya go, so listen real close cuz I can't talk too loud here. You're gonna need money to get by while I'm away. When ya get back to the apartment, here's what ya need to know." He turned his attention to Jesse. "Jess, I want you to grab my toolbox from the closet and go to the workout room. The back wall jus a buncha plywood screwed to the wall studs there. Right behind the dumbbell rack in the middle of that wall, there's a four-foot by eight-foot sheet of plywood that's attached to the wall. First, ya need to remove the weights and pull the rack away from the wall. Then ya need to grab a screwdriver and remove the eight screws holdin' that plywood to the wall. Once ya removed the plywood, you gonna see a long flat piece of metal attached along the bottom of the wall about two feet in height by eight feet wide. It's gonna look like a heatin' vent or bulkhead, but it's not. There's a dozen screws attachin' that metal plate to the wall studs. Take 'em all out. When ya remove the plate, ya gonna see three things. There's bags got money inside. There's bags with valuables. And then you'll see a metal box on its own anchored to the floor."

"What the hell, dad? You robbing banks now too? I'm still trying to process you moving drugs and guns. Hell!" Jesse exclaimed, showing complete exasperation at the flood of information.

"No, nothin' like that son. This jus stuff they give me for doin' a good job. Spoils of the trade, they call it. Told ya, I'm strictly muscle and transportation, son. But also, gotta admit, I been skimming off the boss for years. He got money layin' around all over the place. Some of it end up in my pocket, ya know what I mean. Pick my moments and seize the opportunity. He probably kill me if he knew. I been real careful like, jus take small amounts all the time but it builds up over the years. Got cash stashed away all over the place, only use what I need. Can't be livin' the high life or they figure it out, ya understand? Anyway, not really stealin' from the guy if it ain't his in the first place, ya follow?

"Now listen to me, this is for you, Jeanie." He turned his focus to her. "Important you listen to what I'm sayin now. Between your job and this money, ya should have enough to get by till I get out. Don't be puttin all this money in the bank. Can't do that. Maybe couple hundred dollars now and again, that's it. Ya start putting big chunks a money in the account, they be askin' you questions you don't got the answers to, ya understand?"

Jeanie nodded and listened intently.

"Now, ya gotta pay for everythin' in cash. Best way to use it up. Pay it all in cash, rent, utilities, food, like that, got it? Now Jess, those bags of goodies in there. Ya can turn that into cash real quick if you guys get real desperate. Ya take the jewelry and watches to a pawnbroker, but not jus any pawnbroker. I got a buddy up on Yonge Street, place called Jimmy's Treasures, just north of Dundas Street. Guy who runs it, they call him Jimmy the Fix. He's a buddy of mine. Tell him you're my son and I sent ya. He'll give ya a good deal. Anyways, I'd leave that stuff be for now until ya really need the cash. Emergency only, got it?"

"What's in the metal box?" Jesse asked.

"That box is locked. Ya need a special key to open it. Don't worry about that. Just leave it alone for now. I like to call that my own special life insurance policy in there," Roger said, offering a vague explanation.

Jesse was inclined to press the issue further but then decided against it. The guard turned and knocked twice on the glass. Roger turned to him. The guard raised two fingers indicating two minutes remaining.

"Okay, I gotta wrap it up. I know I jus dropped a giant load of crap on ya both but it's best y'all know everythin'. I hope someday ya can forgive me. Like the doc told me, it's not so important what ya done, it's more important what you're gonna do next. That's what I'm workin' on real hard, jus trying to be a better version of myself cuz I can't change the past. If ya wanna come see me at Christmas break, ya know where to find me. It'd be the best Christmas gift ever, honest to God it would," Roger said, attempting one last appeal before they departed.

"No promises right now, Roger. We got a lot to think about and talk about," Jeanie replied as the guard entered the room.

"Okay, bye, Jeanie. Bye, Jess," Roger said as the guards disconnected him and led him out the door.

□

Jeanie's eyes remained fixed on the road. They were now travelling the 401 West, returning home to Toronto. They had over three hours to digest and discuss what had just happened and they were going to need every minute of it.

CHAPTER 18

"No, daddy, don't! No, stop. Please stop! No, it hurts, stop!"
Jeanie bolted straight up in her bed. Sweat cascaded from her head and down her back. Years had passed since she left her home in Laval but the memories were fresh and the torment invaded her dreams at every opportunity. She despised her father, a burden she carried in her soul. Her heart continued to race but she knew that would pass in a few minutes. The irony struck her. No matter the distance from Laval, he would find her every night, even if it was just in her mind. She punished herself daily with the idea she had brought that same wrath and fate onto Jesse. It was her poor choices and lack of good judgment that allowed Roger to become her husband and ultimately a father. She remained conflicted with the notion that Jesse represented the best her life had to offer yet she was responsible for the pain and suffering he had been forced to endure in his young life. In the end, Jeanie remained resolute she would reconcile that with her God.

Jeanie's thoughts turned to the meeting of the previous day with Roger. She reasoned her choice in men was likely the result of poor genetics handed down through her mother. Roger was the inevitable result of a long family cycle. Unable to sleep further, she rose and headed to the kitchen. It was 6:30 in the morning and she began her daily regimen of toast and coffee. She and Jesse had much to talk about during the trip home but neither would commit to their feelings regarding Roger in spite of his apparent transformation. He appeared completely transparent and contrite, two qualities they had never before experienced where Roger was concerned. If it was all an act, his presentation was very convincing, tears and all.

Jesse awoke a short time later and joined his mother at the table after pouring himself a large cup of coffee. This was very early for him, particularly for a Sunday. Under normal circumstances, Jesse would never surface before 9 a.m. on a Sunday morning.

"Couldn't sleep either, huh?" Jeanie asked staring vacantly across the table.

"Nope. Tossed all night. There's only one thing on my mind. Kinda feels like Christmas morning right now, doesn't it?" Jesse's face lit up.

"I was thinking exactly the same thing," Jeanie confirmed.

They'd elected to tackle Roger's hidden treasure after a full night's sleep rather than when they arrived home the night before. He was unclear regarding the amount of cash and valuables stored in the backroom but they assumed it would be substantial enough to tide them over for quite a while.

Jesse stuffed the last piece of toast in his mouth and washed it down with a gulp of coffee. "I'm ready to rip open our presents now, mom, if you are." His eyes lit up like a young child about to tackle his birthday gifts.

"Let's go then," Jeanie concurred.

Jesse ran to the closet to retrieve his father's toolbox. It was placed in the hall closet on the shelf above the hanger bar. The toolbox was heavy and well stocked. He pulled it away from the closet with ease. They both moved into the backroom and began unloading the dumbbells from the holding rack.

"If this is all bullshit, I'm never talking to him again," Jesse said while shuffling the dumbbell rack away from the wall.

The back wall of the room was unfinished construction with only partial sheets of plywood screwed to the wall studs. Jesse stared at the full four-foot by eight-foot sheet of plywood positioned directly behind the dumbbell rack. There were exactly eight screws as Roger had indicated attaching the wood to the wall. Jeanie handed Jesse a Phillips screwdriver from the toolbox and he made quick work of the fasteners. They removed the large sheet and revealed the inner wall studs. Along the bottom of the wall was a long metal plate that stood about two feet in height and covered the entire width of the opening. It did indeed have the appearance of a heating duct as Roger had indicated.

Jesse continued to unscrew the fasteners and removed the plate from the wall. Inserted between the wall studs were several leather tote bags with zipper openings. Jesse pulled them out one at a time and handed them to his mother. She spread the ten tote bags in the middle of the floor where she and Jesse both squatted staring at their treasure. They looked at each other, their eyes wide in anticipation.

"I don't know about you, but I feel like a pirate who just dug up a treasure chest. Ready to go, mom?" Jesse asked.

"Okay then. Open it. Open it!" she implored him.

They began to unzip the leather totes as excitement built on their faces.

"Oh my God, Jesse." Jeanie was unable to contain her excitement. "This can't be real!"

"We gotta count this. We gotta count it all now!" Jesse's voice rose as he spoke.

They inverted the tote bags and allowed the countless stacks of cash, mostly tens and twenties neatly wrapped in thick elastic bands, to fall to the floor. Jesse uncovered two of the bags filled with a trove of gold rings, earrings, bands, necklaces, and several expensive watches if the Rolex insignia was to be believed. He wondered about the countless men and women to whom the goods belonged before they were stolen.

It took the better part of the morning but they added up approximately $80,000 in cash and goods.

"I guess dad wasn't kidding. Looks like he spent more of his time skimming than working at the club," Jesse said.

"I think I can afford to take a few less shifts at the diner now," Jeanie mused.

They both sat back a moment with eyes glazed over as if they had just completed a large Christmas meal. The moment was surreal and they were momentarily uncertain what to do.

"Maybe I can take Mandy out for a fancy dinner," Jesse said coyly as three twenty-dollar bills disappeared quickly into his pocket in clear sight of his mother.

"You go ahead, sweetie. We'll keep this all safe somewhere. I need to sit down and figure out what to do with all this money. It needs to last us a long time. In the meantime, we live our lives like normal, agreed?" Jeanie reasoned as she looked to her son for confirmation.

Jesse nodded.

Jeanie stared over at the open wall and noticed a metal lockbox located in the far corner along the floor. "What's that?" she asked.

"That's the box dad mentioned. He called it his life insurance policy, whatever that means. Besides, it's locked and he wasn't telling us where the key was."

They both stared at it for a moment then pushed it out of their minds. They had enough to deal with; the mystery box could be left for another day.

Life insurance policy, indeed.

CHAPTER 19

Dr. Ambrosia pulled the test results from his files and spread them out on the table in chronological order to create a storyline. He understood this part of his job would be challenging. Attempting to present and simplify very technical information in a way most non-technical people could understand required a measure of patience and skill. In addition, the subject matter was extremely rare and Dr. Ambrosia himself had performed a great deal of research to make sense of it himself. He felt the visuals he constructed were his best modus operandi under the circumstances.

"Doctor, everyone has arrived now and I'm holding them in the outer wing. Are you ready to receive them?" the nurse asked.

"Thank you, give me five minutes to get organized and then show them in," he instructed.

Jesse arrived at SickKids Hospital with Jeanie, Mrs. Yang, and Amanda in tow. He decided to include Amanda at the last minute. They had become very close and she had expressed a desire to be with him today. The results, examination, and diagnosis had taken longer than expected, which caused everyone concern. Jesse was just happy to finally get some feedback and get it over with, good or bad.

"Can everyone please follow me." The nurse gestured as she opened the door to the inner hallway. They arrived at Dr. Ambrosia's office where he greeted them. "Thank you, everyone. My apologies for the delay of this meeting. My schedule has been very challenging these past few weeks and I had hoped to brief you earlier. But I wanted to consult a few of my colleagues before bringing you all here."

They all sensed from the doctor's intro this would not be a routine debriefing and sat around the large table in his office. There was some tension in the air as they sat in anticipation.

Dr. Ambrosia took a deep breath and began. "Now, I will do my very best to help you all understand the examinations performed and the results we've concluded without confusing you with a lot of very technical jargon.

"The human brain is the least understood organ in the human body," he said, "but we have come a long way to better understand how the brain functions through improved technology and equipment. We ran a number of tests on Jesse, most of which were performed in our laboratory. These lab tests focused on Jesse's ability to absorb, process, and retain information. I'm not going to bore you with all of the testing we did, but I will tell you that Jesse's ability to store and retain information was quite impressive. Normally, brain injuries such as the one Jesse sustained, would cause some degree of cell damage. However, we did not detect this in his case. In fact, we discovered quite the opposite. I'll explain that further in a moment."

Jesse looked to his mother for a reaction. Jeanie felt a sense of relief from the doctor's words as she turned to her son and smiled.

"Just to give you one example of a test we conducted on Jesse. We flashed him five cards in succession, each card containing a number ranging between 1 and 1,000. We then asked him to write those numbers down on a piece of paper in the order he saw them. As he successfully completed each task, we continued to flash additional cards in increments of five. Jesse was able to reconstruct thirty numbers correctly in the order he saw them. Most people struggle with five numbers. We concluded Jesse's data retention and memory to be advanced well into the high 90th percentile of the population."

Dr. Ambrosia then reached for some visuals to begin the next stage of his presentation.

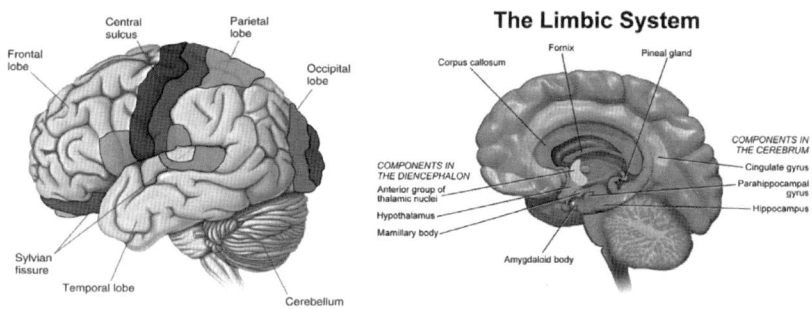

"Next, I want to explain to you some of the basic physiology of the human brain. Don't worry if you don't understand all of this. I really just need you to understand the areas of the brain responsible for memory." He placed the two slides on the table where everyone had a clear view.

"The human brain is divided into a number of regions, each of them responsible for various functions in the human body. The cerebrum here makes up nearly 75 percent of the brain's volume. We'll just focus on this for now. A thin sheet of neural tissue called the cerebral cortex covers the cerebrum. The cerebral cortex contains nearly 90 percent of all the neurons in the brain. It's very important to brain function. The cerebral cortex is divided into a number of regions called lobes. We'll just concentrate on this one here that we call the temporal lobe. The temporal lobe is identified as the region of the brain responsible for memory." The doctor looked around the table momentarily. "Is anyone lost yet?"

Everyone remained silent, deep in concentration. They continued to hang on to his words.

"I want to direct your attention to this region of the temporal lobe called the hippocampus. The hippocampus is an especially interesting area of the brain. It is primarily responsible for memory, more specifically, the transference from short- to long-term memory. The hippocampus is one of the few areas of the brain capable of growing new neurons. I want you to remember this fact as I get into the last part of my presentation, which will bring all of this information together for you."

Dr. Ambrosia retrieved a glass of water and sipped from it before moving ahead. He then placed several brain images in front of his small audience and started again.

"The last test we performed on Jesse is actually the most interesting of all, given this technology is quite advanced with leading-edge, state-of-the-art equipment. In fact, SickKids Hospital is one of only five hospitals in the country that operate this special equipment. The equipment is called an MRI machine. MRI stands for magnetic resonance imaging. Essentially, this machine provides the highest resolution image of the brain available to man. It is very different from the traditional equipment used for brain scans such as the CT scanner, which uses ionized radiation, or x-rays, to produce an image of the brain. The MRI machine is much different. We placed Jesse's head inside a tubular-shaped machine, which creates a powerful magnetic field around the head. Don't worry, it's not harmful," Dr. Ambrosia assured them. "This is what we call a non-invasive test. In fact, it's less invasive than the CT scan, which uses radiation. The MRI shoots radio-frequency pulses through the magnetic field created around the head to produce the high resolution image of the brain. It's completely safe.

"Okay, now you remember we talked about the hippocampus located in the temporal lobe, that's responsible for memory?" He looked to his small audience for confirmation. They all nodded. "Here's a picture of a normal-functioning brain and the hippocampus." He showed them a typical image and red zones indicating activity regions in this area of the brain. "Now here's the image of Jesse's brain. You will notice the red regions of the organ are more pronounced. In fact, his imaging indicates 10 to15 percent more brain activity in this area responsible for memory."

Jeanie spoke up. "Are you trying to say that my son's a genius now?"

Dr. Ambrosia chuckled briefly. "No, not at all. In fact, he's quite normal. However, it appears the brain injury he sustained actually induced neuron growth in this area and, as a result, improved his capacity to retain information. Essentially, Jesse's ability to transfer information from his short-term to long-term memory is superior to the average person. Having said that, we're not sure at this point whether this is a permanent or temporary situation. For this reason, we will be asking you to bring Jesse in every six months so we can continue to monitor his progress."

Jesse sat in his chair trying to process everything he'd just heard. The irony was not lost on him. His abusive alcoholic father was now responsible for the two things in his life in which he was superior to most others his age, human combat and memory. The thought amused him.

"I could probably get into more detail but I believe what I've shown you all is really at the core of what you need to know. Does anyone have questions? I know it's a lot to absorb. I hope I didn't confuse you too much." The doctor scanned the room before bringing the meeting to a close.

"Thank you, doctor," Mrs. Yang said. "I must say this is surely an extreme and rare occurrence. Are their any side effects we should be aware?"

"I just ask that you keep track of any headaches or patterns of discomfort or pain in the head area over the next several months. I would like to know about that as quickly as possible. Also, any disruptions in sleep pattern, anxiety, things of that nature would be of interest to me."

They all thanked the doctor again and departed the office. Amanda whispered to Jesse as she placed her arms around his shoulders, "We really need to get you onto a game show right away while your brain is gold." They laughed as they exited the hospital.

CHAPTER 20

Jesse and Amanda headed back to Lakewood High in the car with Mrs. Yang. Jesse was feeling vindicated and was anxious to meet with Mr. Nardelli to bring some closure to the whole affair. In a strange way, Jesse felt a growing respect for Nardelli and what he was attempting to accomplish at Lakewood, albeit for his own personal gain and ambitions. Nevertheless, it was important for Jesse to gain his respect again and cast away the dark cloud currently hanging over him.

"I think that was the best result we could have hoped for, Jesse," Mrs. Yang said, expressing her thoughts on the meeting. "It certainly explains everything and I will sit with you when we see Mr. Nardelli later this morning. I'm sure he will be relieved as well to know you earned those grades on your own."

"I appreciate you being in my corner, Mrs. Yang. These tests never would have happened without your theory. I'm glad you talked to the hospital about getting me onto their treadmill."

"There was never a doubt, Jess. We just needed a logical explanation."

"I want to thank you as well, Mrs. Yang," Amanda added.

They arrived back at Lakewood High and morning classes were already in session. Amanda headed to her class while Jesse and Mrs. Yang parked themselves in her office. Mrs. Yang checked in with Mrs. Garcia to get an audience with Nardelli to brief him on Jesse's results. She headed back to her office where Jesse was waiting.

"Mr. Nardelli won't be available for about thirty minutes. He's tied up in a few meetings, but Mrs. Garcia will advise us once he's free. In the meantime, why don't you do some of your homework in the office next door?"

"Okay, I'll be right here when you're ready." Jesse set himself up in the side office.

Listening in on Nardelli's meetings and conversations was Jesse's favourite new pastime. He relished the opportunity to get caught up on the latest and greatest at the school. Jesse moved himself close to the shared door. He could hear Nardelli on his speakerphone with Malvoy.

Excellent, I love these two guys. Best entertainment ever!

"Good news, Dominic," he could hear Malvoy chiming in. "We have approval from the board to move ahead with a full re-test for Grade 9 and 10 math and English at the beginning of May. Now, I need to know where you're at with the supplementary instruction plan for that group. I'm sure you don't want to see a repeat of our last results," Malvoy said, stating the obvious.

"Truth is, Anderson, at this very moment, we have adequate coverage on the English literacy side. Not so much on the math front. Math is a completely different animal. I'm trying to rally up some support with the staff but it's been difficult and resources are sparse where math is concerned."

"That's why we pay you the big bucks, Dom. So you can figure these things out. Now look, I campaigned hard for this re-test and it gives you an opportunity to pull yourself out of the toilet. We've got one shot to improve the marks. This is our only window of opportunity."

Nardelli understood the challenge and his pride would not allow him to admit defeat, particularly with Malvoy. "Don't worry about it, Andy, I got it covered," he assured his boss.

"One last thing, Dom. I'm getting a lot of heat from a number of parents from Lakewood through our superintendent there. This whole issue of your junior kids getting bullied and harassed is a real problem. These kids are terrified and the parents are having difficulty getting information from their own children. It's not good, Dom, not good at all. We need to do better for them. Kids should not be going to school in fear every day. You need to get this under control. Now! The problem must be significant if they're going over your head to get some action," he warned.

"I'm fully aware of the problem and we'll get to the bottom of it. It's a complicated issue when these kids don't want to give us any details. They're scared shitless. However, I'm all over it. I'm giving it top priority."

The reality was that he had no firm plan and was extremely frustrated with this ongoing issue, but he wasn't prepared to admit this to Malvoy. It was also ironic that his next scheduled meeting was with a parent, Mrs. Kim, to deal with this exact issue. Mrs. Kim had recently become quite vocal regarding her son Benny's subjection to bullying and harassment. Mrs. Garcia passed him a note indicating Mrs. Kim was already waiting in the outer office for him.

"Listen, Anderson, you know how I so enjoy our meetings and discussions together, but I have a parent waiting to impose her own brand of pain on me. You don't hold a monopoly on that, you know. I really need to attend to our paying customers now." Nardelli attempted to dismiss Malvoy while providing a parting shot, a signature of his.

"Alright, Dominic. You take care of business and we'll be talking soon," Malvoy replied.

"Thanks for the warning," Nardelli shot back and clicked off the call.

Jesse caught himself laughing out loud then quickly stymied himself.

These guys are gold.

"Please show Mrs. Kim into the office, Mrs. Garcia," Nardelli barked through the intercom.

Mrs. Kim was a recent immigrant to Canada and had one son, Benny, who was enrolled in Grade 9 at Lakewood. Her husband worked long hours at the flour mill and she took on the major responsibility of raising their child. Benny was very quiet, slight for his age, and extremely shy. He was a perfect target for such bullying and his mother had reached her tipping point with his situation. Her son, like others, was afraid to disclose too much information about his tormentors for fear of reprisal.

"Good morning, Mrs. Kim. Please sit down. What can I do for you?" Nardelli asked bracing himself.

"You need to help. My boy being bullied every day. I tell you before but nothing happen. They take his money, hurt his arm. He cry all time, but you do nothing," Mrs. Kim appealed in her broken English.

"I've attempted to help your son, Mrs. Kim. However, when I speak with him, I cannot get any details. I know he is genuinely afraid but I'm having difficulty identifying who is doing this. He is not being bullied on our school property best I can determine."

"They threaten him, tell him they kill his dog if he speak. They tell him to keep mouth shut, give them money or they kill his dog. I not know what to do, Mr. Nardelli... I not know..." Mrs. Kim voice started to break down.

Jesse heard Nardelli rise from his chair and move to the other side of the desk to comfort Mrs. Kim.

"Look at me, Mrs. Kim. I will fix this. I commit to you. I will fix this." Nardelli showed conviction but his challenge was great. The problem was not unique and he needed a solution, and soon. Nardelli spent a few more minutes with Mrs. Kim and then assured her he would get back to her.

Jesse absorbed the conversation through the door and it moved him greatly. He understood the concept of living in fear, the constant threat of harm, the feeling of helplessness. Part of him desperately wanted to help, but how?

Mrs. Yang poked her head in. "Okay, Jesse. Mr. Nardelli is ready for us. Let's go."

They headed into the principal's office to share the results they'd received earlier in the day. Jesse was pleased at the opportunity to clear his name but he did so with a heavy heart. His mind was elsewhere as he kept replaying the conversation between Mrs. Kim and Nardelli, over and over in his mind.

CHAPTER 21

Leanne Gosling pursued her son around the apartment like a lion tracking its prey. She was relentless with her barrage of insults and criticism. Goz had braced himself for this as he did every month. He prided himself in his ability to exercise patience and self-control in the face of this seemingly impossible cycle of madness he was forced to endure.

"How many goddam times I gotta tell you about that leakin' tap in the washroom. It ain't gonna fix itself!" Leanne screamed. "I thought I got rid of one useless man years ago and look at me now. Got me another one. You're all the same. Take what you need and give nothing back. Bunch of good for nothings, all of ya!"

Goz had conditioned himself over the years and accepted his role inside the home, for the sake of his siblings. He freely accepted the derogatory comments and degradation to insulate his younger sister and brother from his mother's wrath until the storm would pass. The kids escaped to their bedrooms and made themselves scarce during these difficult days, a survival technique they learned early on.

Leanne's condition had improved tremendously over the years. Doctors tinkered with her medication to treat her bipolar condition and did the best they could. The current version of herself was the best they could achieve and it at least made life bearable within the Gosling home, most of the time. They would persevere through a few days of lunacy until things got back to normal.

Goz grabbed a few hand tools and moved into the washroom to address the persistent plumbing issue. It was more for appearance than anything else. He had already attempted to repair the faucet earlier in the week but the issue required the attention of building maintenance. He had already issued a work order to management but they were backlogged. He reasoned his charade would at least distract her for a while until her attention moved onto something else.

Leanne stood in the doorway of the washroom, anger brewing. She looked down at Goz. Her eyes shot daggers into him as he attended to the faulty pipes below the sink. Goz could feel the wheels of her poisoned mind in motion and braced himself for the next verbal assault.

"What kind of woman's going to marry a useless man like you? Do you even like women? You're not one of them faggots are you? Never seen you bring a girl around here. I bet you are!"

Her comments were piercing and hurtful, but Goz had learned to tune them out, much like white noise. In the early years, her venom took its toll but he came to understand his mother much better with the ongoing support from his adopted father. Hank Gosling left his wife and kids years earlier when Goz had just turned eleven. Hank remained close and involved with his three children in spite of his occupation as a long-haul trucker. He did his best with Goz to help him understand his adopted mother's condition. He knew Goz would become the next target for her abuse in the home as the elder male and did his best to prepare him.

Goz quickly finished up and grabbed his coat. Leanne was lying down now and Goz was looking forward to spending the remainder of the day with his father. He poked his head into his siblings' room, providing some last minute instruction and hugging them before he departed. They would be fine. Leanne's abuse was generally limited to him and he knew things would improve once he vacated the apartment.

Goz sat on the curb in front of his RGI housing complex on Arnold Avenue. He was exhausted, mentally. He saw the approaching tractor coming his way. Long streams of dark smoke escaped the tailpipes as it pulled up to the apartment complex. Hank Gosling drove truck most of his adult life. Goz recalled his father's absence for days at a time while growing up. Nevertheless, Hank represented the only positive influence in his young life following the death of his biological parents. In spite of the challenges home life presented, Hank made the best of the limited time he was there while trying to manage his ex-wife and three children.

Goz grabbed the vertical bar on the tractor's passenger side door and hoisted himself up into the cab. "Hey dad, how's it going?"

"How goes the battle with you, Robby? How's Griselda treating you today?" Hank asked using the disparaging label he'd nicknamed his ex-wife.

"Same old, dad. She's off her fuckin' rocker again. One more day and things should get back to normal," Goz conceded.

"I'm sorry, kid. I'm sorry you gotta deal with that every month. It's not her fault. Her head's just not wired right. Before they found the right drugs, she was ten times as bad. I just wish there was another way," Hank said despondently.

Goz sat quietly in his seat. He drew a deep breath and exhaled. In a strange way, he felt safe and at peace during these rare moments with his father.

"You know, before you came along, we spent years trying to have our own kids but couldn't. When your mom and dad died and you came to live with us, we were so happy to have a child in the house. Your mom was actually doing well back then. Then finally, we had a couple of kids of our own. I suppose the pressure of having a kid wasn't there anymore. I'm not sure. Anyways, your brother and sister came along, one right after the other. That's when things went downhill. Doctors said it was some kind of hormonal thing. We tried to make things work but your mom got worse. There was no fixing what she had wrong. Only solution before someone got hurt was to go our separate ways."

"I'll be honest with you, dad. When you left us years ago, I was real pissed at you. I thought you just bailed on us. I was angry for a long time," Goz said, opening up.

"I know, Robby. I tried real hard to figure out some other way, you know. I thought about filing for custody of you guys but there was just no way. I'm a trucker. It's all I know and it's all I'll ever be. Can't be dragging kids around in my rig every day and give you guys a normal life, just wouldn't work. Then I thought, maybe I'll just hang in there and put up with it for the sake of keeping the family together. Finally, I realized I'd probably end up killing her or she'd kill me. Nope, best thing I could do was leave the home and work hard to provide for you guys, at least financially. Eats me up every day. Trust me kid, if there was another way, I would've done it by now."

"Just makes no sense, dad," Goz said, attempting to reason. "She's perfectly normal all month then turns into this psycho-bitch for a few days. She's okay with the kids but real nasty to me. Sometimes, I just want to drive her through the wall. Don't worry, dad. I forgave you a long time ago. I just had to walk a few miles in your shoes first before I really understood what you went through." Goz looked to his father and they shared a smile. "You know what, kid. When life's got you down and there's no place left to turn, only one thing left to do." He looked at Goz with a sparkle in his eye.

"Dairy Queen?" Goz asked in anticipation.

"You got it, kid. Let's go get some ice cream. Best medicine ever." Hank raised his right hand and shared a high five with his son.

CHAPTER 22

There was a cold nip in the air on a typical December morning. Jesse was in the car, having accepted his mother's offer to drive him and Amanda to school. Normally, he preferred to walk with Amanda but he'd slept in and didn't want to start the week on a bad footing. They pulled up to Lakewood High; there was some commotion going on at the front of the school. Two cruisers were parked in tandem near the entrance and a small crowd started to gather near the front doors.

"Wonder what's going on this morning," Jeanie said.

"That's odd," Jesse added. "We usually don't see the cops till mid-week when our school criminals get on a roll. Way too early for the druggies. They won't wake up till the afternoon," he quipped.

"There's Mrs. Berger out front. She's trying to break up the crowd," Amanda said. "This can't be good. Let's get inside and check it out."

"Thanks for the ride, Mrs. D," Amanda said as they exited the car. "We'll see you later." She waved as the car pulled away.

Jesse and Amanda arrived at the front doors of the school. They received numerous stares as they entered. Jesse walked towards his locker and continued to feel numerous eyes fixed on him. An uneasy feeling was building inside him. As he and Amanda turned the corner to his locker, he saw the welcoming committee.

"What the hell?" Amanda blurted. "They're standing at your locker, Jess. What's going on?"

Jesse didn't respond right away. He looked up to see two uniformed police officers, a canine unit, and Mr. Nardelli standing out in front of his locker.

"Shit, this can't be good," he said in a low register to Amanda. Mrs. Berger was still dealing with crowd control and attempted to disperse the students now starting to swell in the hallway. She barked at the students and made a slight dent but all eyes were fixed on what was about to go down.

Jesse arrived at his locker where Nardelli was waiting. He stopped and stood there in bewilderment.

"What's going on, Mr. Nardelli?" he finally asked in a fit of confusion.

"Jesse, we've received credible information that you've been distributing drugs among the student population here at Lakewood. These officers here have a warrant to search your locker."

"What drugs? Me? Is this a joke?" Jesse asked in disbelief.

The police constable approached Jesse. "Jesse Decruz, we have a warrant to search your locker. We can either cut the lock away or you can open your locker for us. Your choice," he instructed.

The police canine was now in a state of frenzy as it sniffed the outer casing of his locker. The dog arched as it jerked from side to side.

"I have nothing to hide. I'll open my locker right now. No need to cut anything." Jesse approached the lock and rotated the combination tumbler back and forth until it disengaged. He removed the lock and opened the door.

The dog bolted into the narrow opening and motioned to the bottom of the locker near the back under a stack of books. It nestled its nose under the pile and began barking. The officer pulled the dog away and reached underneath to unearth a large plastic bag. As they untied the bag and pulled out the contents, Jesse's eyes nearly popped from his head. Amanda was nearby and gasped in disbelief.

The police officer was now holding numerous small baggies filled with marijuana. Nardelli looked squarely at Jesse for a reaction. Jesse was attempting to process the moment. He was visibly frustrated and confused.

Jesse slowly stepped away from his locker. A nervous smile moved across his face. He felt victimized but there was nothing he could do, not now. He rotated slowly and turned his attention to the large crowd that had assembled in the area. He brought his hands up and began to clap them together in a mocking way. He started slowly then accelerated. Still clapping, he addressed the crowd.

"Excellent work!" he began. "Beautiful set up, whoever you are. Picture perfect frame-up. You should be really proud of yourself, whoever you are!" His gaze became menacing. Amanda raced to his side in tears and hugged him.

Nardelli turned to Jesse. "You need to come with us to my office, Jesse." Then he turned to the crowd and shouted to the gathering, "Show's over everyone. Get to your classes, now!" The students disbursed at the sound of his booming voice.

As the crowd began to recede, Jesse turned his head to the adjacent hallway and then he saw it. There they were, Reed and Wesley the Weasel, both staring in his direction. They quickly averted their eyes, turned, and disappeared down the hallway.

Jesse followed Nardelli to his office with both officers in tow. His head was bowed and shaking in disbelief.

"No calls, no interruptions, Maria," Nardelli instructed his secretary as he led the entourage into his office.

"Based on your reaction, I take it you're not accepting responsibility for these drugs," Nardelli said, addressing Jesse.

"What do you think? It's so obvious this was a frame job!" Jesse exclaimed. "Why was I targeted?" he demanded.

"We received an anonymous tip from a concerned parent at this school. They were afraid to identify themselves for fear of reprisal on their child."

"Anonymous? Very nice. How convenient." Jesse's comment dripped with sarcasm. "Now you're just proving my point."

"We'll be contacting your mother, Jesse. She will meet you down at the 22nd precinct. These officers will escort you there for questioning. I'm sorry, Jesse. I need to suspend you until further notice or until we've cleared you of this situation."

Jesse confronted his principal. "Mr. Nardelli, can you look me in the eye and tell me you actually believe I'm guilty of this?" Jesse fixed his gaze on Nardelli. His eyes began to water. He felt alone and defeated.

"I'm sorry, Jesse. I don't decide innocence or guilt. That's what these gentlemen here are for. My hands are tied," Nardelli offered as the officers escorted Jesse away.

Amanda followed them to the cruiser but was not allowed to accompany Jesse off the school grounds. She made eye contact with him as they pulled away in the cruiser. She saw the devastation and sadness in his gaze; she felt his pain.

CHAPTER 23

"I have a few theories, mom. Nothing I can prove right now, but I will," Jesse said to his mother as they sat at the kitchen table. She and Jesse had spent most of the morning at the police station pleading his innocence to no avail. He had no proof or plausible explanation to offer the police. All he had was a theory. Jeanie was very troubled following the event. This was the second time in as many weeks that she was summoned to the school regarding Jesse; the stress was now wearing on her. "Who could possibly do something like this to you?"

"Someone who's real pissed at me and has no conscience," Jesse offered.

"You have someone in mind?"

"Yep. You know that guy I clocked earlier this year, Mandy's old boyfriend?"

"Did he threaten you, Jesse? Did you tell the police officer this?"

"I can't accuse anybody of anything right now, mom. I got squat for evidence, just a bunch of theories right now. I'm going to get to the truth, believe me," Jesse said with resignation.

"You can't go anywhere without me right now, Jess. You're on probation. You can't even leave the house unless I'm with you," Jeanie reminded him.

"That's okay, mom. I have long arms and good friends. Whoever did this will regret it. People talk and no way something like this happens without somebody saying or knowing something about it."

"Please, Jess. Don't get yourself into bigger trouble. I can't afford to lose you. You're all I got left in this world." His mother looked at him and began to tear up.

"Don't worry, mom. I'm not going anywhere. Just thinking out loud."

Knock... knock... knock.

"There they are now," Jesse announced. He was expecting the whole gang, his entourage, and his support system. Football season was over, which had freed up everyone's spare time. The Bulldogs didn't win the championship as expected but they finished up a respectable season, losing in the semi-finals to Cabbagetown. All in all, their season had exceeded expectations given their star quarterback was sidelined.

He opened the front door to let the gang in. Amanda led the way. Goz and Minoo followed through while the Jackson boys tucked in close behind. They were still embroiled in an earlier argument about whether Bruce Lee could beat Mohammed Ali in the boxing ring. "Well, well, looks like the cavalry is all here," Jesse announced.

Jeanie opened up a large bag of vinegar chips and poured the entire contents into a red bowl. She placed it in the middle of the table where everyone sat around to talk with Jesse.

"Okay, ladies and gentleman, whatever you guys decide to do, just remember, Jesse's on probation and can't leave this apartment unless I'm with him. So don't even try or there'll be hell to pay, understood? We can't afford him getting into any more trouble until we get things sorted out," Jeanie warned. "And one more thing, take it easy on him. It's been a long week." She smiled at her son then departed to her bedroom.

"Alright, get it out of your system now," Jesse announced to the group as he raised his arms above his head in mock surrender inviting the barrage of razzes surely coming his way.

"Alright, Jess. I'll start. I'm just going to say what's on everyone's mind right now but no one else has the balls to say it." Goz paused as he scanned everyone around the table. He fixed his eyes on Jesse for dramatic effect. "You know we all prefer BBQ chips. What's with the salt and vinegar?" The whole gang erupted in laughter. "Also, I might add, salt and vinegar chips are the munchies of choice for habitual pot users." More laughter.

"Ya, it's not good enough you're fuckin' cheating on exams to get high marks. Now you're selling weed to the poor underprivileged children of Lakewood High. It's unbecoming, Jess. Truly," Minoo said, adding to the attack.

"I personally believe he's suffering from low self-esteem. We should all hold hands and sing kumbaya. We're all here for ya brother. This don't make you a bad person." Trey added his false concern. "Whadda you think, JJ?" Trey teed up his brother, knowing whatever came out of his mouth would certainly be either bizarre or hilarious.

"I'm sorry. I jus come over cuz someone said there'd be beer," JJ added innocently as the laughter reached its peak.

"I'm assuming Mandy's got my back so we won't wait to hear from her. Are we all done? Can we move on now?" Jesse asked attempting to bring a close to the abuse. He secretly enjoyed this type of razzing. It was the first time all day he'd smiled and he felt much better having his friends around to support him.

"Alright, anyone want to throw out some theories?" Goz asked, attempting to get back on task.

"Two words," Jesse announced. "Owen Reed."

"Oh, oh, oh!" JJ mockingly raised his hand as if attempting to address a teacher in the classroom.

Minoo pointed to JJ, addressing him. "Yes, the slightly effeminate black boy at the back of the class would like to say something."

"Fuck you, Minoo," JJ said, taking offense at the comment.

"Alright, alright. What you got, JJ?" Jesse asked, sensing he had a point to make.

"I gots three words, Jess." JJ announced playing on Jesse's first theory.

"Okay, let's have it," Jesse pleaded, hoping JJ would get to the point.

"Wesley the Weasel."

"Bingo," Goz confirmed. "I'm with you on that one, brother."

"Are you really convinced those two guys are involved, Jess?" Mandy asked before they continued down this path.

"I don't think it was. I know it was those two guys, Mandy," Jesse said, putting her question to rest. "When I turned around from my locker this morning, there they were, both of them together, staring right at me. Probably laughing their asses off on the inside. They got me real good, no denying it. Soon as my eyes met theirs, they disappeared. No question in my mind they're involved. By the way, it also answers the question why the Weasel's been shadowing me for weeks. Every time I turned around, there he was like a bad smell. That's how they got into my locker. He watched me open it dozens of times. He's likely got the fuckin' combo now. That's how the drugs got in there cuz nobody but me knows that combination," Jesse pointed out.

"So, where do we go from here?" Trey opened the floor up to everyone.

"One of them's got to give it up. My suggestion we go after the Weasel first. We squeeze him and get him to fold on Reed.

He's really the asshole we want. The Weasel's just his patsy and he's weak. We just need to lean on him good," Goz strategized.

"I agree," Jesse added. "No way Wesley masterminded all this. That fuckin' guy needs directions to brush his teeth. He couldn't organize a walk in the park."

"Okay, we need to do this right," Minoo said. "It's all about applying the right amount of pressure. We're going to need a plan."

"Ya need to peel him away from the herd. Gotta get him alone," Trey said, thinking aloud. "I've got a few ideas on that, but it involves JJ."

"Whatchu talkin' 'bout, brother?" JJ's ears perked up uncomfortably at the sound of his name being introduced to the plan.

"Ya, you're going to be key on this plan. The Weasel's got a man crush on you. That's how we get him alone. You're going to be the bait."

"Say what?" JJ snapped back. "I ain't doin' the gay thing, man. Honest to God, Jess. I luv ya like a brother, but I ain't doin the gay thing for no one, understand."

"Settle down, ya hammer head. You're not doin' the gay thing. Listen to me. Here's the plan." Trey walked the group through his ideas. They all agreed after he was finished. The plan could be risky, but properly executed, represented their best shot at getting to the truth.

□

Ring… ring… ring…
Nardelli picked up the phone. "Hello."

"Who the hell is Benny Kim and what the hell is his mother calling me about?" Malvoy demanded. "This is the fourth parent call I've had to field in the past two weeks from your school,

Dominic. How am I suppose to run the Toronto District School Board if I'm handling your operational issues?"

"Mrs. Kim has already been in to see me. I'm handling it," he assured Malvoy.

"You're not handling shit, Dom. Because if you were, I wouldn't be getting phone calls."

"Look, I can't control calls parents elect to make to you directly. Just tell her I'm handling it and that you have 100 percent confidence in me to resolve it."

"In other words, you want me to lie to her. Is this about her kid getting rolled for lunch money? Shit, this situation is totally out of control, Dom. What the hell is your plan?" Malvoy demanded.

"It's getting my full attention, Andy," Nardelli shot back. "I'm going to need law enforcement involved. Most of this is happening off school property."

"On that subject, I got your email today," Malvoy said, switching gears. "You had the police there today? They drove away with one of your students, that Decruz kid."

"Yes, they recovered marijuana from his locker. However, something doesn't smell right about this one, if you pardon the pun. He claims someone planted the weed. I'm inclined to believe him. But right now, he's on suspension until we can get to the bottom of it."

"Sure. They're all innocent until proven guilty, right Dominic?" Malvoy added sarcastically.

"Anyway, I've got it," Nardelli assured him.

"Never a dull moment is there, Dominic?" Malvoy's voice softened.

"From God's lips to my ears," he replied.

CHAPTER 24

Jesse sat quietly in the car as he and Jeanie drove towards Lakewood High. Nardelli had agreed to meet with them both. Jesse hadn't said two words all morning but had remained deep in thought. He had been devising a plan of his own and hadn't slept a wink all night. Jeanie was also quiet on this morning as she mentally prepared herself for battle with Nardelli. She searched for the words to use that might sway him but accepted the fact this meeting would not likely bear fruit.

They arrived early at the school. Jeanie had pushed for this meeting with Nardelli the previous day. He wasn't keen on this get-together but empathized with Jesse. He remained conflicted about the truth behind this whole sordid incident. He had experienced many such meetings before and knew his hands were tied. He expected there was nothing he could offer to improve Jesse's current status. He also understood their family dynamic and felt for them.

Nardelli understood the power of empathy but he also knew the danger of getting too closely involved in the personal lives of his students and their broken families. It was a certain path to occupational burnout. He had learned this early in his career and managed to navigate a labyrinth of issues that presented themselves, particularly at Lakewood High. There certainly was no shortage of pain and suffering among the student population at his school.

"Good morning, Maria. Has Mr. Nardelli arrived yet?" Jeanie asked.

"Oh yes. Mr. Nardelli is an early riser. He's the first person at school every day. He arrives at 6:30 every morning. I'll see if he's ready for you, Mrs. Decruz." Mrs. Garcia moved into Nardelli's office and was gone a few moments. When she got back, she announced, "You can go in now, Mrs. Decruz."

"You stay here, Jesse," Jeanie instructed her son. "I want to talk to him alone first and see how that goes, okay?" She opened the door and disappeared into Nardelli's office.

"Good morning, Mr. Nardelli," Jeanie greeted him.

"I think we've reached a point, you and I, where we can address each other by our first names, Jeanie," Nardelli said, introducing an informal feel to the meeting.

"Thanks. That would be fine, Dominic. I have to be honest with you. This whole situation has made me physically sick. I feel absolutely terrible this morning and I don't know what to do."

"Completely understandable. How else could a mother feel under the circumstances? I'm quite aware of everything your family has been through, Jeanie. It's a lot more than most families should ever need to deal with," Nardelli said, exercising his empathy skills.

"I'm a mother, Dominic." Jeanie sat up and presented a strong face. "A mother knows her children. I can tell you this. Every fibre in my body tells me my son does not deal drugs. Never has, not even close. None of this adds up and he's paying the price for somebody's cruel joke. There's no other explanation," she said, pleading.

"I can tell you from a personal standpoint I tend to accept that scenario as well. Many things don't add up in this case and I was there when he opened his locker. It's hard to fake that type of reaction when he saw the drugs. But, from a professional standpoint, my hands are tied. There are certain protocols I need to follow, Jeanie. If there was only a way around it, I would explore that and get him back in class."

"That's all I'm asking. Can you please find a way to get him back here? His education is so important, especially now since acquiring his new superpowers." Jeanie attempted to lighten the moment.

Nardelli chuckled. "Yes, it's quite amazing to suffer that type of trauma and come out of it better than when you went in. I don't want him to lose pace either and we will need to bridge his education. He will be expected to continue and keep up his studies. We will support him the best we can on our end."

Jeanie sensed there was nothing more she could do at this point and cut the meeting off. "Well thank you, Dominic. I appreciate you being in our corner. Good day." She rose and left the office.

Jeanie entered the outer office to find Jesse pacing the floor in front of Nardelli's office. "You ready to go, Jesse?"

"I asked Mrs. Garcia if I could meet with Mr. Nardelli for about five minutes," Jesse replied.

Mrs. Garcia returned from Nardelli's office and nodded at Jesse. "Okay, Jesse. He can see you for a few minutes."

"I'll wait for you here, Jess." Jeanie looked at her son with a puzzled expression as he entered Nardelli's office.

□

"Hello, Jesse. How you doing, kid?" Nardelli stood and examined Jesse closely. "You look tired this morning. I don't imagine you slept much last night."

"Hard to sleep when you know someone out there has put a target on your back." Jesse fixed his eyes on Nardelli hoping to land some reaction.

"Yes, just had that discussion with your mom. It's not a good situation but, as I explained to her, I have protocol to follow and my options are limited where your suspension is concerned."

Jesse took a deep breath and decided he would launch directly into his appeal.

"What if there is a way, Mr. Nardelli? What if I told you there's a way you could bring me back while this mess works itself out? A conditional pardon of sorts," Jesse pitched.

"No such animal, Jesse. You're on probation right now. No way around it." Nardelli attempted to squash this train of thought.

Jesse was finding his confidence. His plan would either be a home run or a disappointing strike out, nothing in between. He stood up and walked to the side door to Nardelli's office that opened to the shared space between his office and Mrs. Yang's.

"What about your Last Chance Program?" Jesse asked innocently, expecting a significant reaction.

"What? How the hell do you know about that! That's not even launched yet. Don't mess with me here, Jesse. I'm warning you." Nardelli was visibly agitated at the idea his new experimental program was public knowledge. "I want to know how you got that information!" Nardelli demanded.

Okay, Jesse. Do or die here. Go for it!

"It's a combination of things, Mr. Nardelli. It's a combination of your booming voice, this paper-thin door, and the four days I spent in there writing my exams last month," Jesse stated calmly.

"What are you talking about?" Nardelli eyes narrowed.

"What I'm saying is, a person sitting on the other side of this door can basically hear everything that goes on in this office. I'm sorry, but I wasn't eavesdropping on purpose, it just happened." Nardelli's anxiety increased. The protruding vein across his forehead was clearly visible. "I want to know what you heard. Everything, and now!"

Jesse launched right in. "I know about the Grade 9 and 10 literacy marks, the bullying, extortion, and theft problem we have in this school, and, oh ya, and I know about the out-of-control drug problems here at Lakewood High."

Nardelli rose from his seat, walked towards Jesse, and stood in front of him. Nardelli was shorter in stature but far more intimidating. He stared into Jesse's eyes, unsure what to say next.

"Is there anything else?" Nardelli finally asked.

"Yes, one more thing." Jesse decided to place all his cards on the table. "I know about the deal you have with Director Malvoy." He waited for a reaction but there was none. Nardelli slowly walked back to his seat.

"You think your smart, don't you? You think you have this all figured out, don't you? Sit down!" he barked at Jesse. "What's your play here, Jesse? Is this your own brand of extortion on me now?"

"What? No, no, nothing like that!" Jesse quickly dispelled this line of thinking. "Nobody knows anything about any of this. Just me."

"I'll ask you one more time. What's your play here?" Nardelli pressed him as his patience wore thin.

"This is my school too, Mr. Nardelli. You think I enjoyed hearing about the drug problems we have, or the junior kids getting muscled for their lunch money every day, or that our school ends up last place board-wide on testing. It's depressing and really bothers me too." Jesse went on the offensive. "The way I see it, we need each other right now."

"Sure kid, you're the answer to all my problems." Nardelli snorted in derision. "What the hell can you possibly do to help me?"

"Everything. I can help you with everything," Jesse offered.

Nardelli perked up. This was a very bold statement. He wasn't quite sure what to make of it but carried on nevertheless. "Okay, I'll bite. How is Jesse Decruz, Grade 12 student at Lakewood High, going to solve all my problems, the same problems I've been spinning my wheels on all year?" he asked, probing with all the patience he could muster.

"I'm not limited like you. I'm not restricted by protocols and there's nobody breathing down my neck every day watching everything I do and criticizing me on how I do it. I have the time, I have the means, and I have the resources to help you," Jesse explained.

Another bold statement, but Nardelli said nothing.

"I can break it down for you. Let's start with the math literacy problem we have in Grade 9 and 10. Now that I have this beautiful mind, I can get myself up to speed on their entire curriculum for both grades in fairly short order. It wouldn't take long. I could probably be ready in about two or three weeks. With some help, I would be willing to start up an after school math tutoring program and work with those kids, all your Grade 9 and 10 classes. Best part is, I talk their language. If anyone can get through to them, I can. I'll teach them and get them ready for the re-test next May. I'd be willing to do that. I can talk to Amanda Perone and maybe persuade a few other senior math whizzes to help us."

Nardelli watched Jesse closely with intrigue but wasn't showing his cards just yet. "What else you got?" Nardelli asked nonchalantly.

Jesse sensed he had hooked Nardelli's interest and carried on. "Okay, next, we got a big problem here with bullying or extortion, as you call it. You can't solve that problem because it happens off school property. That's not going to stop the parents from blaming you though. I'm not restricted like you. I walk to and from school every day like the rest of these kids." Jesse started to build his case. "I've been thinking a lot about this and I think I have a solution for you."

"You have a solution to this problem. Well, well, I'm all ears," Nardelli replied, taking his claim far less seriously.

"Yes, I can solve this problem for you but you have to agree not to ask me a lot of questions about it. All you need to do is give me a list of kids being harassed and I'll take it from there."

"No, we can't go down that road, Jesse," Nardelli said, anticipating where this plan was going. "I can't approve anything like that. First thing you know, I get hauled in for running some kind of vigilante operation here at Lakewood and exposing my students to unnecessary violence. Forget it. Not going to happen." Nardelli closed the door on the idea.

"No, no, nothing like that, sir. This doesn't stick to you at all. There's nothing to approve. It operates completely off the books. I like to call it Project Shadow. Here's how it works. First, I get the names of students getting bullied. Then I dispatch a shadow to look over that student. Kid doesn't even know there's anyone there. The shadow moves around like a ghost, no one notices. The shadow can be there on the way to school or on the way home. Then, the bad guys pull up and start some trouble with the kid. All of a sudden, a good samaritan shows up, a concerned citizen who wants to help. That good samaritan intervenes, preaches some religion to the bad guys, de-escalates the problem, nice and clean, no one gets hurt. Everyone goes on their way, no harm, no foul. The best part is, the bad guys go away a little more religious than when they came. They're not likely to reoffend, if you know what I mean. The very best part, nothing tracks back to you. Just a bunch of good-hearted citizens doing their civic duty."

Nardelli finally broke a smile. He was quite impressed with the level of thought Jesse had put into this pitch. His interest was now peaked and he did not dismiss the idea. "That's all well and good, Jesse, but in the real world, things never turn out all nice and tidy like that. There's always a mess left to clean up afterwards. Besides, those things are just symptoms of bigger problem in this school."

"I assume you're talking about the drugs, am I right? Drugs are the biggest problem in this school, right?" he asked openly.

Nardelli conceded Jesse had hit on the core of his problem. "What do you know about that? Probably heard me say it a million times while you were sitting there with your hot little ear pressed against the door. What do you have in your bag of tricks where the drugs are concerned?" Nardelli challenged Jesse, believing he had overplayed his hand.

"What if I told you I might have some intel on that? Or should I say, I might know where to get some intel on that problem. You know, how the drugs get in and how they get out." Jesse proposed the idea without any sense of his real ability to deliver.

"If you know something about that, you need to tell me," Nardelli demanded.

"I know nothing about it but I may have a source, a credible source," Jesse replied.

Nardelli was now seriously interested for the first time in the meeting. Having such information would indeed be the Holy Grail towards solving the school's drug problem. The drug issue had baffled him all year and represented the single largest obstacle he faced. Nardelli began to pace about the room. He was intrigued, assessing all he had heard from Jesse so far. In his mind, he had nothing to lose and concluded the opportunity could possibly yield a significant breakthrough. He paused further and played it out in his mind before he spoke.

"Okay, I'll play your game. We've only got a few days left before Christmas break so you will stay out until we come back after New Year's. I need to talk with Mr. Malvoy and get approval from him to place you into the Last Chance Program, which I'm sure I can pull off. In the meantime, you keep your nose clean and stick to your probation till you get back. In fact, why don't you come see me here at school New Year's Day at 2 p.m. I'll be the only one in here so have your mother park around the back and knock on my window. I'll let you in and we'll have a short meeting then," Nardelli instructed him.

"You're working on New Year's Day?" Jesse asked in disbelief.

"Sure, kid. I just can't get enough of this place during the regular work week so I come in on holidays to get my fix," he responded sarcastically.

"Okay, I'll be here," Jesse confirmed. "Thank you, sir." He quickly exited before Nardelli could change his mind.

That's the way to do it, Decruz. Home run!

□

On the way home, Jeanie asked, "You were in there for nearly half an hour, Jesse. What did you talk to him about?"

"I think you may have swayed him, mom. He's talking about letting me back in after Christmas break. He told me to come see him New Year's Day at the school for a meeting. Can you believe it?"

"No, I can't believe it. He made no commitment to me. What did you say to him, Jesse?" Jeanie looked at him sensing there was more to his meeting than he was letting on.

"I just talked to him about maybe setting up an after school math tutoring program to help the Grade 9 and 10 students. Did you know they're going to re-test them in May?" Jesse asked.

"Wow, I didn't even know you were thinking about doing something like that. Maybe that's what turned him around," Jeanie speculated.

"I think you loosened the lid, mom. I just kept turning it. It's not a done deal yet. He needs to get approval from the director. I think that's what the meeting on New Year's Day is all about. I'm keeping my fingers crossed though."

"Well, that certainly will make the holidays a little more merry." A smile grew across her face.

"By the way, mom. I wanted to ask you a question. It's okay if you don't want to, but, how do you feel about visiting dad over the vacation?"

CHAPTER 25

Knock... knock... knock.

"Well, well, if it isn't one of Lakewood High's finest. I remember when I used to go to school, but who has time for that anymore?" Jesse welcomed Amanda into the apartment attempting to amuse her.

"Jerk. Are you going to let me in or should I just stand here freezing my butt off?" Amanda asked shaking the light dusting of snow from her coat.

"My hands are real toasty. I can warm that up for you," Jesse offered.

Amanda ignored the crude comment and quickly brushed past Jesse as she removed her coat and sat down at the kitchen table.

"Honestly, if he's planning to let you back in when we return, why didn't he just let you finish up the week?" Amanda expressed her annoyance at Nardelli's decision.

"I explained all that. He's got to get Malvoy's approval first. I'm sure the guy didn't drop everything else on his plate to deal with my situation. Besides, I deserve an extended vacation, don't you think?" Jesse asked, attempting to lighten her mood.

"Sorry, I'm just so pissed at this whole thing and you seem to be taking it all in stride," Amanda said sounding frustrated.

"So, Mandy, I wanted to talk to you again about this after school math tutoring thing. I know I just dropped this on you without even discussing it. Are you sure you're up to it? I don't want you the feel pressured."

"I think it's an awesome idea and I'm happy to help if it gets you back in school," Amanda reassured him. "It's only a few hours a week. No biggie. You think that swayed things in your favour?"

"I offered him a number of things. You should have seen me, Mandy. I was like a Bay Street lawyer in there making my case. I'm pretty sure my offer to help him on the drug thing was the deal changer. His whole face changed when I brought it up. I didn't really promise anything, just indicated I might have an inside track on things. He was lukewarm on my Project Shadow idea, but I think he'll change his mind once we have a few success stories there."

"Project Shadow?" she asked.

"Oh ya. I never told you about that one. We shadow these kids getting bullied for their cash. Apparently it's a huge problem at our school. We would be like the welcoming committee when the bad guys show up. Get the picture?"

"Kind of sounds dangerous, Jess. Who's we?"

"My boys, of course. Except they don't know anything about it yet till I tell them. Once I get Goz on board, the rest will follow." Jesse sounded confident.

"How are you even going to help Nardelli control the drugs, Jess? Maybe you over-committed on that one," she challenged him.

"Roger," he answered simply.

Amanda paused for a moment allowing the idea to register, then she erupted. "Are you crazy! You're going to get your rehabilitated born-again nut-job for a father involved in this? Your mom will never go for it!"

"I'm not telling her," Jesse admitted. "But she does seem to be warming up to the idea of going to Millhaven right after Christmas with me. Right now my dad would give anything to have us back in his life. All I'm asking for is a bit of information. If he has the low down on drug distribution at our school, he'll give it up. I'm sure of it. I'm trying to figure how to get some alone time with him while we're there. Still working on that one."

"Not sure how you're going to pull that off but good luck," Amanda replied, unconvinced.

"Me either," Jesse conceded.

"On a different subject, are you able to do the Teen Eve Night at Regent Community Centre?" Amanda asked.

The Teen Eve Night was an annual event put on by the Regent Park Community and sponsored by the local police force as an opportunity for community teens to safely celebrate New Year's Eve. This would be the fifth edition of the annual event that had grown quite popular over the past several years. The idea was born following the tragic events of 1980 where two teens were killed following a brawl at a local RGI unit party in the projects. The community council approached local law enforcement and received their support to provide a police presence at the annual event. Parents in the community embraced the idea and showed strong support including volunteer services. They welcomed the idea that their kids had a safe place to celebrate the evening with the expectation they'd make it home alive and well.

"Looks good so far. My mom is getting approval through my probation officer but she needs to drop me off and pick me up. That's the agreement. Just waiting now for the formal go-ahead," Jesse explained.

"That's great!" Amanda said, thrilled with this news.

"Okay, let me pour some cold water on it now. Part of the agreement says I got to leave by 10 p.m." Jesse completed the picture and waited for her reaction.

"That's okay, Jess. We'll come back here and watch Dick Clark's Rockin' Eve on TV. I'll even bring some Jos Louis desserts for you. Maybe we can convince your mom about a few glasses of champagne at midnight."

Jesse saw no hesitation or disappointment on her face. It reminded him why his affection had grown so deeply for Amanda. He wasn't sure what love was but thought this may be how it started. He smiled at her and quickly wrapped her in his arms, finishing with a long amorous kiss. She smiled back at him and buried her face in his chest.

"Before I go, I need to tell you I'm not real comfortable with this Wesley the Weasel plan the guys hashed up the other day. Things can go very badly, Jess, and make it worse for you," Amanda said with a great deal of trepidation.

"The guys know what they're doing, Mandy, and besides, it's better we know the plan than having them go off on their own. There's no way they were letting this go. They were going after these guys regardless. This seems to be the best way to control the situation without getting real messy," Jesse assured her.

"I hope you know what you're doing."

"Don't worry. They don't want me anywhere near this. They agreed no one gets hurt."

As they moved out of the kitchen, Jeanie flew through the front door and immediately hugged Amanda. "How you doing, sweetie?"

"School's out today till the new year. That's how I'm doing!" Amanda smiled.

"Ya, but your boyfriend here can't take you past the front steps," Jeanie reminded her.

"That's okay. Guess we'll need to clear the dust off the Monopoly and Scrabble boards this holiday," she chuckled.

"I don't know where Jesse found you, but he'd be crazy to let you go," Jeanie said affectionately.

"Thanks for that, Mrs. D. I gotta go. Momma's got dinner on. Talk to you both later." Amanda disappeared out the door.

Jeanie removed her coat and put it away in the hall closet. She turned towards Jesse. "Got something for you," she said, holding out a plastic bag.

"What's this?" Jesse asked.

"You're not going to just hang around the apartment the whole break. Thought I would make the next few weeks a bit more productive for both of us." Jeanie handed him the bag.

He looked inside. "Are you kidding me? Beginners Driving Guide? I'm getting my licence?" he asked with excitement.

"Not so quick, kiddo. First you use your new and improved mind to learn everything in this guide, write the test, and get your beginner's. Then you drive around with me for a couple weeks and hopefully we don't kill anyone. Then we schedule a road test for you sometime in January. If all that goes well, then you get your licence."

"Piece of cake, mom. I think I'll look good in the driver's seat of our Monte Carlo," he added.

Jesse had spent countless hours in the front seat of his father's 1978 Monte Carlo pretending to drive the vehicle when he was younger. He had always been curious about driving but never had the courage to ask his father to teach him when he turned sixteen.

"I like your confidence, kiddo. One step at a time. Let's not get carried away, okay?" She took some wind out of his sails.

"Wonder what Roger would think if he knew I was driving his car?" Jesse smirked.

"You can tell him yourself when we see him," Jeanie said checking him for a reaction.

"Straight up, mom?" he asked. "Didn't think you were keen on the idea. What changed your mind?"

"You're right. I'm not keen on it but clearly you are, otherwise you wouldn't have asked me. So, whatever your reasons, we'll go see your dad over Christmas."

"I thought it would be a good way to break the boredom. I'm going to be going stir crazy the next few weeks. I thought a road trip would mix things up for us," Jesse reasoned.

"I set things up with Zach. We'll drive up and make a day of it," Jeanie said.

"You're the best. Thanks mom." He hugged her.

"I got one more bit of good news for you while we're at it," she added. "Your probation officer gave us final approval on Teen Eve, but I got to pick you up no later than 10 p.m. That's the deal."

"Okay, mom. We got a deal."

CHAPTER 26

"Okay, Menusz, I need fifty copies of Jaws, The Godfather, Ghostbusters, and Raiders of the Lost Ark. And I need them by Friday!" Marko Vaskov barked from the hallway of his RGI unit on Pashler Avenue.

"Some of us have to go to school, you know," Minoo shot back sarcastically. "Why don't I just drop out and make this my full-time job."

"Just fuckin' do it and spare me the attitude," Marko replied. "We got another big order coming next week and I need you to clear the backlog!"

Minoo had settled in Canada as a child with his Uncle Marko back in 1976. They came to the country as refugees shortly after Minoo's parents vanished following an anti-government protest during the Croatian Spring in Yugoslavia. The Tito government regime came down hard on dissenters within the country at that time. Minoo's parents were active and vocal within the social movement and paid the ultimate price. The Vaskov family felt it was best for young Menusz and his father's brother, Marko, to start a new life in Canada. His Uncle Marko had skills and was unattached. They settled in the Regent Park community and carved out a living that straddled both sides of the law.

Minoo was an outgoing and hyper kid. He made friends quickly and grew quite popular, particularly with the girls. He was resourceful and street savvy. Having a combination of good looks and an abundance of self-confidence, he prospered in his new country in spite of his personal history and family isolation.

Marko was a polytechnic college graduate in his native Yugoslavia and had become quite proficient in the field of electronics, particularly for TV and stereo equipment repair. Although his English was poor, he assimilated quickly and was able to find part-time work with a local TV repair shop managed by an immigrant Serbian family on Parliament Street. Shortly after he started, he ingratiated himself into the family-run business. He soon discovered there was much more to the family business than simply TV repairs.

The '70s and '80s brought about a revolution in the home entertainment business. And with that, the introduction of video recording equipment and home movie rentals brought about opportunity. Marko's skill and aptitude enabled the small family business to seize that opportunity, more specifically, the reproduction of VHS movies. Over time, the enterprising Marko was able to pilfer, piece by piece, all the components required to build several reproduction units of his own.

As movie rental establishments started to flourish, demand for bootleg movies increased and Marko slowly built a sizeable base of loyal customers. In time, he separated from his employer to pursue his own ambitions. Demand for the cheaper pirated VHS movies grew exponentially and Marko inducted Minoo into his labour pool. In addition, the demand for sales and repair of VHS tape players was on the rise. Marko became wary of the Canada Revenue auditors and elected to operate a legitimate VCR repair business to conceal the revenues he generated from the more lucrative movie reproduction side of his trade. In order to keep up with demand, Marko slowly transferred his technical skills to Minoo who, not surprisingly, had a similar aptitude. Together, they lived a comfortable existence in Regent Park and agreed to live quietly within their means.

Marko and Minoo remained very private. Minoo took extraordinary measures to keep his secret life under wraps. Although he had an affliction where fine clothes and women were concerned, he kept his financial affairs to himself. They were careful to always wait an appropriate amount of time following a major movie release before making reproductions available. Distributing bootleg movies for films that were still playing in the theatres attracted law enforcement. They were careful and resisted the urge to be greedy, electing to maintain a low profile. Minoo trusted his closer friends but he rarely invited them to the apartment on Pashler Avenue. He had become very close with Jesse and Goz but kept his personal life separate.

"Menusz, come here please. I need to talk to you," Marko instructed.

Minoo had several recording devices operating simultaneously. He had mastered his craft and become quite proficient in the fine art of producing high quality bootleg movies. He paused the equipment and joined his uncle in the kitchen. "You want me to work or you want me to talk? Make up your mind," Minoo lamented.

"Shut up and sit down. What I have to tell you is more important right now. What if I told you we could make three times as much money as we're making right now? And the best thing, it wouldn't cost us no money up front, just our time," Marko pitched.

"I'd say, sign me up!" Minoo replied. "What's the catch?"

"No catch. Just a bit more risky but the rewards are high."

"You're not suggesting we make porn movies are you? Quite frankly, I'd do fine but you're way past your prime," Minoo mused.

"I'm serious. We have a perfect opportunity here. I need to know if you're in or out."

"Okay, quit with the cloak and dagger routine. Why don't you explain how this perfect opportunity works," Minoo said, growing impatient.

"It's called hydroponics," Marko said simply.

"What the fuck? You talking about growing our own weed?"

"Think bigger, Menusz. We'd be part of a larger organization. I got a buddy who needs a couple of techs like us to run a warehouse down near the waterfront. They got a slick operation going but they're having some technical issues. They got the hydraulics under control but their electronics are shit. We go in, automate the operation with high-end sensors and timers. We get a huge cut of the action."

"You talking about getting into some big-time drug operation?" Minoo asked again.

"What's the difference between that and what we're doing now?" Marko challenged.

"About five to ten years in prison. That's the difference!" Minoo shot back.

"It's all about risk and reward, Menusz. The rewards are very high."

"I'm sorry. I'm still reeling from the speech you gave me years ago, remember? You said, 'We're going to fly below the radar, Menusz. We're going to make some extra money but we're not going to get greedy. Keep it cool and steady as she goes. That's how we're going to do it.' Remember?"

"Listen, I'm talking about big money, Menusz. Instead of eating hamburger, we eat steak. You understand what I'm saying?" Marko pitched again.

"I happen to like hamburger too," Minoo said dismissively.

"Look at where you're living, Menusz. Do you enjoy living in Regent Park? Is this where you want to live the rest of your life? Take a look outside. We're not living in the Hamptons here, kid. I just want a better life for you and me, that's all I'm saying."

Minoo looked at his uncle. He had never seen this side of him before. Marko was always the pragmatist who measured risk carefully. This conservative approach had always served them well. He also understood he owed everything he had to his uncle. Marko had become a father figure and was always very protective of him. He'd provided him a relatively normal life in Canada following their sudden departure from Croatia. Minoo felt a great deal of dissonance; the proposal unsettled him. He was about to embark on a life that had just destroyed his best friend, Jesse. The hypocrisy conflicted him. In the end, he understood his uncle's pitch was much less a question and much more a statement.

Minoo gave his uncle a look of resignation and said despondently, "Listen Marko, you're the only family I got. You know I love you like my own father. I think this is a really bad idea, but if this is what you really want us to do, I trust you, so count me in."

Marko looked at his nephew and sensed the conflict and sadness in his eyes. He remained silent for a long moment then replied, "I guess we can eat hamburger for a while longer."

CHAPTER 27

"C'mon, mom. Just for half an hour. I promise to drive in the right lane, steady as she goes." Jesse pressured his mother as they rolled down the 401 eastbound towards Millhaven Penitentiary. He had breezed through the written test earlier in the week to acquire his beginner's licence and had been a royal pain to his mother ever since.

"What don't you understand, Jess? You can't drive on the highway with a beginner's licence. It's against the law," Jeanie repeated once again. "Although, I must admit, your road test shouldn't be a problem next month. You've been a quick study. You're a good driver so be patient. Maybe you can take the wheel once we get off the highway at Bath," she said, offering him an olive branch.

Jesse remained quiet for most of the trip and elected to review the Grade 9 and 10 math curriculum. He had a lot of ground to cover to ready himself for the after school tutoring program. He and Jeanie had spent a lot of time cooped up over Christmas vacation in their small apartment and had run out of things to talk about. Time had flown by for Jesse as he busied himself reading profusely. They hadn't discussed much about their upcoming meeting with Roger. They expected this encounter would be far less awkward than the first. They were both curious how he was progressing and the status of his rehabilitation.

Jesse took the wheel as his mother promised after exiting Highway 401. They agreed to grab lunch at McDonald's before arriving at the penitentiary.

It was a chilly morning as they checked in at the gate station entrance. They were familiar now with the entry protocol and waited patiently at the outer station till they were called.

"Can't imagine spending three years of my life in here. It must be like hell to lose your freedom," Jesse pondered in a low register as he scanned the facility.

"You'll never need to worry about that, Jess. You're not a bad guy. Only bad guys end up here," she assured him.

"*Decruz, approach Door 5 please. Decruz.*"

The announcement came over the intercom. They both moved to Door 5 where they were greeted by a large security guard. They followed the guard and weaved through the hallways until they reached the meeting room. Roger was already waiting in the outer room and flashed a smile at his wife and son as they approached. Two guards brought the elder Decruz into the room and locked his chains to the eyebolt anchors on the floor as they did before.

"They still giving me special treatment here as ya can plainly see. Only the best lock and chains for good ol' Rog. I'm like royalty here," Roger joked, breaking the ice. "You both look great. So glad ya came. Thanks, I mean it for real."

"How they been treating you, Roger. You look well. Looks like you put a few pounds on but in a good way, you know what I mean," Jeanie offered.

"Ya, dad. You look pretty good all things considered," Jesse added.

Roger's eyes welled up. He was not accustomed to this type of positive attention. He looked at his son. "Ya called me dad. Last time it was Roger. I appreciate that, son. I know respect gotta be earned. Hope we can mend bridges over the next three years." Roger turned to Jeanie. "How ya doin' financial like. Everything okay there? Ya got the money I told you about?"

"Yep. Got it all in a safe place," Jeanie confirmed. "We should be good for quite a while. Thanks Roger. What have you got there?" she asked pointing at the book he was holding in his right hand.

Roger had entered the room with the book. He raised it and turned it slowly towards them. The cover read *The Holy Bible*.

"I know it's kinda cliché, but I been thankin' God for finding me 'fore it was too late. I read his book every day. Brings me comfort. Kinda joy I never had before, a spiritual joy I suppose."

"They have a chapel here?" Jeanie asked.

"Yep, go twice a week, religiously, if ya pardon the pun," Roger chuckled.

They continued to chat for another fifteen minutes until the guard popped his head through the door.

"Excuse me, Mrs. Decruz. Do you own a blue '78 Monte Carlo?" he asked.

"Yes I do. Is there a problem?" she asked.

"You left the lights on your vehicle, ma'am

Perfect, right on time. Just as I planned!

"I'll stay here and talk with dad while you're out, okay, mom?" Jesse offered.

"Okay, then, I'll be back in a few minutes," Jeanie said and exited the room.

"Hey, don't be treatin' my Monte Carlo badly. I luv that car," Roger quipped as Jeanie departed.

Once Jeanie was gone, Jesse addressed his father.

"Okay, dad. Listen. I don't have a lot of time to explain but I really need your help on something." Jesse kicked in with a sense of urgency.

Jesse quickly explained his predicament at Lakewood High and how he had been set up on a trumped-up pot charge and subsequently suspended. He also explained his plan and his deal with Nardelli in order to get reinstated at the school.

"Long and short of it, dad, there's a bad drug problem at our school and I might have suggested I could help Nardelli with info on how it gets in and out of there." Jesse threw caution to the wind and decided to put it all out there for his father.

Roger listened intently. "Listen kid, ya don't wanna be getting involved in that. Ya need to stay away from it. Dangerous business, besides, I never worked our 'hood for drugs so I don't know how it works there. Ya know what they say. Ya don't crap where ya live. Understand, kid?"

"I won't be getting involved. I'm just a go-between. Nardelli does what he wants with the info. It doesn't stick to me at all. I gotta give him something," Jesse pleaded.

Roger looked intently at his son. He could see this was likely the whole reason he came to visit him. "Your mother know we talkin' about this?"

"Hell, no! You know mom. She'd kick my ass if she knew. Thing is dad, this is the only way I get back into school. It's my only play."

"Okay, okay, let me think." Roger looked at his son again and pondered for a moment. "Got this guy, he cum in here a few weeks back. I know him back from Club eX, a real badass. Apparently the Colombians threw him under the bus. He took the hit for something he didn't do. He's real pissed. Maybe he got loose lips. Maybe, with a bit of persuasion, he sings me a few bars, ya understand. He knows our area in Regent, how things work. Let me try and chum up to him and I see what he got. If

I get somethin', I get a hold of ya. That's all I can promise right now, kid," Roger offered.

"Perfect, dad. Thanks. That's all I'm asking. I really appreciate it." Jesse nodded.

"Hell, now I gotta go to confession. Can't be lying to your mom like this." Roger looked disconcerted as he started rubbing the front of his bible.

"You're not lying, dad. It's only lying if she asks you, but she's not," Jesse said, attempting to rationalize the scenario for his father.

Jeanie had re-entered the room by now. "You left the lights on, Jesse. Lucky we didn't drain the battery. Did you tell your father you have your beginner's licence?"

Jesse quickly turned and looked to his father for a reaction. Roger started to laugh hysterically at his apprehension.

"Hell kid, that car be ten years old by the time I get out. Ya can drive it into the ground for all I care. No skin off my ass." Roger continued to laugh. Both Jesse and his mother watched him closely before joining in.

CHAPTER 28

"I'll meet you right here at exactly 10 p.m. Got it, Jess?" Jeanie waited for confirmation.

"Ya, ya, got it mom. We'll be here, don't worry. Thanks for the lift," Jesse said.

"Thanks for the ride, Mrs. D. I'll make sure we're on time," Amanda confirmed.

"Alright then. It's New Year's Eve. Don't forget to have fun!" Jeanie added.

They headed into the community centre. The hall was decked out in New Year's Eve décor. The music was loud and the hall was filled with revellers. The New Year's community venue had become increasingly popular over the past several years. Parents enjoyed the safety this venue provided while offering quality music, food, and dance at a subsidized cost. The added bonus was a strong police presence.

"Whoa, this place is slammed. Must be every student in Regent Park here tonight. I see Goz over there." Jesse pointed to the northeast end of the hall. "Let's go."

"Did mommy just drop you off, junior?" Goz teased.

"Really, that's how we're going to start the evening?" Jesse wrapped his large hands around Goz's neck in a mock choke.

"And who's this with you? Your chaperone for the evening?" Goz motioned to Amanda.

"C'mon, Goz. Lay off. He's already bummed about the 10 p.m. curfew," Amanda said, defending her boyfriend.

"Where are the boys?" Jesse asked.

"Well, let see. We've got Minoo conducting class over there." Goz pointed to where Minoo was standing with a sizeable entourage of girls around him. They were giggling as he was likely recounting his typical mountain of concocted stories and half-truths.

"And over there, we have the hugely entertaining and ever-so-popular Jackson boys." Goz pointed to the front of the hall. "They've been going at it since we got here." The boys were entrenched in some heated discussion. "Just waiting for the head slap. It's going to be good."

□

"Get your shit together, bro. You got the plan down? You need to chill, baby bro. I need to know you ready for this." Trey attempted to get JJ focused on the evening.

"You kiddin'. I'd rather slit my eyeballs with razor blades, man. Why I gotta be in the starring role tonight?" JJ asked.

"C'mon, man, it's no biggie. You just need to establish trust with the guy," Trey explained.

"Easy for you, man. You not the one romancin' the Weasel tonight," JJ shot back.

"No need to romance him. Just show him some attention. He's like a little puppy dog. Show him a bit of love and he'll follow you around all night," Trey coached his brother.

"Why you wrecking my evening? Minoo should be doing this. Why I gotta do the dirty work all the time?"

"We're doing this for our friend. We're doing this for Jesse. Besides, the Weasel don't like Minoo much, you're our best chance. You're doing it for the team," Trey said, pumping him up.

"Don't be jivin' me, man! Whenever there's a mess to clean up, it's always on JJ."

At that moment, Trey's patience expired. He wound up and delivered a picture-perfect head slap. Goz, Amanda, and Jesse erupted into laughter as they watched the exchange. They moved to the front of the hall to greet them.

"Now, now, children, please. Let's kiss and make up," Jesse said trying to lighten the moment. JJ turned away and walked to the concession to purchase a drink. He was clearly in a foul mood.

"Don't worry about JJ. He'll be okay once he grabs himself a Coke and gets his blood sugar back up. He's just a little annoyed with his role tonight," Trey explained.

"I agree. JJ makes a lot of noise but he always comes through. He's the same way in the dressing room. He's always making noise and working guys up. But once he's out on the field, he gets focused and makes things happen. Always does," Goz confirmed.

Jesse scanned the room. He spotted Wesley who was hanging around the DJ's desk. All indications suggested he was making an annoyance of himself as the DJ was attempting to ignore his presence.

"I've got to freshen up, Jess. Be right back." Amanda headed to the rest room.

Minoo made his way over. "Excuse me, son. Isn't it past your bedtime?"

"Where the hell you come from? Pimps are Us?" Jesse stepped back and chuckled as he ran his hands across Minoo's neon blazer. Minoo had dressed up extravagantly for the evening, complete with a full shiny silver tuxedo and top hat.

"I believe clothes make the man. You are who you dress," Minoo said, bringing perspective to his attire.

"I guess that would make you the monocle guy from the Monopoly game," Goz quipped. They laughed.

"Is everything ready to go, Trey?" Jesse's tone turned more serious and brought them back to the scheduled events of the evening.

"Yep. Momma Jackson's gone till tomorrow. She's staying over at my aunt's place tonight. We got the place to ourselves. Everything's ready to go. I just need to keep an eye on JJ tonight, keep him focused," Trey assured him.

"You got the Polaroid?" Goz asked Minoo.

"Right here," Minoo confirmed, patting his pocket.

"Okay, we got eyes on the Weasel. It's all about execution now," Goz announced.

Amanda returned to the hall and grabbed Jesse by the arm.

"Let's go. My favourite song's playing," she declared.

Led Zeppelin's Stairway to Heaven was now blaring over the speakers as a flood of couples converged to the dance floor to cozy up to the popular slow dance song. Amanda brought her body close to Jesse's and placed her head on his shoulder. They continued to sway back and forth through the eight-minute song. As the song ended, Amanda turned and kissed him and then walked away from the dance floor. Jesse could see Owen Reed in his periphery shooting daggers in his direction. He didn't care. Even Reed couldn't spoil his mood tonight.

"Alright, the eagle has landed," Minoo announced and gestured towards the DJ's area. JJ had just made contact with Wesley. Their plan had officially started.

□

"I didn't know you were coming tonight, JJ. I saw your brother here too," Wesley said, attempting to make small talk with him.

"Ya, this is jus a pit stop for tonight. We got big plans over my place later. Can't really say too much. It's a closed party," JJ said, planting the seed.

"Whaddya mean, JJ. What's goin' on later? You got another party after this? You guys are crazy, man. You doin' an all-nighter?" the Weasel probed.

"Like I said, Wes, can't really say too much. It's a secret. Got some action lined up later on." JJ continued to feed him.

"What kinda action, man? Are you allowed to bring anyone? How many people going?" Wesley was intrigued.

"Small party but big plans. Going to be a lot of fun," JJ continued.

"You think maybe I can go, JJ? I can bring some booze. My contribution," Wesley offered up.

"If there was only a way I could, man, but you know what, let me think about it, Wes, and I'll get back to ya later." JJ went off abruptly, leaving Wesley with a glimmer of hope.

Goz intercepted JJ as he exited into the outer hallway.

"Looks like you and the Weasel getting cozy, JJ. Good job. Where we at?" he asked.

Trey and Minoo were nearby and joined the conversation.

"How's it going so far?" Minoo asked, sensing their plan was falling into place.

"JJ was just updating us now," Trey said.

"Like feedin' candy to a baby. He's jus scratchin' to come to the party," JJ updated. "Right now, I jus leave him hangin' for a bit then we'll get into phase two later."

Jesse and Amanda worked their way over to the group. They were all in deep discussion.

"Hey guys, I was just talking with Mandy about tonight. We still have a chance to pull the plug on all of this. Maybe it's not such a great idea. Things can go bad. I got no problem if you back it out right now. No bad feelings at all." Jesse looked to the group for a reaction.

Goz looked at Jesse in disbelief and grabbed his arm. "Come with me, Jess. I'm taking you to the washroom right now to change your diaper, okay. Cuz that's what we do with babies. We change their diapers for them. Is that what you are, Jess? A big baby?"

"Okay, okay, I get it. Just wanted to give you guys an option but it appears everyone here is committed," Jesse conceded.

"JJ's definitely committed. He's ready to take one up the ass for you, Jess," Minoo stressed.

"Fuck you, Minoo. Why ya gotta be an asshole for, man?" JJ said.

"Okay, then. We gotta go, guys. It's almost 10 and my mommy is waiting for us," Jesse said, offering a self-deprecating comment. "Good luck, boys, and don't be afraid to tank the plan if you're not feeling it. Promise me."

"It's all good, brother. We got your back, man," Trey reassured him. They shook hands and then Amanda and Jesse disappeared out the door. "Okay, back to work, JJ." Goz glanced over at Wesley. "We got to slam dunk this motherfucker!"

JJ worked his way back to Wesley and wrapped his arm around him. "Good news and bad news, Wes," JJ started. "Good news is, found a way to get you invited. Bad news, not sure you got the goods we need. You know what? Forget it. I shouldn't even told you about it. Forget I even brought it up." JJ dismissed his comments and started walking away.

"No! No! JJ, tell me. Whadda you need? I want to go, man!" Wesley clutched his arm, pleading.

"Okay, man. You can't be repeatin' this to no one. I mean it, no one can know, understand?"

"Not a word, man. I ain't sayin' nothin' to nobody. Swear to God." Wesley raised his right hand in allegiance.

"Alright. What our party's seriously lackin' are party favours. You know, the kind that makes you feel no pain. You know what I'm sayin, Wes?" JJ planted the bait.

"Sure, I understand. I can help ya out there. I gotta go somewhere to get it but I can handle that. What you want, man? Got me some weed, dust, coke, hits of acid, whatever you want, man." Wesley was now engaged.

"Sounds trippin', Wes. You know what, how 'bout ya bring a party platter. Let's go for the full experience. It's New Year's Eve after all." JJ sealed the deal. He provided Wesley the time and location. Their plan was now a go.

□

"Five... four... three... two... one... HAPPY NEW YEAR!"

Hundreds of balloons fell from the ceiling and noise filled the hall as the congregation brought in the New Year. The boys made their rounds and gathered at the entrance.

"This fuckin' better work. You know how much pussy I'm missing out on tonight?" Minoo announced as they exited the hall.

"You and me both," Goz added.

"The party jus getting started now, boys. Let's go." Trey gathered the group and they headed back to the apartment.

□

Back on Sackville Street, Jesse and Amanda had just brought in the New Year in front of the tube with Dick Clark's Rockin' Eve and sealed it with a long passionate kiss.

"Got anything left for your mother?" Jeanie asked as she approached her son with open arms.

"Thanks for everything tonight, mom. Sorry to wreck your evening playing taxi cab driver but we really appreciated it," Jesse said apologetically.

Amanda delivered a large hug to Jeanie. "You're the best, Mrs. D. You have been through so much this year. I hope the New Year will be so much better for you both."

"Thanks, sweetie. I appreciate that. Now, one more order of business before I hit the sack." Jeanie opened the fridge and uncorked a bottle of champagne she'd purchased the day before. "I'm sure it don't make me a bad mother if we share a glass of cheer together." She filled their glasses with some bubbly. They clicked them together and toasted to a brighter year for them all.

□

The Jackson boys sat at the kitchen table of their RGI apartment and cracked open some beers. They toasted the evening as they awaited Wesley's arrival.

"Got the Polaroid ready to go, Minoo?" Goz asked.

"Yep, locked and loaded."

"You ready, JJ?" Goz checked. "We don't want him sprinting out of here before it starts."

"Your confidence in me is flatterin', Goz. I'm golden. Just chill out, brother," JJ said. He was starting to feel the confidence the two quick beers he'd just chugged provided him.

Buzz... buzz... buzz...

"Alright, boys, show time. Turn up the tunes," Goz announced.

JJ opened the door. "Hey Wes, welcome to the Shangri-la, brother. C'mon in. I jus wanna know one thing, YOU READY TO PARTY!" JJ screamed in Wesley's face and startled the whole group. "You know everyone here?"

"I thought you said there's a party goin' on here. Where is everyone?" Wesley asked looking around the apartment.

"The party hasn't arrived yet. We got some freaky girls rented for the night. This place'll be burnin' hot soon. You ready for it, man?" JJ leaned into him.

"Really? Girls? They hot?" Wesley asked sheepishly.

"There's gonna be more booty and titties in here soon than you can handle, brother. These are not the type of ladies you bring home to momma, ya understand. Did you bring the party favours we talked about?" JJ asked.

Wesley pulled out a large bag from inside his coat and spread the contents out on the kitchen table.

"Oh, man. Gather round, boys. This party ready to heat up. WOOO!" JJ began to crank up the tunes on the stereo.

"What kinda smorgasbord you got for us here, Wes?" Goz approached the table with Minoo and Trey in tow.

"We got your standard weed, several hits of acid, some angel dust, and a bit of coke that will knock your heads off, man. Honestly." Wesley introduced each item as if it were an entrée. He began to relax and feel more confident in his element. Minoo grabbed the Polaroid.

Click... click... click.

"Why don't you do the honours, Wes. Take a line of that coke right now. We're probably gonna stick with the weed and leave the good stuff for the ladies," Trey instructed.

"Alright, sure you guys don't want some? This stuff is top shelf. Keep you up for a fuckin' week, man," Wesley announced.

"Show us how, man. Go, Wesley, go! Go, Wesley, go! Go, Wesley, go!" they chanted in unison as he fashioned a long thin line of powder using a razor blade. He bent over the table, took a straw to his nose, and snorted the entire line.

Click... click... click.

"Wow, man. You gonna like these girls. They freaks jus like you, man." JJ continued to stroke his ego.

Minoo and Trey disappeared into the bedroom, leaving them at the table. Goz cracked a few more beers and handed one to JJ and Wesley. He raised the bottle up and proposed a toast.

"Here's to whatever the night brings, man. Hope we can remember it all tomorrow." They laughed and chugged the beers down.

JJ grabbed Wesley by the arm and pulled him aside. "Listen, brother. We all gotta do one more thing before the ladies get here."

"What's that?" Wesley asked with little regard to the answer.

"I told ya, these girls are real freaks. They want a picture of each of us when they get here. Picture of us in our birthday suits, you know what I mean," JJ said.

"Are ya fuckin' kiddin me, JJ? Where the hell you get these bitches?" Wesley asked.

"Don't ask, man. Jus do it. Trey's in the bedroom now getting his pic done. Minoo's the camera guy tonight. When Trey comes out, you go next. Got it?" "Whatever, man. Can't wait to meet these bitches." Wesley was giddy.

Trey emerged from the bedroom shirtless. He flashed Wesley a smile as he carried his shirt and socks in his arms. His theatrics were convincing.

"You're next, Wes." He gestured to Wesley.

Wesley appeared a bit apprehensive but his resistance and reasoning were now severely compromised by the narcotics and alcohol. He looked at everyone, burst out laughing, and headed into the bedroom.

"Okay, Wes. Strip right down to the wood. Don't be shy now. It's all for a good cause," Minoo assured him.

Wesley did as he was instructed.

Click... click... click.

Wesley returned to the room. Goz looked over at Minoo who gave him the thumbs up; then he whispered to Trey, "Get the bath started."

JJ continued to keep Wesley occupied. They carried on for another ten minutes until Goz gave him the nod.

JJ suddenly moved towards Wesley bringing his face very close to his. "You know what, Wes? You don't smell so good. I think it's time you take a bath."

"What ya talkin''bout, man. I don't need a—"

Suddenly, Wesley felt another set of arms on him. JJ and Goz quickly moved against him. They manhandled him with ease as they carried him into the washroom where the bathtub was now filled with water.

"What the fuck? Get off me, man! Get off! What the fuck's goin' on?" Wesley struggled to no avail. He was no match against the two larger football players holding him on either side. They aggressively moved him to the side of the bathtub and collapsed his legs from behind. Wesley was now on his knees with Goz directly in his face.

"Here's what's going on fuckhead! Listen real close cuz I got zero time and patience for you right now!" Goz grabbed Wesley's hair at the back of his head as Wesley continued to struggle. JJ provided a head slap for good measure. There was terror in Wesley's eyes. He was unable to grasp completely what was happening.

"You and Reed made a big mistake. You guys were crazy to believe you could get away with it. You planted those drugs in Decruz's locker and you stood there and watched the cops walk him out of the school. Worst fuckin' decision you assholes ever made. Part of me just wants to bury your head in this water and watch your lungs fill. Maybe I will and maybe I won't. Depends entirely on you, Wesley boy." Goz painted him a picture in a slow and deliberate fashion.

"I don't know what the fuck you're talkin' about, man," Wesley shot back.

"Would you say that's the wrong answer, Trey?" Goz looked to Trey.

"Yep, I would say that's the wrong answer," Trey replied.

"Okay, down you go," Goz instructed.

JJ and Goz leaned him over the side of the tub, completely submerging his head. Wesley kicked and struggled vigorously until they pulled him back up.

"It's going to be a long evening, Wes, if you keep lying to us. We can do this all night if you want. I'm going to ask you again. Who planted the drugs?" Goz questioned him again, turning up his tone.

"Honest, man. We had nothing to do with it. I'm tellin you the truth!" Wesley pleaded. He continued to panic attempting to escape their grasp.

"Bye-bye, Wes." Goz and JJ snapped his head back down into the water. This time they kept him submerged for several more seconds until Trey chimed in, "Don't want anyone dying here tonight, boys, and don't think momma would appreciate it much."

They pull him up again. Wesley struggled to find his breath. "Okay, okay, okay, stop! I did! I did it!" Wesley began sobbing.

"It's a good start, Wesley, but you're not really the prize we're looking for. We want Reed," Goz said, revealing their true intentions.

"Reed had nothing to do with it. It was all me. I did it. Decruz dissed me one too many times so I was pissed at him. It was suppose to be just a joke but things got out of hand. Didn't mean to jam him up like that!" Wesley was now talking fast and furious confessing his role.

"You still don't smell so good, Wes." Goz replied and they dunked him one more time. They pulled him back up. "Tell us about Reed now!" Goz screamed directly into his ear this time.

Wesley began sobbing uncontrollably. "I told you man, it was me, jus me."

"Hey, Trey, I'm getting real hungry. Can really go for some toast right now. Can you bring the toaster in here please," Goz instructed Trey. They looked down at Wesley. His panic elevated in spite of his impaired condition. Trey returned from the kitchen with toaster in hand.

"Thanks, Trey. Can you plug that in over here, please," Goz continued calmly and turned his attention to Wesley. "I'm going to ask you one last time then you and the toaster are taking a long bath together, Wesley," Goz warned ominously.

"You're fuckin' crazy, man! You really gonna kill me over this? I don't know what you want me to say." Wesley bowed his head, sobbing, and resigned himself to his fate.

"Okay, that's the way you want it," Goz said patiently. They waited till Wesley was settled before speaking again.

They pulled him up back on his feet, walked him back to the kitchen, and sat him on a chair. Goz positioned another chair directly in front of him and straddled it moving himself closer to speak with Wesley.

"Look at me," Goz instructed. Wesley continued to wipe tears from his eyes. "Here's what you're going to do. Are you listening to me?" Goz attempted to gain his full attention.

Wesley looked up and simply replied, "Ya."

"First day back to school, you're going to walk into Nardelli's office and confess. You're going tell him what you told us. It was all a joke that just went badly. You tell him those were not Decruz's drugs. Got it?" Goz glared.

"Ya, I got it." Wesley replied simply. He was just relieved he was not going to die on this night.

"Oh, one more thing, Wesley," Goz continued. "If you tell anyone about what happened here tonight, or you don't visit Nardelli first day back, show him, Minoo." Goz motioned to Minoo to complete his point.

Minoo pulled from his pocket several pictures he had developed earlier on with the Instamatic. He spread them out on the table. They were all there, pictures of Wesley doing drugs and, most notably, the full frontal nude pic he'd posed for earlier.

"You recognize the guy in those pictures, Wesley? Needless to say, you were the star tonight. If you don't do exactly as we say, or you tell anyone about tonight, these pictures will show up everywhere. I mean everywhere, Wesley boy. You'll see them at school, at home, hell, we'll hang them on the fuckin' billboard coming into town. You understand?" Goz asked, completing the narrative.

Wesley simply nodded and bowed his head in defeat.

"Now, take all your drugs and get the fuck out of here," he instructed.

After Wesley had departed, they all looked around the table at each other. There were no high fives or any sense of celebration. They had taken a big chance and now their fate was entirely in the hands of the person they had just tortured.

Goz remained stoic and simply said, "Okay, boys, good job. Just a waiting game now."

They remained silent and said nothing as they sat back and sipped the rest of their beers. They were neither proud nor disgusted by what they had just done. They would have no problem sleeping on this night. They rationalized their behaviour out of a strong sense of loyalty and dedication to their friend, plain and simple.

CHAPTER 29

Knock... knock... knock.

"Come on in. You don't look so good," Jesse said, ushering his friend through the front door. "You're up pretty early for New Year's Day. Didn't expect you to surface till noon."

"Your mom out?" Goz asked.

"Ya, she's at some friends for New Year's brunch. She won't be back for a bit. She's driving me to school later. Got a meeting with Nardelli at 2 p.m.," Jesse explained.

"Okay, good. Gotta fill you in on last night," Goz said quietly in obvious signs of pain.

"You okay? Your colour's not so good."

"Can I get a coffee, please? We got into it last night after Wesley left. Way too many beers. My head's hurtin' like a bitch this morning." Goz eased himself onto the kitchen chair.

"So spill. Did things go down as planned? It's been on my mind all night. What happened?" Jesse grew impatient for details as he put on a coffee pot for Goz.

"Ya, everything went pretty much to plan. My only concern is the Weasel. He's definitely a wild card. No telling what that fuckin' nut job will do now." Goz began to explain what had happened. "We buried his head underwater a number of times. Even brought out the toaster. Fuck, didn't think I was that badass but it just kinda popped into my head if you pardon the pun. Definitely scared the shit out of him."

"I'll bet. So where did we end up?" Jesse asked.

"Well, got some good news and some bad news." Goz remained evasive. "Good news is he admitted to planting the drugs."

"And, the bad news?" Jesse asked.

"Bad news, he wouldn't implicate Reed. Swears Reed had nothing to do with it."

"Shit, that was our end game. You believe him?"

"Hell no. There's no way the Weasel stickhandled this whole thing by himself. But shit, we threatened to give this asshole a toaster bath and he still wouldn't give it up. Guess he's going to eat this one himself," Goz said, providing his perspective.

"Any chance he sings about his ordeal at the Jacksons' place?"

"Where it sits right now, he confesses to Nardelli first day we're back. That's the deal or we threatened to publish his best Polaroid moments of the evening to the whole world. Ha, ha. He wasn't very keen on that. Anyhow, it can go either way. This guy's got a loose screw, no question about it. But I think we got a better than 50 percent shot it goes in our favour."

"Holy shit, you guys are badass. Wish I could've been there for all that. I owe you guys big. In fact, we will dine in style. My treat." Jesse shook his hand.

"The Keg?" Goz suggested.

"Sure, three-inch steaks all around. By the way, how did JJ do last night?" Jesse smiled as he asked.

"He was awesome. Football's not his only talent. He played the Weasel like a finely tuned instrument. Had him lock, stock, and barrel." Goz laughed, recounting the event, bringing Jesse up to date and leaving nothing out.

□

"I took a big hit for you last night, man," Wesley said to Owen Reed.

"What do you mean? What happened to you? I saw you take off with JJ last night. You don't hang with him. What was all that about?" Reed asked.

"It was a fuckin' ambush, man. That's what it was. They set me up real good. Tried to drown me. Fuck, tried to kill me. They dangled a fuckin' toaster over a filled bathtub with me in it. Shit! They're fucked up, man."

"Shit, what d'you do?" Reed asked, looking concerned about where the discussion was headed.

"I gave it up. I'm not going to die over this. I confessed."

Reed fixed his eyes on him. "Did you mention me?"

"Nah, they tried hard to get me to pin it on you but I held my ground," Wesley said with loyalty.

"That's fucked up, Wes. You need to tell the cops about this. They can't get away with that," Reed encouraged him.

"Yes they can," Wesley shot back immediately.

"What do you mean? They tortured you! They can't get away with that."

"They got pictures of me. Bad pictures of me doing stuff. Bad stuff," Wesley explained.

"Bad stuff, like what?"

"Like running a line of coke up my nose, and other stuff," Wesley said, holding back the details.

"What else is worse than doing drugs?" Reed continued to push for details.

"Ya, worse than doing drugs. I don't wanna talk about it. Let's just say they got me by the short and curlies and there's nothing I can do about it. First day back, they want me to give it all up to

Nardelli. I gotta confess the whole Decruz thing or the pictures get published. I'm fucked," Wesley said with a sense of defeat.

Reed pondered the situation. He saw an opportunity to cut his losses and bring an end to the situation. He did the math and determined the best course of action that would have the least impact on him; he was prepared to sacrifice the Weasel and close the book on the whole incident. He turned back to Wesley.

"Okay, here's what you're going to do, Wes. Best case for everyone. You already confessed and now they got your neck in a noose. You're going to confess to Nardelli. Tell him the whole thing was just a prank that went too far. Be real remorseful-like. He'll take pity. You ain't been in trouble with him before. Worse case, you get your hand slapped, maybe a few days suspension and it's all done. For your trouble and loyalty, I'll pay you $200 for taking the hit. No sense us both going down for this. It's the best thing for everyone at this point," Reed summed up, looking to Wesley for a reaction.

Wesley had already given the situation some thought and was resigned to confessing in any case. He was $200 richer in the process, not a bad consolation, he thought. "Ya, I don't see any other way out. Makes sense."

□

"You ready to go, Jess?" Jeanie yelled from her bedroom.

It was nearly 2 p.m. when Jesse pulled on his coat. "Ya, let's go mom. Don't want to be late."

They jumped into the car and made their way to Lakewood High.

"Honestly, we must have the most dedicated principal in Toronto. Who goes to work on New Year's Day?" Jeanie asked.

"This guy's got so much on his plate, mom. I wouldn't want his job for anything. And his boss, this Malvoy guy, he's a tyrant.

He's all over him all the time. The pressure must be incredible."
Jesse attempted to defend Nardelli's work ethic. "Actually, I'm
kinda worried about whether he convinced Malvoy to let me
back in. That's not a done deal either."

"We'll know soon enough. I'm keeping my fingers
crossed, Jess."

They arrived at the school, drove around the side of the building, and parked next to Nardelli's vehicle at the back. He was
there already as advertised. Jesse exited the car, made his way to
Nardelli's office window, and knocked. Nardelli rose from his
desk and motioned to Jesse to meet him at the front entrance.
Jesse retrieved his mother and they made their way to the front.

"Happy New Year, Jeanie, Jesse," Nardelli greeted them both
as he opened the front door and shook their hands.

"I'm not sure what they're paying you, Dominic, but it's not
nearly enough," Jeanie said.

"The more I do today, the less hectic things are when we start
back. All part of the job," Nardelli explained. "Okay, folks, have
a seat, please." He pulled out an armchair for Jeanie and they sat
across from Nardelli's large desk.

"Let's start with the good news. Jesse's suspension has been
lifted. He starts back here Day 1 as part of the Last Chance
Program." On hearing the good news, Jeanie embraced her son.
"Now, the program is a bit of a misnomer but it is new. Jesse is
our first test case for the program, which means we're taking a
chance on you, Jesse. You will report to me each morning fifteen
minutes before school starts. We'll meet and discuss a plan for
the day, and then we'll meet for a debrief fifteen minutes after
school. We'll continue this way until I'm satisfied we no longer
require a daily meeting. You've agreed to assist us with an after
school tutoring program, which I will admit swayed things in
your favour. I suspect our meetings will focus on this for the
first week. I'm anxious to launch this, Jesse. Our Grade 9 and 10

math program is in deep trouble right now and your proposal grabbed our interest. Okay, any questions?"

"Thank you, Dominic. We really appreciate this, truly," Jeanie said.

"I won't let you down, sir," Jesse added.

"We're counting on that," Nardelli said. "Unless you have any questions, that's all I really have. We're done here. Short and sweet."

Jeanie and Jesse rose from their chairs and shook his hand again. When Jesse reached the door, he turned back towards Nardelli.

"I'll meet you in the car, mom. I just need to ask Mr. Nardelli a quick question."

"Yes, Jesse? You forget something?" Nardelli asked, looking puzzled.

"Benny Lee," Jesse stated. "I need his address. I just want to keep an eye on him if you don't mind."

"Jesse, we already discussed this. I'm not comfortable with that."

"I promise you. No one will know you have anything to do with it. Let's just call it a pilot project. You got nothing to lose and everything to gain, sir."

Nardelli look at him pensively. The Benny Lee situation was problematic and he had yet to resolve it. The case was particularly troublesome as it had reached Malvoy's level. Mrs. Lee had become what they referred to as a squeaky wheel, and she was not likely to back away until the problem was resolved. He pondered the situation as he bent down and started to click the keys on his computer. He grabbed a piece of paper and pencil and transcribed some information from the screen. He handed the paper to Jesse.

"Okay, I'll take a chance. If this thing blows up in my face, you're out of the program, Jesse. You understand? You can't afford any more trouble and neither can I," Nardelli warned as he surrendered the slip of paper.

Jesse reviewed the slip that contained Benny's home address. "Got it, thanks," Jesse said simply and left the office.

CHAPTER 30

Knock… knock… knock.

"Yes, come in!" Mr. Alverez yelled.

"Hi, we need to talk," Owen Reed said, entering the locker room office.

"What's up, Owen? You don't look so good."

"We got a situation, Manny. Not sure I handled it right. You need to know what's going on." Reed sat down.

"I got a busy day, Owen. First day back. Lot's to do, so you need to make this quick. What's up?" Alverez looked at Reed impatiently.

"It's about that stuff I bought from you last month. I got to come clean about what went down." Reed began to explain. He rehashed the whole story and set up, including the latest involving Wesley and his pending confession to Nardelli.

"Please tell me this whole thing is a joke. Help me understand. You planted drugs in someone's locker and today they're telling Nardelli about it?" Alverez asked in disbelief. "And Decruz's buddies muscled him into a confession? Unfuckinbelievable! He can't go to Nardelli with this."

"It's a done deal. He's got a meeting set up today. There's no way out. They got pictures, incriminating pictures. Wesley's got no way out. Good thing though, he's eating this whole thing himself. No connection to me or you. He's taking the full hit," Reed said, attempting to rationalize it.

"Wake up, numb nuts! You really think it ends there? You think Nardelli just accepts the confession and closes the books? Fuck!" Manny Alverez shouted raising his arms above his head in exasperation. "They got Decruz on probation. What do you think's going to happen when Nardelli approaches the cops with this story? Now you got law enforcement going to ratchet down on this Wesley Dragos guy. He's nine cents short of a dime to my understanding. The kid's going to sing like a bird." Alverez finished his thought glaring at Reed.

"I thought about that so I paid him off $200. You know, insurance money so that don't happen," Reed explained further.

"Oh ya, well, you just wasted $200, kid. You think that'll keep him quiet, do you?" Alverez gave Reed a look of derision. "If this thing goes sideways on us, they'll have more drug sniffing dogs wandering through this school than we can possibly handle. You getting the picture, Owen? You need to leave now. I got to think. I'll be in touch." Alverez quickly dismissed Reed.

□

Jesse and Amanda headed out from his Sackville apartment. This was Jesse's first day back since they'd hauled him away in a police vehicle the previous month. They were both excited to be back to the daily routine of walking together to school.

"Where we going, Jess? School's this way." Amanda pointed as Jesse led them on an alternate route. Jesse explained his deal with Nardelli to look over Benny Lee.

"I thought he shut you down on that idea," Amanda said.

"He did. But I told him I was doing it anyway. I suggested we do a trial on this one. This Benny kid's mother's making a lot of noise. She already went over his head to Malvoy. I think Nardelli's actually on board with it but he won't admit it, not until he can see results."

Jesse directed them to River Street where the Lee family lived in the government housing projects. They waited across the street from his building until Benny emerged.

Benny was small for his age. An easy target, Jesse thought. Jesse was moved by his mother's plea to Nardelli during her last visit to the school. It affected a part of him that was very familiar in his own life. He understood the injustice of abuse at the hands of those in a position of strength or authority. Jesse had less and less tolerance for this as he matured. He'd committed that he would not idly stand by if he was able to make a difference.

"Are you going to do this every day, Jess? You're going to follow this kid back and forth to school when nothing may ever happen again?"

"Chances are it's going to happen again. When it does, I just need to be here. Just once, that's all it takes. I need to put a face to these assholes. It's probably just some pothead looking for quick money. Look at that kid, Mandy." Jesse motioned to Benny as he exited the apartment building. "How's he going to defend himself? He's 90 pounds soaking wet, like a helpless little puppy."

Amanda smiled at Jesse. She had witnessed this nurturing side of him before; empathy was his most endearing quality. Jesse had a good heart, she concluded.

"I guess it's no different than what you did for me, Jess. You saw I was in trouble and you just reacted. You helped me out of a bad situation without being asked." Amanda hugged him.

Benny reached the sidewalk from his apartment complex and headed to school. Jesse and Amanda followed closely behind until they arrived. Today would be a non-event but Jesse was committed. He would do this as long as it took. There would be a tomorrow and a day after that.

□

"You can go in now, Wesley. Mr. Nardelli is ready to see you," Mrs. Garcia announced.

Wesley Dragos entered Nardelli's office. He was trembling and anxious at the thought of this meeting with his principal.

"Mr. Dragos, what can I do for you today, son?" Nardelli greeted him.

The meeting lasted only fifteen minutes but Wesley confessed to everything, leaving Nardelli dumbfounded.

"I've been in public education a long time, Wesley, and I thought I'd heard everything. But I must admit, what you're telling me this morning is very disturbing. I'll give you credit for having the courage to come forward but I suspect the police will want to talk with you some more about this," Nardelli explained.

"What do you mean? I just admitted everything. I'm ready for a suspension. I know I did wrong. Why the police got to get involved?" Wesley's face turned ashen as he began to panic.

"Well, for one thing, we need to explain to the police that they have the wrong person on probation. No need to panic, son. The fact you came forward with this with a relatively clean record, they'll have some mercy on you. You'll probably get off with a warning or perhaps a short probation. It's too early to tell but I'll put in a good word for you," Nardelli said, trying to calm him. "You can go now, Wesley. We'll be in touch."

□

Nardelli held his end-of-day meeting with Jesse. They had chatted briefly in the morning and he was pleased to have this opportunity to clear him of the drug charges.

"Sit down, Jesse. I just a have a few things to discuss with you. I think you'll be pleased." He looked at Jesse with a slanted smile. "Before we get to the good news, I need to know when you think you might be ready to launch the math tutoring program. I know you've already read most of the material and you met today with the head of our Math Department."

"Amanda and I had a good meeting today with some of the math faculty. They've been really supportive and gave us a lot of tools we can use for instruction. We're still reviewing some of the curriculum. We should be ready to launch the week after next if that's okay." Jesse looked to Nardelli for confirmation.

"That's perfect, way ahead of my expectations, Jesse. Now, what I'm about to tell you may change all of this." Nardelli's comment caught Jesse off guard. He appeared confused as he waited for the news.

"How do you mean?" Jesse asked.

"It would appear you've been vindicated from the crime you were accused of. Wesley Dragos came forward this morning and confessed to the whole sordid affair about your drug possession. Appears he had some issues with you and made some bad choices. Fairly extreme choices, I might add. I have a meeting set up in half an hour with the police to explain everything. They'll take over from there. I suspect your probation will be lifted in fairly short order afterwards. In addition, you're free of any obligations you made to the Last Chance Program and any other commitments you made to me."

"Wow, I don't know what to say. I'm real happy my name's been cleared." Jesse felt the weight of his ordeal lift. "As far as my commitments go, I intend to do everything I said I would, Mr. Nardelli," he said, recommitting to his principal.

Nardelli was taken aback. He felt tremendous respect for Jesse at that moment and was not expecting this reaction.

"You're telling me you want to continue with all of this?"

"Yes, everything. This is my school too, Mr. Nardelli. I followed Benny Lee to school this morning. It's not right that kid lives in fear every day. I wanted to put a stop to it and I was kind of disappointed nothing happened. But, I'm going to do it again tomorrow and the day after that. As long as it takes. Also, Amanda and I will follow through and help these kids learn math. And I told you I'm going to help if I can with the drug situation. I meant every word of it," Jesse stated with conviction.

Nardelli sat back in his chair as a large smile spread across his face. "Well Jesse, I must admit, you are quite a unique individual and you continue to impress me. I will thank you in advance. You can walk through my door anytime if you need help. I mean it. Just ask. Thanks for your dedication, kid." Nardelli shook his hand and Jesse left the office.

□

"We have a sticky situation here," Alverez said over the phone. "I need to deal with it. There's nothing to worry about. Just keeping you in the loop."

Alverez provided a reader's digest version of the Wesley Dragos scenario.

"Needless to say, you need to contain this, Manny," the voice on the other end of the phone said. "I don't pay you to leave loose ends hanging, you understand? Let me be very clear. This goes badly, it falls on you, so clean up your mess now," the voice warned.

"Understood. I'll take care of it," Alverez confirmed. "It's under control."

CHAPTER 31

"I still can't believe it, Jess. I'm so happy but real angry at the same time. How could somebody do that?" Jeanie asked as she prepared toast and coffee for her son. "And then he walks into the principal's office three weeks later and gives it up? Don't make sense at all. What did you do to this kid to get him so angry?"

"He's just real messed up, mom. He's never been right upstairs whole time I've known him. Probably dropped on his head when he was born," Jesse answered flippantly.

"Well, I hope they get him some professional help or counselling. A kid who does something like that sounds dangerous. You stay away from him, Jess. I don't want you taking any revenge on this kid. By the way, Mr. Nardelli said your parole officer will contact me sometime today and make it official. They're busting you out of this prison," she said with a chuckle.

"I'm just glad it's over. I won't touch him, mom. Promise. You know how much I love you, mom, but it's going to be nice to walk out this door without having me on your leash."

"No Mandy today?" Jeanie asked.

"She's going in early this week to prep some math lessons for our after school math program. We've been planning together

SUNRISE AT DUSK

with the math faculty. We should have it up and running week after next."

"I think you and Mandy are doing an amazing thing for those kids, Jess. I'm real proud of you. I know Mr. Nardelli appreciates the help. He said something about applying for Grade 13 credits for this program of yours if it's successful."

"One step at a time, mom. We haven't even started yet, but you're right. Getting some credits for the program would be icing on the cake. One less class to take next year."

Jesse finished his breakfast and headed out to River Street to shadow Benny Lee. He and Amanda had agreed she would distance herself from this activity. Jesse didn't want to compromise her in any way in the event things got out of hand. She'd attempted several times to dissuade him to no avail. Jesse had made up his mind; he would see it through.

Jesse waited for Benny to surface then followed him for several blocks. He noticed someone approaching Benny from behind; he maintained his distance and watched things unfold. Jesse didn't recognize the individual. He was black, approximately 5'10" with a thin build and a tall afro, and he walked with a slight limp on his right leg. Jesse approached closer to watch the interaction and noticed Benny recoil as his assailant clawed at his knapsack.

Okay, Jesse, showtime.

Jesse sprinted across the road like a panther and walked up behind Benny. He placed his hand on Benny's shoulder, which startled his tormentor. Benny looked back quickly and Jesse shot him a huge smile.

"How you doing, Benny? How's my buddy today?" Jesse asked nonchalantly.

Benny, unable to grasp what was happening, could only manage a one-word response. "Fine," he said timidly.

"Who's your pal here, Benny?" Jesse said. "I'd like to meet him."

He waited for a response but Benny was visibly frazzled, uncertain how to respond.

"What's your name?" Jesse asked leaning in with a menacing stare.

The guy looked up to see Jesse meant business. He answered simply, "Darren."

"Nice to meet you, Darren," Jesse said offering his hand.

Darren looked up sheepishly at the larger Decruz. Uncertain what to do, he extended his right hand to meet Jesse's.

Jesse began to squeeze his hand tightly and asked, "Where do you go to school, Darren?"

Darren felt his hand caught in a vice grip and grimaced in pain as he attempted to respond. "Cabbagetown" was all he could muster.

Jesse finally released his hand. "I think you're going the wrong way, Darren. I believe Cabbagetown is that way," Jesse said, pointing in the opposite direction. Jesse turned to Benny and asked, "Has Darren borrowed money from you recently, Benny?" Benny looked terrified and, again, did not respond.

Jesse turned back to Darren and placed his large right hand on his shoulder. He clutched the muscle running between his neck and right shoulder squeezing with force. "Let me ask you, Darren, and I need you to be honest with me now. Have you been borrowing money from Benny here? It's okay. It doesn't make you a bad person, so long as you pay back your debt." Jesse continued to clamp down on him until he was unable to endure the pain any further.

"Ya I did! I did!" Darren finally responded hoping to stem the pain Jesse was inflicting.

"How much money did you borrow?" Jesse asked calmly still holding him in his grasp.

"Ten bucks, I think," Darren responded prompting Jesse to squeeze harder. "No, maybe twenty bucks, ya, twenty bucks, I'm pretty sure," Darren surrendered. Jesse stared at him. "I'm waiting," he announced. Darren pulled the cash from his pocket and handed it over to Benny who was watching the exchange, wide-eyed. "What do you say, Benny?" Jesse prompted him.

"Thank you," Benny said simply.

"Okay, Benny. Stay right here. I'll be right back," Jesse instructed.

Jesse clutched Darren by the arm, walked him slowly several yards away from Benny, and stopped. He looked down at Darren and the smile fell away from his face. He brought himself closer in a menacing fashion. "Listen to me very closely, you fuckin' parasite," Jesse said in a hoarse whisper. "You ever talk to this kid again, you so much as walk on the same side of the road or even look at him the wrong way, I will fuckin' end you. Do we understand each other?"

Darren's eyes were now wide open and attentive. He responded, "Yep, okay."

"Okay what?" Jesse prompted.

"I won't bother him no more," Darren offered.

Jesse placed his hand on top of Darren's large afro leaving a discernable imprint. "Excellent. You have a good day, Darren," he said loudly enough for Benny to hear. Darren disappeared quickly down the street.

Jesse headed back towards Benny and leaned down to comfort him. "Hi, Benny. I'm Jesse. I'm your new friend. We're going to walk to school together today and maybe even tomorrow if that's okay with you. Can you make me a promise, Benny?"

"Yes," Benny said as he looked up.

"I want you to promise me you will tell me if anyone ever bothers you again. Do we have a deal?" Jesse placed his hand out.

Benny looked tentatively at his large hand, causing Jesse to break out in laughter. "Don't worry, I'm not going to squeeze your hand. Good friends always shake hands. We're friends, aren't we, Benny?

Benny looked up again and finally a smile spread across his face as everything came into proper context. "Ya, you and me are friends, Jesse."

□

Jesse arrived at the school where numerous emergency responders were parked directly across the road from Lakewood High. The parkette was a popular hangout for students during the week and headbangers on the weekend. In a tiny remote area of the park where trees obstructed the view from the road, kids would often escape to toke up or make deals. Police were present at the entrance of the parkette and Nardelli was standing alongside them, speaking to several officers. There were paramedics and an ambulance parked up on the grass. There was a large student presence and many people on the perimeter watching events unfold. Jesse noticed Goz and Minoo in the crowd and quickly made his way over.

"What the hell's going on now?" he asked his friends.

"Not sure," Goz responded. "Someone said there's some guy overdosed in the park. Haven't pulled him out yet. I think he's still alive. Working on him now."

"Nardelli's about to blow a gasket. He's been marching around the grounds for about fifteen minutes now. He was over there where the guy was lying and then they chased him out. Must be bad," Minoo summarized.

The crowd continued to grow as the paramedics finally moved the victim out after another twenty minutes. The scrum of paramedics loaded the patient and approached the ambulance. As the gurney came into view, they could see the patient looked familiar. Jesse, Goz, and Minoo positioned themselves closer to the ambulance. They now had a clear line of sight to the stretcher. It was Wesley Dragos.

□

Ring... ring... ring...

"Talk to me," the voice instructed.

"Just wanted you to know our problem has been resolved. The situation is now under control," Alverez responded.

"Excellent," said the voice. *Click.*

CHAPTER 32

Malvoy marched right past Maria Garcia with hardly an acknowledgement and quickly closed the door behind him as he entered Nardelli's office. Nardelli was already on the phone and glanced up to see him approach. He knew this day would be long but wasn't expecting the fireworks to begin so early. He made quick work of his phone call and turned his attention to his less-than-amused superior.

Malvoy was wearing his black power suit, carrying his briefcase in one hand and the morning newspaper in the other. Nardelli was well aware of this pending visit and the likely subject matter of their discussion. Malvoy was exhibiting his no-nonsense demeanour, one that lacked patience and empathy. Nardelli recognized it right away, bracing himself for the inevitable.

"Good morning, Anderson. Let me guess. You forgot my phone number and decided to pay me a personal visit instead?" Nardelli asked, throwing caution to the wind.

"Don't fuck with me this morning, Dominic. Look at this, page goddam one!" Malvoy pitched the morning edition of the *Toronto Star* onto Nardelli's desk. The *Star* ran a full-page story from the previous day's events titled in bold letters, **Lakewood's Newest High**. There was no mention of names but Nardelli was front and centre on the front page. The picture was supplemented by a full story exposé of Lakewood High, complete with a chronology of the persistent drug-related incidents over recent years at the school.

"Congratulations, Dom. You're the talk of the town today. Doesn't get much better than this," Malvoy stated sarcastically.

"Yep. Read it this morning. Really don't like the way the light hits me in this picture, not flattering at all. They caught my bad side." Nardelli decided to add fuel to the fire.

"Oh, that's what we're going to do this morning, Dom? You think this is funny? You think this is a goddam joke, do you?" Malvoy's stress level was rising along with his voice.

Okay, Dominic, time to de-escalate. Bring him down.

"No, it's not funny. It's not a joke. In fact, it's quite sad. That same kid was in here a few days ago confessing to his part in the drug frame-up of Jesse Decruz. After he confessed, he became distraught with the idea of being questioned by the police and the consequences of that. Since then, I've come to know from the school counsellors here that Wesley Dragos is not a very stable individual. He's an oddball kid and unpredictable in many ways. In retrospect, it's not that surprising he acted out this way but we had no way of knowing the depth of his despair. I don't have a crystal ball. Wish I did. Good news is, he will recover but he'll be out for quite a while."

"Well that's just wonderful. The media is making a great big meal out of this. It's a public relations nightmare. I need to do some damage control. The *Star* has agreed to meet with me later today to get our official response from the board. I'm going to spin it the best way I can but we can't afford to take another hit like this. My phone hasn't stopped ringing all morning."

"If it's the last thing I do here, Anderson, I will get to the bottom of the drug issue at this school. I promise you. My entire success or failure at Lakewood High will depend on the impact I make at eradicating the drugs from this school," Nardelli said, committing himself.

It was a bold and unconditional statement, Malvoy thought. "I believe you. I need to believe you. Otherwise I have no reason for getting out of bed every morning. I'm an ambitious guy, Dominic. I guess I don't need to explain that to you. But, it sickens me to know the scourge of these drugs affects the good, decent kids every day in our high schools. I need to believe we are winning the war. Their lives depend on us and I feel like we're failing them." Malvoy expressed a rare moment of vulnerability.

Nardelli sat quietly. He remained pensive and the words landed hard in his mind. It was time to raise the bar and meet the challenge. He responded simply, "Okay, Anderson. We're on the same page." They nodded in full agreement and ended their meeting on that note.

Mrs. Garcia entered the office as Malvoy exited. "Mrs. Lee's on the phone, Mr. Nardelli," she announced.

Ah shit, here we go again. More bad news.

Nardelli waited a moment to collect his thoughts before picking up the call. The day was barely two hours old and he had already reached his threshold. He snapped up the line. "Good morning, Mrs. Lee. How are you this morning?" Nardelli braced himself.

"Very good, very good, Mr. Nardelli. I call to tell you much thanks. I thank you muchly for taking care of Benny. He so happy when he come home yesterday. He no scared anymore. I thank you so much," Mrs. Lee said, stating her gratitude over again.

Nardelli sat puzzled. He remained quiet and elected to listen further. Someone was thanking him now, but he hadn't the faintest idea why.

"Benny have new friend, Jesse. Jesse help him yesterday. He come home with twenty dollar. Bad boy pay him back. Jesse walk home with him after. Make me so happy, Mr. Nardelli. You say you help me and you did. I thank you so much again."

"You're very welcome, Mrs. Lee. I'm just pleased we were able to help Benny. Thank you for the kind words. If you wouldn't mind, Mrs. Lee, could you please give Mr. Malvoy a call and let him know as well. I believe he is familiar with your son's situation and would be very interested to hear your thoughts."

"Yes, I will do, Mr. Nardelli. Good bye. Thank you again," she said and hung up.

"Maria, can you have Jesse Decruz come see me right away, please?" Nardelli barked over the intercom to his secretary.

□

Roger Decruz picked up the phone at Millhaven and placed a call.

"Hello, Zach Simon speaking," a voice answered.

"Hey, Zach. It's Rog. Need your help. Can ya get a hold of Jesse? I need to talk with him private-like. Can't let the Mrs. know. Jus me and the boy. Gotta talk to him right away, got it? Set up a meeting time I can call him."

"Okay, Rog. Got it. I'll let you know," Zach replied and hung up.

□

Jesse entered Nardelli's office. He had become much more comfortable entering the Lion's Den, as he referred to it. They developed a mutual respect once Nardelli decided to champion the math tutoring program. It was a small win he desperately needed but it would require his ongoing support until it was properly launched. In spite of his confidence, Jesse was always a bit apprehensive where Nardelli was concerned. There was no telling which way the wind was blowing in his office. This day was no exception. The entire student body was very much aware of the morning article published in the *Toronto Star*.

"Hard to believe what happened with Wesley," Jesse said, opening the discussion. "Everyone's talking about it today."

"If you don't mind, Jesse. I'm all talked out where Wesley Dragos is concerned. Let's just agree it was tragic and leave it at that," Nardelli replied.

"Ya, I'm sure it's going to be a zoo for you today. Sorry," Jesse consoled him.

"The reason I called you in, I received a very interesting phone call this morning. Mrs. Lee spoke with me for several minutes." Nardelli hesitated, waiting for a reaction from Jesse.

"Benny's mother?" Jesse asked.

"Yes, one in the same. She called to thank me and spoke of Benny's new friend. In fact, his new friend has the same name as you." Nardelli smiled.

Jesse smiled back sheepishly. He had hoped to get Nardelli caught up ahead of time but neglected to do so.

"You want to tell me about it, Jesse?" Nardelli asked, inviting an explanation.

"Sorry, I meant to let you know yesterday but I figured you had enough on your plate with everything going on around here. I didn't realize his mother would call you already. Anyways, there's not much to tell. I shadowed Benny to school for several days and yesterday we had some success. It turns out this skinny black kid from Cabbagetown's been harassing him for a few months. We had a little talk, the two of us."

"Did you put your hands on him, Jesse?" Nardelli asked pointedly.

"I shook his hand, I placed my hand on his shoulder, and I patted him on the head when we parted. That's about it." Jesse remained aloof with the details but had a slight smirk on his face. Nardelli chuckled at Jesse's response. "Do you think this kid will bother him anymore?"

"Let's just say, if this kid runs into Benny on the street, he's more likely to run the other way than towards him," Jesse offered.

Nardelli examined him and said nothing. He rose from his chair and walked to the large side window of his office, looking out pensively.

"If I was going to endorse this program, how does it work exactly, and who do you have in mind for it?" Nardelli probed.

"I would only involve people I know, people I trust. I have four close friends in mind. They are big and intimidating. I think that's important so things don't get physical," Jesse replied.

"Do they know about this yet?"

"No, sir. No sense involving them until you're on board."

"Do you think they'll agree to do this?"

"Yes, 100 percent. I just need to ask them. They won't say no," Jesse confirmed confidently.

"Well, I like your confidence. Why don't you gather them up, get a hold of Mrs. Garcia, and have her set up a short meeting with me and your crew. Will you do that?" Nardelli asked.

"Yes I will," said Jesse with a smile.

"One last thing, Jesse." Nardelli reached into his desk and pulled out a blank white envelope. "I want you to have this."

Jesse reached for the envelope and looked at Nardelli quizzically.

"Open it up," Nardelli instructed.

Jesse slowly opened the flap and reached inside the envelope retrieving two tickets. He looked down to see a couple of gift certificates to Barberian's Steak House, a high-end restaurant in Toronto's downtown core.

"For me, Mr. Nardelli?" Jesse looked up at him in astonishment. "One thing you need to understand about me, Jesse. I tend to show my appreciation to those who help and support me. I suppose it's part of my old-school Italian background. I was planning to give these to you and Amanda in a few weeks but it seems appropriate to give them to you now. Why don't you plan a nice dinner with her and celebrate, on me."

"Thank you, sir. This is not necessary. I'm just happy to do what I can," Jesse replied.

"I know you are and I'm happy to do this for you. Enjoy," said Nardelli.

□

Jesse met up with Amanda after school. He was feeling particularly good about himself and carried a disposition to match.

"Somebody's in a real good mood today. What's the deal, Jess?" Amanda asked.

"I got a gift for you. Correction, I have a gift for us," he said pulling the white envelope from his jacket pocket.

"What's this? You forget to give me something at Christmas?"

"Open it," Jesse said impatiently.

Amanda reached in and pulled out the gift certificates. "Are you kidding me? Barberian's? That's huge! That place is real expensive. How did you get these?" she asked in amazement.

"Nardelli. He wanted to show his appreciation for our work. Wants us to go out and celebrate. What do you think?" Jesse asked anxiously.

"Hell ya. Owen and I will let you know how it goes." Amanda chuckled at her own joke.

"Good one." Jesse rolled his eyes.

They continued walking home, planning their steakhouse date for the coming weekend when they were approached from behind.

"Jesse, hold up. I need to talk to you," a voice called out.

Jesse shot around and saw Zach Simon approach. "Zach, what's up? What are you doing here?"

"Your dad needs to talk with you right away," Zach said. "Is your mom working tonight?"

"She'll be home by 10 p.m. Does he need to talk with her?" Jesse asked.

"No, just you. That'll work. Can you be home at 7 p.m.? He can call you then."

"Ya, I'll be home. Did he say what he wants to talk about?"

"No, but it sounded important. I'll let him know. Thanks, Jesse." Zach departed as quickly as he'd appeared.

"What's all that about?" Amanda asked, looking at him.

"Not sure. Guess I'll find out at seven tonight."

CHAPTER 33

Ring... ring... ring...

"Hello," Jesse answered quickly, anticipating the call.

"Hey, Jess. Your dad here. You alone?"

"Ya, mom's at work. Won't be back till ten. Zach said you needed to talk to me. What's going on?"

"Listen, kid, only got ten minutes, need to talk real quick. This about what you asked me last month. Did me some diggin' around and got some intel for ya. Now, before I get started, I really don't think it's a good idea for ya, son, to be gettin' too involved with this drug stuff. These are bad people we're talkin' about. Don't want ya gettin' jammed up on the wrong side of these characters," Roger warned.

"I'm committed, dad. No turning back for me. I'm all in right now and, besides, nothing you say is going to track back to you or me. Shit, our high school made front page of the *Star* this week. We got a big drug problem at this school, dad."

"Ya, I get it, son. I know ya jus wanna fix things there. I just wouldn't forgive myself if somethin' bad happen to ya, son. Finally got myself in a better place and now I feel like I'm jumpin' back in the fire. I just got a bad feelin', is all." Roger continued to show his apprehension.

"I'm sorry to drag you into to this, dad. It's worth the risk. It's like you told us last time we were out there, being honest was your best chance at healing and getting better, and I believe you. Here's your chance to get better. What better way to make amends than saving a bunch of kids at our school?" Jesse reasoned.

"You're right, Jess. I never looked at the other side of the equation before. Ya know, the kids that get hooked, the damage it do. I just looked at the money side. If it was jus me, I don't care. I jus don't want nothin' bad happenin' to ya, son. Ya gotta be real careful cuz ya don't know who's in and who's out on this. Can't trust nobody, ya understand? I'm gonna explain to ya what's goin' on at your school and it probably gonna blow your mind, people involved and the corruption," Roger forewarned.

Jesse braced himself at his father's foreboding words. "Just tell me, dad. Sometimes you just gotta do the right thing and let the chips fall where they will."

Roger proceeded to explain the entire operation at Lakewood High including the key players and the distribution channels. Jesse listened intently. His stomach fell as his father made one revelation after another; it sickened him. He processed all the information, even though it was difficult to accept. The only redemption he felt was his strengthening resolve to help Nardelli eradicate the drugs and corruption that had consumed his school.

"Ya get all that, Jess? Pretty much sums it up. Any questions?"

"I think I'm going to be sick, dad. Are you 100 percent sure on the facts?" Jesse asked.

"Sure as I'm sittin' here at Millhaven, kid. Makes me sick too. I was part of the problem. No tellin' how many lives we cost with them drugs. I own it too so I gotta wear it. No escapin' my responsibility. All I can do is try make it better," Roger confessed. "Listen, kid. Gotta drop off the line. They're ready to cut me off here. Luv ya, son. Be careful, promise me."

"Thanks, dad, I will. Talk to you soon." Jesse hung up.

Jesse sat quietly at the kitchen table, attempting to digest his conversation with Roger. He felt despondent. He had learned early in life you couldn't always trust those in positions of responsibility. Roger had implicated a person he had the upmost respect for. It was a kick in the gut. He knew the truth would devastate his friend, Trey, and Nardelli for that matter. It would be a betrayal of monumental proportions. Jesse sat paralyzed, trying to reason and make sense of it all. He fought the urge but finally surrendered to his tears.

□

Knock… knock… knock.

Jesse had invited the whole gang over. He needed to introduce and recruit his friends into Project Shadow. He decided he would say nothing to his friends about Roger's phone call earlier, not even Amanda. He took a deep breath and opened the door.

"What took so long, Jess. Did we interrupt your meeting with the palm sisters?" Goz launched in.

"Don't be so crude," Amanda shot back as the rest of the gang filed in cracking up at the comment.

"Ya, hope they gettin' equal time now," JJ piped in. "Don't want left palm gettin' jealous of the right palm!"

"Got any chips, Jess. BBQ if you got it?" Minoo asked.

"I'll grab the beers," Trey announced as he opened the fridge door and leaned in.

"Hang on a fuckin' second! No, we don't got BBQ, only vinegar. On the top shelf over there. And if you dare crack a beer, I'll bust your hand. Get the fuck out of my fridge. Shit, don't they feed you apes at home?" Jesse attempted to get everyone back on track.

"I heard they still have Wesley in intensive care," Amanda announced.

"Are you trying to make us feel bad, Mandy? The guy made his own bed. Hard to feel sorry for him," Goz retorted.

"Can't help but think the guy who got away clean on this whole thing was Owen. For sure he was involved," Minoo added.

"Don't worry. It'll come around. Always does. He'll get his," Trey said.

"As much I love a good Owen bashing, I called you guys over for a reason so grab the chips, get a drink, like a pop, no beer, sit down, and shut up." Jesse attempted again to corral everyone.

Jesse began to explain his deal with Nardelli and the trust he had built up with him before Christmas. He detailed the entire ordeal with Benny Lee and the basic concept around Project Shadow. More importantly, he shared the potential benefit of getting on the right side of Nardelli and their ability to make a difference in their troubled school. He appealed to their sense of making things right at Lakewood, a mindset he felt he shared with this group of friends.

"So help me understand. You made a deal with Nardelli to get yourself back in after he suspended you? Man, you got a huge pair. I wish I could have been in his office to hear that go down," Goz said.

"Ya, this Project Shadow thing was all part of the deal," Jesse revealed.

"Hang on! Your suspension got lifted once Wesley confessed. You don't owe him anything. Am I missing something?" Minoo asked.

"You're absolutely right, Minoo. I could've walked away from it. Nardelli even gave me a chance. I could've been like everyone else at this school, just look the other way and pretend everything is just fine. Just look after myself and ignore all the bullshit going on around me." Jesse's tone took a serious turn and caught everyone off guard. They had never quite seen him like this before and his passion now grabbed their attention. "Who fuckin' cares if the Benny Lees of Lakewood High walk to school every day in fear that someone's going to shake them down for money, and who fuckin' cares if our Grade 9s and 10s are the dumbest shits in the whole school board, and who cares if half the fuckin' student population come to school drunk and high every day. It's just another generation of Rogers in progress, our school's contribution to society, right? It's okay. Somebody else's problem, somebody else will clean up the mess, right? We have a choice here. We can try to make a difference or we can walk away. Either way is fine with me. Honestly, I won't think of you any less. You're all still my friends. I made my choice though. I told Nardelli I'm in, no matter what, 100 percent," Jesse said, completing his pitch to the group.

Goz raised his arm, made a fist, and stretched it across to the middle of the table. "I'm in too," he committed.

Everyone else followed suit in short order and pledged their allegiance to the cause. Jesse was the last to enter. He placed both his large hands over the other five at the centre of the table. "Thanks guys. I mean it," he said simply.

□

Jeanie returned home after her shift at the diner. Jesse was seated on the couch watching the end of the hockey game. The Toronto Maple Leafs had a comfortable lead over the Boston Bruins as he switched off the TV.

"Hi, mom. How was your shift?" Jesse greeted her.

"The clientele were very stingy tonight, pretty light on the tips. How was school today?" she asked.

"Had a meeting with Nardelli today. We've been talking about starting up a program to help some of the kids at school who are getting bullied. I had the guys over tonight. They're going to be part of the program." Jesse elected to disclose just the bare details to his mother.

"Wow, Jess. You sure you have time to do all this extracurricular stuff? I sure hope Dominic appreciates all this personal time you're giving him."

"Check out that white envelope on the table." Jesse motioned to the kitchen table. "Open it," he told her.

Jeanie opened the envelope. "These are gift certificates to Barberian's. Dominic gave you this?"

"Yep, wants me to take Amanda out for dinner. He says he wants to show his appreciation for what we're doing."

"Is there a certificate in there for me? Never been to Barberian's before. Heard it's pretty nice."

"Sure, you can take mine, mom. You and Mandy go out for dinner," Jesse offered jokingly.

"Would never do that to you, kiddo, but thanks for the offer," she said, dismissing it.

"Thank God." Jesse exhaled in relief. They both laughed.

"That reminds me. I have something for you too, Jess," Jeanie announced as she opened her purse and handed him a manila envelope.

Jesse examined the envelope. It had no discernable markings. He opened it and pulled out a document. It was from the Ministry of Transportation. He read it. "It's my booking for a driver's road test in three weeks from now!" he announced.

"Yep, you're ready, Jess. You're a better driver than I am. I'll take you there on that date. Already arranged it with work."

"Thanks, mom. Best news ever." He rose and gave his mother a hug. "Just one thing left to do," he said.

"What's that, Jess?" she asked.

"Need to decide what kind of car I'm going to buy." He looked at his mother in amusement.

CHAPTER 34

Jesse led his crew into Nardelli's office as Mrs. Garcia waved them through. Jesse looked behind at them. "Last chance to back out boys," he announced and shot them a huge smile. "Good morning, Mr. Nardelli." Jesse greeted the principal as he advanced through the office door with his crew in tow.

"Morning, gentlemen. Grab a chair and gather 'round," Nardelli instructed. "I'm assuming Jesse's filled you in already on the details of Project Shadow and the results of our trial with Benny Lee?" He looked at them for confirmation.

"Yes, he did," Goz replied for the group.

"I'll be honest with you. I wasn't a big fan of Jesse's plan at first. This seemed a bit vigilante to my mind. Before I give you the rest of my thoughts on this project, I'm going to ask you a simple question and I want you to be completely honest with me because there is no right or wrong answer. What I want to know is, what's your motivation? What's in this for you?" Nardelli stood up from his desk and took a dominant position over the small group.

The question caught them off guard. This was not something they had given any great deal thought, although Jesse's pitch the previous evening was still very fresh in their minds.

"Simple answer is, Jesse asked us," Goz said, taking the lead.

Nardelli examined them. "So you're telling me the only reason you're doing this is because Jesse asked you?"

"No, that's not the only reason we're doing this," Minoo interjected. "Let me explain, Mr. Nardelli. With all due respect, you need to understand we all grew up in this neighbourhood. You're just passing through. We watched kids smaller and weaker than us get bullied every day growing up. It's just the way it was in the 'hood. We never thought much about it because it wasn't happening to us. We were a bit bigger and stronger, you know what I mean? Maybe we're older and smarter now, don't know. That kind of stuff gets under our skin now. Maybe it's time we stop sitting on the sidelines and do something about it."

Nardelli digested the comments and turned his attention to Trey and JJ. "How about you guys?" he asked.

"Not sure what your home life was like, Mr. Nardelli," Trey began, "but our lives were no different than Jesse's here. We grew up with an abusive father. We never knew when we were going to get our next beating. We know a little something about living in fear. When you're young, small, you can't do nothing about it. You just accept it. Just the way life was for us. Well, we're older now, stronger. Maybe we can do something about it now. Maybe we balance out the power for some of these kids, you know."

Nardelli's heart grew heavy listening to their experiences. He realized his life was very different. He'd lived a more privileged life in spite of the mental abuse he was subjected to by his disciplinarian father. He accepted that their abuse was likely more physical, severe, and frequent than his own personal experience. "Do you agree with your brother, Jamal?" he asked JJ.

The group fixed in on him. JJ was always the wildcard. You never knew what was going to come out of his mouth. "I agree with everything Trey just said, 'cept for one thing, Mr. Nardelli. I think dad beat me cuz I annoyed the hell out of him, probably deserved every bit of it. But Trey, I think dad beat him cuz he was just butt ugly," JJ explained. The room erupted in laughter, Nardelli included.

Nardelli regained his composure after sharing a long laugh with the boys. "I appreciate the honesty, boys. It's important for me to understand why you are here. I'm going to endorse this program as part of our anti-bullying initiative but I'm going to modify it slightly in order to sell this to my staff and superiors. First, we need a new label for the program. Project Shadow sounds a bit nefarious. I'm open to suggestions. Anyone?" he asked the group.

"How 'bout Project Kick Ass'?" JJ contributed. The comment caused Nardelli to chuckle.

"No, that's exactly what we want to avoid, Jamal," Nardelli explained. "Our goal is to eliminate any appearance of conflict or altercation."

"How about Project Guardian Angel?" Goz offered.

"I like it," Jesse added.

"So do I," Nardelli confirmed. "Are we unanimous here, fellas?" Nardelli looked around. The group nodded in agreement.

"Perfect. Project Guardian Angel it is. Next order of business. I want to discuss process. This activity will work in teams of two. There is strength in numbers and, based on the size of you fellas, we eliminate the possibility of conflict. I will start by providing each team with a student's name. You guys will team up and shadow the student. If the student is confronted, you intervene, peacefully. No one gets hurt. Understand?" Nardelli looked at them, waiting for confirmation.

"You're taking all the fun out of this, Mr. Nardelli," Minoo added jokingly.

"I'm very serious, fellas. You have a great opportunity here to improve the lives of these weaker kids as you just explained to me. If you start knocking heads, I'm going to pull the plug on the program." Nardelli brought clarity to his point. "One last thing. This is for you, Jesse. I don't want you actively involved in this program, son. I'm sorry, but you just came off a head injury and I don't want to compromise you in any way. I'm not prepared to take that risk. Besides, you've already got your hands full with the after school tutoring."

Jesse thought about challenging his decision but Goz jumped in before he could say anything. "We agree 100 percent, Mr. Nardelli. Jesse's out. Besides, five is not divisible by two."

"Fine. I'm out," Jesse conceded.

"Thanks, boys. I will contact you when we're ready to go," Nardelli said, dismissing them.

Jesse lingered behind as his friends exited the office. "I'll talk to you guys later," he whispered to Goz as he left the office.

"We need to talk, Mr. Nardelli. It's important." Jesse turned to Nardelli who had already returned to his seat.

Nardelli examined him. Jesse seemed unsettled so he invited him to sit down. "Is something wrong, Jesse?"

"You need to prepare yourself for what I'm about to tell you, Mr. Nardelli," Jesse announced ominously.

"Well, this doesn't sound good. Can you close my door, please. Go ahead, Jesse. Lay it on me," Nardelli prompted.

"Just a few conditions. You can't ask me my source because I won't tell you. Also, none of this can trace back to me. Once I tell you, I walk away from it and you do what you need to do with the information."

Nardelli felt uncomfortable with the direction of the conversation but he had built a trust level with Jesse. "Okay, Jesse, agreed. But I need to know what you're talking about first."

"I told you I was going to help you if I could on the drug situation here. It looks like your suspicions about Lakewood High were spot on. In fact, it's probably worse than you imagined," Jesse stated. Nardelli's expression turned grave. "Unfortunately, I hate to be the one to tell you this school is ground zero for drugs in the region, and even worse, you have people here on the inside who are involved. People you trust. People I trust," Jesse added.

Nardelli said nothing, just stared at him. "Those are serious allegations, son. Are you absolutely sure?"

"As positive as I can be," he responded. "My source is solid."

"Who's involved, Jesse? Who from my staff is involved?" Nardelli's temperature rose.

Jesse began to tear up but regained his composure. He was aware of Nardelli's bond with Manny Alverez but elected to lead with the bomb. "This is going to destroy you, sir, but the main pivot at this school is Mr. Alverez."

Nardelli fixed on Jesse as he sat motionless in shock. He'd always had the utmost respect for Mr. Alverez, a person he had often confided in and trusted in the past. "Are you trying to tell me Manny Alverez, our physical education teacher, is involved?"

"Yes, sir. Not just involved, he pretty much runs things. Also, your two evening shift janitors are involved."

"Are you talking about the husband and wife team we've had here for the past six years, Carlos and Gabriela Perez?"

"That's right. They're working with Mr. Alverez."

"Christ! Who else knows about this, Jesse?"

"Nobody. Just the person who told me and now you."

Nardelli came out of his chair, poured himself a glass of water, and drank it all. He paced for a moment before returning to his desk. He pulled out a binder and started to write feverishly. He finally looked up and asked, "Okay, Jesse. How does it work? And leave nothing out."

Jesse drew a deep breath. "First Saturday of every month, they receive a shipment at the school. It arrives during the afternoon along with other food supplies for the cafeteria. Alverez and the Perez team are always here for that shipment. You can check your records. They're always on board. The drugs are coming into the school in a shipment of coffee. The coffee containers are filled with coffee grounds but there's a false bottom on some of the cans. That's where the drugs are stored. The janitors unload the shipment and secure the coffee cans in storage.

"Alverez takes it from there. He takes inventory and starts to redistribute to the area traffickers in this region, including other schools. He moves the product in his gym equipment. He uses his van to move it offsite. You'll notice his vehicle is always conveniently parked near the storage door at the back of the school. They are very careful. They have lookouts everywhere to make sure nobody is around. That's probably why they've never been caught."

"Why would they take the chance and move the stuff through a school?" Nardelli asked.

"Because nobody would suspect someone would do that. Also, they want to bring the supply to where the demand is. Students buy about 80 percent of all the drugs. They bring it in here and redistribute to each school strictly for logistics. You'll find the same coffee cans at every school around this area."

"Are you trying to tell me I can walk down to our storage room right now and put my hands on some of these drugs?" Nardelli asked in amazement.

"Yes, sir. But you don't want to do that," Jesse warned.

"Why not?" Nardelli challenged.

"They probably have some early warning system in place. Besides, why catch a few minnows when you can catch the whale?"

Nardelli contemplated his comment. "You're absolutely right except for one thing. They're not minnows. They're rats. It sounds like we have an infestation here and I'm appointing myself the exterminator. Listen, Jesse. Don't repeat this to anyone. I need to get a bunch of people involved and we need to contain it. Is there anything else I need to know?"

"One last thing. You don't know who to trust. Apparently the corruption runs deep so be careful who you tell. The less people who know, the better. You should go as high up as possible with law enforcement. I'm told the corruption is more likely happening at the lower levels."

"Thanks, Jesse. I won't divulge my source. You have my word," Nardelli committed.

Jesse left the office. He felt the weight of the world come off his shoulders but now it was the storm to come that worried him.

□

Ring... ring... ring...

"Hello, Malvoy here," he answered.

"Anderson, it's Dominic. We need to talk right away, face to face. I'm coming over right now. Don't leave your office."

CHAPTER 35

Nardelli arrived at the Toronto District School Board headquarters, his mind still turning. The short trip from Lakewood High was a complete blur. He could not recollect his journey there while processing the numerous revelations Jesse had made.

Nardelli prided himself in recognizing true character, something he had sadly miscalculated with Manny Alverez. The results left him feeling both violated and vulnerable, a state of mind he could not accept. That feeling was now morphing into raw anger and rage. Nardelli had worked hard over the years to manage his anger issues, his Achilles heel. It would now challenge him beyond anything in recent memory. He marched up the steps of the school board building, consuming three stairs per stride. He elected to climb the staircase to Malvoy's third floor office instead of using the elevator.

Malvoy's head was buried in a pile of metrics stacked on top of his desk as Nardelli entered the office. He looked up sharply. "What's wrong, Dominic? You look completely frantic."

"You got something in here I can hit? I just want to hit something, Anderson! I'm so fuckin' mad right now!" Nardelli was exhibiting a rare loss of composure. He continued to pace about and looked up at Malvoy from time to time.

"It's after hours right now, Dominic. Let me pour you a scotch. Looks like you can use one." Malvoy retrieved a bottle hidden in the bottom of his desk drawer and poured them each a generous four fingers. Nardelli accepted the glass and quickly disposed of its contents. "Careful big fella, that's twelve-year-old scotch. You're going to hurt yourself. Come on. Sit down and talk to me," Malvoy prompted him, sensing his torment. He poured him another glass.

Nardelli finally looked up at him and took a deep breath. "You do this job long enough and you think you've seen everything. Well, today shoots that theory all to hell. I just had a bomb dropped on me, Anderson."

"Okay, let's have it." Malvoy braced himself.

"Lakewood High is no longer a school. It's a drug distribution centre, and it's been going on for a long time apparently."

"Okay, Dom. Rewind a bit. Sounds like you're starting in the middle of the story. Give me some context, please."

Nardelli had calmed himself now and gave Malvoy the entire story complete with names and all the sordid details. Malvoy was left speechless and dumbfounded.

"This is big, Andy. It starts at Lakewood then gets moved to all the area schools. We're the tumour and the other schools are the surrounding organs where the cancer is spreading." Nardelli attempted a crude metaphor to make his point.

Malvoy rose from his seat and chugged the remainder of his drink. The initial shock had now worn off. He was in full spin mode. He was the master of spin. Malvoy was never a great problem solver but his administrative skills were unparalleled. His facial expression turned to one of confidence and resolve.

Nardelli looked at him. "I got to be honest with you, Andy. I've never seen you take such shitty news so well. I expected you to take a nosedive out of your window by now. You're certainly an enigma."

Malvoy sat himself in a chair next to Nardelli and examined him. "You're looking at this all wrong, Dom. You're treating this whole thing like a defeat. It's a victory. You've only been here for less than six months and already you've figured this all out. What about all the administrators running that zoo before you came along? What did they do about it? It was happening right under their noses. It's their failure, not yours. You're right. It's a big fucking mess, no argument. But, we're going to be the solution, not the problem. The media will be all over it and we'll be out front and centre taking credit for finally fixing it. That's what success looks like, Dom. That's what affirmative action looks like. If there's one thing I'm very good at, Dominic, it's dealing with the media. When you control the media, you control the narrative. You understand what I'm saying? If there's one thing I have no tolerance for, it's the unknown. We're in the driver's seat now, Dom. I can see the path in front of me. We're going to blow the lid off this whole fucking thing and everyone is going to know we were the ones who fixed it. Sure, it's going to be a shitstorm and we'll get some backsplash on us. But in the end, we'll be credited for cleaning up a huge problem that's been here forever. You just watch the community rally behind us. People love a success story. Good defeats evil, the underdog prevails, get the picture, Dom? Lakewood High is about to receive the enema it desperately requires. It's the dawn of a new day, a true metamorphosis. That's the story that gets written, Dominic."

Nardelli's lips started to curl up as he smiled at him. Only Malvoy could turn this situation into a positive. He quickly weighed his options and realized Malvoy's approach was likely the best scenario they could hope to achieve. "You know what, Anderson? It's a marvel to watch your mind at work. Okay, where do we go from here?"

"First, I'm assuming your source is solid. We can't bring this to law enforcement without probable cause. Are you able to share your source with me?" Malvoy asked.

"Can't do it, Andy. This individual is fearful for his life. This activity is tied to very dangerous people, something we need to be aware of ourselves," Nardelli shot back.

"I know the sergeant in charge of the emergency task force who deals specifically with drug enforcement. He may need to involve the RCMP but I'll start with him and go from there. Stay close to your phone, Dominic. Once I get their attention, this is going to heat up real quick. Are you ready?" Malvoy looked at him.

"Let's do it," Nardelli confirmed.

Malvoy approached Nardelli and placed his hand on his shoulder. "Believe it or not, I actually feel good right now. Actually feels like we're finally in front of the power curve instead of two paces behind. We're finally steering this ship."

"I told you it was going to get worse before it gets better. However, I agree with you. Better the devil we know than the one we don't," Nardelli said, framing it.

"Two more?" Malvoy asked as he raised the scotch bottle against the two empty glasses. Nardelli nodded. Malvoy went back to his seat and turned to Nardelli again. "On an unrelated matter. I received a phone call from Mrs. Lee this morning. You know anything about that?"

"Yes, I asked her to call you. We ran a pilot project and shadowed her son for a few days. The results were positive. I believe it's an effective plan and will get us the results we need. I haven't briefed you yet with everything else going on here. You'll have my report on your desk in a few days with details of the plan. We're calling the initiative Project Guardian Angel. I'm folding it into our anti-bullying program," Nardelli briefed.

"Sounds interesting. I look forward to hearing about it. But right now you need to excuse me, Dom. I have a sergeant I need to call. I'll be in touch."

CHAPTER 36

Lakewood's finest math-challenged Grade 9 students began to file into the classroom. None of them looked very happy. The math faculty had worked out a manageable schedule for Amanda and Jesse. Grade 9s and 10s would participate on alternate weeks. Each week would consist of three classes running from Tuesday to Thursday for one hour after school. Each class would rotate in a different group of students.

Mathematics was not a strong subject at Lakewood High, a condition highlighted following the mandatory testing conducted earlier in the year. Their school ranked lowest across all high schools within the Toronto District School Board, a statistic both Malvoy and Nardelli were determined to expunge. The program hinged on a re-test scheduled for the coming May. The success or failure of the re-test would rely primarily on the shoulders of two senior students. This was no small task.

Mr. Cranston stood next to Amanda and Jesse. He was the head of the Math Department at Lakewood and had been coaching them both for weeks leading up to this day.

"I see no joy on their faces," Amanda said under her breath to Cranston and Jesse as the students continued to fill the seats.

Cranston leaned in. "This is not a voluntary program. We've received permission from each of their parents to provide this additional instruction. The majority of the parents were more than happy to sign the consent forms. Probably so they could enjoy an extra hour of peace before all their little bundles of joy came home."

Jesse laughed openly at the comment but Amanda's demeanour remained tentative. The gravity of their task was now starting to wear on her and fear was quickly consuming the confidence she'd had earlier in the day. Jesse sensed her uneasiness as the room began to fill. All the back seats were now occupied and the latecomers were forced to occupy the seats closer to the front of the class, clearly the less popular location within the classroom.

Cranston provided some last-minute instruction. "I'll introduce the program then hand it over to you both. Just remember, if this thing starts to go sideways on you guys, I'll be in my classroom a few doors down. Also, Mr. Nardelli has made himself available if you encounter any behaviour issues. Unfortunately, you're not dealing with the cream of the crop with this group."

Mr. Cranston brought some order to the group and provided a short introduction to the program explaining the roles Jesse and Amanda would take in their instruction. Once he finished, he introduced Amanda to kick off the class and then departed the room.

Amanda stood at the head of the class. "Good afternoon, my name is Amanda Perone and this is Jesse Decruz. We'll be helping you over the next three months in math to prepare you for the mandatory testing scheduled for this coming May. Now what I would like you to do—"

"You guys aren't even teachers. You're students just like us. Why we learning math from a couple of students?" a voice from the back of the class said, interrupting her.

"What's your name?" Jesse asked pointing directly at the young male student.

"Marlon."

"Well, Marlon, let me say a few things about that. First, and this applies to everyone in the classroom, it's common courtesy to raise your hand if you want to speak so we know who we're talking with. Secondly, you're right. We are students, but we are students who are very good at math, a subject you need help with otherwise you wouldn't be here." Jesse attempted to take back control.

"This stuff makes no sense. How you gonna teach us when real teachers can't get us to understand?" A female voice spoke out this time.

Jesse approached the female student and stood over her using his physical presence for effect. "I believe someone forgot rule number one already. We're never going to get to the math lessons if we can't follow some basic rules," Jesse said calmly.

"Sorry, it's Sandra."

Amanda approached Jesse and held his arm slightly to intervene. "The answer to your question, Sandra, is simple. Because we are students, we understand what you're asking and how to explain things to you in a way you can understand. Sometimes teachers talk over your head. They don't realize it but it happens all the time. Their explanation probably confuses you more. That's where we come in. We know how to talk to you, explain things," she said, attempting to clarify.

They exchanged back and forth for several minutes but continued to be challenged by other students. The discussion turned into a free-for-all. Amanda and Jesse were starting to lose control of the classroom. The volume level rose as students began discussing and arguing among themselves.

Amanda's expression turned to desperation as she looked to Jesse. "Shit, we need to call Cranston or Nardelli in here, Jesse. This is turning into a disaster."

"We're not running to Cranston or Nardelli ten minutes in. That's a complete fail on us," he stressed. "Makes us look completely incompetent." He looked up at the students. Half of them were now out of their chairs. It was anarchy, he thought with amusement.

He looked back to Amanda. "You trust me?"

"What?" Amanda replied looking at him in confusion.

"Do you trust me?" he asked again.

"Yes," she replied simply.

"Just follow my lead and do what I say."

Jesse moved back to the front of the class and raised both his large hands to the top of the chalkboard and dug his fingernails in. He slowly and deliberately ran his fingernails down the chalkboard from top to bottom. All the students, including Amanda, held their hands to their ears, attempting to mute the repulsive noise coming from the front of the class.

"Sit down! Everyone sit down, now!" Jesse raised his voice commanding their attention. "Alright, we get it. You don't want to be here. You know what? We don't want to be here either, but we are. You know why we're here? Because we don't like the fact that Lakewood High has the lowest math scores across the board. It's not acceptable and it shouldn't be acceptable to you either." He was now attempting to tap into any sense of pride they may have. "Maybe you've given up on yourselves but we haven't, your teachers haven't, and your parents haven't. That's why you're here. You have another chance to change the score. You've got nothing to lose and everything to gain."

Jesse composed himself and looked out over the class. The room was now silent. He had caught them off guard with his outburst. "Let me ask you a question. How many of you don't want to be here?"

Three-quarters of the class raised their hands. As they did, the remainder of the students followed their lead.

"Okay, how many of you think we're not smart enough to teach you this math? And don't worry, you won't hurt our feelings."

Hands began to rise slowly, somewhat apprehensive. Approximately half the class had their hands in the air now.

"Okay, I may have lied. My feelings are hurt," Jesse blurted. The room filled with laughter.

"Fair enough. We're going to make a deal with all of you. We're going to switch this around. You're going to test us first, and if we fail your test, you can walk out of here right now and go home." Jesse issued the challenge much to the surprise of the group, including Amanda. She had no idea where he was going with this.

"Here's how the test works. Amanda will provide each of you a blank sheet of paper. You will write a random number between one and a hundred on that sheet of paper and place it facing up on your desk." Jesse looked to Amanda prompting her to begin distributing the paper to each student.

Jesse waited until everyone was done. "Has everyone finished writing their number down?" he asked. Surprisingly, the students were engaged in his game and complied nodding in confirmation. They looked at each other in confusion trying to make sense of the game Jesse was leading them through.

Jesse whispered to Amanda, "Just follow me and do what I do." Jesse began navigating slowly up and down each row visiting each student's desk. First he examined the student's face and then the number they had written on the sheet of paper. They continued up and down each row doing the same at each desk until they had completed all thirty-two students.

"Okay, here's the deal," Jesse said. "You're all going to stand up now and hold your piece of paper behind your back so we can't see it. Amanda and I will point at you and tell the class the number you wrote on your piece of paper. Once we've guessed your number correctly, you will sit down. If we get all thirty-two numbers correct, you guys give us your complete undivided attention for the next three months. If not, you can all go home, deal?"

"You can't remember everyone's number, that's impossible," Marlon shouted out from the back of the room.

"Apparently you can't remember rule number one, Marlon." Jesse glared at him. "If that's the case, then I assume you have no problem making the deal with us." Jesse looked to the rest of the students. They all nodded.

One by one, Jesse pointed to each student then consulted with Amanda. They took turns guessing the correct number. The students watched in amazement as they worked their way through the entire group. One by one, they matched the number and watched each student sit back down. Two students in the back remained, Marlon and his friend, Derrik. Jesse pointed to Marlon. "Marlon's number is 48," Jesse announced.

Marlon flashed a huge smile to his classmates and turned over his paper. The number 65 was written on the sheet. "Wrong answer. We get to go home!" Marlon announced. The class cheered.

"I said, if we guess your number incorrectly, you go home," Jesse said, repeating the rules.

"My number is 65. You got it wrong," Marlon repeated.

"No, your number was 48 until I watched you switch your paper with your buddy, Derrik," Jesse announced, watching Marlon's smile wash away from his face. "I want Derrik to show everyone the piece of paper you passed to him." Derrik sheepishly revealed the piece of paper he was holding. It was number 48.

The students smiled, then erupted in applause. They were impressed and amazed by what they had just witnessed. Amanda shot Jesse a quick smile. She was less impressed, but then again, she knew his secret.

□

Goz and Minoo walked slowly down Sumach Street. They were on guardian angel duty today. They were keeping a close vigil over Charmaine Jones for the third day in succession. Charmaine was a recent Jamaican immigrant student at Lakewood and had fallen victim to some area thugs.

Nardelli was very pleased with the progress to date from Project Guardian Angel. Between the two teams, they had registered half a dozen successful interceptions by now, all without incident. He was concerned, however, with the Charmaine Jones case. Her situation was like no other and posed a legitimate risk. Her assailants included a pair of gangbangers from midtown, the best they could determine. Nardelli was able to glean some information from Charmaine and determined they were likely both of Caribbean descent. Their ages were advanced and not likely students, possibly early twenties. The dominant of the two was heavier, wore a bandana, and sported a snake tattoo on the side of his neck. His partner was similar height but lanky with dreadlocks.

Nardelli huddled with Goz and Minoo before their sortie. He was concerned and gave them strict instructions to determine the presence of any weapons first before engaging. They were also instructed to avoid any type of physical confrontation and to pull the plug on the operation if the interaction escalated. Goz and Minoo agreed to the terms but they understood self-defence would trump any and all conditions they had agreed to. They did not feel the need to remind Nardelli of this minor detail.

Charmaine walked south on Sumach Street and saw two males approaching from the west as she passed Oak Street. Goz and Minoo picked up their pace to get a closer look. The pair matched the description they were given. The first male was heavy set, standing at around six feet. His head was wrapped in a black bandana and a tattoo was visible on his neck. His partner was thinner, about the same height, with a full head of dreadlocks that cascaded down below his shoulders.

"You ready?" Goz looked to Minoo.

"Party time!" Minoo announced.

"Follow my lead. I'll take Hardy. You take Laurel," Goz instructed referring to the '30s fat-and-skinny comedy duo.

They quickly crossed the road to intercept the pair who had already halted Charmaine's progress. Goz quickly inserted himself between Charmaine and the heavier thug. He fixed his stare on his opponent. Minoo positioned himself behind the pair ready to pounce on a moment's notice. Minoo had seen this look in Goz's eyes many times in the past. If past experience was any indication, the situation was not likely to end well for these two.

"Well, well, what we got here, the welcoming committee? You know these choir boys, Zeus?" the tattooed banger asked his partner.

"Never seen them before, Pooh Bear," Zeus replied.

Goz smirked at the sound of his name. It certainly made sense as he closely examined his portly adversary.

"You girls have a name?" Pooh Bear engaged them disparagingly.

"Ya, I'm Starsky and that's Hutch over there," Goz shot back, motioning to Minoo.

"These ladies got a sense a humour, Pooh Bear. Couple a fuckin' comedians we got here," Zeus added.

"Why don't you and Pooh Bear head back to the zoo from where you escaped," Minoo barked.

"Ya, looks like Pooh Bear's had his head stuck in the honey pot one too many times," Goz insulted. Minoo chuckled at the comment.

Pooh Bear's expression changed immediately. His look was menacing and they sensed the situation was about to take a turn. Charmaine quivered as she stood nearby watching the foursome. She was terrified and unsure what to do. Goz looked at her, and then motioned to Minoo with his eyes.

Minoo picked up on the queue. "Hey Charmaine, you're going to be late for school. You better get going now." Charmaine obeyed and departed in haste.

Goz inched closer, hoping to intimidate Pooh Bear but he stood his ground. It became clear this pair were not standing down. Nardelli's words resonated in his mind. Goz held back resisting the urge to attack first. He would need more.

"What kind of fuckin' name is Zeus? Was Hercules already taken?" Goz antagonized further, waiting for a physical response.

"You gonna make your move or we gonna dance all night?" Pooh Bear shot back.

"I think he wants to dance with you, Pooh Bear. Maybe he's sweet on ya," Zeus added.

Pooh Bear kept his eyes fixed on Goz. He slowly reached down with his right hand and lifted the bottom of his leather jacket above his belt exposing a sizeable hunting knife. Goz and Minoo were both in clear view of the weapon. "Maybe you want some of this?" he challenged.

Goz remained perfectly still. Minoo fixed on Goz's eyes. He was about to explode out of his position and readied himself to take Zeus out.

"Or maybe you're just one of them faggots. Is that what you are Starsky? Are you one of them fudge packin' faggots?" Pooh Bear asked.

Goz's face turned red as the words pierced his mind straight to the grey matter that had filed away every vile comment his mother had ever made against him. Years of unbridled rage erupted from inside of him.

In one lightning-quick reflex motion, Goz cocked his right arm back and shot his fist straight up catching Pooh Bear full force with a devastating uppercut to the jaw. Pooh Bear's head snapped back violently as he collapsed backwards, falling to the ground like a 200-pound bag of wet cement. His head bounced once on the sidewalk as his body came to rest. That was it. Game over. Pooh Bear was out cold. Minoo had already wrapped his arm around Zeus's neck and had him in a strong sleeper hold. He kept the pressure on until he felt the strength from Zeus's legs release. Minoo dropped Zeus onto the grass as he gagged, struggling to regain oxygen.

"Shit, this is not good," Goz said looking down at Pooh Bear. He dropped to his knees attempting to revive the behemoth.

"I'm pretty sure that wasn't in the guardian angel handbook," Minoo quipped.

"Quit with the fuckin' jokes and help me wake this fat fuck up!" Goz demanded.

Goz slapped his face slightly on either side trying to get a reaction. Finally, after several seconds, Pooh Bear started to stir.

"That's a good Pooh Bear," Goz exclaimed as he exhaled a nervous breath.

They examined him again. Fatality averted, they concluded. Goz and Minoo quickly rose, turned, and hightailed it down Sumach Street.

CHAPTER 37

Nardelli entered the police van parked on the adjacent property to Lakewood High School. Malvoy was already positioned along with Danny O'Shea, who was the lead sergeant in charge of the sting operation. Malvoy was engaged in conversation with O'Shea as they reviewed the numerous video monitors set up in the surveillance van. Nardelli could see Malvoy was giddy as a child on Christmas morning. He had been anticipating this day, the culmination of several weeks of careful planning. Nardelli did not share his enthusiasm. They were about to blow the lid off the school's drug operation. Nardelli knew he would no doubt be dealing with the messy aftermath in the wake of this sting for many weeks, possibly months to come.

"Gentleman, are we all ready?" Nardelli announced.

"Danny has this all under control. If everything goes as planned, we should have a clean house by tonight," Malvoy proclaimed in a fit of anticipation.

"What are we looking at here?" Nardelli asked as he scanned the numerous remote monitors mounted to the interior of the van.

"What you're seeing is the pathway the drugs will be taking into the school based on our intelligence of the situation," O'Shea explained. "As you know, we've carefully installed camera equipment at the back of the school and inside straight through to the back of your cafeteria storage area. You're employees are on board now. We've had the three subjects under surveillance for the past several weeks and I can tell you their movements are consistent with the intel you provided us. We've gathered a list of their associates at other schools and in the neighbouring area. This operation has been a virtual treasure of information for us. I'm just pleased they do this handover on weekends. It eliminates the complications that come along with students and teachers in harm's way."

Nardelli felt sick to his stomach. Manny Alverez was not just another faculty member to him. He had befriended Alverez early on in the year. Alverez was the type of teacher who always volunteered his time and worked tirelessly with students on various school athletic teams and programs. He was head of the Phys. Ed. Department, head coach for the boy's junior football team, and assistant to the senior football team. He had become a mentor of sorts over the years for numerous students. These included students who desperately needed positive male role models in their lives, including students like Trey Jackson. Nardelli would quite often visit with Alverez in his office next to the gymnasium after school hours. Ironically, Alverez would carefully prepare an excellent cup of coffee for them both as they chatted. The same coffee that came from the cans containing the drugs, Nardelli reasoned. He became aware of this betrayal nearly a month earlier but the wound was still fresh in his mind. He avoided Alverez at all costs for fear he might physically attack him as he carried the knowledge of his betrayal. It robbed him of countless nights' sleep leading up to this day.

"Can I ask you a question? Why coffee containers? Why do they use coffee containers?" Nardelli posed the question to O'Shea.

"Kills the smell. Our best canine units can't even sniff it out if it's packaged properly. These cans are half coffee and half drugs. The false bottom is halfway down the can. They would probably pass inspection even if they cracked open the top half off the can. It's all coffee unless you empty the entire container. Quite ingenious actually."

O'Shea was interrupted by his handheld radio as the voice on the other end channelled through. "*Okay, Danny, showtime. Subject vehicle is five minutes out.*"

"We have agents positioned on the second floor of the school looking out to the back of the property. There's another squad positioned in a storage locker next to the cafeteria. They will storm the area from two directions once I give them the green light," O'Shea explained.

"You ready, Dom?" Malvoy asked as he seated himself in front of the monitors, waiting for the show to begin.

"I just have one request, Danny. Once you have them in custody, I would like to see Alverez face to face. Can we do that?" Nardelli asked.

"It's not advisable, Dominic. These situations get pretty heated. I suppose that would ultimately be up to Anderson," O'Shea weighed in as he glanced over at Malvoy.

Malvoy looked at Nardelli. He understood the relationship with Alverez and the importance of closure for Nardelli. "I have no objection, Danny."

The cube van labelled Jake's Catering Services entered the school property and weaved slowly to the back of the building. The van rotated its position and backed up directly onto the egress door stationed near the school cafeteria. A single driver occupied the van. The driver was white, in his early twenties, and unlikely part of the operation. He would be apprehended with everyone else until his active involvement could be eliminated.

Malvoy, Nardelli, and O'Shea watched the monitors intently as the two janitors, Carlos and Gabriela Perez, moved into place. They started to offload the catering truck. The driver remained outside as he lit up a cigarette waiting for his load to be emptied. Carlos did most of the heavy lifting as the coffee shipment was moved from the truck onto a trolley and then through to the storage area. O'Shea picked up his two-way radio and readied himself to give the signal. The last of the containers was removed from the truck and brought inside the building.

"*Storm! Storm!*" O'Shea yelled over the radio.

SWAT teams moved swiftly from the upper floors of the school and the adjoining locker room next to the cafeteria. A sea of squad cars flew onto the property with sirens blaring. The cube van was now sealed off; the driver was quickly apprehended and cuffed. Inside the surveillance van, Malvoy and Nardelli were glued to the monitors as they watched an endless tide of black uniforms storm into the outer area of the cafeteria. They watched as the three suspects attempted to scramble to safety but to no avail.

"*Subjects are secure.*" The message came across on O'Shea's handheld.

"*Roger that, we'll be right down,*" O'Shea confirmed.

"Okay, gentlemen, let's go. Stay behind me please and do not present yourself until I tell you," he cautioned Nardelli and Malvoy.

The three men worked their way onto the school property and into the rear area of the school where the cafeteria was situated. O'Shea led them to the cafeteria storage where he was met with his squad leaders from both SWAT groups.

"Good work, boys. I'm going to need a can opener," he instructed them. O'Shea moved into the storage locker with

Nardelli and Malvoy close behind. O'Shea grabbed a utility knife and cut into the bubble wrap tearing it away from the coffee cases. He began to pull the cans, one by one, from the case. He examined each can carefully from the bottom. "Now, there is usually a distinct etching on the bottom of the can. Usually a number. This indicates whether it's hot or not," O'Shea explained.

"Hot?" Malvoy asked.

"When it contains drugs," O'Shea clarified.

O'Shea continued to examine numerous coffee cans and then presented them to Nardelli and Malvoy. "See this, gentlemen, this red number here etched at the bottom of the can. 321. This is likely the marker." O'Shea continued pulling out all the cans with the same marker at the bottom.

"You guys ready for this?" O'Shea asked as he took the can opener and locked it into the bottom of the can. He continued to twist the opener until the bottom was completely cut away. The contents spilled a sealed clear bag containing a white substance onto the floor. He continued to open other cans with the same result.

Malvoy stood over the coffee cans in disbelief. Nardelli also watched quietly shaking his head from side to side in disgust.

"Unbelievable" was all Nardelli could muster. A sadness fell over him but he understood that things would likely get better from this point forward.

"Unbelievable indeed," Malvoy parroted.

"Mostly pot and cocaine. Typical haul for a market that caters to high school kids." O'Shea continued to educate the two. "I can see this is troubling to you both. That's quite understandable. However, I see it every day so nothing really surprises me anymore."

"I want to talk to him. Alverez. I want to talk to him now," Nardelli demanded as his face turned red. The prominent vein across his forehead was now clearly visible.

O'Shea looked to Malvoy who simply nodded in agreement. "Follow me, gentlemen. We have them secured in the outer office."

Nardelli picked up one of the bags of cocaine and followed him out.

O'Shea knocked on the door and was met by one of his agents. They entered the room. Nardelli locked his eyes on Alverez. Malvoy hung back and allowed Nardelli his moment.

Nardelli walked slowly towards Alverez, who was cuffed with his hands behind his back. Alverez looked at Nardelli momentarily then averted his eyes, unable to face him.

Nardelli positioned himself directly in front of Alverez who refused to make eye contact. "You don't even have the guts to look me in the eye?" he challenged him.

Alverez slowly moved his gaze to Nardelli. His eyes filled with tears and shame. He said nothing. There was nothing to say.

"You know what you are, Manny? You're a malignant tumour spreading your fuckin' cancer to everything you touch," Nardelli announced holding the bag of cocaine directly in his face. "There's only one way to deal with cancer, Manny. You get rid of it. You make it go away forever."

"I'm sorry," Alverez finally managed.

"Too late, Manny. Too late for apologies. Besides, you're saying sorry to the wrong guy. Your apologies need to go to those kids' parents. It's their kids you poisoned with this crap. In fact, why don't you write a letter to Mr. and Mrs. Dragos when you're sitting in prison? Their son Wesley nearly killed himself last month, probably OD'd on the same fuckin' drugs you're selling. But don't worry. You'll make a whole new set of friends in prison. They love the drugs in there. You'll be very popular while they all spoon you to sleep every night." Nardelli finished and turned to walk away.

Alverez suddenly looked up, refusing to accept his judgment. He screamed, "Fuck you, Nardelli!"

Nardelli whipped around in a fit of rage. He hoisted the bag of cocaine over his shoulder and delivered the package full force to Alverez's head. Everyone watched in astonishment as the contents of the bag exploded on contact, leaving Alverez covered with the fine white powder all over his body.

CHAPTER 38

Malvoy entered Nardelli's office wearing a huge grin on his face. Nardelli looked up to acknowledge him. They had spent a good deal of time together over the past several days, talking with media and faculty. Lakewood High was the talk of the town.

"I'm not quite sure how to handle this, Anderson. You're smiling and in good humour this morning. Perhaps you can yell or criticize me for something. I'd be much more comfortable with that," Nardelli said, attempting a slag.

"You're not going to spoil my good mood, Dom. Have you read the *Star* this morning?" Malvoy asked placing the paper on his desk opened to page three.

"Yes, first thing this morning," Nardelli confirmed.

"I told you this would turn into a win for us. There's nothing but good press in this article. Praise all around for rooting out the evil. We're heroes, Dom. Look at this picture of us. It's a powerful statement, don't you think?" Malvoy continued to stare at the cover picture of them both standing behind a table filled with recovered drugs from the sting operation. The article provided full details of the takedown and arrests made at Lakewood High and the surrounding area schools caught up in the sting.

The paper showcased Malvoy complete with a personal interview and commentary. It was the type of coverage he revelled in.

"Just glad they didn't cover my altercation with Alverez. That would have been a disaster," Nardelli added.

"You should have seen your face after you gave him that cocaine shower, Dom. Classic," Malvoy said chuckling at the memory.

"Just hope Alverez doesn't launch an assault charge on me. A conviction wouldn't look good on my record," Nardelli pointed out.

"I got your back, Dominic. If and when it goes that far, I'll provide my deposition and put it all in proper context. Worst-case scenario, you get your hand slapped. No biggie," Malvoy said, dismissing the thought. "This is going to play well in the news cycle for weeks. Heads are starting to roll already at other schools. It's all starting to crumble like a house of cards. I couldn't buy better press than what we're getting right now. I think you're witnessing the official launch of my political career, Dom. Be happy for me."

Nardelli smiled at Malvoy, amused at his excitement. He rose from his desk and offered his hand in congratulations. "Just don't ask me to kiss your ring. That's where I draw the line."

"By the way, I need you tomorrow afternoon. The *Globe and Mail* wants to do a story on us. That's national, baby. Doesn't get much better than that."

"If I'm going to do all this extra work, you're going to need to pay me a lot more, Andy. Just saying," Nardelli kidded.

"Alright, gotta go. I'll be in touch." Malvoy exited.

◻

Jesse and Amanda headed out to school as they did every morning. Jesse was pensive and remained quiet while Amanda updated him on her planned lessons for the upcoming math tutoring session scheduled that afternoon.

"What's up, Jess. You're real quiet today. Something bothering you?" she probed.

"Sorry, didn't sleep well last night. Got lots on my mind," he offered.

"Okay, I'm just going to say it. I can't help but believe you may have had something to do with this drug bust that went down at the school." She looked at him for a reaction. "I'm not stupid, Jess. You mentioned talking to your dad about that a while back and then all of a sudden, all hell breaks loose at school. It's too much of a coincidence." Amanda had connected the dots.

Jesse's face grew alarmed. "Mandy, promise me you won't repeat that to anybody. I mean, nobody must know, you understand? You need to forget I ever told you that. People can get hurt. I'm serious. Just promise me you won't ever ask me about that or mention it to anybody," he pleaded.

"I promise. I promise," Amanda said, reading the concern on his face. She sensed his uneasiness with the subject and decided to drop it completely.

"Big day coming up this Saturday," Amanda said, attempting to change the subject.

"My driver's test, ya. I'm a bit nervous but it'll be good to have some wheels when we need to go somewhere." Jesse's mood switched.

"You'll do great. Your mom says you're a natural. By the way, that gives us another place to make out." Amanda shot him a wink.

Jesse smiled. "Now I have a whole new reason for passing." He wrapped her up in his arms as they continued on to school.

CHAPTER 39

Owen Reed slouched over in his chair, having survived his second round of beatings at the hands of his Colombian captors. Blood flowed freely from his mouth and his eyes were now swelled beyond recognition. The restraints were cutting into his wrists and ankles, both numb from lack of circulation after two hours in captivity. He sat quietly in the centre of the abandoned warehouse, wondering what the next hour would bring. He wondered whether this would be his last hour of life.

"He's not talking. I'm getting nothing," Reed's captor updated the boss. "He's taking a lot of punishment but offers nothing. I think we're wasting our time."

"What do you think?" the boss turned to his partner for input.

"I think we go at him one more time and see what he coughs up. Maybe we get a name, something. Pain is usually a good motivator. It's hard to say, boss. I don't think he's involved either," the second captor concluded.

The boss paced about impatiently looking out of the small window of the abandoned building on the shore of Lake Ontario.

"Somebody's going to pay for this. We will get my blood for this betrayal. I assure you. I will get my ounce of blood. Okay, then. Go at him hard once more. When you're done, cut him loose. And boys, make sure you remind him the consequences of going to the police," the boss instructed.

They both nodded and returned to the warehouse.

Reed tensed up at the sound of footsteps re-entering the open space. His bruised and battered body had just settled in time for the next round of punishment. He became frantic with the anticipation of what was to come.

"I don't know anything. I told you I don't know who talked! I'm telling you the truth, I don't… uh—" Reed took several more blows to the torso and hunched over coughing up more blood.

"You will tell us what you know or this will be your last day on earth," his captor said calmly.

Reed broke down and began to cry. He endured several more blows to the head and checked out. He sat motionless for a long while.

After several minutes, Reed began to stir again and slowly returned to consciousness. He was met by a large bucket of cold water. He sat up alert once more but his destiny remained the same.

"Bring me the pliers," the first captor instructed the other who quickly complied. He returned with pliers in hand. They stretched out Reed's right hand, his throwing hand, and secured it to the arm of the chair with bindings. They lowered the pliers to his index finger and opened the mouth of the tool so he could feel the sharp edges on either side of his finger.

"Please! Please! Don't, please!" Reed screamed.

"I will give you one last opportunity to cooperate. Then you can begin to look back fondly on your football career," his captor said.

"It was Nardelli! Nardelli figured it out! I don't know how but Nardelli figured it out! He's the guy. He's the one!" Reed blurted out attempting to save his own skin.

His two tormentors looked at each other and backed away momentarily. They retreated to the corner of the warehouse engaged in discussion. They exited out the door. Reed looked down tentatively at his right hand and counted five fingers, then exhaled in relief.

They returned ten minutes later and covered Reed's mouth and nose with a moist cloth. The smell was repugnant.

Lights out.

CHAPTER 40

Jeanie and Amanda waited patiently for Jesse inside the driver's examination centre. It was nearly thirty minutes since Jesse departed the centre for his road test. Jesse had been anticipating this day for weeks and barely slept a wink the previous night at the thought of gaining his G-licence.

"What's taking so long?" Amanda asked Jeanie as they waited for Jesse to return. "I thought they just took you around the block on these tests." She was both excited and nervous for Jesse.

"Every instructor is different. Some tests are short and others go long. Just luck of the draw, I guess. Hope he does well on the parallel parking. I know that was nagging at him," Jeanie said.

"Hope he passes. If he doesn't, there won't be enough Vachon cakes in Toronto to cheer him up," Amanda countered.

"How about we change the subject, Mandy. Tell me about your math tutoring. Jesse says you guys are starting to make some progress."

"Ya, it started slow but now we have a few more volunteers from Grade 13 helping us. It made a big difference. It's all about spending one-on-one time with these students. They're finally getting the personal attention they need. The results have been good."

"Mr. Nardelli called me out of the blue the other day just to thank me. He wanted to tell me how much he appreciated Jesse's help on the program," Jeanie said proudly.

"He called my mom as well. I really like Mr. Nardelli. Most kids are afraid of him but they don't see the side of him we do. He really does care about the students."

"By the way, Jesse told me you guys had a great time at Barberian's Steak House. I almost talked him into taking me but, sadly, you won that battle." Jeanie smiled.

"Oh my God, he was in heaven. We went for the full experience. Started with a shrimp cocktail. The shrimp was about the size of a baby's arm. We followed that with a full entrée including a three-inch steak and Caesar salad. Finally, we finished with this decadent carrot cake. It was to die for," Amanda recounted. "I think we were both suffering from severe food hangovers the next day," she laughed.

Jesse entered the examination centre parking lot with his instructor. The women attempted to gauge his facial features to no avail. The two sat in the parked vehicle for another five minutes as the instructor had his head down writing notes in his log. They finally emerged from the parked car. Jesse was handed a document and made his way back into the examination centre. His expression was blank as he looked at his mother and girlfriend while entering the building. As he approached the area where they were sitting, he turned the document towards them allowing them to see the word stamped in enlarged font at the top right-hand corner of the page. **PASS.**

The two immediately jumped to their feet and embraced him. "Congratulations, Jesse. I'm so proud of you," his mother blurted.

"Me too," Amanda offered as she kissed him.

"It was touch and go there for while. I didn't do so well on my first crack at parallel parking but I was able to convince him to give me another try. The rest is history," Jesse explained with a huge smile on his face. "There's just one thing I need to know, mom," Jesse continued.

"What's that?" Jeanie asked.

"Can I have the car tonight?" he asked. Amanda chuckled.

"Long as you fill it with gas, it's all yours," Jeanie said, surrendering. "In fact, why don't you drive us home? The gas is on me."

Jesse recounted his road test on the way home. They pulled up to their Sackville Street apartment and Jesse entered the parking lot. He looked over to see Goz and Trey hanging out at the front of the building. They exited the car and Jesse replayed the same shtick for his friends, holding up his road exam results for them both to see. High fives were made all around.

"Well done, JD. Did you threaten to beat up the instructor dude or did you get it the old fashioned way?" Goz asked.

"Straight up, man. It was all me, never a doubt." Jesse strutted. "Wasn't expecting you guys today. What's going on?" he asked.

"Gotta talk to ya, man. Alone," Trey said as he gestured his head towards the girls.

Jesse turned to his mother and Amanda who were walking their way. "I'll be inside in a few minutes. Just need to talk with the boys for a bit."

The woman acknowledged them and moved inside the apartment.

"We got a call this morning from a couple guys on the football team," Goz began. "Apparently Owen Reed was found all beat up downtown last night. They brought him into emergency at St. Mikes."

"You guys trying to cheer me up or is this just a bad joke?" Jesse asked with a hint of doubt.

"No word of a lie. We just got back from the hospital. We went with some of the boys this morning to see him. His parents were there. They're really broken up," Trey said.

"You should see him, Jess. He's real messed up. Looks like he went fifteen rounds with Ali and lost. His face is all fucked up. Swollen eyes, cuts, bruises. They did a good job on him whoever they were," Goz said.

"Who did that to him?" Jesse asked.

"Don't know. Some homeless guy found him last night unconscious in an alley just off Jarvis Street south. Got beat up bad. Broken ribs, they were real thorough. He's going to be okay but he'll be in the hospital a while," Trey said, attempting to fill in the blanks.

"Well, it's not like he's got a fan club or anything. Bound to happen when you spend most of your life being an asshole. I suppose they did me a favour and evened the score. Hope it's nothing permanent though. Don't wish that on anyone," Jesse offered.

"This whole thing don't smell right, JD. There's too much shit going down. It can't just be a coincidence. First Wesley goes down, then the big drug bust, now Reed. Any chance this is all connected somehow?" Goz asked.

"Ya. Like a conspiracy or something," Trey added.

"You guys watch too much TV," Jesse deflected. "Thanks for coming by. I'll talk to you some more at school Monday."

CHAPTER 41

Boom!

The inertia from the blast shattered the large panes of glass along the entire back section of the office, propelling Nardelli right out of his chair. He landed halfway across the office area face down on the carpet. Nardelli lay motionless for several minutes in amongst the thousands of charred pieces of glass strewn about the room.

What the hell just happened?

The sound of the blast was deafening. Nardelli slowly rocked his body to the side holding his right ear. Blood was evident on the carpet but the source wasn't altogether clear. He gingerly picked himself up into a kneeling position, attempting to make sense of where he was and what had just transpired. He felt some pain at the back of his head along the upper scalp. He placed his hand firmly against the back of his head. Mystery solved regarding the blood source.

Nardelli propped himself up using some broken furniture as a lever and started to pick the glass out of his hands, head, and facial area. He dug his index fingers into his ears hoping to improve his audio. All he could manage was a constant ringing.

His vision was slightly blurred but likely a result of the stucco falling from the ceiling. He quickly examined his limbs, all four present and accounted. He retrieved the box of Kleenex lying on the ground and pulled the remaining tissues from the container, applying them firmly to the injured area of his head. He moved slowly and deliberately towards the back of the office. He could feel the cold rush of wind from outside moving into the office space; it flowed freely through the openings that had once contained windows.

Nardelli focused his sight at the back of the schoolyard and discovered the source of the blast approximately thirty feet away. As he moved himself closer to the opening to get a better look, he could now see his vintage 1958 Studebaker Golden Hawk engulfed in flames. He loved the classic vehicle and had spent countless hours waxing and detailing it over the past year. He was not sure what assaulted his senses more, the head injury or the sight of his burning vehicle.

"Motherfuckers!" Nardelli screamed at the top of his lungs as he leaned out of the window opening.

He was thankful the blast had occurred now, at 7 a.m. The schoolyard would be filled with students in about an hour's time. The collateral damage would have been devastating.

Nardelli looked about his broken office and located his desk phone in the corner of the room. The unit had come away from the wall jack but appeared to be in reasonable condition. He reconnected the wire into the wall jack and waited for a dial tone. Success! He dialed 9-1-1.

Within ten minutes, emergency vehicles converged on Lakewood High School—ambulance, fire, and police. The paramedics quickly attended to Nardelli's injuries carefully removing all the charred glass from his body.

"You're very lucky, sir. This could have been much worse. We see broken glass injuries all the time. Your injuries are mostly superficial. It was fortunate your back was to the explosion," the medic explained.

"Yes, I suppose I was much luckier than my vehicle out there," Nardelli quipped.

"I saw that coming in. Looks like a real classic. Is that a '50s Studebaker?" the medic asked.

"You seem to know your cars. It's a '58 Golden Hawk. Don't make those anymore," Nardelli explained, impressed with the young medic's knowledge of classic vehicles.

"Ya, my dad's a bit of a collector. He's got a '57 Ford Thunderbird sitting in his garage. Drives it two or three times a year, that's it. I don't get it." The medic attempted to keep Nardelli engaged in conversation.

Nardelli smiled at the young medic. "You need to be one of us to understand. It's a bit of an obsession, an expensive habit actually."

Danny O'Shea appeared and addressed the medic. "Can I have Mr. Nardelli for a few minutes?" "He's all yours. I'm done here," the medic said. "We'll need to drive you to hospital, sir, for further examination once you're done," he instructed Nardelli.

"I suppose you're on speed dial for this kind of thing?" Nardelli asked, looking at O'Shea.

"What happened, Dominic? This looks a lot like a mob job. Cars don't normally blow themselves up. We've got the bomb squad looking at it now but that would be my guess."

Nardelli began to explain the sequence of events to O'Shea when Malvoy marched through the door. He raced over to Nardelli and placed his hand on his shoulder.

"You alright? Look at this goddam place. Looks like a war zone." Malvoy looked around in exasperation.

"This is what happens when you incarcerate the janitors, Andy. Place goes all to hell," Nardelli said, attempting to make light of a grave situation. "By the way, you owe me a new Studebaker."

"Jesus Christ, Dom. What the hell is going on, Danny? Talk to me." Malvoy looked at them both in bewilderment.

"It's not hard to figure this one out, Anderson. This is likely pay back for the drug bust. We've got our bomb squad checking things out now. I had no idea they would take it this far. There's usually a few death threats issued before it gets to this point," O'Shea explained.

Nardelli's expression immediately changed and he quickly averted his eyes following O'Shea's comments.

O'Shea looked at him and recognized the guilty expression. "For Christ's sake, Dominic. Are you holding back on us? Not very smart," he scolded him.

Nardelli rose from the chair. He slowly walked to the filing cabinet in the corner of the room and retrieved several documents from a file folder. He returned and handed them to O'Shea.

O'Shea pulled several pages from the folder. Malvoy stood over O'Shea's shoulder reading the contents of the documents.

"Goddammit, Dominic! These are death threats!" Malvoy announced in disbelief.

"When were you planning to share this with us?" O'Shea asked.

"I thought now would be a good time," Nardelli said sheepishly.

"I should hope so," Malvoy added. "Where do we go from here, Danny? They've got my attention now. I'm all yours," Nardelli offered.

"We'll assign a police detail to you immediately. You need protection. We'll be out there aggressively shaking the bushes. We have several snitches on our payroll. We'll see what pops. In the meantime, you need to stay put at home so we can protect you until we figure this out."

"Absolutely not. That's not going to happen, Danny. I've got a lot of people at this school who need and depend on me.

They're not going to scare me down some rabbit hole until you figure things out. Not going to happen, and it's not negotiable." Nardelli remained solid.

"You should listen to him, Dom. They just blew up your goddam car! We're dealing with nut jobs here! You can't fuck around with this, Dominic!" Malvoy said, appealing to his sense of reason.

"You heard me, fellas. Life goes on and so do I. I'll be back here tomorrow morning, doing my job. Probably in a different office," Nardelli mused looking around his current office space.

"Well, I can't force you to stay home but my guys will shadow you. You'll need some protection. I wish you would reconsider," O'Shea appealed once more.

"We've shut things down today, Dominic. We have staff turning the kids away as they get here and I'll take care of the communication to the parents," Malvoy added.

"What's your communication going to say?" O'Shea asked with trepidation.

"I'm going to be honest with them, Danny. We had a car fire, which caused some damage to the building," Malvoy said matter-of-factly.

"Perfect. You always did have a way with words, Andy," Nardelli added, causing the men to chuckle.

"Yes, that sounds fine. No need to alarm the community until we learn more about this," O'Shea confirmed.

□

Jesse and Amanda arrived at Lakewood and witnessed the commotion and barricades surrounding the property. Several fire trucks were positioned along the side of the school. Jesse noticed Goz and Minoo among the spectators congregated near the entrance of the parking lot. They made their way over.

"What the hell now? Is this going to be a weekly thing?" Jesse asked, looking to his friends.

"They told us there was a car fire along the back of the school and some damage to the building. School's cancelled today!" Goz announced.

"Okay, then. No need to tell me twice. Let's go. We're off to the record store." Jesse suggested. They all turned and began their journey to Yonge Street.

CHAPTER 42

"Hard to believe Mr. Nardelli's car burned up that way. He drove an old car, didn't he? Probably faulty wires or something," Jeanie reasoned.

"It wasn't an old car, mom," Jesse countered. "It was a classic, a vintage '58 Studebaker. Probably cost more than we make in a year. Whole thing doesn't make sense. Wonder if someone torched it. That's my bet."

"Anyways, I'm glad school's back on tomorrow. Things need to get back to normal there. Gotta go, kiddo. My shift starts in thirty minutes. Spaghetti and sauce are warming up on the stove for you. I'll see you when I get back tonight." Jeanie kissed her son as she left the apartment for work.

Jesse served himself a healthy portion of spaghetti and drowned the noodles in sauce. He loved his mother's spaghetti sauce and reasoned she likely had Italian somewhere in her bloodline. He quickly devoured the serving when the phone startled him.

Ring... ring... ring...

"Hello?"

"Jesse, it's your dad. Is your mom there? I need ta talk with ya in private." His voice sounded urgent and unsettled.

"Hey, dad. Ya, she's working tonight. Won't be back till ten. What's wrong?" Jesse asked. "You don't sound right."

"I think you're in trouble, kid. We're in trouble. Both of us got a problem we gotta fix right away. Not much time to waste." His voice sounded manic.

"Slow down, dad. What do you mean we have trouble? What's going on?" Jesse had never known his father to sound nervous or vulnerable. It alarmed him.

"Sit down, son. Grab yourself a pen and paper. Ya need to listen real careful to what I'm gonna tell ya," Roger instructed.

Jesse did as he was told and sat down at the table. "I'm ready, dad. Tell me what's going on."

"I know what's been goin' on there, Jess. I know 'bout the drug bust and I know about your Principal Nardelli. He's in deep shit right now."

"Ya, his car burned up this morning. Has this got something to do with that?" Jesse asked.

"His car didn't burn up. It fuckin' blew up! Colombians are after him now. Jus a matter a time before they snatch him up. They don't take lightly to anyone cuttin' into their profits. This little drug sting of Nardelli's cost them lots of money. Destroyed an entire network. They lost a lot of good soldiers in the process," Roger clarified.

"Are they trying to kill him?" Jesse asked in disbelief.

"Hell no, that was jus a shot across the bow. If they wanna kill him, it be done by now. They jus tryin' to scare the shit out of him right now, probably doin' a good job too. That's why they did it before school. They not interested in hurtin' any kids. They jus sendin' him a message. Damn, a bomb like that probably detonated remotely. Bet the triggerman was less than a hundred yards away from the school when he pushed the button. They only interested in one thing, Jess. They wanna know who talked. They wanna know who ratted them out. That's the only thing on their minds right now. They keep goin' till they find out."

"Nardelli would never rat me out, dad. He's not like that. He promised me. Besides, I'm sure the cops are protecting him, right?" Jesse asked unconvincingly.

Roger began to laugh. "Listen kid, ya don't know who they got paid off in law enforcement. They wanna get to him, they find a way. These guys are bad motherfuckers and they got long memories. They keep goin' till they smoke out the rat. Once they get a hold of him, they got ways of makin' him talk. Trust me, kid. Maybe Nardelli loves ya now, but when someone got his testicles in a clamp, all bets are off. That's why I'm callin' ya son. There's jus one degree a separation from him to you now, ya understand what I'm sayin'? Once Nardelli sings your name, they gonna connect the dots to me too, then lights out for good ol' Rog. Don't need to be rocket scientist to figure that one out." Roger painted him the picture.

"Shit dad, you telling me I'm fucked? There's no way out?" Jesse's anxiety was climbing.

"Settle down, kid. There's always a way out. Gotta be done right, though, or it's over for all of us including your mom."

The words landed hard on Jesse. He immediately went into protective mode at the thought of harm being directed against his mother. It was a thought he could not bear. "Okay, dad. I'll do anything. What do I need to do?"

"What I always taught ya, son? What's the best way to deal with people who wanna hurt ya?" he quizzed Jesse.

Jesse pondered the question and then it came to him. "The best defence is an offense."

"Bingo, kid. What ya gotta do is dangerous but I see no other options right now. Ya gotta take these guys down. Gotta cut the head off the snake. Take them out before they get to Nardelli."

"Anything, dad. I'll do it. Just tell me what I need to do." Jesse committed to his father.

"Okay, ya remember that metal safe in the wall I told ya about? Ya know, my life insurance policy?"

"Ya, I remember. We never got into that box. It's locked," Jesse confirmed.

"That's right. Now I need ya to get in there. You're gonna go into the workout room and push up the ceiling tile next to the fluorescent light at the centre of the room. Ya need to slide your hand along the topside of the light ballast until ya feel a key. It's connected to the ballast on a magnet. Pull it off. That's the key ya need to open the metal box. Once ya open the box, ya gonna find a few things in there. Pull out the ski mask and surgical gloves. Ya gonna need those. Ya markin' all this down, son?" Roger asked as he worked through his instructions.

"Got it, dad," Jesse assured him. "Keep going," he said as he continued to file the information in his memory.

"There's a log book in there. Ya need to pull that out cuz it's got all the important numbers ya gonna need. Now, I need to explain somethin' else to ya, son. Everythin' I'm about to tell ya can't be repeated. Ya gotta swear."

"I swear, dad. Just tell me," Jesse said impatiently.

"Ya gonna need to get into Club eX. That's your end game. Everythin' ya need to bring these fuckers down is in there. A Colombian named Diego Garvon heads the operation. His headquarters is in the basement of Club eX. Ya never wanna meet this guy. He's a bad motherfucker. He the kinda guy who'd cut his mother up if she crossed him, ya know what I mean. I spent some time with him. He's holed up in that basement office all day long. He's like a snake. Likes to stay in his hole all day till it gets dark, jus the way he is. Anyways, he got an office down there, like Fort Knox. Got security cameras down there, locks, codes, you name it. In his office, he got a large picture on the wall of his native home in Bogota, Colombia. Behind that picture is a wall safe. That's where he keeps the Holy Grail."

"Christ, dad! Are you asking me to break into Fort Knox and steal the Holy Grail?" Jesse asked in disbelief. "I can't do that!"

"Wish I was, kid. It's not impossible once ya got the secret sauce. In the metal box at the house, ya need to pull out the logbook. In the logbook, there's instructions and a key that will open the rear door at the west end of Club eX. Once ya in there, ya need to input the security code into the keypad on the north wall. If ya don't, all hell breaks loose. Code is on the instruction sheet. Then ya make your way down the hallway along the back of the building until ya see a stairwell to the basement. Ya go down the stairs and work your way to Garvon's office. It's a big ugly black door. Can't miss it. Enter the six-digit code on the keypad outside to open the door. Once you're in, ya gotta input it again on the keypad inside the office otherwise it sets off a silent alarm. Ya only got ten seconds, kid, so ya gotta be quick. All the codes and instructions are in the log book, okay? Make your way to the painting. Take it off the wall. There's another six-digit code ya input to open the safe. Once you're in, there's a blue binder with a whole bunch of pages with numbers. Don't worry about what it all means, just a bunch of gobbledygook to the untrained eye. Ya need to copy down all the numbers you see on the last entry page only. Don't be tearing the page out. Write it all down. Don't worry about the rest. Jus copy all the numbers entered on the last page. Once ya copy everythin' down, make sure ya put everythin' back the way it was and hightail it out of there. When ya get back home, get a hold of Zach to contact me. I'll explain what to do next."

"I don't know, dad. I'm not sure I can pull this off," Jesse said nervously.

"You'll be fine. Ya need to go on a Sunday night. Nobody there on Sunday night, usually," Roger explained.

"Usually?" Jesse asked.

"Jus stay away from east side of the building at the back. There's a loadin' dock there. Outside chance someone might be offloadin' something there but not likely. Jus don't wanna be taking chances," he explained. "Listen, son. Jus stay calm. Relax. You can do this. Jus like I taught ya. If ya stay calm and keep your wits, ya can do this. I played out all kinda scenarios, son. I see no other option. This our best chance of surviving. I'm sleepin' every night, son, with my bible under my arm. I got God on our side. He's protectin' ya. He and I got an understanding," Roger assured him.

"Okay, I'll go this weekend." Jesse resigned himself to the task.

"Oh, one more thing, Jess. Almost forgot. Ya gotta come in from the west side of the building at the back. It's best you come down the alleyway through the parking lot at the back of the warehouse west of Club eX. It's abandoned. Best way for ya to scope things out at Club eX before ya do anythin'. Once ya satisfied no one there, put the ski mask and gloves on and keep them on. They got surveillance cameras out there. Keep your head down and move steady towards the door. Jus keep your head down and don't take your mask off. Don't know if they got cameras inside. Wouldn't surprise me. Ya understand all that, son? Ya got any questions?"

"Yep. Who's gonna take care of mom when I disappear?" Jesse asked sounding fatalistic.

"You'll be fine, kid. I got faith in ya. Listen, Jess. I already know I'm goin' to hell. If something ever happened to ya, kid, jus means I'm gonna be there a lot longer. If ya need to talk with me some more before the weekend, contact Zach. He can get ya in touch with me. And, Jesse, be careful, son. I luv ya," and with that, Roger hung up.

Okay, Jess. Stay calm. Just process this and get your shit together.

Jesse immediately moved to the back room and did as his father instructed. He retrieved the key from the light ballast to open the metal box located in the wall. He found everything his father explained, including a few other things he didn't mention, namely, a gun and a knife. He retrieved the building key, and memorized all the codes and instructions he required. He also found a schematic for the interior of Club eX. He spread the document on the floor, focused, and made a mental picture in his mind. He grabbed the gun and knife, examined them, and decided to return the gun to the metal box. He placed the knife in his pocket. Jesse was both focused and scared as hell, all at the same time. A tear ran down his cheek. He knew there was no other viable options and accepted his fate. This plan was the best chance he had to save himself and his mother.

CHAPTER 43

Sunday night arrived quicker than expected. Jesse was out of sorts all week as he struggled with the task at hand and the gravity of his situation. He wanted desperately to speak with Nardelli throughout the week to give him a heads up. He had even approached the office a few times but then retreated. The thought of Nardelli being interrogated by the Colombians sickened him. Both Amanda and his mother detected a change in his demeanour. Jesse simply dismissed it as a stomach flu and that he was under the weather.

"Did you take some aspirin, Jess? You don't look well. Maybe I should take your temperature." Jeanie attended to her son as he sat on the couch watching TV with a blank expression.

"I'll be fine, mom. Just need some rest. I'm going to head off to bed now. I'll be better in the morning, promise," Jesse assured her.

"Well then, I guess I'll call it a night," Jeanie replied. She kissed him and headed off to bed.

Jesse planned to sit up in his bedroom until his mother fell asleep. It was fortuitous his mother was a heavy sleeper or the evening would be much more challenging on the front end. He waited for about a half hour until his mother was no longer stirring. He walked softly to the door, grabbed his knapsack, which he'd pre-packed earlier in the day, and then quietly exited the apartment.

Jesse navigated south on Sumach Street, which merged into Cherry Street. He continued down Cherry Street just south of Front Street where Club eX was located. In spite of his physical size, travelling alone at night on this side of town was tenuous at best. He maintained a steady trot. It was harder to stop a moving target, he reasoned. He arrived at his destination. The streets were barren at this time of night. There were only a handful of unsavoury characters present but they paid him no attention.

You can turn back right now, Jesse. Do it next week when you find your courage.

Jesse stood directly across the street from Club eX. He examined the entry point to the west—an old abandoned warehouse. He mapped out his route and headed across the street, entering the alleyway to the west of the abandoned building. It emptied into a parking lot near the back. The laneway was very dark as he moved tentatively through the narrow passage. As he neared the rear of the building, he felt a presence behind him. He quickly turned around at the sound of bottles rustling. He focused, and then he saw them, three figures in the darkness. His heart started to pound as adrenaline filled his body.

Shit! Stay calm, Jesse. Control your heart rate. Keep your wits about you. What would Roger do right now?

The three figures moved quickly towards him. His initial instinct was to run but then decided against it. That's not what Roger would do, he thought.

The hazy figures came into focus. "Well, well, well, what do have we here? It's little Ritchie Cunningham. You lost, Ritchie?" the middle thug asked him.

Jesse resisted his urge to take flight and decided he would hold his ground and fight. He found his calm. He brought his heart rate down and focused on the task at hand. Ironically, Roger had trained him years ago for this very scenario. *Being outnumbered don't mean shit, kid,* his father would say. He went on to explain how your vulnerability provides you the upper hand since they believe you will simply comply. That's a big mistake on their part. Never show them your fear. Talk down to them. Go on the offensive and use distraction whenever possible. Roger explained to Jesse that three against one was, more often then not, really two against one. He explained the need to compartmentalize your enemy. Pick out the leader, then the right-hand man, and then the weak link. Give them names if you must, but sort them out right away.

Jesse fixed his focus on the leader. He stood in the middle. He was shorter but stocky with a good build, balding, and wearing a black leather jacket. Let's call him Fonzie, Jesse thought. Fonzie's right-hand man was tall, lanky, and homely looking. Let's call him Lurch. The weak link stood to Fonzie's left. He was skinny with greasy curled hair, poor teeth, and eyes positioned too close together. He would call him Squiggy.

"I asked you a question, Ritchie. You deaf or something?" Fonzie asked again, this time flashing a large smile revealing brown teeth.

"Why don't you boys move along before I lose my temper," Jesse responded calmly as he stared directly at Fonzie. He exhibited no emotion or fear.

Jesse's response caught them off guard. Fonzie looked side to side at his crew. "Can you believe this guy? He wants us to move along." He turned back to Jesse. "Sure, Ritchie, we'll move along once you pay the toll. Tonight's toll on this road includes everything in your pockets. You got about five seconds to comply," Fonzie warned.

"Tell you what. Why don't you take your lap dogs, Lurch and Squiggy there, by the arm, turn them around right now and walk away. I promise you boys won't spend the rest of the evening in the hospital. I'll even give you ten seconds to comply," Jesse countered.

Fonzie's mood turned sour as he removed his right hand from his leather jacket and flashed a large switchblade. "I'm not playing no more, Ritchie. Empty your fuckin' pockets now or I'll fill you with six inches of metal. You understand?" Fonzie raised the blade towards Jesse's face.

"If you don't remove that blade from my face, I'm going to shove that thing so far up your ass you'll be brushing you teeth with it," Jesse warned him. He kept his focus on Fonzie, his intended target.

Roger had taught him this delay tactic as an effective way to buy time and plan an attack. Jesse was formulating his next move but needed more time. He was ready but needed one last distraction to execute the plan.

"You know, it's really cold tonight, you really should bundle up. You're going to catch a cold." Jesse motioned to Fonzie's exposed neck.

Fonzie laughed at him but remained steadfast, keeping his stance with the blade raised to Jesse's face.

A few tense moments passed. "Okay, okay, you got me. I'm taking my wallet out. Don't do nothing stupid. Take the money." Jesse removed his wallet from his back pocket and slowly handed it to Fonzie.

As Fonzie reached for the wallet, Jesse allowed it to slip from his hand to the ground. Fonzie diverted his eyes momentarily watching the wallet as it fell. Jesse shifted his entire weight onto his toes. In one cobra-like motion, he pounced forward with great speed and accuracy against his target. Jesse extended his arm straight up and forward with tremendous force as his large fist landed directly against Fonzie's exposed neck. There was a sickening crunch as his adversary dropped the knife and crumbled to the ground struggling to breathe through his collapsed esophagus. Jesse pivoted his body and delivered a sidekick down firmly against Lurch's left knee. The large ogre buckled in severe pain as his ACL snapped. By the time Jesse turned around, Squiggy was already in a full sprint up the alleyway towards the street. Roger was right again. No such thing as three against one. Jesse retrieved his wallet and quickly disappeared around the back of the building, leaving the damaged duo sprawled out on the cold ground.

Jesse reached the edge of the property. He took a deep breath and scoped out the rear of Club eX. There was no sign of life anywhere, just a stray cat looking for a quick meal in the numerous trash containers at the east end of the building near the loading dock. He reached into his knapsack and pulled out the mask and gloves, placing them on his head and hands as Roger instructed. Adrenaline was still running through his veins. He paused momentarily to regain his composure and get back on task.

Jesse walked at a steady pace towards the rear door at the west end of the building. He approached the door, keeping his head lowered, and grasped the key in his right hand, delivering it through the keyhole. The key turned easily as he pulled the door open and closed it immediately behind him. Jesse looked to his right and then his left. He found the keypad on the wall, entered the code, and received a green indicator on the remote display. He exhaled in relief. The hallway produced a distinct odour, a strong mix of stale beer and cigarettes.

Jesse stood quietly for a moment, listening for any noise or sign of life within the building, but heard nothing. He closed his eyes and pictured the schematic he had examined earlier. He placed the picture in his mind and started to move along the back wall to the east. He arrived at the stairwell leading to the basement and worked his way down to the lower level. He doubled back to the west and found the large black door. Garvon's office. He punched in the code and turned the handle to enter the office as the indicator beeped and turned green. He closed the door behind him and quickly punched the code again into the keypad on the interior of the office this time. He waited for a moment and received no signal. There was no confirmation from the keypad. His heart moved to his throat and adrenaline once again began to fill his veins. After approximately ten seconds, the indicator finally turned green. He felt the blood suddenly flush from his face in relief.

The office was dark. Jesse elected to use the flashlight he packed instead of the overhead office lights. He moved to the wall picture, removed it, and keyed in the final code to open the safe. He took a moment to appreciate his improved memory. Having memorized all of the codes had made his task less challenging logistically.

The wall safe was filled with cash and other valuables. He ignored both. Jesse located the blue binder just as Roger indicated. He removed it from the safe, placed it on the floor and positioned the flashlight so the light cascaded against the open pages. He flipped through the various sheets. All of them looked similar, with seemingly random numbers and codes on each page. There was no apparent pattern, he concluded. He finally turned to the last entry and focused his eyes on the document for a long moment. He closed his eyes momentarily then opened them again. He closed the binder and returned it to the safe just as he found it. Jesse rose and quickly backtracked his steps, exiting the office and working his way back to the upper level. As he turned the corner heading towards the exit, he was startled as something crossed his path. Jesse's heart skipped a beat as a large black cat brushed past him and disappeared down the hallway. He moved quickly to the west door and exited.

Lights from police vehicles suddenly blinded Jesse. He slowly turned towards them, prepared to accept his fate.

Almost got away with it, Jesse. Just wasn't quick enough.

When his eyes came back into focus, he fixed his gaze to the source of the lights. They were coming from the adjacent property. He stood still for a moment then reasoned the emergency vehicles, which now included police and ambulance, were likely attending to Fonzie and Lurch next door.

You gotta go, Jesse. Get out of here now while you can.

Jesse had no choice. He moved swiftly to the east end of the building against his father's warning and examined the dock. Thankfully the area was vacant. He moved around the corner and made his way back towards the street, removing his mask and gloves as he turned north back up Cherry Street. Jesse accelerated into a steady trot, which he maintained all the way back to Sackville Street. As he entered his apartment, he felt the stress and emotional exhaustion lift from his body. Roger was right again. God certainly was on his side tonight.

CHAPTER 44

"Come on in, boys." Nardelli waved the troupe in through his office door. Jesse led the way followed by Minoo, Goz, and the Jackson brothers.

They looked about Nardelli's office. The finishing touches were nearly completed in his newly renovated office space following the bomb blast.

"Lookin' good, Mr. Nardelli. You oughtta blow up the library next. Now there's a space sure can use a facelift," JJ blurted. Trey shot him an angry look at the inappropriateness of the comment.

But Nardelli had become accustomed to JJ's personality. He had worked with him and the others on Project Guardian Angel. JJ's candour amused him. Nardelli had developed an affection for the Jackson brothers as he came to understand their upbringing and challenging home life in Regent Park.

"How about we finish my office first and then we'll take it from there," Nardelli replied.

"This office looks much nicer than your new car, Mr. Nardelli," Minoo teased as he examined his new wheels through the back window. "Looks like the insurance company ran out of money on that ride. Don't look like no Studebaker to me," he chuckled.

"That's the rental the insurance company insisted on. It's a Russian brand. It's called a Lada. It's not vintage, definitely economy," Nardelli said, embarrassed, as he peered out the window in despair at his new temporary vehicle.

"No disrespect, Mr. Nardelli, but that car is a Lada ugly right there, sir," Goz added as the room broke into laughter. They looked over at Nardelli, who joined in with them. The vehicle had become a great source of ridicule from fellow staff members and faculty at the school.

"No argument there, boys. Okay, if we're all finished evaluating my fashion style in automobiles and interior design, let's get started," Nardelli said, attempting to get everyone back on point. "I wanted to personally update you on Project Guardian Angel since we are now into the second month. You've probably noticed I haven't reached out to you in a little while."

"I thought things were going well on the project. The boys have intercepted a bunch of kids so far," Jesse pointed out.

"Yes, you're right, Jesse. We've had exactly nine interceptions to date. The best news is, there have been no incidents of any violence to my knowledge and the problem appears to have dried up."

Goz and Minoo shot each other a quick glance. They knew they had dodged a bullet. Their encounter with Pooh Bear and Zeus remained unavowed. They suspected, however, the pair were likely plotting their own brand of retribution. That was a problem for another day. Until then, they would enjoy this victory.

"That's why I called you all here. I wanted to let you know this project has been hugely successful and you are all officially out of work right now. That's the good news. I'll be honest, Jesse. I was very apprehensive about this project at the beginning but I believe the results speak for themselves. It would appear our project has been an excellent deterrent for this criminal activity. I'm proud of all of you."

"That didn't take very long. I was just starting to enjoy it," Trey quipped.

"Now, having said all that, I will continue to reach out to you if we have any new incidents. But as of now, the slate is clean. I also asked you here to properly express my gratitude. This was a problem that caused me and Mr. Malvoy a tremendous amount of grief, to say the least. I'd like to offer each of you a small token of our appreciation." Nardelli pulled out four envelopes and handed them to Goz, Minoo, and the Jackson brothers.

They all dove into their envelopes and pulled out the tickets. Gold seats at the Maple Leaf Gardens for the coming Saturday night hockey game against the Montreal Canadians.

"Woohoo! These are the hottest tickets in town!" JJ's eyes nearly popped out of his head; he was unable to contain his excitement. The group shared his reaction. Nardelli understood access to such seats at this venue were more suited to the rich and famous than four financially challenged kids from the projects of Regent Park.

Each of them thanked Nardelli profusely. The joy he witnessed on their faces gave him pause and a rare moment of emotion.

"Next time you see Mr. Malvoy in the hallways, you can thank him as well. He is well connected with an executive at Maple Leaf Gardens. Even I don't have the kind of influence required to score gold tickets like this," Nardelli added.

Once their elation settled, the boys glanced over at Jesse. It occurred to them he was the odd man out. The whole idea had originated from him yet he had not received the same recognition. Nardelli watched them carefully as the mood softened and he sensed the growing elephant in the room. Jesse was genuinely happy for his friends but the irony was not lost on him either, yet he said nothing.

"Oh yes, almost forgot. I'm not sure what to do with this," Nardelli said as he pulled out a fifth envelope from the inside of his suit jacket pocket and handed it to Jesse.

Jesse flashed a huge smile as he opened the envelope to find another gold ticket inside. "Ya, baby, that's what I'm talkin' about!" Jesse announced as he held the ticket above his head and delivered high fives all around, starting with Nardelli.

CHAPTER 45

Ring… ring… ring…

"Hello, dad?" Jesse answered quickly, expecting his father's call.

"Hey, Jess. Zach said ya needed to talk. I been dying to hear from ya, kid. Praying for ya all day Sunday. What happened?" Roger asked impatiently.

"I had a few surprises along the way, but over all, mission accomplished. I got to tell you, dad. I was scared shitless. I could never be a criminal. Just not in me."

"That's okay, kid. I'm criminal enough for the both of us. No need to follow in your dad's footsteps. Won't hurt my feelings none. Tell me what happened, what ya found. Did ya get into the safe?" he asked eagerly.

"Yeah, the blue binder was in there, just like you said. I wrote down a bunch of numbers but got no idea what it all means. Just a bunch of mumbo jumbo to me. Hope I copied the right stuff."

"Ya done good, Jess. I gotta pen and paper ready to go here. So, ya gonna tell me what all the numbers are, then I gonna explain to ya what it is," Roger instructed.

"Okay, if you're ready, dad, here we go. These were the numbers on the last page." Jesse began to recount the various alphanumeric codes he'd recorded for his father.

2446548
9452874
CLHY7599330
JSY246
TXB842
MJR466
PTL479
BEK565
CGT941
622

"That's it, dad. That's all I got," Jesse concluded.

"Perfect, son. That's all I need. Jus give me a sec. I gotta figure things out," Roger replied and the line went quiet.

Jesse was puzzled but pleased the information was valid. He waited patiently till Roger came back on.

"Okay, Jess, I'm gonna explain to ya how it all works so pay close attention. This is all about drugs coming into Toronto from Colombia. All that mumbo jumbo you jus gave me, that's the Holy Grail I was talking about before. That's all ya need to figure out the roadmap how it all happens. That first number, 2446548. It's not a number. It's a date. They use the Julian calendar to set the dates when the drugs coming into the country. That's the Julian number for April 27th. That's when the next shipment coming in. The next number, 9452874, is the IMO number. It's the shipping vessel number that's carrying the drugs in. That's how they identify the cargo ship hauling the goods here. All these ships come into the Port of Montreal. The next number, CLHY7599330, is the sea can the drugs are in. Sea can is just what they call the large metal container the shipment comes in. The CLHY and 7599330 together refer to the shipping company and registration number. Company called Colombia Highway. They own the sea can. These sea cans are offloaded in Montreal by large cranes and dropped right onto a tractor trailer so they can drive 'em on the road. The cans travel in bond from Montreal to Toronto. That jus means that Canada Customs hasn't inspected and released the shipment yet. All goods imported into the country need to be cleared by Canada Customs before the freight goes to the customer. The sea can is driven to a large sufferance warehouse on The Queensway in Mississauga. That's where they hold all the shipments in bond until Canada Customs inspects and clears them for delivery. Now the next six numbers are actually bar codes they put on the skids. These bar codes identify the hot shipments. Drugs are inside coffee cans on those skids. Garvon got his boys employed inside that warehouse on The Queensway. They get heads up the shipment's comin'. Once it arrives, they scan all the skids for barcodes. The cold ones go through Canada Customs. The hot ones disappear, ya understand."

"Garvon's got people working for him in a bonded warehouse?" Jesse asked.

"Garvon got people paid off everywhere, kid. Right up and down the food chain. That's why I always say, ya never know who to trust. It's best be involving as few people as possible when ya talkin' about this stuff."

"How did you find out about how this all works?" Jesse asked.

"Garvon gotta trust some people too. He made a big mistake when he trusted me," Roger chuckled. "Okay, pay attention to the last part here, Jess. They gonna pull those six skids aside and load them on a separate truck. They gonna make it look like they never exist, jus disappear like that. Truck leaves The Queensway and drives over to Club eX where it gets received and processed. After that, it gets distributed to every junkie in Toronto, I suspect. Ends up in their veins."

"What's 622 mean?" Jesse asked about the final number.

"Oh ya, almost forgot. That's the number they etch on the bottom of the hot cans. All the drug cans gonna have the number 622 etched on the bottom, usually red in colour. Okay, Jess, I gotta wrap this up. They lookin' at me now to get off the phone. Ya go ahead and tell Nardelli all this. It's real important they track the can from Montreal. He gonna need to be involving the RCMP. No way local law can handle all this. Your Nardelli sounds like a pretty smart guy. I suspect he know what to do once he got the info."

"Are they still after him, dad? Is he still in danger?" Jesse asked with a hint of concern.

"Not hearing too much right now, kid. He got police protectin' him right now. They followin' him everywhere for sure, but that don't mean shit. These guys are patient and got a long memory. They jus waitin' for their moment. They figure a way. Eventually, they gonna get to him. Gotta go now, Jess. Godspeed son. I be praying for ya, kid," Roger concluded and hung up the line.

Jesse sat at the table quietly trying to absorb the conversation. He imagined the type of life his father had lived with the constant danger and stress he faced on a daily basis working for criminals. This type of life boggled his mind. He understood his task. There was no turning back now and time was of the essence. He would go see Nardelli Saturday.

CHAPTER 46

Jesse headed out Saturday morning towards Lakewood High. He understood Nardelli's schedule and work habits by now. He knew he could find him there working. A Saturday rendezvous also provided the opportunity to speak with him privately without the endless interruptions his normal workday would bring. He carried the knowledge Roger imparted earlier in the week with great trepidation. The burden played on him mentally. He had been short with Amanda and his mother throughout the week. His mental health was suffering. He desperately needed to unload the information eating away at him.

Jesse approached the school. There were a few kids playing basketball on the east side of the building but, for the most part, the outer facility was vacated. He slowly moved towards the back property along the west wall. As he turned the corner near the back of the school, he saw Nardelli's rental car parked in its normal spot. The sight of the Lada caused him a moment of levity. Goz's earlier comment to Nardelli regarding its lack of visual appeal brought a smile to his face. It was certainly a far cry from his vintage '58 Studebaker. He advanced towards Nardelli's office window when he was abruptly startled.

"Freeze! Hands up now!" a voice shouted from behind.

"Hands over your head now!" another voice screamed.

Jesse froze immediately in his tracks. Without turning around he complied with the instructions and raised his hands above his head.

"Now lie down on your stomach. Keep your hands above your head where we can see them. Do it now!"

Within seconds, Jesse felt a knee and the full weight of his new master against his back. It reminded him the fractured ribs he had sustained at the hands of his father seven months earlier were still very much present as pain registered through his torso. He felt two sets of hands frisking his person top to bottom. The next feeling was a set of handcuffs locking his wrists together. He was finally turned around and caught a glimpse of the two very large officers holding their firearms in his direction.

"What's your name, son, and what are you doing here?" they asked him.

"Jesse Decruz. I'm here to see Mr. Nardelli. I'm a student at this school," he quickly provided.

Nardelli was alerted by the sound of commotion outside his office in the schoolyard. He arrived at the window just as the takedown occurred. He immediately recognized Jesse and opened the vented window to yell out. "Let him go! He's here to see me. Let him up now!" Nardelli barked through the narrow opening.

One of his security detail moved closer to the window to speak with him. "Says his name is Jesse Decruz. Here to see you. You know him, sir?"

"Yes, yes, take those cuffs off of him right now and send him to the front entrance please," Nardelli instructed.

Jesse was released and he brushed himself off. He returned to the front of the building as instructed where Nardelli was waiting.

"Sorry about that, Jesse. We've assigned a few security guards at the school since the fire," Nardelli informed. "What are you doing here?" he asked as they entered his office.

"Security guards don't pull weapons on some kid loitering around the school. I know those guys are here to protect you, Mr. Nardelli," Jesse said.

Nardelli stared at him for several seconds before responding. "Yes, I suspect you know a lot more than you've been telling me, Jesse."

The comment caught him off guard. He attempted to play coy but Nardelli's inference was quite telling. "What do you mean?" Jesse asked.

Nardelli brushed off the question and turned it around. "I'm going to ask you again, why are you here, Jesse? What are you doing here on a Saturday morning? I'm sure you're not here for additional instruction," Nardelli persisted.

Jesse decided there was no sense in delaying the inevitable. "You're in trouble, sir, serious trouble, and there's only one way out of it. That's why I'm here," he unloaded.

"Keep talking," Nardelli instructed, sensing the truth was about to be told.

"I know about the bomb. I know the police are protecting you. And I know why they're after you now," Jesse blurted.

"Well, it looks like we're finally being honest with each other, doesn't it, Jesse? You know, I didn't get to my position because of my keen sense of style and good looks," Nardelli continued in a self-deprecating manner. "I know how to problem solve, figure things out, piece things together. It's a talent I have," he explained. "I figured you out a while back. When you first came to me with information on the drugs here at Lakewood, it didn't take me very long to figure it out. I did some research on you and I know the history with your father. After that, I just started to connect the dots and it all fell into place. I'm sorry for the life you've had to live and endure so far, Jesse. It's a lot more than any kid should have to experience. But, you're in too deep right now, much deeper than a seventeen-year-old kid should ever be. You need to back away from this now and let law enforcement handle things. I'm serious. You don't want to be in the position I'm in right now. It's not good for your health," Nardelli warned.

"It's too late, Mr. Nardelli. I'm already in way over my head. I can't un-hear and un-see everything I've already heard and seen. The fact that you know my source makes the situation even more dangerous. I don't think you completely understand everything yet, sir."

Nardelli hesitated, unwilling to show his hand. He allowed Jesse to continue. "Why don't you tell me what you know about all this."

"I know the Colombian drug cartel is trying to get to you right now. There's a bad dude named Diego Garvon who operates out of Club eX. He's the kingpin and he won't stop until he gets to you," Jesse stated ominously.

"That's the first I'm hearing that name. Why's he tracking me down?" Nardelli asked.

"The drug bust they did here last month put a huge dent in their operation, bigger than you think. A lot of his people went down because of it. This Garvon guy doesn't believe you figured it all out by yourself. He's convinced someone on the inside ratted him out. He doesn't want you dead, at least not yet. He wants to get to you and find out who talked. They won't stop till they find out. The way it was explained to me, once they get you, they'll get the information they need from you. They're ruthless, Mr. Nardelli. These guys are nut jobs. Once they do, lights out for you, my father, and me. I don't want to be part of this. Unfortunately, I got skin in the game now. That's why I'm here."

Nardelli stood quietly processing the information. "Since we're being honest with each other, what you're telling me is fairly consistent with the information the police have given me so far. However, your explanation is far more detailed. I wasn't aware who was after me and where he worked. That's certainly news to me. I'm assuming the police likely know this Diego Garvon character but they're purposely keeping me in the dark for security reasons, I suppose."

"There's a lot more to this that you don't know, sir," Jesse continued.

"No, Jesse. You need to stay away from this. As of right now, they don't know you and your father are involved. There's no need to put yourself in harm's way. I want you to stay—"

"You're not listening to me, sir!" Jesse interrupted. "These guys will not stop until they get to you. Never! You're in grave danger and these two rent-a-cops you have outside here are no contest against the cartel. Do you understand?" Jesse appealed to him, raising his voice.

"What are you saying, Jesse?" Nardelli looked at him confused.

"The only way to end this is to take them out first. Otherwise, they'll never stop trying to get to you," Jesse explained.

"That's what our law enforcement is doing. What more can we do?" Nardelli responded.

"Law enforcement doesn't have what I have." Jesse finally played his hand.

"What do you have, Jesse?" Nardelli pressed.

"I have everything we need to take them down, the whole operation, the whole playbook. But we're going to need a lot more muscle. We need to be real careful though. Apparently, the Colombians have a lot of people on their payroll. They have people in legitimate positions. It's hard to know who to trust, even in law enforcement," Jesse cautioned.

"Okay, Jesse, tell me what you know and I'll stickhandle it from here," Nardelli offered.

Jesse jotted all of the numbers and codes onto a piece of paper for Nardelli. He explained the meaning of each code and the date of the next shipment just as Roger had explained it. Nardelli listened in amazement as Jesse explained each step of the operation. He resisted the urge to ask how his father was able to acquire such sensitive information. That question, he reasoned, would not yield a clear answer in any case.

"You're right. We're going to need some serious resources to deal with this. Your anonymity is safe with me, Jesse. I promise," Nardelli assured.

They continued to converse briefly then ended the meeting. Jesse left the office hoping he had done the right thing. The situation was about to get very real and very dangerous, he concluded.

Nardelli picked up the line and dialed Malvoy at home. "Hello, Anderson. Stay where you are. I'm coming over right now."

CHAPTER 47

Mrs. Yang slipped silently through the back door of the Grade 10 math tutoring class currently in progress. Jesse and Amanda were both attending to students at the moment and didn't notice her entrance. She was impressed with the students' level of engagement and the quality face time they were able to provide. The math and English re-test was scheduled three weeks out and this was crunch time. Nardelli had asked her to stop by from time to time and take stock of their progress and readiness for the pending examinations.

Jesse surfaced first and noticed her at the back of the room pacing about. He shot her a quick smile and moved on to the next student struggling with an algebra problem. Amanda was wrapping up her one-on-one lesson with Pharah Augustin, a recent Haitian immigrant who settled in the Regent Park area. She was especially challenging as English was a second language in addition to her questionable home life. Amanda had taken a special interest in Pharah, who, in spite of her personal challenges, exhibited tremendous potential and a winning attitude. Mrs. Yang took note of Amanda's nurturing side and her capacity for empathy and support. Jesse, on the other hand, was less nurturing but the students responded to his personality and easy manner. He was able to reach many of the students that a seasoned math instructor could not. She reasoned lack of resources and one-on-one time contributed to that shortfall.

Amanda dismissed the class and walked to the back of the classroom to meet with Mrs. Yang. Jesse followed behind.

"Hello, Mrs. Yang. Did you drop by to hand us our paycheques?" she asked playfully.

"Probably same amount as last week, Mandy. I think we're in a rut," Jesse added.

"Very amusing, you two. I'm just here observing and, I must say, you both have a real knack for this type of work. You're naturals. I'm very impressed," Mrs. Yang complimented.

"You should have been here on day one. It almost turned into a disaster, but Jesse was able to save the day with his beautiful mind. It was definitely touch-and-go at the beginning," Amanda replied.

"I'm very serious about you two. If you have any ambitions to enter the educational field, I believe you could be very successful. I encourage you and would be willing to provide you a recommendation anytime," Mrs. Yang added.

"I'm not sure about Mandy but I see how difficult kids can be. It's a tough profession and doing this three times a week gives me a whole new respect for the real teachers who work at this school full time," Jesse stated.

"I appreciate that, Jesse. The reason I dropped in, Mr. Nardelli wanted me to gauge our level of readiness for the re-test next month. We're only three weeks away now."

"We're getting there, Mrs. Yang. There's always going to be those tough kids we just can't reach but, for the most part, they're responding," Amanda said.

"Spending face time with them makes all the difference in the world. Our teachers don't have that time during the day. That's the game changer," Jesse added.

"Well, I'm proud of both of you. This is the most unselfish thing you could do to help your peers. You're making a tremendous difference with these kids, and Mr. Nardelli shares the same feeling," Mrs. Yang praised.

"Thanks, Mrs. Yang. Speaking of Mr. Nardelli, is he still around? I wanted to talk with him before he leaves today," Jesse said.

Mrs. Yang chuckled, "You're kidding, right? Mr. Nardelli is always here. Unless you're planning to see him after 8 p.m. tonight, I'm sure you'll find him in his office."

Jesse and Amanda continued to chat briefly before Mrs. Yang departed.

"I'll be right back, Mandy. Just need to talk to the boss for a few minutes. We'll leave when I get back." Jesse headed out towards Nardelli's office.

Knock... knock... knock.

"Enter!" Nardelli barked from his seat in the office. "What's up, Jesse? Need a ride home in my lovely new Lada? If we take out the back seat, I'm sure we can fit you in there," he joked.

"Do you ever go home, Mr. Nardelli? Seriously, you may as well install a bed in here and save yourself the commute every day," Jesse observed.

"I once figured out how much I make per hour. Comes out to somewhere around $2.50 an hour," he laughed. "I'm starting to think my hours of work annoy the police detail who are protecting me out there. Those poor guys sit in their vehicles all day just looking after me. I'd rather be doing what I do all day than that."

"They're out there now?" Jesse asked with curiosity. "I don't see them."

"They're paid to be invisible, Jesse. You're not supposed to see them," Nardelli stated matter-of-factly. "What can I do for you, kid?"

"I know April 27th is coming up and the police are likely busy planning for that day. I have more information I thought I should pass on to you. It might be helpful." Jesse handed Nardelli a few pages from his pocket.

"What's all this?" Nardelli asked as he examined the documents.

"These are all the security codes and a schematic to Club eX. I thought they might be helpful to the police. I've marked out the security codes for each entry point and also some detail about Garvon's office down in the basement of that building. He's got a safe behind the large painting in his office. The code to get into the safe is right here." Jesse pointed to the numbers on the paper.

"I guess you weren't kidding when you said you were too far in on this. I fear for you, Jesse. I want to remind you to keep your distance and do nothing to place yourself in any more danger. I'm serious, son," Nardelli said, addressing him in a paternal way. "I'll pass this on to the authorities. I'm sure they'll be pleased to receive this kind of intel."

"Are you doing okay, sir? I don't know how you manage to sleep at night knowing there's a target on your back," Jesse stated.

"I sleep with one eye open, Jesse, if I sleep at all. You need to call it a day now, kid. I see Amanda standing outside my office. I'm sure she's not waiting for me. Have a good day, Jesse, and thanks for the information."

CHAPTER 48

Ring... ring... ring...

Nardelli was startled awake from a dead sleep, a privilege he had not enjoyed for several days. His Type A personality and obsessive work habits rarely afforded him a restful slumber. Added to this, he was now living in the crosshairs of a ruthless drug cartel. It was any wonder he could close his eyes at all. He stretched out his right arm over the vacant pillow to retrieve the phone perched atop the side table.

"Hello, Dominic speaking," Nardelli responded in a groggy voice.

"Hello, Dominic. I'm so sorry to awaken you but surely you didn't think we forgot about you already, did you?" The ominous voice spoke slowly and deliberately. "It's just a matter of time, Dominic. Perhaps tomorrow, maybe next week, or maybe we're just outside your front door right now. I promise you, it will be a surprise. Do you really believe a sleepy police officer sitting in his vehicle half a block away from your house poses a challenge to us? If we really wanted to snatch you up, we would have already. But this is much more fun, don't you think?" the voice taunted.

"Why don't we settle this like a couple of real men or maybe your dick is so small you don't qualify any more," Nardelli said with contempt.

"All in due time, Dominic. I can assure you the size of my dick is the least of your worries. We'll have plenty of opportunity to become acquainted. Right now, I'm enjoying our courtship, aren't you?"

"So tell me. What happened to you?" asked Nardelli, going on the offensive. "Did your daddy shackle you to the floor and keep you locked up in the basement when you were young? Or maybe your crazy uncle on your mother's side fucked you up the ass every night. Please tell me what kind of depraved life you've lived to become the pathetic parasite you are today. I really need to know."

"I look forward to sharing with you the details of my depraved life, Dominic. Very soon. In fact, now that you've expressed an interest in my life, I will make it my top priority to share with you the deepest depths of my depravity. I'd love to chat some more with you, Dominic. However, in about ten seconds they'll be able to track my location so I really need to let you go for now. Until next time. Sleep well, Dominic." *Click.*

Nardelli sat quietly on the edge of his bed, his hands physically shaking. The call had unnerved him, this one much more than the previous two he'd received over the past month. He reached into the drawer of his side table and pulled out his .38 special, a weapon handed down from his father. His father had gifted him the gun before departing Canada to retire in his homeland of Italy. Nardelli Sr. had always had a fascination with firearms, an interest Nardelli neither had nor shared with his father. He accepted the weapon out of respect but it had never seen the light of day, until now.

Nardelli slid off the bed and quickly moved to the front window overlooking his Brentwood Road split-level home in

Etobicoke. He peered out the window holding his body low. He could barely see his security detail in the parked vehicle several doors away. Probably eating or sleeping, he thought. He then moved to the back of the house and did the same. All was quiet but it didn't provide him the calm he needed. He felt trapped and alone, vulnerable, a state of mind he considered weak, not worthy of him.

Ring... ring... ring...

Nardelli jerked as if receiving a jolt of electricity. He moved to the phone and picked up the receiver, but said nothing.

"That wasn't wise, Dominic. You shouldn't be antagonizing this guy. He's dangerous and unstable," Danny O'Shea scolded him.

"What am I supposed to do, Danny? That's the third call in a month. If these fuckers are trying to get into my head, I don't mind telling you, they've succeeded," Nardelli shot back.

"Just hang in there, Dominic. We're monitoring all your calls. Just another week and we'll be dealing with all of them. We're almost there," O'Shea explained. "We couldn't trace this call either. These guys are good. They know exactly how much time they have before shutting it down. The good news is, we're fairly certain who the players we're dealing with are so we have them on a short leash. I want you to know we have you covered."

"On that subject, please tell me this guy sitting in the car about 300 feet away from my house is not sleeping. And what the hell is he going to do if these assholes decide to storm my house?" Nardelli asked in a rare moment of paranoia.

"First of all, Dominic, they would never do that, especially knowing your home is being cased by police. Even if they were so brazen to attempt your abduction, we have numerous squads on alert. They would respond to your home inside of two minutes. The calls are simply made to elevate your fear and anxiety until they decide it's time to scoop you up," O'Shea assured him.

"Easy for you! The sooner we raid these degenerates, the braver I'll be. I may as well kiss the rest of this evening goodbye. There's no chance I'll be falling asleep again."

"I'm here if anything else happens or you just need to talk some more. Do me a favour though, Dominic."

"What's that?" Nardelli asked.

"No more schoolyard challenges or references to his penis. And leave his father and uncle out of your conversations. You can't be throwing gas on a burning fire and expect to extinguish it. Understood?"

CHAPTER 49

Malvoy and Nardelli sat quietly in Nardelli's office. This was the calm before the storm; the culmination of nearly eight weeks of planning. Malvoy had engaged Danny O'Shea, who coordinated the Toronto Police Service along with the RCMP special task force in charge of covert operations. The planned takedown would be a coordinated effort between the two organizations that promised to deliver a significant blow to the Toronto east end drug trade.

O'Shea entered Nardelli's office followed by a large representative of the RCMP task force who more closely resembled a CFL line guard.

"Good day, gentlemen. This is Sergeant Allan Quinn from the special covert services branch of the RCMP. He will have command authority over today's operation. My team will be supporting him throughout the raid," O'Shea explained.

"Mr. Malvoy. Mr. Nardelli." Quinn accepted their handshakes then sat down next to Nardelli's desk. "I understand, Mr. Nardelli, we have you to thank for the intelligence that led to this operation. We've had Diego Garvon and his people under surveillance for nearly two years now. He's been very slippery and, up until now, we've had very little concrete intelligence surrounding his operation and how it works. I must say, the level of detail on his network and logistics has helped us tremendously, particularly with the Montreal connection. I would dearly love to discuss that further with your source."

"I appreciate that sergeant but my source is not available for questioning. That was a strict condition for his cooperation," Nardelli said, dismissing the idea.

"Fair enough. I know you've endured a number of threats on your life since the bomb attack. I can respect your decision to honour that condition. If this all goes well today, I suspect the contents of Garvon's wall safe will be a Pandora's box of information for us."

"We've had the shipment under close surveillance since it hit the Port of Montreal," O'Shea added. "We've inserted special agents inside the sufferance warehouse on The Queensway and are tracking the drug shipment every step of the way. It's been very smooth thus far but this is where the rubber hits the road. From this point on, things become very unpredictable and dangerous."

"What else do you need from us, Danny?" Malvoy asked. "Dominic and I were planning to stay here and remain available in case you need to contact us for any reason."

"That's perfect, Anderson. We don't want you anywhere near this. We're dealing with heavily armed and dangerous individuals. We have no idea what they know at this moment. We have police protection for you both stationed just outside the school as a precaution. Stay put and stay close to the phone until we contact you again," O'Shea instructed and then departed.

□

Quinn pulled out his radio and barked instructions to his SWAT team leaders. *"Okay, showtime ladies. I want the blue team to enter the property from the west and remain at the northwest corner at the rear. I want the red team to enter from the east and park at the northeast corner at the rear with eyes on the dock area. Green team will remain at the front of the building parked curbside for containment."*

"Roger that," the replies came back.

"Wait for my signal, then come in together." Quinn provided last minute instructions.

Quinn and O'Shea's vehicle led the way down Cherry Street followed by the three SWAT vans. The Toronto Police Service quickly moved into action to close off the roads in both directions and eliminate any through traffic. Quinn accelerated forward and did a quick U-turn as they reached Club Ex. He parked the vehicle across the street and set up his command centre.

The SWAT vehicles positioned themselves as instructed. Quinn readied himself and then issued the call. *"Storm, storm, storm!"* he shouted.

SWAT agents from the blue team began to spill out in formation as they approached the dock area along the back wall from the west. The squad leader reached for his side belt and pulled out a flash bomb. He motioned to his team with his right hand above his head. Then he reached down, pulled the safety lever, and threw the flash bomb inside the receiving dock area.

Boom!

The detonation was deafening and the flash was blinding. Anyone caught in its wake would most certainly be immediately disabled. The team waited several seconds then stormed into the building.

The blue team squad leader radioed in. *"We've breached the dock area, moving down the hallway towards the basement stairwell."*

"Okay, red team, follow in behind and support," Quinn barked.

Before the blue team squad could reach the stairwell, bullets began flying as they met resistance from Garvon's men moving quickly up the stairwell and from the front of the building. The blue team were caught up in the narrow hallway leading to the stairwell and had to turn back immediately. *"Retreat, retreat!"* the squad leader yelled.

Sparks from semi-automatic weapons were now flying off the walls and floor. Two squad members were hit. They were quickly grabbed by team members and dragged to safety before taking additional fire.

"Blue team report," Quinn instructed.

"Two men down, sir. Both took hits to their vests. They're winded but they'll be fine," the blue squad leader reported.

"Green team, storm from the front!" Quinn issued new orders.

The green team at the front of the building blew the doors and quickly spilled into the building in formation, dropping numerous flash bombs along the way. Sharpshooters took their positions and made quick work of Garvon's men positioned near the stripper stage.

"All teams, storm the basement," Quinn issued further instructions.

The squadrons converged from all entrance points. They moved quickly and picked off with precision a number of Garvon's soldiers perched throughout the facility.

Diego Garvon watched from the basement using numerous remote monitors set up in his office. He watched his men being picked off one by one as the squads made their way to the stairwell. They began descending the staircase towards his office. Garvon opened the top drawer of his desk and retrieved a large bag of white powder. He spilled a generous amount onto his wooden oak desk. He fashioned a long line of the powder using a business card. Holding a straw in his right hand, he lowered his head to the desk and took the entire line through the straw and into his nose. He raised his head, shaking it violently several times. His eyes widened and his courage magnified. Garvon sprinted to the office closet and pulled out a long buckled rocket container, assembling the rocket launcher with great skill and speed. He loaded the launcher with a grenade and, balancing the long tube on his shoulder with the help of a shoulder saddle, moved towards the door of his office and waited.

"Any sign of the King Snake?" Quinn asked his red squad leader, referring to Garvon.

"Negative, we're moving to the basement now. Top floor is secured."

SWAT agents moved to the basement and filled the hallway leading to Garvon's office. They stood outside and the squad leader yelled through the door, "Come on out, Garvon! It's over. You're surrounded. There's nowhere to go!"

Garvon stood behind his desk and steadied his body. A potent mix of adrenaline and cocaine coursed through his veins. He felt the rush invade his mind. "I'm not doing your fuckin' job for you! You want me? Come in and get me!" he challenged.

He took direct aim at the office door then slowly depressed the trigger, launching the grenade.

Boom!

Garvon's office door vapourized as the force of the explosion knocked everyone near the entrance of the door onto the floor. Those who were still able-bodied grabbed the injured and retreated back up the stairs. Garvon loaded another grenade onto the launcher. He quickly glanced at the monitor to see the hallway in front of his office was now clear. He advanced to the door opening, pivoted towards the head of the hallway, and launched his weapon again.

Boom!

This time the grenade exploded near the end of the hallway where some stragglers were still retreating up the staircase.

Garvon returned to his office to retrieve an automatic weapon. *"What the hell is going on in there? Report! Report!"* Quinn yelled into his radio.

By this point, most of the agents were now back upstairs. The injured were carried or dragged to the dock area and delivered to the SWAT vehicles for medical attention.

"He's deployed a rocket launcher, Sarg. We had to retreat. We need to smoke him out. It's too dangerous to storm that area right now," the green squad leader reported.

"Fuck! This is exactly what I was afraid of, the unknowns. That's what makes this type of operation unpredictable!" Quinn shouted to O'Shea. *"I need a casualty count,"* Quinn barked over the radio.

"Six down, Sarg. One serious, the others will survive."

"Okay, smoke him out. Hit him hard with the smoke bombs," Quinn instructed.

"Roger that."

Three SWAT agents advanced towards the dock and receiving area, prepared to deliver smoke bombs into the building. They didn't make it halfway to the dock before bullets from Garvon's automatic weapon began flying, downing two of them. The SWAT teams returned fire and continued to contain Garvon until the injured men could be retrieved.

The red squad leader reported in. *"We're drawing automatic fire, Sarg. We need to hang back until we get eyes on King Snake."*

"What's his last location?" Quinn demanded.

"He was on the opposite side of the east wall along the receiving dock. Sir, I have an idea, but I need your authority to proceed."

"Talk to me," Quinn ordered.

"There's an entire line of propane tanks secured along the back side of the east wall. Not sure if they're full or empty. We could launch grenades against those tanks, which will neutralize anyone in the

dock area. The only problem, sir, it could destroy the whole building. Also, collateral damage is possible."

Quinn weighed his options then issued the order. "*Do it. Take them out now.*"

Agents positioned behind the van loaded three launchers with grenades. They waited for cover fire from the squad, moved into position, and unloaded their payload towards the propane tanks.

Boom! Boom! Boom!

The explosives detonated with such power the entire wall disintegrated and the dock area was engulfed in hellfire.

Garvon suddenly emerged, penetrating the wall of fire, holding his automatic weapon. He began discharging it indiscriminately in the air yelling at the top of his lungs. His clothes were now fully engulfed in fire as he continued to discharge his weapon. All SWAT teams immediately returned fire, downing him in a flurry of ammunition, finally putting Garvon out of his misery. The green squad leader ran towards Garvon spraying him with fire retardant but it was too late.

"*King Snake has been decapitated, Sarg,*" the red squad leader reported, indicating Garvon had expired.

"*Good work. Let's secure the facility, contain those fires, and bring them all in,*" Quinn said, wrapping up the operation. Within minutes, emergency response vehicles converged on Club eX.

O'Shea picked up the phone and called Nardelli's office. "Good news, Dominic. You should sleep like a baby tonight."

CHAPTER 50

Jeanie poured herself a cup of coffee and sat down to read the morning paper. Jesse held vigil over the toaster, waiting for his delivery of burnt toast. The toaster had seen better days. Yielding a proper slice of toast had become less an expectation and more a pleasant surprise in the Decruz kitchen. He attempted to fish his breakfast out with a knife but grew increasingly impatient waiting on the temperamental contraption.

"Oh my God, Jesse, look at this!" Jeanie announced. "They raided Club eX yesterday. Apparently a drug ring was operating out of there. Unbelievable! Looks like your dad will be looking for other work when he gets out."

Jesse lunged towards the table and scanned the lengthy article in the newspaper. The report indicated several casualties but there was no mention of names. "Look at this picture. The place looks like a war zone. Half the building is gone," Jesse announced in disbelief.

"Says three employees at the club were killed in a gun fight. I always knew that place was bad news. Hard to believe your father worked there for nearly twenty years," Jeanie said as she continued to peruse the article.

Jesse quickly inhaled his breakfast. He needed to get to Nardelli's office right away as curiosity was killing him. He needed to know the final outcome and fate of Diego Garvon.

"I gotta go, mom. I forgot I had a meeting with Mr. Nardelli this morning. Can you tell Mandy I'm sorry, but I gotta blast without her this morning? Thanks, mom." Jesse disappeared as he vacated the apartment in haste.

Jesse peeled down Sackville Street with purpose, jogging the entire way to Lakewood High. He rushed through the front doors and worked his way to Nardelli's office. Nardelli looked up as he entered the room.

Out of breath, Jesse pulled up a chair and stared intensely at Nardelli. "Did they get him?" he asked impatiently.

Nardelli provided a dramatic pause, flashed a smile, and then gave Jesse the thumbs up. "We got him. He went out in a blaze of glory. Literally. I don't have a lot of details right now. Suffice it to say, his organization is finished. They scooped up a lot of bad guys along the way, thanks to you, Jesse."

Jesse closed his eyes and sat back in the chair. He drew a deep breath of relief. "I'll be honest with you, sir. I was really worried for you. I'm the guy who dropped all of this in your lap. If something would have happened to you, it would have all been on me."

"Doesn't work like that, Jesse. There are two types of people in this world. There are those who step up and those who hide. There's a famous Shakespearean quote you might remember. 'A coward dies a thousand times, a hero dies but once.' You and I are not cowards, Jesse."

"Right, I remember that quote. Julius Caesar," Jesse recalled.

"While I have you here, we're about one week away from the Grade 9 and 10 re-examinations. What's your best prediction on our math literacy chances?" Nardelli asked.

"I'm going to predict we'll do better than we did at the start of the year." Jesse smiled.

"Wow, you're really going out on a limb there kid," Nardelli quipped.

"Seriously, I believe Amanda and I got through to a lot of them. It took a while, but I think, overall, they'll be much better this time out," Jesse said, attempting to clarify his thoughts.

"Whatever happens, you guys provided an outstanding service to those kids and our school. I have nothing but the deepest respect for you both. And while we're at it, thanks to you, I might make it to my 40th birthday now." Nardelli stood and offered his hand. The two shook and wrapped up their meeting.

Jesse returned to the apartment after school. He opened the fridge door, examined the contents, and pulled out the leftover spaghetti from the previous evening.

Ring... ring... ring...

Jesse picked up the phone. "Hello?"

"Hello, this is Decruz Enterprises. Can I interest you in a new vacuum cleaner, sir?"

"Hi, dad. I don't think sales is in your future, sorry," Jesse answered amused.

"Hell, kid, that's jus mean spirited. Ya really need to be nicer to the unemployed and incarcerated," Roger shot back as he chuckled in amusement. "Jus thought I should start thinkin' about another career since Club eX got exterminated."

"That's one hell of a prison grapevine you have there at Millhaven. Is there anything you don't know or hear about, dad?" Jesse asked in amazement.

"I jus wanta tell ya, Jess. Havin' Garvon outta the picture brought a great deal of joy to my heart. Couldn't happen to a nicer guy. I was wearing out the pages of my bible praying for ya, son."

"Are we out of danger, dad? Should we still be worried?" Jesse asked, concern showing in his voice.

"Ya don't need to worry about the Colombians. They gonna stay in their hole for a good long time. Damage is done. You guys should be fine now. Me, on the other hand, my name probably gonna pop up from whatever documents they pulled from the Club. Maybe not. I dunno. Hard to say. Bottom line, Jess, this was the only play we had. Let the chips fall. That's all I gotta say about that. Anyway, jus called to congratulate ya, son. Ya done real good. I think ya got a real future for this kinda thing," he chuckled. "Jus kiddin, son. I been thinking a lot 'bout you guys and what purpose I got left in my life. I think me being in here been good for me. Opened my eyes for the better. Gotta go, Jess. Luv ya, son. We talk again soon," Roger added and dropped off the line.

CHAPTER 51

Faculty, parents, and students began to file into the large gymnasium at the west side of the school building to celebrate Lakewood High School's annual year-end assembly. Seats began to fill quickly as attendance was much better than expected. Lakewood had gone through a transformative year. The school had garnered a great deal of attention from the media, law enforcement, politicians, and school board brass. Malvoy and Nardelli had become local celebrities of sorts and periodically appeared on TV and radio. They were invited to many media events and interviewed in various news publications. Although the media attention focused primarily on the drug challenges faced by the school, the narrative had morphed into good-news stories around the dramatic changes and massive clean up that Lakewood and the surrounding schools had gone through over the past year. Local reporters were onsite to cover the assembly; Malvoy couldn't pass up the opportunity. He had alerted them ahead of time to his attendance and a special announcement he would deliver.

Jesse had scouted the seating plan before the start of the assembly and secured a string of chairs in the fifth row. He sat with Jeanie and Amanda while his boys filled out the remainder of the section.

"Oh my God, this place is jammed. Where they all come from?" Jeanie observed as she glanced at the sea of humanity behind her.

"I know, never seen the gym this full before. Hey guys, check it out." Jesse motioned to the Jackson boys seated near the end of the row with their mother, Winnie. She was embroiled in an argument with JJ. Another classic moment was about to be born.

"I give it another five minutes before we see the head slap," Goz predicted.

"Won't take that long," Minoo added. "Look at Trey, he's ready to crawl under his seat right now with embarrassment." They began to laugh.

Nardelli approached the lectern and gestured to Mrs. Garcia to flick the lights to signal the beginning of the assembly.

"Good afternoon, everyone. I'd like to get started and welcome all the parents, faculty, students, and special guests from the local media here today. For those of you who don't know me…"

The audience laughed. Everyone knew Nardelli; the introduction was moot.

"For those of you who don't know me," Nardelli repeated. "I'm Mr. Nardelli, principal here at Lakewood High School. It's my pleasure to welcome you to our annual year-end assembly. We have a full agenda this afternoon so let's get right to it, shall we? Needless to say, we've had quite an eventful year at Lakewood. I have several more grey hairs and a questionable ulcer to prove it."

There was more laughter from the audience.

"I'd like to say it was all good, but that would be less than truthful. I've never been shy to talk about the many challenges we face here at Lakewood High. My goal this year was to make a difference, a positive change, because the status quo was no longer an option. Winston Churchill had a famous quote. He said, 'If you are going through hell, keep on going.' It describes our journey this year. We've certainly been through hell but we came out the other side. I made some enemies along the way, but that's okay. I didn't come here to win a popularity contest. In the end, I think we finished much better than we started."

The audience leapt to its feet, everyone clapping and cheering. Nardelli stood solemnly at the lectern. He had underestimated his popularity. The audience reaction caught him off guard and tears began to well up in his eyes. He attempted to regain his composure as the ovation went on for a few minutes. When the audience finally took their seats again, he continued.

"Thank you, thank you very much. One man alone cannot affect the type of change we experienced this year. It takes a community. It takes those special people who have the courage to step up and be counted, and it takes special leadership. At this time, I would like to introduce one of those special leaders. He's been a mentor of mine and he provided a tremendous amount of time and support to Lakewood High and to me this year. Ladies and gentleman, our Director of Education for the Toronto District School Board, Mr. Anderson Malvoy."

The clapping followed Malvoy all the way to the lectern.

"Thank you, Mr. Nardelli, for those kind words, and thank you all for having me here today. I generally don't make a habit of attending individual high school assemblies but, this year, I made an exception with Lakewood High because this school is exceptional. I have several special announcements to make today but before I get into that, I wanted to share with you some statistics I believe will impress you. Lakewood didn't just transform itself this year, it experienced a true metamorphosis." Malvoy reached into his pocket and pulled out a document. "I'm going to go through just a few of the highlights for you now. At the beginning of the school year, Lakewood's student suspension rate was well over twice the Toronto district average, with an average approaching 6 percent. I'm please to announce the suspension rate is now averaging below 2 percent, that's nearly a 70-percent reduction in the back half of this school year. Drug-related suspensions are down 80 percent. Student complaints for bullying are down 75 percent. Violent incidents on school property are down 60 percent, and the list goes on."

The audience clapped and cheered in appreciation.

"I use this as a segway to a most impressive accomplishment achieved this year among our student body. I have in my hand the examination results recently completed by our Grade 9 and 10 student body for math and English literacy last month. Many of you may recall the school board marks were first published in the *Toronto Star* back in October last year. Lakewood, unfortunately, scored the lowest marks board-wide in both subjects, a statistic we all took to heart. After a great deal of consternation and negotiation among the board trustees, we received approval, along with several other high schools, to re-test our students this past month. The results of those exams indicated that Lakewood now falls within the 50th percentile in English, and most notably, we have achieved the 60th percentile for math. Both these milestones represent unprecedented achievements and performance improvement."

The audience applauded again.

"This type of change requires great leadership. I want to congratulate Mr. Nardelli and his team for this unparalleled turnaround. This leads me to my final announcement. I wanted to be here personally to make this announcement as it does affect my executive leadership team. The Toronto District School Board is always looking for exceptional talent, true visionaries, people who will forge the future in education in our city. We've found such a person right here at Lakewood. I'm proud to announce today we are appointing Mr. Dominic Nardelli to our executive team as the new Deputy Director of Education responsible for New Programs."

Liking what they were hearing, the audience clapped and cheered.

"Mr. Nardelli has proven himself this year. He has introduced a number of new and innovative programs right here at this school, yielding outstanding results. Those very programs will act as models and best practices board-wide as we move forward into the new school year. I want to pledge to all of you here today, we will provide a quality replacement for Mr. Nardelli. That replacement will be someone worthy to carry on the good work he started and accomplished here at Lakewood. Thank you all and I will pass this back over to Mr. Nardelli."

"Well, I certainly wasn't expecting that. Do you think I should accept the position?" Nardelli asked, smiling as he scanned the audience for approval.

The audience was a chorus of booes and voices yelling, "No!"

Nardelli laughed as he looked over at Malvoy. The crowd enjoyed the moment of levity. "Thank you, I'll take that as a no," he mused.

"I have a special announcement of my own this afternoon. I represent my father's scholarship trust, which he established several years ago after retiring from the school board. It has been my privilege to award these scholarships over the past number of years. They are known as the Nardelli Scholarship Awards. For those of you who don't know, my father was the former Director of Education for the Toronto District School Board. He had a tremendous appreciation and respect for those students who went above and beyond their regular roles as students to distinguish themselves as leaders among their peers. He established these scholarship awards to recognize these very special students. Specifically, these $5,000 scholarships are awarded to the top male and female students within the Toronto district who contributed the greatest benefit towards their fellow students throughout the year. Each school nominates a male and female student they feel are most deserving of the award. The board of trustees reviews all submissions and votes on the winners. For the first time ever, both male and female student scholarship recipients are from the same school. In fact, they are both students right here at Lakewood High School."

The audience erupted into clapping.

"Ladies and gentlemen, in recognition of their selfless contribution this year in establishing an after school peer-to-peer math tutoring program, your 1986 Nardelli Scholarship Award recipients are Amanda Perone and Jesse Decruz."

Once again, the audience leapt to its feet, clapping and cheering. Jeanie jumped to her feet and immediately began to cry. She joined Goz and Minoo in mauling Jesse before he could even rise from his seat. The announcement caught Jesse off guard and he sat frozen in his chair until Goz and Minoo pulled him up. The crowd remained standing as Amanda and Jesse finally made their way to the stage. Nardelli greeted them with a huge smile. He handed them a framed award and their scholarship cheques as the photographers gathered around to snap pictures. Once the audience settled down, Nardelli continued.

"I want to add a personal thought here. Amanda and Jesse can take a great deal of credit for the preparation of our Grade 9 and 10 students on the math examinations conducted last month; the results speak for themselves. In addition, the trustees were most impressed with this particular program. They want to see it expanded board-wide next year and we've received approval to provide a full credit towards Grade 13 accreditation for senior students who sign up and successfully complete this program."

He finished speaking and the room was filled with the thunderous sound of applause. After Nardelli dismissed the assembly, students mingled and wandered about. Jesse and Amanda were at the centre of numerous scrums as they received congratulations from faculty and students alike.

Malvoy made his way over to speak with them. He congratulated Jeanie on her son's accomplishment. "Can I speak with you both a second?" Malvoy asked, interrupting the scrum to pull Amanda and Jesse aside.

"I wanted to congratulate you both personally. You are most deserving of this award, truly. The math results exceeded everyone's expectations, including my own. Next year, we'd like to roll this program out to other high schools across the board and we can't think of anyone better to do that than both of you. Essentially, you two would train the trainers to mirror the program you established here. We've approved a budget for this program and would compensate you for travel and expenses. In addition, you would qualify for the Grade 13 credit we talked about. No need to commit right now but I wanted to put it out there for you so you can think about it over the summer.

"Thanks, Mr. Malvoy. It's a generous offer and a great opportunity. We'll definitely think about it," Jesse replied as Amanda nodded in agreement.

They returned to their friends and continued the celebration. "Okay, everyone," Jeanie announced to the small group as they exited the gymnasium. "There will be a pizza-and-wings party at our place this coming Saturday. Everyone's invited."

CHAPTER 52

Although Jesse enjoyed his newly found rock star status at school, he preferred the smaller more intimate gathering of close friends his mother had planned for him at the apartment. Amanda had arrived already and was preoccupied with Jesse while Jeanie was busy on the phone organizing a batch of Duff's famous Buffalo chicken wings and pizza for the party.

Knock... knock... knock.

Jesse answered the door to let the gang inside.

"Hey, Jess, I'm a bit strapped this week. Any chance you can dip into that scholarship fund and spare a good buddy some cash?" Goz asked.

"Here we go," Jesse said to Amanda rolling his eyes.

"JJ and I are willing to work cheap as your entourage. You know, keep the groupies away. Wouldn't charge you much," Trey added.

"I dropped your name at the disco last night. I'll tell ya, man, got me right to the front of the line," Minoo chirped.

"Leave Jesse alone," Amanda said, defending Jesse. "He's had a tough week. It's tough being famous, you know."

"It's okay, Mandy. It's just jealousy, plain and simple. Very unbecoming, fellas," Jesse shot back.

Jeanie finished up with the order and entered the kitchen.

"Hey, Mrs. D, how ya doin'? Ya didn't put no pineapple on them pizza's, did ya?" JJ asked. His comment was met with a head slap.

"You paying for them pizza's, fool?" Trey barked at his brother.

"Na, I ain't payin for 'em."

"Then keep your trap shut. She can put strawberries on them if she wants." Trey threw Jeanie a wink.

"Is that something you would like, JJ?" Jeanie asked, playing along.

JJ, glancing over at Trey and sensing another attack was imminent, responded, "Sure, that sound great, Mrs. D."

Knock… knock… knock.

"You expecting anyone else, Jesse?" Jeanie asked as she walked to the front door.

"No, mom. Everyone's here."

Jeanie opened the front door. "Hi, Zach, come on in. What brings you here?" she asked.

"I heard there was a party so I decided to join in. Hope you don't mind."

"Hey, Zach." Jesse approached and shook his hand. He looked over at his mother in confusion but was unable to gauge her reaction.

"Congratulations, Jesse. I heard you had quite a week. You're dad's very proud of you. In fact, he'll be calling you in a few minutes to chat."

"You really need to explain to me how that prison grapevine works. It's like he's living in my back pocket," Jesse stated in amazement.

"I could tell you how it works, but then I'd have to kill you," Zach chuckled. "Sorry, just a bit of prison humour."

Jeanie pulled Zach aside to speak with him privately. "Everything ready to go?" she whispered.

"Yep, all ready," he confirmed.

Ring... ring... ring...

"And there he is, right on schedule," Zach announced.

Jesse picked up. "Dad?"

"Congratulations, son. I'm so proud of ya, kid," Roger said.

"Thanks, dad. You got someone here following me around? How did you know about that?"

"Can't take credit for this one, Jess. It was actually your mother called me this week. She's in on it. She told me all about it. I told her not to say nothin' till I called today," Roger explained. "I can hear yer having a party over there. Wish I could be there with ya like a normal father. Well, can't do nothin' about that, now can I?" he asked with resignation.

Jesse looked over at Jeanie who was standing with Zach. They were both watching him intently as he spoke with his father. He thought it was odd but carried on conversing with Roger.

"Listen, dad. There's something I wanted to say to you weeks ago but the time wasn't right," Jesse started, then he hesitated.

"What's that, son?" Roger asked.

"I wanted to tell you... I wanted to say... I wanted you to know... I forgive you, dad. I'm finished being angry and I'm ready to forgive." The words choked in his throat as the emotion translated to his face. He could hear his father sobbing on the other end. His mother and Zach watched, sensing an intimate moment was occurring. Roger remained silent as he collected himself.

"Ya have no idea how much that means to me, son. I spent nearly eight months in here holding my bible, asking the Lord Almighty for forgiveness and he jus released me from my pain, right now."

"I've been to Millhaven twice, dad. Watched them drag you into that room in shackles and lock you to the ground like an animal. I got a tiny glimpse of the world you lived in over the past twenty years and I have to say, it's not pretty. Maybe life dealt you a bad hand, I don't know. And maybe you still got to make peace with your God. But I think I'm man enough now to let go of my anger and give you at least some peace," Jesse said, opening up.

"God bless ya, son. What I pray most for you now, don't want ya following the same path I took in life. I want a normal life for you and your mother. Best way to explain. Most people watch the sun rise every morning and enjoy the light of the day it bring till the sun go down at night. That's how a normal life need to be. I lived my life in reverse. I never paid attention to the sunrise or the joy it brung. Not until the sun set on me and I'm standing in the dark, did I finally see the light. You and your mom, you guys are my sunrise, and I never saw it till it was too late. Maybe it was God helped me see the light, I dunno, but the truth is plain as day to me now. All I'm tryin' to say, Jess, don't let the sun pass ya by without feeling its light and warmth on your face. And while you're at it, don't forget to smell the roses too." Roger remained quiet for a long moment.

"I need to dry myself off here, Jess. The guys here gonna think I'm a girl or something with all these tears. Anyway, reason I called, I gotta gift for ya that Zach delivered. I already cleared everything with your mom. She know about it. I jus wish I could be there to see your face when ya get it. Zach got him a Polaroid and gonna take pictures for me so I got me somethin' in my cell to look at every day. Go ahead, kid. I'm gonna stay on the line with your mom. She gonna describe it for me while Zach give ya my gift."

Jesse handed the receiver to Jeanie and walked over to Zach with an obvious look of confusion. What could Roger possibly gift him?

"Can I have everyone's attention, please," Zach announced to the small group as they gathered around to listen. "Jesse's father would like to apologize for not being here today to celebrate with all of you but he's currently indisposed." The intro generated laughter around the room. "He may not be here physically but he's certainly here in spirit and wanted to share his pride in Jesse by presenting him a small gift in front of all his close friends in recognition of his accomplishments this year."

Zach reached into his pocket and pulled out an envelope and handed it to Jesse, who examined it, opened it up, and pulled out a key. Everyone looked on, puzzled.

"I don't get it. My gift is a key?" Jesse asked innocently.

"No, your gift is what the key opens," Zach explained cryptically. "If you open the front door, you'll see your gift."

Jesse walked to the front door and opened it up. His eyes widened as he stood paralyzed looking at the white 1984 Ford Mustang GT350 convertible parked at the curb. "This is a joke, right? You're not serious," he looked at Zach in disbelief.

Everyone spilled out of the apartment and rushed towards the vehicle. Jesse led the way. He opened the driver's side door and slid his hand along the red leather interior. He sat in the driver's seat and fired it up. "Oh man! Only 50,000 clicks on this baby!" he announced. The group converged on the vehicle and looked on in amazement. Amanda joined him in the front seat while Goz and Minoo quickly occupied the back.

"Let's go baby!" Goz screamed. "Let's take this bad boy for a ride."

"Hang on a sec," Jesse shouted as he jumped out of the vehicle and ran back into the apartment where Jeanie was describing the moment to Roger.

Jesse quickly retrieved the phone from his mother. "Are you kidding me, dad? An '84 Mustang GT?"

"It's all yours, kid. Ya deserve it. All ya gotta do is get Zach to sign over the ownership and it's all yours."

"You're the best incarcerated dad a kid could ever have," Jesse blurted as they shared a laugh. He thanked his father profusely before finally hanging up.

Jesse ran back out the door and approached Trey and JJ. "I'll be right back to pick you guys up, but right now, I need to burn some rubber." He quickly straddled his legs over the door and landed in driver's seat, ready to pull away. Before he could put the vehicle in gear, he heard a loud shout from the apartment.

"Hang on, hang on!" Zach yelled as he rushed towards the group gathered at the front of the car. Zach readied his Polaroid. "Alright, everybody gather around the car and smile." Zach fired off several group pictures then announced, "Okay, you're good to go," and gave Jesse the thumbs up.

Jesse rammed the stickshift into gear, pushed the accelerator to the floor, and released the clutch. The front end of the Mustang GT heaved as it accelerated and peeled away down Sackville Street with horns a-blazing.

ACKNOWLEDGEMENTS

I would like to express my sincere thanks and appreciation to the following individuals who inspired, encouraged, and supported me throughout this project:

First and foremost, to my wife, Marianne, who has always been the best part of me. Her positive energy and encouragement drove me to the finish line. Her creative spirit challenges my conventional ways pushing me out of my comfort zone and has made me a better version of myself.

To my daughters Lauren and Michelle, who give me purpose in life and keep me young at heart. They continue to be my biggest cheerleaders and provided valuable input during the manuscript stage. Thank you for always being in my corner and making my life, as a father, a proud and fulfilling experience.

To my good friend, Steve Kretz, with whom I've shared many great life experiences. Among other things, I thank him for our countless post-workout trips to Tim Hortons where we sat, discussed, and resolved all the problems of the world over a cup of coffee. Thanks for hanging with me and being my sounding board, even when I didn't know what I was talking about.

To my lifetime buddies, Tom McDonald and Carmen Derose, for allowing me to steal their nicknames for characters portrayed in this book. Our history early on in life was unique and inspired some of the dialogue and ideas depicted in the story. I offer special thanks to Tyler Thomas for his valuable feedback and insight during the manuscript stage of this project.

To my mother, Rejeanne Fournier-Lauzon, who taught me life is not always a bed of roses but you can achieve in life what you want if you're prepared to work for it. Thank you for instilling a strong work ethic, confidence, and providing me the moral fiber and compass to navigate life without fear or regret.

Finally, to all the vastly talented individuals at FriesenPress who guided me through this project and made the final product the best it could be. You are all true professionals and it's been an honor working with you all, thank you.

Alain Fournier

ABOUT THE AUTHOR

Alain Fournier enjoys stories where the underdog prevails against all odds. He's a proud family man, married to the same woman for thirty-four years, with two beautiful daughters. Now retired from the aerospace industry, Alain leads a very active life involved in various sports and maintaining a healthy lifestyle. Always open to learning something new, Alain and his wife are avid travellers who enjoy touring the world and immersing themselves in different cultural experiences.

Printed in Canada